EXPLOSION IN A CATHEDRAL

*the text of this book is printed
on 100% recycled paper*

By Alejo Carpentier

THE LOST STEPS

EXPLOSION IN A CATHEDRAL

EXPLOSION IN A CATHEDRAL

a novel by

ALEJO CARPENTIER

translated by
JOHN STURROCK

Las palabras no caen en el vacio
The Zohar

HARPER COLOPHON BOOKS
Harper & Row, Publishers
New York, Hagerstown, San Francisco, London

Original title: *El Siglo de las Luces*

First HARPER COLOPHON edition published 1979

ISBN: 0-06-090651-0

79 80 81 82 83 10 9 8 7 6 5 4 3 2 1

For my wife Lilia

I SAW THEM ERECT the guillotine again to-night. It stood in the bows, like a doorway opening on to the immense sky— through which the scents of the land were already coming to us across an ocean so calm, so much master of its rhythm, that the ship seemed asleep, gently cradled on its course, suspended between a yesterday and a to-day which moved with us. Time stood still, caught between the Pole Star, the Great Bear and the Southern Cross—though I do not know, for it is not my job to know, whether such in fact were the constellations, so numerous that their vertices, their sidereal fires, mingled and combined, shuffling the allegories they symbolised. And even the brightness of a full moon paled beside the whiteness—how portentously renewed at that moment!—of the Milky Way.

But the empty doorway stood in the bows, reduced to a mere lintel and its supports, with the set-square, the inverted half-pediment, the black triangle, and its bevel of cold steel, suspended between the uprights. Its naked, solitary skeleton had been newly raised above the sleeping crew, like a presence, a warning, which concerned us all equally. We had left it far astern in the cold winds of April, and now it had reappeared over our very bows, going ahead of us like a guide, resembling, in the necessary precision of its parallel lines, its implacable geometry, some gigantic instrument of navigation. But no banners, drums and crowds attended it here; it was not the object of the emotions, fury, weeping and drunkenness, of those who had surrounded it like the chorus in a Greek Tragedy, as the tumbrils creaked towards it, and the drums gave an accompanying roll. Here the Door stood alone, facing into the night above the tutelary figurehead, its diagonal blade gleaming, its wooden uprights framing a whole panorama of stars.

The waves came to meet us and parted, brushing along the sides of the ship; they closed again behind us, with a noise so continuous, rhythmical and persistent that it came to resemble that silence which a man thinks of as silence because he can hear no other voice like his own. A vital silence, full of a steady throbbing, and not, as yet, the silence of the lifeless corpse.

Suddenly the blade fell with a hiss, and the cross-piece stood out clearly, like a real lintel above two jambs. The Plenipotentiary, whose hand had activated the mechanism, muttered "We must protect it from the saltpetre". And he closed the Door, by throwing a huge tarpaulin over it. The breeze smelled of the land now—of humus, dung, corn and resin—of the island which had lain for centuries under the protection of Our Lady of Guadalupe, whose image is to be seen both in Cáceres in Estremadura and in Tepeyac in Mexico, standing erect upon a crescent moon supported by an archangel.

Behind me lay an adolescence whose familiar landscapes were now, after three years, as remote as was the sickly, puny creature I had been until the night when Someone had arrived amongst us with a thunderous knocking; as remote as was my former confidant, guide and mentor from the sullen Mandatory who now leaned pondering on the gunwale—beside the black rectangle in its inquisitorial cover, which swung like the pointer of a balance in time to the waves.

From time to time the water grew bright with the flash of scales, or with the passage of some floating wreath of sargasso.

CHAPTER ONE

I

Behind him, in mournful diapason, the Executor was again running over his list: responses, cross-bearer, oblations, vestments, tapers, baize and flowers, obituary and requiem. One man had come in full dress uniform, a second had wept, a third had said that we were as nothing; yet the sadness of death had not ceased to dominate the boat as it crossed the bay under a torrid, mid-afternoon sun, whose light was reflected from every wave, sparkled dazzlingly in the bubbling foam, blazed on to the open deck, burned under the awning, got into everyone's eyes and pores, and was unbearable for the hands which leant for rest upon the gunwale.

Dressed in his improvised mourning, smelling of yesterday's dye, the boy contemplated the city. At this hour of shimmer and long shadows, it looked strangely like a gigantic baroque chandelier, whose green, red and orange glass lent colour to a jumbled rocaille of balconies, arcades, domes, belvederes and lattice-covered galleries, bristling all over with scaffolding, timber, cross-beams, forked props and builder's poles now that the inhabitants (enriched by the last war in Europe) had been gripped by the building fever.

It was a town constantly exposed to the invading air, thirsty for land and sea breezes, with its shutters, lattices, doors and flaps all open to the first cool breath. Then the tinkling of lustres, chandeliers, beaded lampshades and curtains, and the whirling of weathercocks would announce its arrival. Fans of palm fronds, Chinese silk, or painted paper, would be motionless. But when this transient relief was over, people would return to their task of setting in motion the still air, once more trapped between the high walls of the rooms. Here light congealed into heat, from the moment the swift dawn first admitted it into even the most inaccessible bedrooms, penetrating curtains and mosquito-nets; especially now, in the rainy season, after the fierce midday downpour, a regular cascade of water accompanied by thunder and lightning, which soon emptied the clouds and left the streets flooded and steaming in the returning sultriness.

In vain the palaces proudly displayed their splendid columns and coats of arms carved in stone; during the rainy months they rose out of mud which clung like an incurable disease to their masonry. When a carriage went past, doors and railings were covered with fountains of splashes from the puddles which filled every hollow, undermined the pavements and spilled over to replenish each other with filthy water. Although they were adorned with precious marble and fine panelling, with rose windows and mosaics, and with slim voluted grilles so unlike iron bars that they looked more like iron vegetation twining round the windows, these manorial houses could not escape the primaeval slime which spattered up over them from the ground as soon as the roofs had begun to drip. Carlos reflected that many of those who had attended the wake must have had to cross at the street-corners on planks laid over the mud, or by jumping on to stepping-stones to avoid leaving their shoes behind them.

Strangers praised the town's colour and gaiety after spending three days visiting its dance halls, saloons, taverns and gambling dens, where innumerable orchestras incited sailors to spend their money, and set the women's hips swaying. But those who had to put up with the place the whole year round knew about the mud and the dust, and how the saltpetre turned the door-knockers green, ate away the iron-work, made silver sweat, brought mildew out on old engravings, and permanently blurred and misted the glass on drawings and etchings, already curling up with damp.

Over on San Francisco Quay a North American ship had just tied up, whose name Carlos spelt out automatically: *The Arrow*. The Executor went on picturing the funeral to himself; it had certainly been magnificent, worthy in every way of such a good man, with all those sacristans and acolytes, the splendid vestments and religious pomp; and the clerks from the warehouse too, who had wept discreetly, in a manly way, from the Psalms of the Vigil until the Memento for the Dead. But the dead man's son had not been present; he had given way to grief and fatigue, after riding hard since dawn along main roads and interminable short cuts. He had hardly reached the hacienda, where the solitude gave him an illusion of independence—he could play his sonatas there all night by candlelight, without annoying anyone—when the news came, and he had had to return at a horse-killing speed, but not in time to follow the funeral procession. ("I do not want to go into painful details," the other man had said, "but we couldn't wait any longer. Only your dear sister and I were there to watch beside the coffin.")

Carlos thought of the mourning, the year's mourning, which would condemn his new flute, bought from the best flute-maker, to remain in its black oilcloth case, because one must seem to conform to the stupid idea that no music should sound where there was grief. His father's death was going to deprive him of everything he enjoyed, side-tracking his plans, cutting him off from his dreams. He would be condemned to look after the business; he, who understood not a thing about figures, would sit dressed in black behind an ink-stained desk, surrounded by lugubrious book-keepers and clerks, who knew each other too well to have anything left to say to each other.

He was still bemoaning his fate, and promising himself that as soon as a suitable ship turned up he would make his escape without warning or farewells, when the boat came alongside a jetty, where Remigio was waiting, with a gloomy expression and a badge of mourning fastened to the brim of his hat. As soon as the carriage drove off down the first street, throwing up mud to right and left, the smells of the sea were left behind, swept away by the odour from the huge buildings full of hides, salted meat, cakes of wax, loaves of black sugar, and long-hoarded onions sprouting in dark corners, beside the fresh coffee and cocoa that had been spilled on the scales. The sound of cow-bells filled the evening air, accompanying the usual migration of recently-milked cows to the pastures outside the town. Everything gave off a strong scent at this time of day—it was nearly dusk and the sky would soon be set aflame for a few minutes before dissolving into a rapid nightfall : the firewood that would not burn, the trodden cow-dung, the damp canvas of the awnings, the leather in the saddlers' shops, the birdseed in the canary-cages hanging in the windows. The damp roofs smelled of clay, the still wet walls of old moss, the street-corner fritter-stalls of oil that had been many times boiled, the coffee-roasting machines of a Spice Island bonfire, as their dark smoke wreathed slowly up to the classical cornices, where it hung between the crenellations, before dissolving like a warm mist about the head of some saint on a belfry. But the dried beef, there was no mistaking it, smelled of dried beef; omnipresent beef, hanging in every cellar and storehouse, its acrid smell dominating the city, invading the palaces, impregnating the curtains, challenging the incense in the churches, intruding into performances at the Opera House. The dried beef, the mud and the flies were the curse of this emporium, visited by all the world's ships, but where, thought Carlos, only the statues, set on their mud-stained plinths, were suited by their surroundings.

As an antidote to so many cooking smells there suddenly emerged, from an air-vent in a small cul-de-sac, the noble aroma of the tobacco piled in sheds there, battened down, compressed, bruised by the knots in the palm fibre which encircled the bales—the thick leaves were still a tender green, with specks of pale gold in the down that covered them—alive and growing still in the midst of the dried beef which surrounded and divided it.

At last breathing in an aroma which he liked, and which alternated with the smoke from another coffee-roasting machine at work near a chapel, Carlos thought sadly of the life of routine that now awaited him. His music would be silenced, and he would be condemned to live in this marine city, an island within an island, where every possible outlet to adventure was stopped up by the sea; it would be like finding himself wrapped prematurely in a shroud fashioned from the stench of beef, onions and brine, the victim of a father whom he reproached— and it was a monstrous thing to do—for the crime of having died too soon. At this moment the boy was suffering as never before from the claustrophobia induced by living in an island, by being in a country where there were no roads leading to other lands along which to wander, ride, or make one's way, crossing frontiers, sleeping in a different inn each night, roaming wherever fancy led, fascinated by a mountain that was soon for-gotten in the sight of another mountain, or by the body of an actress perhaps, met with in a city unknown only the day before, whom one could follow for months, from one playhouse to another, sharing the bohemian life of the company.

The carriage heeled over to take the corner, which was protected by a cross turned green by saltpetre, and stopped in front of a nail-studded door, from whose knocker hung a black bow. The entrance hall, the vestibule and the patio were carpeted with jasmine, tuberoses, white carnations and immor-telles, fallen from the wreaths and bouquets. Sofia was waiting in the huge drawing-room, hollow-eyed, her face distorted, dressed in mourning which was too big for her, so that it encased her like a cardboard wrapper; she was surrounded by Clare nuns, decanting flasks of melissa water, essence of lemon, salts and infusions, in a sudden ostentatious flurry of solicitude for the new arrivals. Voices rose in chorus, advocating courage, acquiescence, resignation to those who had to remain here below while others were already experiencing that Glory which never fails nor ceases.

"I will be your father now," whined the Executor, from the corner where the family portraits were. Seven o'clock sounded from the belfry of the church of the Espiritu Santo. Sofia made a gesture of dismissal, and the others understood it and retreated towards the hall in mute condolence. "If you need anything," said Don Cosme. "If you need anything," chorused the nuns.

All the bolts on the big door were slid to. Crossing the patio where the trunks of the palm trees rose amongst the arums, like columns in a different style of architecture from the rest, to merge their fronds with the gathering darkness, Carlos and Sofia went to the room next to the stables, perhaps the dampest and darkest in the whole house, but the only one where Esteban could manage at times to get a whole night's sleep, without undergoing one of his attacks.

But they found him now hanging by his hands from the highest bars of the window, his body lengthened and crucified by his efforts, his head fallen forwards, his ribs standing out in sharp relief, naked but for a shawl wound round his waist. From his chest came a dull wheezing, oddly pitched on two notes at

15

once, which from time to time died away into a moan. His hands sought for a higher bar to grip, as if his lean body, ridged with purple veins, wanted to elongate itself even further. Helpless in the face of an illness which defied medicines and poultices, Sofía passed a handkerchief dipped in cold water over the sick boy's forehead and cheeks. Soon his fingers released their hold, slipping down the iron bars, and Esteban, taken down from his cross by the brother and sister, dropped into a wicker arm-chair, staring with a fixed but absent gaze out of dilated black pupils. His finger-nails were blue, and his neck had disappeared between shoulders so hunched that they almost closed above his ears. With his knees as far apart as they would go, his elbows raised in front of him, and the waxen texture of his anatomy, he looked like an ascetic in a primitive painting, engaged in some monstrous mortification of the flesh.

"It was that accursed incense," said Sofía, sniffing at the black clothes which Esteban had left on a chair. "When I saw him beginning to choke in church . . ." But she suddenly stopped when she remembered that the incense whose fumes the sick boy had been unable to endure had been burning at the solemn funeral of someone who had been described, during the parish priest's oration, as a dearly beloved father, a mirror of goodness and an exemplary man.

Esteban had now thrown his arms over a sheet which had been rolled up like a rope and suspended between two rings fixed in the wall. The pathos of his collapse was made crueller by his being surrounded by all the things with which Sofía had tried to distract him during his attacks ever since his childhood : the little shepherdess mounted on a musical-box; the monkey-orchestra with a broken spring; the balloon with aeronauts, which hung from the ceiling and could be raised and lowered by means of a string; the clock which started a frog dancing on a bronze platform; the puppet theatre with its backcloth of a Mediterranean port and its Turkish policemen, its servant girls and its monks lying scattered about the stage, one with his head back to front, another with his scalp shaved clean by cockroaches, another without any arms or legs, and the harlequin spewing sawdust out of his eyes and nostrils.

"I shan't go back to the convent," said Sofía, spreading her lap to support Esteban's head, which had dropped gently to the floor, seeking the unfailing coolness of the flag-stones. "My place is here."

II

THEIR FATHER'S DEATH had certainly affected them deeply. Yet, now that they found themselves alone, by the light of day, in the big dining-room with its blackened still-lives—pheasants and hares between bunches of grapes, lampreys with flasks of wine, a pie so crisp that it made one want to sink one's teeth into it—they might have had to confess to being overcome by an almost sensual feeling of freedom, as they sat round a meal ordered from the nearby hotel, since they had not thought to send anyone out to the market. Remigio had brought in trays covered with cloths, beneath which could be seen porgies cooked with almonds, marzipan, young pigeons *à la crapaudine*, truffles and candies, all very different from the soups and stuffed meat which usually came to the table.

Sofia had come down in a dressing-gown, and was delightedly trying everything, while Esteban was being restored to life by the warmth of a *garnacha* wine that Carlos pronounced to be excellent. The house, which they had always looked on with eyes grown accustomed to its reality, as something at once both familiar and strange, was taking on a peculiar importance and making demands on them, now that they knew they were responsible for its preservation and continuance. It was obvious that their father—who had been so bound up in his business that he even went out on Sundays, before Mass, to arrange contracts and to anticipate Monday's buyers by purchasing goods from the ships—had seriously neglected the house, after it had been prematurely deserted by their mother, a victim of the deadliest influenza epidemic the city had ever suffered.

There were paving stones missing in the patio; the statues were dirty; the mud from the street had penetrated far into the hallway; the furniture in the sitting-rooms and bedrooms was reduced to pieces that did not match and looked more suited to an auction sale than to be decorating a respectable house. For years there had been no water in the fountain and its dolphins had remained silent, while indoors panes of glass were missing from partitions. There were some pictures, however, to lend dignity to the damp-blackened walls, although they showed a violent mixture of subjects and schools, attributable to the haphazard manner of their acquisition—there had been no opportunity of choosing from amongst the unsold items of a collection put up for auction. This residue might have some value, might even be the work of masters and not copyists; but one could never hope to find out in this city of businessmen, because of the lack of experts who could appraise modern work or recognise the grand classical manner beneath the cracks of a maltreated canvas. Beyond a Massacre of the Innocents which might well be by a pupil of Berruguete, and a Saint Dionysius which might well be by an imitator of Ribera, hung a sunlit garden full of black-masked harlequins, a picture which Sofia found enchanting, although Carlos maintained that the artists of the early part of this century had travestied the harlequin figure for the mere pleasure of playing with colours. He preferred realistic scenes of harvest and vintage, although he recognised that several pictures without any story, hanging in the hallway—a cooking-pot, a pipe, a basket of fruit, a clarinet lying beside a sheet of music—did not lack a certain beauty due entirely to their execution.

Esteban had a taste for the imaginative and fantastic, and would day-dream for hours in front of pictures by modern artists representing monsters, spectral horses, or impossible scenes—a tree-man with fingers sprouting from him, a cupboard-man with empty drawers coming out of his stomach. But his favourite painting was a huge canvas by an unknown Neapolitan master which confounded all the laws of plastic art by representing the apocalyptic immobilisation of a catastrophe. It was called "Explosion in a Cathedral", this vision of a great colonnade shattering into fragments in mid-air—pausing a moment as its lines broke, floating so as to fall better—before it dashed its tons of stone down on to the terrified people beneath. ("I don't know how you can look at it," his cousin used to say, though she was strangely fascinated herself in reality by the terrible suspense of this static earthquake, this silent cataclysm, this illustration of the End of Time, hanging there within reach of their hands. "It's because I'm used to it," Esteban would reply, without knowing why, but with that automatic insistence which can lead us to repeat an inferior pun that makes no one laugh, for year after year whenever the circumstances recur.)

At least the French painter of the picture beyond, by placing a monument of his own invention in the middle of a deserted square—a sort of Asio-Roman temple, with arcades, obelisks and crests—had introduced a note of peace and stability after catastrophe, before one entered the dining-room, with its still lives and imposing pieces of furniture : two china cupboards of monastic proportions, proof against termites; eight tapestry chairs, and the great dining-room table, supported on Salomonic columns. But as for the rest : "Rubbish from the junk stalls," Sofia had pronounced, remembering her own narrow mahogany bed, and how she had always dreamed of a bed in which she could twist and turn about, and sleep crossways, curled up, or with arms outstretched, whichever way she fancied.

True to the habits he had inherited from his country-dwelling forebears, their father had always slept in a room on the first floor, in a wretched canvas bed with a crucifix at its head, between a large walnut chest and a small chamber-pot of Mexican silver, which he emptied himself every morning, with the majestic sweeping movement of a sower, into the runnel that carried away the urine in the stables.

"My ancestors came from Estremadura," he would say, as though this explained everything, and he was proud of an austerity which knew nothing of parties or social graces. Dressed in the black he had worn ever since the death of his wife, he had been brought home from his office by Don Cosme. He had just put his name to a document when a stroke laid him out on his still wet signature. Even in death he had kept the hard, impassive features of a man who never did others a favour, nor asked for favours for himself. In recent years Sofia had hardly seen him, except at formal family luncheons, on occasional Sundays during her few hours' freedom from the Clare convent.

As far as Carlos was concerned, once his early studies were

over, he had been kept constantly journeying out to the hacienda, charged with orders for felling, clearing and sowing, which could well have been sent in writing, now that the estate was so much smaller and was principally given over to the cultivation of sugar-cane. "I've ridden two hundred and forty miles to bring back twelve cabbages," the boy observed, as he emptied his saddle-bags after one such trip up-country. "That's how Spartan characters are moulded," replied his father, who was as fond of relating Sparta to cabbages as he was of explaining the prodigious levitations of Simon Magus on the bold hypothesis that he had some knowledge of electricity, and who always postponed the plan for Carlos to study law, out of an instinctive fear of the new ideas and dangerous political enthusiasms that were wont to flourish in university faculties.

He concerned himself little with Esteban. This frail nephew, orphaned since early childhood, had grown up with Carlos and Sofia like another son; everything the others had he had also. But ailing men irritated the merchant, especially if they belonged to his own family, for the very reason that he himself was never ill, but worked from dawn to dusk throughout the year. He used to look into the sick boy's room from time to time, and frown with disgust when he found him in one of his attacks. He would mutter something about the damp, about people who insisted on sleeping in caves like the ancient Celtiberians, and then, after thinking longingly of the Tarpeian Rock, he would offer a present of fresh eggs from the North, recall memories of famous paralytics and finally walk off, shrugging his shoulders and growling out condolences, words of encouragement, advertisements for new medicines, and excuses for not being able to spend more time looking after those who were left stranded on the banks of a creative and progressive life by their afflictions.

After they had spent some time in the dining-room trying first this and then that with no semblance of system, taking figs before sardines, and marzipan with olives and sausage, the "little ones", as the Executor called them, opened the door leading into the next house, where the business and the warehouse were; it had been closed for the last three days because of the mourning. Beyond the desks and safes, passages had been cleared between the mountains of sacks, barrels and bales coming from all over the world. At the bottom of Flour Street, with its smell of foreign mills, came Wine Street, with its casks of *Foncarral, Valdepeñas* and *Puente de la Reina*, dripping red wine from every faucet, and giving out a smell like a wine vault. Rigging and Tackle Street led to a corner stinking of salt fish, whose wrappers sweated brine on to the floor. Returning along Deerskin Street, the young people came back to the Spice District, with its drawers proclaiming, merely by their smell, that they contained ginger, laurel, saffron and pepper from Veracruz. Parallel lines of La Mancha cheeses led to Oil and Vinegar Court, at the end of which, under the vaulting, an assortment of merchandise was kept : packs of cards, cases of barbers' instruments, bunches of padlocks, red and green parasols, cocoa mills, Andean blankets brought from Maracaibo, a pile of sticks of dye, and books of gold and silver leaf from Mexico. Nearer at hand were low trestles on which rested sacks of birds' feathers—soft and puffy like huge eiderdowns; Carlos threw himself down on them, making swimming motions with his outstretched arms. An armillary sphere, whose hoops Esteban spun distractedly with his hand, stood like a symbol of Commerce and Navigation in the midst of this world of things that had arrived here by so many different sea-routes. Here too the stench of dried beef predominated, though less offensively, because it was stored in the furthermost recesses of the building.

The brother and sister returned down Honey Street, to the open space where the desks were. "How disgusting it smells !" murmured Sofia, her handkerchief to her nose, "How it smells !" Standing on some sacks of barley, Carlos was contemplating the view from under the roof, and thinking fearfully of the day when he would have to set about selling all this, selling and buying, negotiating and haggling, knowing nothing about prices, unable to tell one cereal from another, forced to go back to the beginning through the thousands of letters, bills, invoices, receipts and estimates stored in the drawers.

A whiff of sulphur caught Esteban's throat, filling his eyes and making him sneeze. Sofia felt sick with the reek of wine and herrings. Supporting her cousin, who was threatened by a fresh attack, she made her way quickly back to the house, where the Mother Superior of the Clare convent was lying in wait for her with an edifying book. Carlos was the last to return, carrying the armillary sphere, which he meant to set up in his room. In the shade of the shuttered drawing-room the nun talked composedly about the falsehoods of the world and the joys of the cloister, while the young men amused themselves moving tropics and ellipses round the sphere.

A new life was beginning, in the sultry heat of a particularly oppressive evening, with the sun drawing up fetid moisture from the puddles in the streets. Reunited once more over dinner, under the fruit and fowls of the still-lives, the young people made plans for the future. The Executor had advised them to spend the period of mourning at the hacienda, while he cleared up the dead man's business affairs—they had generally been conducted by word of mouth, so that some contracts would have been recorded only in his memory. This would mean that Carlos would find everything in order when he returned, or whenever he should decide to take a serious interest in the business. But Sofia remembered that previous attempts to take Esteban to the country "to breathe the clean air", had only made him worse. When all was said and done it was in his low-ceilinged room next to the stables that he suffered least.

They talked about possible travels. Mexico, with its thousand domes, lay glittering across the Gulf. But it was the United States, and the rapid advance of progress, which fascinated Carlos, who very much wanted to see New York Harbour, the battlefield at Lexington, and the Niagara Falls. Esteban dreamed of Paris, with its art exhibitions, its intellectual cafés, its literary life. He wanted to take a course in Oriental languages at the Collège de France, a line of study which might not be particularly useful for making money, but would be thrilling to someone like him, who wanted to read certain recently discovered Asiatic texts from the manuscripts. For Sofia there would be performances at the Opéra and the Théâtre Français, in whose foyer something as beautiful and famous as Houdon's bust of Voltaire could be seen. In their imaginary travels they went from the pigeons of San Marco to the Epsom Derby; from performances at Sadler's Wells to a visit to the Louvre; from well-known bookshops to famous circuses; from the ruins of Palmyra and Pompeii to the displays of Etruscan horses and marble vases in Greek Street. Anxious to see everything, they could decide on nothing, but the young men were secretly attracted by a world of licentious pleasures, already craved by their senses, and which they would manage to find and enjoy while the girl was out shopping or visiting monuments.

Without having reached any decision at all, they said their prayers and kissed each other tearfully, feeling that they were orphans, alone in the universe, friendless in a soulless city indifferent to painting and poetry and given over to trade and ugliness. Oppressed by the heat and the smells of beef, onions and coffee which reached them from the street, they went up on to the roof, wrapped in their dressing-gowns, and carrying blankets and pillows on which at last they fell asleep, after talking, with their faces turned upwards to the sky, about habitable—and surely inhabited—planets, where life would per- haps be better than it was on this earth, everlastingly subjected to the processes of death.

III

SOFIA COULD NOT get away from the nuns, who kept urging her—insistently but unhurriedly, gently but repeatedly—to become a servant of the Lord. But in reaction to her own doubts she took special pains to be a mother to Esteban, a mother who was so possessive in her new functions that she did not hesitate to undress him and bathe him with a sponge, when he was unable to do it himself, overcoming his embarrassed reluctance with a firmness which brooked no argument. This illness of some- one whom she had always looked on as a brother helped her in her instinctive resistance to withdrawing from the world, by making her presence here a necessity. As for Carlos, she pre- tended to ignore his robust health and took advantage of the slightest cough to put him to bed and make him swallow very strong punch, which put him in an excellent mood.

One day she went through the rooms of the house, pen in

hand, the mulatta servant carrying the inkpot aloft behind her as though it were the Holy Sacrament, making an inventory of all the useless lumber. She laboriously drew up a list of all the things they needed to furnish the house respectably, and handed it to the Executor, who was still bent on acting as "a second father" and satisfying the orphans' least wants.

On Christmas Eve crates and bundles began to arrive which were put in the rooms on the ground floor as they appeared. From the principal drawing-room right through to the coach-house, they were invaded by things still half-protected by their packing-cases, or wrapped in straw and wood-shavings, awaiting a final sorting-out. Thus a heavy side-board, brought in by six negro porters, remained in the hallway, while a lacquered screen was left leaning against the wall, with the nails not yet removed from its casing. China cups were still in the sawdust they had travelled in, while the books destined to form a library of new ideas and new poetry were strewn everywhere, a dozen here, a dozen there, piled carelessly on top of arm-chairs, or on occasional tables still smelling of fresh varnish. The cloth of the billiard table was a meadow stretching between the glass of a rococo mirror and the stern profile of an English inlaid desk.

One night, explosions were heard from inside a packing-case; the strings of a harp which Sofia had ordered from a Neapolitan dealer were snapping with the humidity. Since all the rats in the neighbourhood were making themselves at home everywhere, the cats came and sharpened their claws on the choicest examples of the cabinet-maker's art, and unravelled the carpets where unicorns, cockatoos and greyhounds flourished.

But the disorder reached its height with the arrival of apparatus for a physics laboratory which Esteban had ordered so that he could replace his automatic toys and musical boxes with a pastime that would combine pleasure with instruction. There were telescopes, hydrostatic balances, pieces of amber, compasses, magnets, Archimedean screws, model winches, speaking tubes, Leyden jars, pendulums, balance-beams and miniature cranes, to which the manufacturer had added (to compensate for the absence of certain articles), a mathematical box, containing all the most advanced instruments. Thus some nights the young men would eagerly set up the oddest pieces of apparatus, their faces buried in the sheets of instructions, exchanging theories, waiting for the dawn to confirm the efficacy of a prism, and marvelling to see the colours of the spectrum outlined on the wall.

Gradually they grew accustomed to living by night, inspired by Esteban, who slept better during the day and preferred to sit up until it grew light, because if he should drowse off during the early morning hours he was very likely to bring on a prolonged attack. Rosaura, the mulatta cook, prepared their lunch for six o'clock in the evening, and left them a cold supper for midnight.

Day by day a labyrinth of packing cases was being built in the house; everyone had his own corner in it, his own floor, his own level, so that they could either isolate themselves or meet to discuss a book, or some piece of apparatus which had suddenly begun to work in a most unexpected manner. There was a sort of ramp, an Alpine path, which led from the door of the drawing-room over a cupboard laid on its side, and climbed up to the Three Crates of Crockery, standing one on top of the other, whence one could contemplate the countryside below, before ascending by a rugged pathway of broken boards and laths, bristling like thistles (with protruding nails for thorns) up to the Grand Terrace, made out of the Nine Crates of Furniture, where the nape of the explorer's neck was pressed against the beams of the ceiling.

"What a lovely view!" Sofia used to cry, laughing and hugging her skirt to her knees, when she reached the summit. But Carlos maintained that there were other, more dangerous ways of making the ascent, by attacking the massif of bales on the other side, and climbing, mountaineer fashion, until one hauled oneself up on top, arms outstretched and panting bravely like a Saint Bernard dog. They used to sit on a path or a plateau, in a hidden corner or on a bridge, reading whatever took their fancy: old newspapers, almanachs, guide-books, natural history perhaps, a classical tragedy, or a modern novel, set in the year 2440, which they stole from each other from time to time. Or Esteban, perched on a pinnacle, might give a blasphemous imitation of the ranting of some well-known preacher, glossing a passionate verse from the Song of Songs, and enjoying Sofia's annoyance when she stopped her ears and shouted that men were all pigs.

The sundial in the patio had become a moon-dial, marking topsy-turvy hours. The hydrostatic balance was used for weighing cats; the little telescope, projecting through the broken glass of a skylight, made it possible to see things in nearby houses, which brought an equivocal laugh from Carlos, a solitary astronomer on top of a wardrobe. Meanwhile the new flute was taken out of its case in a room padded with mattresses, like the cell of a madman, so that the neighbours should not hear it. There, with his music-stand set at an angle to him, and surrounded by the sheets of music that had fallen on the carpet, the young man indulged in long nocturnal concerts which improved his tone and his fingering—when he did not succumb, that is, to the urge to play country dances on a recently acquired fife.

Often, moved by mutual affection, the young people swore that they would never separate. The nuns had inspired Sofia with an early horror for the ways of men, and she grew angry when Esteban, for a joke—and perhaps to put her to the test—talked about a future marriage, which was to be blessed with a whole brood of children. The introduction of a "husband" into the house was considered in advance as an abomination, as a transgression against the flesh which they all three of them held in sacred bond, and which must remain inviolate. Together they would travel, and learn about the wide world. The Executor would take admirable care of the "nasty things" which smelled so horrible on the other side of the dividing wall. Indeed he had shown himself very favourable to their projected travels, and promised that letters of credit would follow them everywhere. "You must go to Madrid," he had said, "to see the Post Office and the dome of San Francisco el Grande, because you won't see architectural marvels like that here." Distance had ceased to exist, with the speed of communications in the present century. It would be up to the young people to make a decision, when the countless requiems for their father's eternal rest were over. Carlos and Sofia attended them every Sunday before they went to bed, walking through still deserted streets to the church of the Espiritu Santo.

They decided not to finish opening the packing cases and bales for the present, nor to arrange the new furniture; the very thought of the task depressed them, especially Esteban, whose illness forbade him all physical exertion. Moreover, early morning invasions of upholsterers, varnishers and other strangers would have broken into their habits, which were out of step with more normal time-tables. One was an early riser if one got up at five o'clock in the evening to greet Don Cosme, who was more paternal and obsequious than ever now, as far as carrying out their commissions went, offering to procure whatever they wanted, and to pay whatever might be necessary. He told them that the affairs of the warehouse were going splendidly, and he was always most concerned that Sofia should have ample money for the house-keeping. He praised her for having taken on a mother's responsibilities in looking after the young men, and fired a light but well-aimed volley in passing at the nuns, for persuading young girls of good family to shut themselves away, so as to lay their hands on their money—but Sofia could pride herself on being a splendid Christian without that.

Their visitor would then withdraw with a bow, assuring them that, for the moment, Carlos' presence was not necessary to the business, and the others would return to their possessions and their labyrinth, where everything had a secret code name. A certain pile of packing-cases in danger of collapse was "The Leaning Tower"; the trunk that formed a bridge between two wardrobes was "The Druid's Causeway". If anyone mentioned Ireland, they were referring to the corner where the harp was; if they spoke about Carmel they meant the sentry-box, made out of half-open screens, where Sofia used to seclude herself to read spine-chilling mystery novels. When Esteban set up his physics apparatus, they said that Albertus Magnus was now at work. Everything was transformed into a perpetual game which established them at one more remove from the outside world, within the arbitrary counterpoint afforded by lives led on three different planes : the terrestrial plane, so to speak, belonged to Esteban, who was little given to mountaineering because of his illness, but permanently envious of anyone who, like Carlos, could leap from packing-case to packing-case on the mountain-tops, hang from the panelling, or rock in a Veracruz hammock slung from the rafters in the ceiling. Meanwhile Sofia carried on her existence in an intermediate zone, situated some six feet from the ground, her heels level with her cousin's temples, moving books from one hiding-place (or "lair" as she called them) to another. Here she could stretch out as she liked, undo her buttons, let down her stockings, or pull her skirts right up to her thighs if she was too hot.

Their supper was generally held at dawn by the light of candelabra, in a dining-room swarming with cats. Reacting against the decorum they had always had to observe at family meals, the young people behaved like barbarians, seeing who could carve worst, snatching the best portions from one another, trying to tell the future with wish-bones, shooting potatoes at each other under the table, suddenly putting out the candles so that they could steal a pie from someone else's plate, sitting badly, slumped sideways, with their elbows on the table. Anyone who was not hungry would play patience or build card castles while eating; anyone who was in a bad mood would bring his novel to table. When the young men banded together to criticise Sofia for something, she used to let fly in the coarse language of a muleteer, although in her mouth the low swear words acquired a surprising purity and lost their original meaning to become no more than expressions of disagreement. She was getting her own back for innumerable convent meals, eaten with eyes fixed on her plate, after the Benedicite had been said.

"Where did you learn that?" the others would ask her, laughing.

"In the brothel," she replied, as naturally as if she had really been in one.

Eventually, tired of misbehaving, or violating the rules of good manners, or of playing billiards with nuts on the table-cloth (stained with wine from a spilled glass), they would wish each other good-night as day dawned, carrying off fruit, a handful of almonds or a glass of wine to their rooms in a false dusk full of street cries and matin bells.

Siempre sucede
—Goya

THE YEAR OF mourning passed and the young people began the year of half-mourning, without changing their way of life at all, but growing increasingly attached to their new habits, and endlessly absorbed in reading, as they discovered the world through books. They remained in their own ambit, forgotten by the rest of the town, unheeded by the world, casually discovering what was happening from some foreign newspaper arriving months late. Scenting the presence of a possible "good match" in the shut house, certain leading families had tried to make advances to them, issuing several invitations, and apparently distressed that the orphans should live such solitary lives. But their friendly advances met with cold rejection. The young people used their mourning as an excuse to remain outside all commitments or obligation, and to ignore a society which, in its provincial narrow-mindedness, presumed to submit all lives to a common norm, going to the same places at the same times, lunching at the same fashionable confectioners', spending Christmas on sugar plantations, or on fincas in Artemisa, where the rich planters vied with each other in erecting mythological statues on the edges of their tobacco plantations.

They were nearly at the end of the rainy season, which had filled the streets with fresh mud, when, one morning, in the half sleep which began his night, Carlos heard someone knock loudly on the front door. This would not have attracted his attention if, a few moments later, there had not come a knocking at the coach-house door, and then at all the other doors of the house. The impatient hand then returned to its starting-point, and thundered on all the doors for a second, and a third time. It was as if someone determined to gain admittance were circling round the house searching for some place where he might be able to squeeze in, and this impression of being surrounded was made all the stronger because the knocks re-echoed where there was no outlet to the street, and filled all the remotest corners of the house.

People who wanted information usually went to the warehouse, but as this was Easter Saturday, and a holiday, it was closed. Remigio and Rosaura must be at the Mass for the Resurrection, or shopping in the market, since they did not answer. "He'll soon get tired," thought Carlos, laying his head back on his pillow. But when he at last realised that the knocking was going to continue, he pulled on a dressing-gown and went angrily down to the hall. He looked out into the street just in time to catch sight of a man hurriedly turning the nearest corner, carrying an enormous umbrella. On the floor was a card that had been slipped under the door :

VICTOR HUGUES
Négociant
PORT-AU-PRINCE

After cursing this unknown person, Carlos returned to bed, and thought no more about him. When he awoke his eyes fell on the card, dyed a curious green by a last ray of sunlight that was filtering through the green glass of a sky-light.

The "little ones" were once more united among the packing-cases and the bales in the drawing-room, and Albertus Magnus was absorbed in his experiments in physics, when the same hand as in the morning began to lift the door-knockers all round the house. It must have been about ten o'clock at night, early for them but late according to local habits. Sofia was suddenly frightened : "We can't receive a stranger in here," she said, for the first time becoming aware of the peculiarity of everything which had come to constitute for them the natural framework of their existence. Moreover, to let an unknown person into their family labyrinth would have been like betraying a secret, surrendering some esoteric knowledge, destroying a spell.

"Don't open it, for God's sake !" she implored Carlos, who was already standing up, wearing an angry expression. But it was too late. Remigio, woken out of his first sleep by the sound of the knocker on the coach-house door, showed the stranger in, a candlestick held high. He was a man of indeterminate age—he might have been thirty, perhaps forty, perhaps much less—with a face set in that sort of fixity which is always produced by premature wrinkles on forehead and cheeks, imprinted there by the mobility of features adept at passing abruptly—and this was apparent with his very first words—from an extreme tension to an ironic passivity, from uncontrollable laughter to a hard, self-willed expression, which reflected his dominant anxiety to impose his own opinion and convictions. For the rest, his deeply-tanned skin and his hair casually combed in the modern style completed a healthy and vigorous picture. His clothes were too tight for his corpulent torso and muscular arms. His legs were solid and sure in their movements. If his lips were plebeian and sensual, his dark eyes shone with an imperious, almost unbearable intensity. The man had an air of originality about him, but at first glance this could as easily arouse aversion as liking. ("All that louts of his type can do, when they want to get into a house," thought Sofia, "is to thunder on doors.")

After saluting them with a stiff bow, which did little to make them forget the discourtesy of his insistent and noisy knocking, the visitor began to talk rapidly, leaving no time for interruptions, declaring that he had letters for their father, of whose intelligence he had heard wonderful things; that this was a good time for new commercial agreements; that the local businessmen, with their right to free trade, ought to establish contact with those on other islands in the Caribbean, that he had brought with him a modest gift of a few bottles of wine, of a quality unknown there . . .

When he received the news, shouted at him by all three of them, that their father had long been dead and buried, the stranger, who expressed himself in an amusing jargon, partly Spanish, but mixed with some French and phrases in English, stopped with an "Ah!" of condolence; so concerned, disappointed and so checked in his verbal momentum that the others, without realising that it was disgraceful to laugh at such a moment, broke out into loud guffaws. It had all happened so quickly, so unexpectedly, that the disconcerted trader from Port-au-Prince added his laughter to the rest.

A "For heaven's sake!" from Sofia, who had come abruptly back to reality, straightened their faces. But the mental tension had been relaxed. The visitor moved forward, without having been invited to do so, and, oddly enough, did not seem to be in the least surprised by the picture of chaos which the house presented, nor by the unusual costume of Sofia—she had amused herself by putting on one of Carlos' shirts, whose tails reached down to her knees. He gave an expert tap of the finger on the porcelain of a flower vase, stroked the Leyden jar, praised the workmanship of a compass, turned the Archimedean screw, muttering something about the levers which raise the world, and started talking about his travels, which had begun as a cabin-boy in the port of Marseilles, where his father—all honour to him—had been a master baker.

"Bakers are very useful members of society," commented Esteban, well-pleased by a foreigner who could arrive in these parts without boasting about his noble blood.

"Better to lay roads than make porcelain flowers," remarked the other, with a classical quotation, before going on to talk about his nursemaid from Martinique, who had been as black as coal and, as it were, a presage of the paths he would follow later, since, although as a boy he had dreamed of Asia, all the ships which would take him on board were bound for the Antilles or the Gulf of Mexico. He talked of the coral forests of the Bermudas; of the wealth of Baltimore; of Mardi gras in New Orleans, just like that in Paris; of the spirits they made from mint and watercress in Veracruz; then he had gone on to the Gulf of Paria, by way of the Island of Pearls and far-off Trinidad.

With the rank of mate he had gone as far as distant Paramaribo, a city that might well be envied by some others which gave themselves airs—here he pointed to the ground—for it had broad avenues of orange and lemon trees, whose trunks were inlaid with sea-shells by way of additional decoration. Magnificent balls were given on board the foreign ships anchored at the foot of the Fort Zeelandia, and the Dutch girls there—he said, winking at the young men—were very prodigal with their favours. One could sample every wine and liqueur in the world in that iridescent colony, where the banquets were served by negresses decked in bracelets and necklaces and wearing skirts of Indian silk, with delicate, almost transparent blouses stretched tight over their hard, quivering breasts. And to placate Sofia, who was frowning at this picture, he lent it opportune dignity with a quotation from a French poem alluding to the Persian slave-girls who wore a similar costume in the palace of Sardanapolis.

"Thank you," muttered the girl furiously, although she acknowledged the skill with which he had extricated himself. As for the Antilles, the man went on, changing latitudes, it was a wonderful archipelago, where one came across the strangest things : enormous anchors abandoned on lonely beaches; houses fixed to the rocks with iron chains, so that the cyclones could not sweep them into the sea; a huge Sephardic cemetery in Curaçao; islands inhabited by women who lived alone for months and years on end, while the men were working on the mainland; sunken galleons, petrified trees, unimaginable fish; and, in Barbados, the tomb of a nephew of Constantine XI, the last emperor of Byzantium, whose ghost appeared to solitary wayfarers on stormy nights.

Sofia at once asked their visitor, with great seriousness, whether he had ever seen mermaids in the tropical seas. And before the stranger could answer, the girl showed him a page in *Las Delicias de Holanda,* a very old book where it was told that once, after a storm which breached the dykes in West Friesland, a sea-woman had appeared, half-buried in the mud. They took her to Haarlem, dressed her and taught her to spin. She lived there for several years, never learning the language, and always instinctively attracted to the sea. When she cried it was like the moan of someone who is dying.

In no way disconcerted by this information, the visitor told them about a mermaid discovered years before in Maroni. She had been discribed by a Major Archicrombie, a very reputable soldier, in a report that had got as far as the Academy of Sciences in Paris : "An English Major can't have been wrong," he added, with almost annoying gravity.

Noticing that the visitor had just risen several points in Sofia's estimation, Carlos brought the conversation back to the subject of his travels. But all that he had left to talk about was Basse-Terre in Guadeloupe, with its fountains of running water and its houses which reminded one of Rochefort and La Rochelle. Did the young people not know Rochefort or La Rochelle?

"They must be horrible," said Sofia. "We shall have to spend a few hours in places like that on our way to Paris. But let's talk about Paris. I suppose you know it like the back of your hand?"

The stranger looked askance at her and, without answering

her question, told her how he had gone from Pointe-à-Pitre to San Domingo, with the object of starting a business, and had finally established himself in Port-au-Prince, where he had a prosperous shop, a shop with many goods in it: skins, salted meat ("How dreadful!" exclaimed Sofía), casks, spices, "more or less *comme la vôtre*". He stressed the French phrase, jerking his thumb over his shoulder at the dividing wall, with a gesture which the girl considered the height of insolence.

"We don't look after all this ourselves," she observed.

"It wouldn't be *easy* or *leisurely* work," replied the other, immediately going on to explain that he had just come from Boston, a big centre of commerce and a splendid place to procure flour at a better price than in Europe. He was now awaiting a large shipment, of which he would sell part on the spot and send the rest to Port-au-Prince.

Carlos was on the point of dismissing this intruder courteously, now that he was getting on to the hateful subject of buying and selling, after his interesting autobiographical introduction, when, rising from his arm-chair as if he were in his own house, the man went over to the books piled in a corner. He pulled out a volume, and showed obvious pleasure at being able to link the name of the author with an advanced political or religious belief: "I see you are very much *au courant*," he said, at once undermining the others' resistance. Soon they were showing him the editions of their favourite authors, which the stranger fingered with deference, sniffing the grain of the paper and the calf of the bindings. Then he approached the clutter of the physics laboratory and proceeded to assemble a piece of apparatus from the parts lying scattered on various pieces of furniture: "This is used in navigation too," he said.

Then, since the heat was considerable, he asked permission to take off his coat, to the amazement of the others, who were disconcerted at seeing him penetrate with such familiarity into a world which seemed terribly unfamiliar tonight, with this alien presence standing by the "Druids' Causeway" or the "Leaning Tower". Sofía was on the point of inviting him to dinner (though ashamed to have to reveal that in this house they dined at midnight, off food suitable to the mid-day meal) when the stranger, adjusting a quadrant, whose function had hitherto been a mystery, winked towards the dining-room, where the table had been laid before his arrival. "I've brought my own wine," he said. And fetching the bottles, which he had left on a seat in the patio when he came in, he set them on the table-cloth with a flourish, and invited the others to take their places.

Sofia was scandalised afresh at the incredible effrontery of this intruder, who was assuming the role of a paterfamilias in the house. But the young men were already sampling an Alsatian wine with such a show of satisfaction that, thinking of poor Esteban—he had been very ill lately, and seemed much taken with this visitor—Sofia adopted the attitude of a proud and gracious lady and passed the trays to the man whom she called "Monsieur Juig" in sibilant tones.

"Huuuuuuuug," corrected the other, drawing out the "u", and cutting the "g" abruptly short, but Sofia would not amend her pronunciation. Although she had been told how the name should be pronounced she took a malicious delight in distorting it a little more each time, into "Iug", "Juk" and "Ugües", and finally into unpronounceable sounds which made her burst out laughing over the Holy Week cakes and marzipan that Rosaura had brought—and which now suddenly reminded Esteban that it was Easter Saturday.

"Les cloches! Les cloches!" exclaimed their guest energetically, pointing aloft with an obviously scornful forefinger, to indicate that there had been much ringing of bells, both great and small, in the town during the course of that morning. Then he went out for another bottle—of Arbois this time—which the now somewhat tipsy young men greeted with tumultuous delight, going through the motions of blessing it. When their glasses were empty they went out into the patio to breathe the night air.

"What's up there?" asked Monsieur Juig, going resolutely over to the wide staircase. And in no time he was on the next floor, having mounted the stairs with huge strides, leaning out from the gallery under the roof, where a wooden balustrade ran between the pillars.

"If he dares to go into my room I'll kick him out again," murmured Sofia. But their bold visitor approached the last door, which was ajar, and gently pushed it.

"That's a sort of loft," said Esteban. And it was he who

now led the way into a room where he had not been for years, lamp in hand. Various trunks, boxes, chests and travelling bags were stowed against the walls, with an orderliness which provided an amusing contrast when one remembered the chaos reigning below. At the back was a sacristy cupboard, made of magnificently grained wood which attracted Monsieur Juig's attention: "Solid, handsome." Sofia opened the cupboard so that he might feel the solidity and see how thick the doors were. But the stranger now showed more interest in the old clothes hanging from a metal rod: clothes that had belonged to members of their mother's family, who had built the house; to the academician, the prelate, the naval ensign, the magistrate; their grandmother's dresses, faded satins, austere cloaks, lace ball-gowns, muslins green with saltpetre, calicos and Indian silks; fancy dresses, worn only once, a shepherdess, a fortune-teller, an Inca princess, a lady of long ago.

"Wonderful for charades!" exclaimed Esteban. And suddenly, all agreed on the same idea, they began to take out these dusty relics, amidst a great flurry of moths, and to slide them down the polished mahogany stairs. Soon afterwards, in the main drawing-room, now turned into a theatre, the four of them were taking it in turns to interpret different characters and guess who they were. Merely by changing the clothes about, modifying their shape with pins, accepting a nightgown as a Roman peplum or an ancient tunic, they were able to represent heroes from history or from novels—sometimes with the help of a ruff made to represent a laurel wreath, a pipe doing duty as a pistol, or a stick hanging at the waist like a sword.

Monsieur Juig, with an obvious preference for antiquity, played Mucius Scaevola, Caius Gracchus and Demosthenes—a Demosthenes who was quickly identified when he was seen to go out into the patio in search of small stones. Carlos, with a flute and cardboard cocked hat, was recognised as Frederick the Great, however much he tried to prove that he had wanted to be the flautist Quantz. Esteban imitated the experiments of Galvani with a toy frog brought from his room, and brought his own performances to an end there and then, because the dust from his clothes made him sneeze alarmingly. Sofia, guessing that Monsieur Juig would be very little versed in things Spanish, took a malicious revenge on him by playing Inez de Castro, Juana la Loca and the Famous Kitchenmaid, and finally made herself look as ugly as possible, contorting her face and putting on a stupid expression, in order to bring to life an unidentifiable character who turned out, amidst the protests of the others, to be "any Bourbon princess".

When it was nearly daylight Carlos proposed that they should have "a big massacre". After adorning them with grotesque masks of painted paper, they hung the costumes with thin pieces of thread on a wire stretched between the trunks of palm trees, and then began throwing balls at them to knock them down.

"Massacre them!" cried Esteban, leading the assault. And prelates, captains, court ladies and shepherds tumbled down, amidst laughter which was forced upwards through the narrow patio, and could be heard all down the street.

Daylight surprised them in the grip of a joyful frenzy, still playing insatiably, hurling paperweights, cooking pots, flower vases and volumes of an encyclopaedia at the costumes which the ball had failed to dislodge. "Massacre them!" Esteban was shouting. "Massacre them!"

At last Remigio was asked to get the carriage out and take the visitor to the nearby hotel. The Frenchman took his leave, protesting his affection and promising to return when night came. "He's quite a character," said Esteban. But it was time for the others to dress in black and go to the church of the Espiritu Santo, where another Mass was being said for their father's eternal repose. "Supposing we didn't go?" said Carlos, yawning. "They'll say the Mass just the same."

"I will go by myself," said Sofia severely.

But after some vacillation, she found an excuse in the imminence of a very normal indisposition, drew the curtains of her room and went to bed.

V

VICTOR, AS THEY now called him, came to the house every evening, and proved himself a master of the most unlikely skills.

One night he was inspired to put his hands into the flour-bowl and make croissants which showed his command of the art of bakery. On other occasions he concocted exquisite sauces, using ingredients which it seemed most improbable would mix. He transformed cold meat into a Russian dish by skilful use of fennel and ground pepper; and he would add boiling wine and spices to any of his confections before baptising the result with grandiloquent names inspired by famous chefs. The discovery of the Marques de Villena's *Arte Scisoria*, amongst various rare books which they had received from Madrid, led to a week of mediaeval delicacies, during which a sirloin of pork would take on a magnificently venatorial appearance.

Besides this he managed to assemble the most complicated pieces of apparatus in the physics laboratory—almost all of them now worked, illustrating theorems, analysing the spectrum, throwing off pretty sparks—and he would hold forth about them in the picturesque Spanish he had acquired in his travels in the Gulf of Mexico and the islands of the Caribbean, where words and phrases multiplied with surprising fertility. At the same time he made the young people practise their French pronunciation, getting them to read a page from a novel or, better still, some comedy or other, in which they each took different parts as in the theatre. And how Sofia laughed when Esteban, in a dusk which to her was dawn, declaimed, in the marked southern accent he owed to his mentor, the lines from *Le Joueur*:

> *"Il est, parbleu, grand jour. Déjà de leur ramage*
> *Les coqs ont éveillé tout notre voisinage."*

One stormy night Victor was invited to sleep in one of the bedrooms. And when the others got up the following evening, shortly before the cocks of the neighbourhood tucked their heads under their wings, they were met by an incredible sight: his chest exposed, his shirt torn, sweating like a negro stevedore, the Frenchman had just finished pulling out what for so many months had been left half-unpacked, and was arranging the furniture, carpets and vases to suit his own fancy, with the help of Remigio. Their first impression was disconcerting and melancholy. The whole scenery of their dreams was collapsing. But the young people gradually began to enjoy this unexpected transformation, which gave them more space, created more light, and revealed the soft depths of an arm-chair, the delicate inlay of a sideboard, or the warm tints of the Coromandel. Sofia went from room to room as if she were in a new house, looking at herself in unknown mirrors set facing each other, which multiplied her reflection until it was lost in a nebulous distance. And since some corners had been stained by damp, Victor was perched on top of a step-ladder, touching them up with paint here and there, and spattering his eyebrows and cheeks.

Overcome by a sudden frenzy to arrange everything, the others threw themselves on what was left in the packing-cases, unrolling carpets, unfolding curtains, pulling crockery out of its sawdust, throwing everything that was broken out into the patio—and perhaps regretting that they could not find more broken things to dash against the wall of the warehouse. That morning there was a Grand Dinner in the dining-room; they made believe it was in Vienna, because for some time now Sofia had loved reading articles extolling the marble, glass and rocaille of that incomparably musical city dedicated to Saint Stephen—the patron saint of Esteban, who had been born in this house one December 26th.

Afterwards they held an Ambassadors' Ball in front of the bevelled mirrors of the drawing-room, to the sound of Carlos' flute—as this was such a special occasion he cared little for what the neighbours might think. They served trays of punch sprinkled with cinnamon, prepared by the Crown Minister. Esteban, in his position as peevish and much decorated dauphin, remarked that everyone was dancing atrociously at this party: Victor strutting about like a sailor on the quarter-deck, Sofia inept because the nuns did not teach dancing, Carlos looking like a revolving mechanical doll as he spun in time to his own music.

"Massacre them!" shouted Esteban, bombarding them with hazelnuts and sweets. However, all was not well with the teasing dauphin, for suddenly a wheezing in his trachea signalled the start of an attack. Within a few minutes his face was lined and aged by a rictus of pain. Already the veins in his neck were swelling, his knees were as wide apart as they would go, and his elbows turned forward so that he could lift his shoulders, as he fought for the air which he could not find anywhere in that huge house.

"We must take him where it's not so hot," said Victor. Sofia had never thought of that. While their father was alive, austere man that he was, no one would ever have been allowed to leave the house after evening prayers. Taking the asthmatic boy in his arms, Victor carried him to the carriage, while Carlos took down the horse's collar and harness.

And now, for the first time, Sofia found herself out of doors among great houses made taller by the darkness, which accentuated the depth of shadows, the height of the pillars and the width of the roofs, with their eaves projecting over grilles surmounted with an iron lyre, siren or goat's head beside a coat of arms full of keys, lions, crowns and Santiago scallop-shells. They came out into the Alameda, where a few street lamps were still burning. It appeared strangely deserted with its closed shops, its shadowy arcades, its silent fountain, and the ships' lanterns rocking at the mastheads, which rose like a forest of serried trees beyond the wharfs. With the soft sound of the water, as it lapped against the piles of the jetties, there came a smell of fish, oil and marine decay. A cuckoo-clock sounded from the depths of a sleeping house, and the night watchman chanted the time, melodiously proclaiming that the sky was clear and cloudless.

After taking three slow turns Esteban made a gesture expressing his desire to go farther. The carriage drove off towards the Astillero, where the ships under construction looked like giant fossils with the soaring ribs of their hulls. "Not this way," said Sofia, noticing that they were already beyond the jetties, and had left the skeleton ships behind to enter a district where the people looked increasingly sinister. Victor ignored her and brought his whip lightly down on the hind quarters of the horse. There were lights nearby. And on turning a corner they found themselves in a street thronged with sailors, where several dance halls were pouring out music and laughter through their open windows. Couples were dancing in time to drums, flutes and violins, with a shamelessness which brought a flush to Sofia's cheeks; though mute and scandalised, she was unable to tear her eyes away from the crowded rooms dominated by the acid voice of the clarinets. There were mulattas wriggling their hips and turning their rumps on anyone who followed them, only to run quickly away from the aggressive gesture which they had incited. On the stage a negress, with her skirts up over her thighs, was tapping out the rhythm of a *guaracha*, which kept returning to the poignant refrain of "When, my love, when?" A woman was showing her breasts, for the price of a glass of wine, while next to her another, lying on a table, threw her shoes up to the ceiling and shook her thighs free from her petticoats. Men of all types and colours were making their way into the taverns, plunging their hands into the mass of buttocks.

Victor avoided the drunks with a coachman's skill and seemed to be enjoying this squalid turmoil; he picked out the North Americans by their swaying gait, the English by their songs, the Spaniards because they drank their wine out of wineskins and *porrons*. At the entrance to a hovel, several prostitutes in night-dresses were grabbing hold of the passers-by and allowing themselves to be fingered, embraced, lifted up; one of them, thrown backwards on to a wretched bed by the weight of a black-bearded colossus, had not even had time to close the door. Another was undressing a skinny cabin boy, who was too drunk to manage his own clothes.

Sofia was ready to cry out with disgust and indignation, even more on Carlos' and Esteban's account than her own. This world was so strange to her that she saw it as a vision of hell, unconnected with the world she knew. The promiscuities of these harbour denizens who knew neither faith nor law had nothing to do with her. But she noticed something restless, something unusual and expectant—not to say acquiescent—in the expressions of the men, which exasperated her. It was as if "it" did not repel them as deeply as it did her; as if a sign of understanding had passed between their senses and these bodies, so different from those of the normal world. She imagined Esteban and Carlos dancing there in that house, writhing on those bedsteads, mingling their clean sweat with the coarse exhalations of those women.

Standing up in the carriage, she snatched the whip from Victor and delivered such a blow with it that the horse leaped into a gallop, upsetting a street vendor's cooking pots with the

41

shaft. Simmering oil, hake, bread rolls and meat pies were spilled out, raising howls from a scalded dog which writhed in the dust, skinning itself still further on the broken glass and splinters of fish-bone. Uproar broke out up and down the street, and several negresses came running after them in the darkness, armed with sticks, knives and empty bottles, and hurling stones which rebounded from the roofs, detaching pieces of tile from the gables as they fell. When they saw the carriage vanishing their insults became almost amusing, so exhaustive were they, so far did they go in blasphemy and insolence.

"The things a young lady has to listen to!" said Carlos, as they took a roundabout course back to the Alameda. When they reached the house Sofia disappeared into its shadows, without saying good-night.

Victor presented himself as usual that evening. After a momentary respite Esteban's attack had been growing in severity throughout the day, reaching such a pitch that now they were thinking of sending for the doctor, a decision of exceptional gravity in this house, because the patient had learned from long experience that medical prescriptions, when they had any effect at all, only made his condition worse. Hanging from the bars of his window, facing the patio, the boy had removed all his clothing in his desperation, and was naked, perhaps without realising it; he presented a tragic picture. With his ribs and collar-bones sticking out so sharply that they seemed to have come through his skin, his body made one think of certain recumbent figures in Spanish graveyards, which have been emptied of their entrails and reduced to skin stretched tightly over a framework of bones.

Defeated in his struggle for breath, Esteban let himself drop to the floor, and leaned against the wall, his face purple, his finger-nails almost black, looking at the others with the eyes of a dying man. His wildly racing heartbeats throbbed in every vein. His face seemed to be smeared with a waxen paste, his gums were white and his tongue, unable to find any saliva, was pressed against teeth that were beginning to chatter.

"We must do something!" shouted Sofia. "We must do something!"

After a few minutes of apparent indifference, Victor ordered the carriage, as if moved by a sudden decision, and announced that he was going for someone who possessed extraordinary powers in overcoming illness.

He returned after half an hour, accompanied by a powerfully-built but soberly and elegantly dressed half-breed, whom he introduced as Doctor Ogé, a famous doctor and a distinguished philanthropist, whom he had met in Port-au-Prince. Sofia made a slight bow in the newcomer's direction, without offering him her hand. The relatively light colour of his complexion made it look as though this were an artificial skin covering a real negro's face, one of those with wide nostrils and woolly hair. Anyone wholly or partly black was to her by definition a servant, a stevedore, a coachman, or an itinerant musician, even though Victor, noticing her peevish gesture, explained that Ogé came of a well-to-do family in San Domingo, had studied in Paris, and had qualifications which guaranteed his skill. Certainly his vocabulary was meticulously chosen; he used old, obsolete turns of phrase when he spoke in French, and he drew an excessive distinction between "c"s and "z"s when he spoke in Spanish, while his manners showed a constant attention to the rules of politeness.

"But he's a negro!" whispered Sofia into Victor's ear with a gasp.

"All men were born equal," he replied, pushing her gently away from him. This only increased her resistance. Even if she acknowledged it as a humanitarian ideal, she could not bring herself to accept that a negro could become the family doctor, or that one could surrender the body of a relation to a coloured person. Nobody would entrust a negro with the building of a palace, the defence of a criminal, the direction of a theological controversy or the government of a country. But Esteban, breathing stertorously, called out in such desperation that they all went to his room.

"Let the doctor go to work," said Victor peremptorily. "We've got to end this attack somehow."

The half-breed did not look at the patient, did not examine him or touch him, but remained motionless, sniffing the air in a curious way. "It would not be the first time it had happened," he said, after a while. And he looked up at a little ox-eye window, set in the thick wall between two of the rafters which supported the ceiling. He asked what was behind the wall. Carlos remembered that there was a narrow yard, very damp and full of broken furniture and useless lumber—a sort of open-air corridor, separated from the street by a thin railing covered with creepers—into which no one had been for many years past. The doctor insisted on being taken there.

After making a detour through Remigio's room—he was out fetching medicine—they opened a creaking blue door. The sight that now met their eyes was very surprising; parsley, nettles, mimosa and woodland grasses were growing in two long parallel beds around several very flourishing mignonette plants. A bust of Socrates, which Sofía remembered having once seen, as a child, in her father's office, was set in a niche, as if displayed on an altar, surrounded by curious offerings, such as magicians use for their spells: cups full of grains of maize, sulphur stones, snails, iron filings.

"*C'est ça,*" said Ogé, contemplating this miniature garden as if it had great meaning for him. And moved by a sudden impulse he began to pull up the mignonette by the roots, piling it between the flower-beds. Then he went into the kitchen, brought back a shovelful of glowing coals, and started a bonfire on which he threw all the vegetation that was growing in the narrow yard. "We have probably found the cause of the illness," he said, launching into an explanation which seemed to Sofía just like the lore of a necromancer. According to him certain illnesses were mysteriously connected with the growth of a grass, a plant or a tree somewhere nearby. Every human being had a "double" in the vegetable kingdom, and there were cases where this "double", to further its own growth, stole strength from the man with whom it was linked, condemning him to illness while it flowered or germinated. "*Ne souriez pas, Mademoiselle.*" He had been able to verify this many times in San Domingo, where asthma afflicted children and adolescents, and killed them either by suffocation or by anaemia. But sometimes it was enough to burn any plants growing near the sufferer, either in the house or in the vicinity of it, for surprising cures to be effected.

"Witchcraft!" said Sofía. "It must have been."

Remigio now appeared, and became suddenly agitated when

he saw what had been happening. Violently, almost disrespect-fully, he threw his hat to the ground, exclaiming that they had burned *his* plants, which he had been growing for a long time to sell at market, for medicinal purposes. They had destroyed his *caisimón*, which he had been at great pains to get acclima-tised, and which cured all afflictions of a man's genitals if the application of its leaves was accompanied by a prayer to Saint Hermenegildo, who had been tortured in that part of the body by the Sultan of the Saracens. What they had done had gravely offended the Lord of the Forests, whose "portrait"—and he pointed towards the bust of Socrates—recognisable by the sparse beard, sanctified this place, which no one in the house had ever used for anything. And, bursting into tears, he ended by groan-ing that if the Master had put a little more faith in his herbs—and he had made a point of offering them to him when he saw him being led astray, what with his final passion for introducing strange women into the house, at times when Carlos was away at the finca, Sofia at the convent, and the other one too ill to notice anything—he would not have died the way he did, on top of a woman, undoubtedly because he had bragged too much about a virility that was denied to men of his years.

"To-morrow you leave here!" shouted Sofia, cutting short this loathsome scene; she felt crushed, sickened, by this stupefy-ing revelation, unable to come to terms with it. They went back to Esteban's room, Carlos, who had not yet grasped the implica-tions of what Remigio had said, deploring the time they had wasted in useless fuss. But something wonderful was happening to the sick land; from having been protracted and high-pitched, the wheezing which filled his throat was now becoming inter-mittent, occasionally ceasing altogether for several seconds on end. It was as if Esteban could now take short sips of air, and with this relief his ribs and collar-bones had returned to their rightful places and no longer protruded from the contours of his body.

"Just as some men are murdered by raspberry canes or Good Friday thistles," said Ogé, "this boy was being slowly killed by those bunches of yellow flowers which were feeding off his substance." And now, sitting in front of the patient, gripping his knees between his own, he fixed him with an imperious gaze, as, with an undulating movement of the fingers, his hands seemed to pour an invisible fluid into his temples. An astonished gratitude showed on Esteban's face; it was no longer congested, but turning white in first one part then another, although a blue vein still stood out here and there in abnormal relief. Changing his methods, Doctor Ogé massaged the orbits of the young man's eyes with the fleshy part of his thumbs, his hands describing identical circles. Suddenly he stopped and drew them to himself, closing the fingers and holding them suspended level with his own cheeks, as if completing a ritual action. Esteban slipped sideways on to the wicker ottoman, overcome by a sudden torpor, and sweating from every pore. Sofia covered his naked body with a blanket.

"A tisane of ipecac and arnica leaves when he wakes up," said the medicaster, going over to adjust his clothes in front of a mirror where he met the questioning stare of Sofia, who was following him with her eyes. There was a lot of the magician and the charlatan in his theatrical gestures, but for all that he had accomplished a miracle.

"My friend belongs to the Harmony Society of Cap Français," explained Victor to Carlos, as he uncorked a bottle of Portuguese wine.

"Is that a musical organisation?" asked Sofia. Ogé and Victor looked at one another and burst out laughing together. Irritated by this inexplicable hilarity, the girl went back to Esteban's room, where the sick youth was sleeping heavily, his breathing normal, and his finger-nails recovering some of their colour. Victor was waiting for her in the doorway of the drawing-room: "The negro's honorarium," he said, in a low voice. Ashamed of her oversight, Sofia hastened to fetch an envelope from her room, which she held out to the doctor.

"Oh, jamais de la vie!" the half-breed exclaimed, rejecting the payment with an angry gesture, and starting to talk about modern medicine; although she had for a number of years been very ready to admit that certain powers, certain inadequately understood forces, could work on a man's health, Sofia directed an angry glance at Victor. But it fell into the void; the Frenchman had his eyes fixed on Rosaura, the mulatta, who was strutting across the patio, her rump bulging in a light blue floral dress. "How interesting," the girl murmured, as if she were attending to Ogé's discourse.

"Plaît-il?" asked the other.

A palm frond fell into the middle of the patio with a noise like a curtain being torn. The wind was bringing them a smell from the sea—a sea so close that it seemed to spill over into the streets of the city. "We shall have a cyclone this year," said Carlos, trying, as he inspected one of Albertus Magnus' thermometers, to convert Fahrenheit into Réaumur. A suppressed uneasiness reigned. Words were divorced from thoughts. Each of them spoke out of a mouth which did not belong to him, even though it might be opening above his own chin. Albertus Magnus' thermometer did not interest Carlos; Ogé did not feel that anyone was listening to him; Sofia could not rid herself of a gnawing irritation against Remigio—for stupidly revealing something she had suspected for some time, and which made her despise the miserable masculine inability to support the quiet, dignified solitude of a bachelor or widower's life. And this irritation against the indiscreet servant grew as she realised that the negro's words had given her a reason for admitting to herself that she had never loved her father, whose kisses, reeking of liquorice and tobacco, reluctantly planted on her forehead and cheeks when she was returning to the convent after those tedious Sunday luncheons, had been hateful to her ever since the days of her puberty.

VI

SOFIA FELT ALIENATED, estranged from herself, as if she were standing on the threshold of an epoch of change. Some evenings she had the feeling that the light had taken on a different coloration, and was giving things a new personality. A Christ came from the shadows, to stare at her out of sad eyes. A hitherto unnoticed object proclaimed the delicate quality of its workmanship; a schooner would suddenly take shape in the grained wood of a chest of drawers; a picture seemed to speak another language when she suddenly noticed that a figure in it had been restored; her harlequins were no longer so confined by the foliage of their park, while she was exasperated by the checked motion, the everlasting fall which never fell, of the broken, scattered columns in the "Explosion in a Cathedral".

Books arrived from Paris, much coveted and eagerly ordered from a catalogue a few months before, but were now left half-unwrapped on a shelf of the book-case. She went from one thing to another, abandoning some useful task to repair something valueless—sticking broken vases together, sowing plants which would never grow in the tropics, amusing herself with a botanical treatise, then digging into a boring work all about Aeneas and Patroclus, whom she abandoned in their turn to rummage in a trunk full of remnants. She was incapable of persevering with anything, of finishing a piece of mending, the household accounts, or her translation—unnecessary in any case —of *An Ode to Night*, by the Englishman Collins.

Nor was Esteban the same as before. Many changes had taken place in his character and his habits since the portentous night of his cure—it was a fact that since the destruction of Remigio's unsuspected garden his illness had not troubled him at all. Having lost his fear of a nocturnal attack, he was now the first to leave the house, and got up earlier every day. He ate when he felt an appetite, without waiting for the others. In revenge for all the diets imposed on him by the doctors, a perpetual greed led him to the kitchen, where he would put his hand into the stewpot, seize the first piece of puff-pastry from the oven, or devour the fruit which had just been brought from the market. Tired of pineapple juice and orgeat, which he associated with the memory of his sufferings, he quenched his thirst, whatever the hour, with huge draughts of red wine, whose colour rose into his face. He was insatiable at table, especially when he lunched alone at mid-day; when, chest exposed, sleeves rolled-up, shod in Arab slippers, he would take the nutcrackers and attack a tray of shellfish with such violence that the pieces of shell flew off against the wall. By way of a dressing-gown he wore a bishop's cope, taken from the wardrobe of family clothes, whose satin was delectably cool against his bare skin; a rosary girdled him in place of a belt, and his hairy knees stuck out from below the amaranth. And this bishop was always on the move, playing skittles in the gallery of the patio, sliding down the banisters of the staircase, hanging from the balustrades, or laboriously trying to mend the chime of a clock which had been silent for twenty years. Sofía, who had bathed him so many times during his attacks, paying no heed to the downy shadows which were beginning to darken his body, now felt growingly embarrassed, and was careful not to look out on to the flat roof when she knew that the boy was taking an open-air bath, or lying on the tiles to dry in the sun, without even having taken the trouble to lay a towel across his hips.

"He's becoming a man," Carlos would say, delightedly.

"A real man," Sofía echoed, knowing that, for the last few days, he had been shaving off the adolescent down with a barber's razor.

By re-ascending the ladder of time Esteban had given back their true meaning to the hours that had been reversed by the habits of the household. He got up earlier every day, until he was sharing the servants' early morning coffee. Sofía was astonished by him, frightened by the new personality that was growing inside someone who had been a sickly, pitiful creature a few weeks ago, and who now went about inhaling and exhaling perfectly, cured of his phlegm and his congestion, displaying an energy which was belied, however, by his bony shoulders, his weak legs, and a general physique emaciated by his long illness. The girl felt the anxiety of a mother who notices the first signs of virility in her son—a son who more and more frequently took up his hat and went and roamed the streets on some pretext or other, concealing, needless to say, that his excursions always led him to the streets round the harbour, or to the furthest reaches of the Alameda, near the church—a route which circumscribed the Arsenal quarter.

Timidly at first, venturing as far as the first corner one day, and as far as the second the next, so as to divide up the distance he had to cover, he finally reached the street of the gambling dens and the dance halls, which were oddly peaceful at this time of the evening. Women who had just got up or bathed came to their doors breathing out tobacco smoke, and banteringly importuned the lad, who fled from the more aggressive ones, but shortened his stride in front of those who whispered offers to him which only he could hear. From the houses behind them came a cloying aroma of perfume and soap, of languorous bodies and warm bedrooms, which set his pulse racing, as he realised that the decision of a moment would suffice to enable him to penetrate into a world full of mysterious possibilities.

Between an abstract notion of the physical mechanisms and the real consummation of the act, lay the enormous distance which only adolescence can measure—along with the vague sensation of guilt, of danger, of something beginning, which was implied in the act of embracing the body of another. For ten days he walked as far as the end of the street, almost resolved to go into a house where an indolent young girl was always sitting on a footstool, in tactful silence. Ten more times he returned and walked past her without summoning up sufficient courage, while she waited for him unconcernedly, sure of having him either that day or the next, and knowing that she had already been chosen. Finally, one evening, the blue door of the house closed behind him.

Nothing that happened to him in that hot, narrow room, unadorned except for some petticoats hanging from a nail, seemed to him either very important or very extraordinary. Certain modern novels, of unheard of crudity, had revealed to him that true voluptuousness obeyed impulses that were subtle and shared. Nevertheless he returned there every day for several weeks; he needed to prove to himself that he was capable of doing—without either remorse or physical failure, though with a growing curiosity to experiment on other bodies—what youths of his age did quite naturally.

"Where did you pick up that frightful perfume?" his cousin asked him one day, sniffing at his neck. Shortly afterwards Esteban found a book on his bedside table dealing with the terrible diseases inflicted on men as a punishment for the sins of the flesh. The boy kept the book without acknowledging the allusion.

Sofia had grown accustomed to spending long evenings alone, now that Esteban was out so often, and Carlos, driven by a new whim, went to the riding school on the Campo de Marte, where a famous horseman was giving exhibitions of the Spanish style of riding, training the horses to rear up nobly on their hind legs like those in equestrian statues, or to mark time gracefully with their hooves, by working the bridle in the Portuguese style.

Victor always turned up at dusk. By way of a greeting, Sofia would ask after the shipment of flour from Boston, which had never arrived.

"When it comes," said the trader, "I shall go back to Port-au-Prince with Ogé. He's got several things to attend to there." This prospect terrified the girl, who was afraid that Esteban might suffer some recrudescence of his illness.

"Ogé has pupils here," observed Victor, to calm her, although he did not enlighten her as to where the lessons were taking place, nor as to what view of him was taken by the Board of Physicians, who were very strict about matters of affiliation.

He often talked to her about Don Cosme, whom he considered to be a very poor businessman: "He's a *gagne-petit* who can't see beyond the end of his nose." And although he knew Sofia's repugnance for anything in any way connected with the business on the other side of the wall, Victor took to advising her. As soon as they were old enough to do so, she and her brother should get rid of the Executor, and entrust the management of their affairs to someone more capable, who could make the business flourish. He then enumerated the new commodities from which there were great profits to be made.

"It might be my dear father talking, who is now with God in Glory," said Sofia, to put an end to this tedious discourse—in a voice so false and unconvincing that the very sound of it betrayed her sarcasm. Victor burst into the laugh which always accompanied any abrupt change of mood when he talked, and began to speak about his travels—Campeche, Marie Galante or Dominica—listening to himself with obvious pleasure. He was a disconcerting mixture of vulgarity and distinction. According to the turn the conversation was taking, he could pass from the boisterous eloquence of the Midi to an excessive verbal economy. Several individuals seemed to dwell within him. When he talked about buying and selling he would make the gestures of a banker, with hands that had been transformed into the pans of a balance. A moment later he would be deep in a book, quite motionless, wearing an intense frown, his eyelids seeming not to move over dark eyes that were riveted burningly on the page. When he took a fancy to do some cooking, he became a chef, balancing colanders on his forehead, making himself hats out of dish-cloths, drumming on the saucepans. Some days his hands were hard and grasping, and he had a habit of closing his fist around his thumb which Sofia found disagreeably revealing. On other days they became soft and delicate, caressing an idea as if it were a sphere suspended in the air. "I'm a man of the people," he would say, like someone displaying his family coat of arms. Yet, when they played charades, Sofia had noticed that he chose the parts of ancient legislators and tribunes, taking himself tremendously seriously, perhaps convinced that he was a great actor. Several times he had insisted on performing episodes from the life of Lycurgus, a character for whom he seemed to feel a special admiration. Clever in matters of commerce, knowledgeable about the mechanics of banking and insurance, a trader by profession, Victor nevertheless supported the distribution of land and property, the surrender of children to the State, the abolition of private fortunes, and the minting of an iron coinage which, like that of Sparta, could not be hoarded.

One day, feeling particularly cheerful and well, Esteban proposed an improvised party in the house, to celebrate "The Restoration of Normality in Eating Times". A great feast was to be held at eight o'clock precisely, and the guests would hurry to the dining-room from different corners of the house and occupy their seats within the time it took for the clock of the Espiritu Santo to strike eight. Anyone who failed would have to pay various forfeits. As for the formal dress, that was upstairs, in the wardrobe of costumes.

Sofia chose to disguise herself as a Duchess who had been ruined by pawnbrokers, and set to, with the help of Rosaura, to unstitch the underskirt. Esteban had already had his episcopal costume in his room for some time. Carlos was to come as a naval ensign, while Victor chose a magistrate's toga—"*elle me va très bien*"—before going off to the kitchen to prepare the wild pigeons that were to form the second course.

"So we have representatives of the Nobility, the Church, the Navy and the Judicature," said Carlos. "Diplomacy is missing," remarked Sofia, and, laughing, they agreed to make Ogé take the part of Ambassadorial Plenipotentiary of the Kingdom of Abyssinia.

But Remigio, who was sent to find him, returned with the most disconcerting news. The doctor had gone out early in the day, and not returned to his hotel. And now the police had just appeared to search his room, with orders to take away all his books and papers.

"I don't understand," said Victor, "I don't understand."

"Couldn't they have denounced him for practising medicine illegally?" asked Carlos.

"His *illegal* medicine is the one which cures the sick!" cried Esteban, beside himself.

Unusually agitated, and urgently hunting for his hat, which could not be found, Victor went out in search of news.

"It's the first time I've seen him upset by anything," said Sofia, passing a handkerchief over her sweating temples. It was exceedingly hot. The air seemed to hang motionless around the inert curtains, the withered flowers and the plants, which might have been made of metal. The leaves of the palm trees in the patio had taken on the heavy look of wrought iron.

VII

VICTOR RETURNED A little after seven o'clock. He had discovered nothing about Ogé's whereabouts, but he thought that he was a prisoner. Or perhaps, having been warned in time that he had been denounced—what for, no one yet knew—he had had the good fortune to find some friendly house where he could hide for a time. It was certain that the police had searched his room, taking away books, papers, and portmanteaux containing personal effects. "To-morrow we shall see what's going on," he said, abruptly changing the subject to something he had heard being discussed while he was walking through the streets: a hurricane would strike the city that night. The warning was an official one. There was much activity on the quay; the sailors were talking about a cyclone, and taking emergency measures to protect their ships. People were laying in supplies of candles and food. Everywhere they were starting to board up doors and windows.

In no way alarmed by this news, Carlos and Esteban went off to fetch hammers and wood. At this time of the year all the inhabitants of the city were expecting the cyclone—designated thus, in the singular, because there was never more than one which was really devastating, and if it veered in its course and failed to arrive on this occasion, then it would come next year. The important thing was to know whether it would strike the town directly, ripping off roofs, breaking the windows of churches and sinking ships, or whether it would pass by to one side and devastate the countryside. Those who lived on the island accepted the cyclone as a dreadful meteorological reality, which ultimately none of them would escape. Every district, every town, every village could remember a cyclone which seemed to have been intended for it alone. The best that one could hope for was that it would be of short duration, and not too severe.

"Ce sont de bien charmants pays," grumbled Victor, making fast the leaves of one of the outside shutters, and remembering that San Domingo too knew this annual threat.

A sudden brutal gust of wind eddied outside. The rain was already falling, solid and vertical, on the plants in the patio, with such fury that it made the earth spout from the flower-beds. "Here it comes," said Victor. A vast noise enveloped and encircled the house, and the different tunes made by the roof, the window-blinds and the skylights combined in a watery concert : solid water and broken water, water spattering, tumbling from a height, spouting from a gargoyle, being sucked into the mouth of a gutter. A respite ensued, but more oppressive, more heavily charged with silence than the early part of the night. And then came the second downpour—the second warning— more aggressive even than the previous one, accompanied this time by disproportionate gusts of wind, which were developing into a sustained assault. Victor went out on to the gallery of the patio; the wind blew over its roof without pausing or checking, carried forward by the forces that had brought it whirling, hurrying, spinning ever faster, from the furthest reaches of the Gulf of Mexico or the Sargasso Sea. Using an old sailor's trick he tasted the rain-water: "Salty. From the sea. *Pas de doute.*" He made a gesture of resignation, and then, to show that the next hours would be an ordeal, he went to fetch bottles of wine, glasses and biscuits, before settling himself in an arm-chair, surrounded by books. Lanterns and candles were placed beside the lamps, which threatened to go out with each gust of wind. "Better keep awake," said the Frenchman, "a door may give way, or a window blow out." A pile of planks, together with a set of carpenter's tools, rested within reach of his hand. Invited to share the asylum of the drawing-room, Remigio and Rosaura joined together in a prayer which frequently invoked the name of Santa Barbara.

It was a little after midnight when the eye of the hurricane entered the city. An immense roaring was heard, and in its wake the crash of buildings collapsing. Things went bowling along the street, others flew over the church-towers. Bits of beams, shop signs, tiles, glass, broken branches, lanterns, casks, ships' rigging fell from the sky. Imaginary door-knockers were battering on every door. The windows trembled between assaults. The house quivered from the foundations to the roof, groaning in every beam.

And it was at this moment that a torrent of filthy, muddy water overflowed into the patio, from the stables, the backyard, the kitchen, and from the street too, choking the drains with a sludge of horse manure, cinders, refuse and dead leaves. With shouts of alarm, Victor rolled up the big drawing-room carpet. He threw it up on to the stairs, and then approached the filthy water, whose level was rising all the time; it was already penetrating into the dining-room, and lapping the entrance to the other rooms. Sofia, Carlos and Esteban ran to pick up various pieces of furniture, which they piled on sideboards, tables, chests of drawers and wardrobes. "No!" shouted Victor, "There!" And wading knee-deep into the stinking water he opened the door which led into the warehouse. It had begun to flood there too; many things were already afloat, and drifted gently past as they shone the lantern. Victor set the men and the mulatta to work, pointing to what must be rescued, giving orders, shouting, directing their efforts. Bundles of perishable goods, bolts of cloth, packets of feathers, and more valuable merchandise, were thrown up on top of heaps of sacks, where the water could not get to them. "The furniture can be repaired," Victor shouted, "these might be ruined." Seeing that the others had understood, and were working where the urgency was greatest, he went back to the house, where Sofia was huddled on a divan, terror-stricken and in tears. There was already six inches of water all around her. Victor took her in his arms, carried her up to her room and threw her on to the bed: "Don't move from here. I'm going back for the furniture." And he began to run up and down stairs, carrying carpets, screens, stools, chairs, anything he could rescue. The water was already up to his knees. Suddenly there was the crash of something falling; on one side of the house the roof was shedding its tiles on to the floor of the patio like a handful of playing cards. A pile of debris and broken crockery now obstructed the door, cutting them off from the warehouse. Sofia leaned over the upstairs banister screaming in terror. Victor went up again, carrying a trunk full of odds and ends, and, thrusting the girl firmly into her room, dropped exhausted into an arm-chair: "I can't do any more." But to calm her and give her the comfort she so greatly needed, he told her that the worst of the cyclone had now passed over, that the others were safe in the warehouse on top of the piles of sacks, and that there was nothing to do but wait for dawn. The great thing was that the doors and windows had not given way. It would not be the first time after all that this sturdy old house had withstood a hurricane. In an almost playful tone he pointed out to Sofia how really filthy she was; her dress had been soiled by the dirty water, her stockings were muddy, and dead leaves had lodged in her wet, bedraggled hair. She went off to her dressing-room and soon returned in her nightdress, her hair somewhat tidier.

Outside, the sustained onset of the hurricane had now broken up into gusts, some weak, others fierce, but increasingly spaced out. What was now falling from the sky was a watery mist which smelled of the sea. The noise of things being pushed, dragged, tossed about and knocked down was diminishing.

"The best thing you can do is to go to bed," Victor said to Sofia, bringing her a large glass of wine. Then, with startling casualness, he removed his shirt and stood there stripped to the waist.

"Just as if he were my husband," thought Sofia, turning to the wall. She was going to say something, but sleep jumbled her words.

She awoke early—it was still dark—with the feeling that someone was lying beside her. An arm rested on her waist, an arm which became heavier as it tightened its grip. In her sudden confusion she could not grasp what was happening; after the terror she had experienced it was pleasant to feel herself enveloped, shielded, defended, by the warmth of another human being. She was on the point of going back to sleep again when she became aware, with a sudden icy thrill, that such a situation could not possibly be allowed to go on. She turned over abruptly and her body came into contact with the nakedness of another body. A nervous spasm shook her. She struck out with her fists, her elbows, her knees, trying to find something to scratch, something to bruise, but she still could not escape that strange contact with the unknown weight which pressed upon her stomach. The man's hands tried to grab her wrists; a menacing sound of heavy breathing brushed her ears; unaccustomed words came to her out of the darkness. In the struggle they became locked, knotted, grappled together, but the man gained no advantage. Fired with a new and enormous strength, which seemed to flow from her threatened womb, the woman hurt him with each movement she made, her body hard and clenched, never weakening or relaxing. At last the man abandoned his intent, signalling defeat with a dry laugh which ill concealed his annoyance. The woman continued the battle vocally, heaping on him indignant protests and sarcasms which displayed a prodigious capacity for humiliating, for inflicting wounds where they would hurt most.

The bed was relieved of a weight. The man was walking about the room, imploring her not to be too severe on him. In his attempt to excuse himself, he invoked reasons which astonished the girl who lay listening to them, doubly victorious. She had never imagined that this mature man, so worldly-wise and so much master of his past, could bestow the stature of a woman on her, who still felt so close to her own childhood. Now that her body was safe from the immediate peril, Sofia found herself being drawn towards a greater one : that of hearing herself being addressed by this voice speaking from the shadows—often with intolerable sweetness—opening the doors of an unknown world for her. The play-time of adolescence had come to an end that night. Words were beginning to take on a new meaning. What had happened—what had not happened—was acquiring a vast significance.

The door creaked, and a human form, outlined against the light of a watery dawn, went slowly away, with dragging legs, as if exhausted. Sofia was left alone, in her distress, her heart pounding, her hair dishevelled, and with the feeling that she had come through a terrible ordeal. Her skin had an unusual odour—perhaps real, perhaps imaginary—which she could not get rid of : a crude, animal smell, which she did not find entirely unpleasant. Her room grew lighter. Beside her were the hollows where someone had left the imprint of his body. The girl began to arrange the bed, pounding it with both fists to bring the feathers up again. That done, she felt profoundly humiliated; the prostitutes who lived down by the Arsenal no doubt straightened their beds like this after lying with an unknown man. And virgins too, when they awoke, deflowered and sullied, after their wedding night. This had been the worst of all, this arranging, this smoothing down, which had something of complicity, of acquiescence, about it; a shameful reparation, the secret movements of a lover anxious to erase the disorder left by an embrace.

Sofia lay down again, overcome by such drowsiness that Carlos found her sobbing, but so fast asleep that his knocking would not wake her.

"Leave her alone," said Esteban, "she's got her own troubles."

VIII

DAY DAWNED SLOWLY (though it was still not as light as was normal at this hour) above a roofless city, full of rubble and debris—a mere skeleton of bare rafters. Hundreds of poor homes had been reduced to the four corner-posts, and to tottering wooden floors standing in a quagmire, like scenes of poverty on the stage, on which resigned families were taking an inventory of the few articles that remained to them. The grandmother, rocking in a Viennese chair, the pregnant woman, afraid her labour pains might start now at her moment of dereliction, the consumptive or the asthmatic, sitting wrapped in blankets on the edge of the boards, all looked like actors in a fairground whose parts were already over. The masts of sunken schooners emerged from the dirty waters of the harbour, between capsized smaller craft, which drifted aimlessly about and collected in bunches. The corpse of a sailor was being dragged ashore, his hands caught in a tangle of ropes. By the Arsenal the cyclone had swept along close to the ground, scattering the planks of the ships that were building, and demolishing the flimsy walls of the taverns and dance saloons. The streets were muddy ditches. Several old palaces, for all their sturdy masonry, had been vanquished by the wind, and had surrendered their skylights, doors and shutters to the hurricane, which had penetrated within the walls and attacked them from inside, tearing down porticos and façades. The furniture from a famous cabinet-maker's—"Little Saint Joseph's", down by the quay—had been carried off by the wind, and dropped out in the open country beyond the city walls, beyond the orchards even, out where hundreds of palm trees were lying in the inundations caused by swollen streams, like the shafts of ancient columns torn down by an earthquake.

Yet, despite the magnitude of the disaster, people were accustomed to this periodic scourge, which they considered as an inevitable convulsion in the tropics, and they began to work like ants to seal up, repair and level out. Everything was wet, everything smelled wet, everything made one's hands wet. To dry out, to drain, to drive the water from wherever it was lying, that was everyone's task for the day. And by mid-afternoon, when the job of getting the houses clean again had been accomplished, carpenters, masons, glaziers and locksmiths began to offer their services.

When Sofia came out of her deep sleep, the house was full of workmen, fetched by Remigio—some busy retiling the skeleton of the collapsed roof, others removing the last of the debris which had filled the patio. There was a coming and going along corridors and galleries with mortar, plaster, and beams carried on shoulders, while Esteban and Carlos, moving between the warehouse and the house, were making an inventory of damaged furniture and ruined merchandise. Victor was installed in the drawing-room, dressed in a suit of Carlos' that was too small for him, and absorbed in a minute examination of the ledgers from the warehouse. When he saw Sofia he buried his face in the pages, pretending that he had not noticed her arrival. The girl went to the kitchen to attend to her own duties, and to the scullery, where Rosaura, who had not yet been to bed, was rescuing earthenware pots, plates and other kitchen utensils from the mud which was now hardening on the floors.

Sofia seemed dazed by all this activity, by this invasion of the house, by the unusualness of a situation which had disorganised the normal order of things and established a chaos in the rooms reminiscent of the past. During the night new Leaning Towers had sprung to life, new Druids' Causeways, new mountain paths climbing between the packing-cases, furniture, loose curtains, and rolled-up carpets piled on top of cupboards. But the surrounding smells were no longer those of the past; and the strangeness of everything, the violence of an event which had jolted everyone out of their habits and routine, now helped to aggravate the countless, contradictory disturbances produced in Sofia, when she woke up, by the memory of what had happened the night before. This formed part of the vast disorder in which the city had been plunged; it had integrated itself into the scene of the cataclysm. But there was one fact which outweighed in importance the collapse of walls, the destruction of belfries, the foundering of ships—she had been *desired*. This was so unusual, so unexpected, so disturbing, that she could not admit its reality. Within the space of a few hours she had emerged from adolescence, feeling that her body had matured in the presence of a man's desire. He had looked on her as a woman, before she had looked on herself as a woman, or imagined that others might concede her the status of woman. "I am a woman," she murmured resentfully, as if weighed down by an enormous burden which had been placed on her shoulders, and she looked at herself in the mirror as if she were looking at someone else, someone different and beset by adversity, finding herself tall, ungainly and insignificant, with those too-narrow hips, those skinny arms, and the asymmetry of her breasts which, for the first time, made her feel angry about her figure. The world was full of perils. She was leaving a road free from dangers to take another—a testing road, where everyone would make comparisons between her real and her reflected selves, a road which one could not travel without harm and giddiness.

Night fell quickly. The workmen departed, and a vast silence —the silence of ruins and mourning—fell on the chastised city. Sofia, Esteban and Carlos went exhausted to bed, after a meagre repast of cold meat, during which very little was said except by way of comment on the havoc wrought by the cyclone. Victor was absorbed in scrawling figures on the tablecloth with his thumb-nail, adding them up, subtracting them, rubbing them out; he asked permission to remain in the drawing-room until later, or rather, until next morning. The streets were impassable. There would be marauders and pick-pockets about their dark trade. Moreover he seemed very anxious to finish examining the books. "I think I've found something which will interest you a good deal," he said. "We'll talk about it to-morrow."

It had not yet struck nine the following morning when Sofia, aroused from her sleep by the hammering, sawing, noise of pulleys, and voices of the workmen who filled the house, came down into the drawing-room and found something strange happening. The Executor, with a half-smile on his face, was sitting in an arm-chair facing two other arm-chairs a certain distance away, in which sat Carlos and Esteban, looking like two judges in a courtroom, frowning, over-serious, over-expectant. Victor was pacing up and down the room, his hands clasped behind his back. From time to time he would stop in front of the accused, staring hard at him, and summing up his thoughts with a *"Oui!"* emitted from between his teeth in a sort of growl. Finally he sat down in a chair in the corner. He consulted a small note-book, in which he seemed to have made some notes (*"Oui!"*), and began to speak in a casual, indulgent voice, polishing his finger-nails against his sleeve, playing with a pencil, or suddenly becoming very interested in something that was happening to the little finger of his left hand.

He began by pointing out that he was not a man given to interfering in other people's affairs. He praised the diligence which Monsieur Cosme had shown (he called him "Monsieur Côôôme", extending the circumflex interminably), in satisfying all his wards' wishes, in ordering whatever was required and taking care that the household lacked nothing. But this diligence, *n'est-ce pas?*, could have been used in advance to lull mistrust.

"Mistrust—what of?" asked the Executor, as if quite unmoved by what the other was saying, and he pulled his chair over towards the young people in little jerks, as though to make his integration with the family more obvious. But Victor's gestures and tone of marked intimacy towards the young people effectually categorised the other man as an intruder : "Since we have just been reading Regnard, *mes amis,* you will remember the lines which you might apply to me to-day :

> *"Ah, qu'à notre secours à propos vous venez!*
> *Encore un jour plus tard, nous étions ruinés."*

"Ah, a French farce," said Don Cosme, laughing at his witticism, in the midst of an uncomfortable silence.

Sometimes, on Sundays, Victor went on, while the boys were asleep (and he pointed to the door into the warehouse) he had been in the adjoining building, prying about, observing, counting, adding, making notes. And in this way (he had the mind of a business-man, he didn't deny that) he had been able to ascertain that the total stock of certain goods did not correspond with what appeared on the documents that the Executor handed regularly to Carlos. He knew ("Shut up!" he shouted at Don Cosme, who was trying to say something) that business was more difficult now than it had been, and that free trade had its snares and problems. But that was no reason (and here his voice swelled in a terrifying way) for presenting the orphans with false statements of account, especially as he knew they would never read them. Don Cosme tried to rise from his chair. But Victor rose first and with huge strides went and stood over him, his forefinger rigid. His voice was now hard and metallic; what had been going on in the warehouse was a scandal, a scandal that had lasted since the death of Sofia and Carlos' father. By means of a simple inventory drawn up by him before witnesses, he would show that this false confidant, this dissembling protector, this thieving executor, was making his own fortune at the expense of these unfortunates, these mere children, whom he had been deceiving criminally, in the knowledge that they were too inexperienced to manage their own affairs. Nor was that all; he knew of risky speculations which their "second father" had made with his wards' money, of purchases accomplished through men of straw (whom he called *canes venaticos,* thunderously evoking Cicero's *In Verrem*).

Don Cosme was trying to stem this verbal avalanche, but the other man, perspiring and terrifying, and seeming to have grown taller, pursued his allegations at an ever-mounting pitch. He had loosened his collar, with such an abrupt gesture that the two loose points hung down over his waistcoat, exposing a throat taut in every fibre with the final efforts of his stentorian peroration. For the first time Sofia found him handsome, as he stood there like a tribune, his fist falling on the table to mark the culmination of a period. Suddenly he moved back towards the rear wall, and leaned against it. He crossed his arms with an expansive gesture, and after a very brief pause, which the other man did not know how to turn to advantage, he concluded, drily and cuttingly, in a haughty, scornful voice : *"Vous êtes un misérable, Monsieur."*

Don Cosme seemed to have shrunk; he was curled and huddled in the depths of an arm-chair too wide to serve as a frame for his exiguous form. An angry trembling kept his lips moving silently, while his finger-nails scratched the velvet of the seat. But he suddenly stood up and barked a single word at Victor, which sounded in Sofia's ears like an explosion in a cathedral : "Freemason !" The word flared up and burst out again with a terrifying sound : "Freemason !" Then it was repeated over and over again, in a voice that grew higher and angrier, as if it were enough to disqualify any prosecutor, to make any allegation groundless, to absolve whoever proffered it from all guilt. Seeing that his opponent's only reply was a defiant smile, the Executor spoke of the shipment of flour from Boston, which had never arrived and never would arrive, because it was only a pretext to cover the activities of a man who was an agent of the freemasons in San Domingo, along with that other half-caste Ogé, the mesmerist and sorcerer, whom the Board of Physicians would denounce for having practised an extravagant deception on these young people, a deception whose worthlessness Esteban would be aware of one of these days, when his illness returned. And Don Cosme now went over to the offensive, circling round the Frenchman like an infuriated hornet: "These are the men who pray to Lucifer; these are the men who insult Christ in Hebrew; these are the men who spit on the crucifix; these are the men who hold an abominable feast on the night of Holy Thursday, when they carve a lamb, crowned with thorns and laid face downwards on the table with nails through its feet. It was for this that the Holy Fathers Clement and Benedict excommunicated these infamous men, and condemned them to burn in hell-fire."

And in the awed tones of someone revealing the mysteries of a witches' Sabbath which he has witnessed, he spoke of the infidels who denied the Redeemer and worshipped one Hiram Abif, architect of the Temple of Solomon. In their secret ceremonies they paid homage to Isis and Osiris and took for themselves the titles of King of the Tyrians, Builder of the Tower of Babel, Kadosh, and Grand Master of the Templars —this last in memory of Jacques de Molay of the nefarious practices, who had been convicted of heresy and burned alive, for worshipping the Devil in the form of an idol called Bafomet. "They do not pray to the saints, but to Belial, Ashtaroth and Behemoth." They were infiltrating everywhere, combating the Christian faith and the authority of legitimate governments in the name of "philanthropy", of an aspiration towards happiness and democracy which merely concealed an international conspiracy to overturn the established order. And looking Victor in the face he shouted the word "conspirator" at him so many times that he became exhausted by his efforts and broke off into a fit of coughing.

"Is all this true?" asked Sofia, in a small, timid voice, alarmed and dazzled at the same time by the unexpected appearance of Isis and Osiris against the portentous backcloth of the Temple of Solomon and the Castle of the Templars.

"The only thing that's true is that this house is crumbling away," said Victor quietly. And, turning to Carlos: "The case of dishonest guardians was already foreseen in Roman Law. We'll take it to the Courts."

The word "Courts" brought the Executor violently to his senses. "We shall see who goes to prison first," he croaked. "I have it on good authority that there is soon to be a round-up of freemasons and undesirable foreigners. The stupid tolerance of the old days is over." And, taking his hat: "Drive this adventurer from the house, before you're *all* imprisoned."

He bowed with a "Good-day to *all*" which reiterated his threat, and left the drawing-room, slamming the door so violently that it rattled all the glass in the house.

The young people were waiting for an explanation from Victor, but he was now busy putting sealing-wax on the thick string with which he had tied up the ledgers: "Keep them here," he said, "they're your proof." Then he looked thoughtfully out into the patio—full of workmen finishing the repairs under the watchful eye of Remigio, who was very proud at finding himself elevated to the rank of builder's foreman. Suddenly, as if he needed to forget himself in some physical activity, Victor picked up a mason's trowel and joined the workmen, setting to work to build up and level off the wall where it had been severely damaged by the falling tiles. Sofia watched him as he clambered on to a scaffold, his face flecked with plaster and mortar, and thought of the legend of Hiram Abif. Despite the anathemas she had heard pronounced in church, despite the lamb crowned with thorns, the blasphemies in Hebrew, and the Popes with their terrible Bulls, she felt rather fascinated by this secret, of which Victor, looking now like a builder of temples, was the depositary. She suddenly saw him as a traveller in forbidden lands, as the holder of esoteric secrets; as an Asian explorer who had come upon some unknown work by Zoroaster; as a sort of Orpheus, who had passed through Avernus. She remembered now having seen him play the part of an architect of ancient times, treacherously murdered with a wooden mallet, in one of their games of charades. She had seen him dressed as a Templar, too, in a tunic adorned with a cross, mimicking the execution of Jacques de Molay. The Guardian's accusations appeared to contain a certain degree of truth. But this truth now seemed attractive to her, because of the secrecy, the mystery, the esoteric activities which it implied. A life devoted to the service of a dangerous belief was more interesting than one confined to waiting piously for some sacks of flour. A conspirator was preferable to a merchant. This glimpse of an adventurous life revived her adolescent addiction to disguises, passwords, secret writing, private codes and intimate diaries garnished with clasps.

"But . . . are they as terrible as they say?" she asked. Esteban shrugged his shoulders; sects and secret societies had always been calumniated, from the early Christians, accused of slaughtering children, right up to the Illuminati of Bavaria, whose only crime had been to want to do good to the whole of humanity.

"Naturally, if they're on bad terms with God," said Carlos.

"God is only a hypothesis," said Esteban.

Suddenly, as if compelled to free herself from an intolerable pressure, Sofia cried out, "I'm tired of God, tired of the nuns, tired of tutors and guardians, of lawyers and documents, of thefts and beastliness. I'm so tired of everything, I don't want to go on living."

And jumping on to an arm-chair by the wall, she took down a large portrait of their father and dashed it to the ground, with such violence that the frame came away from the backing. Then, as the others watched her with assumed indifference, she began to drum her heels furiously on the canvas, causing slivers of paint to fly about. Once the picture had been thoroughly destroyed, thoroughly torn, and thoroughly violated, Sofia dropped into a chair, panting and frowning.

Victor had dropped his mason's trowel in his surprise—Ogé was hurrying into the patio. "We must get away," he said, relating briefly what he had been able to learn while hiding in the house of a *brother*. The cyclone, by diverting the attention of the authorities to more pressing problems, had interrupted an impending political move against the freemasons. They had had instructions from the capital. There was nothing to be done here at present. The sensible course was to take advantage of the current confusion, when people's only thought was to rebuild walls and clean out the streets, and leave the town. They could watch what turn events took from somewhere outside.

"We have a finca for that," said Sofia, in a decisive voice, going off to the larder to prepare a basket of provisions. There, amongst the cold meats, mustard and loaves of bread, they all agreed that Carlos should remain in the house and try to gather information. Esteban went to take down the horse's harness, while Remigio was sent off to the carriage rank in the Plaza de Cristo to procure two remounts.

IX

CREAKING, BOUNCING AND lurching, the carriage rumbled along broken roads, under a fine drizzle which made the black oil-cloth gleam, and penetrated with the swirling wind as far as the back seat, drenching the clothes of Esteban and Ogé, who were perched on the box. At times they leaned so far over that they seemed likely to capsize; or sank so deep into the water at a ford that the side-lights were splashed. There was mud everywhere; they escaped from the red mud of the cane country only to enter the grey mud of the waste lands. Remigio, who was riding behind on one of the remounts, crossed himself as they passed the graveyards with their tombstones.

Despite the disagreeable weather the travellers were laughing and singing as they drank Malvasia wine and ate sandwiches, pastries and bonbons, and feeling strangely happy in this new atmosphere smelling of green pastures, full-uddered cows and the clean wood of camp-fires, far from the brine, dried beef and sprouting onions whose fumes vied with each other in the narrow streets of the city.

Ogé was singing a Creole song :

> "Dipi mon perdi Lisette
> Mon pas souchié kalenda,
> Mon quitté bram-bram sonnette,
> Mon pas battre bam-boüla."

Sofia was singing, in English, a pretty Scottish ballad, and had assumed a horrifying accent for the benefit of her cousin, who paid no attention. Victor was singing too, very much out of tune but taking himself very seriously, something which kept on beginning : "Oh Richard! Oh mon Roi!", but never got any further because he did not know the rest.

In the evening the rain increased and the roads grew worse;

one of them began to cough, and another grew hoarse, while Sofia shivered in her wet clothes. The three men took it in turns on the box, and this continual changing of positions inside and out prevented any consecutive conversation. The great question —the great enigma—as to the true nature of Victor and Ogé's activities remained unanswered; no one had broached the subject, and the reason why they were singing so much along the way was possibly that they were waiting for a favourable moment to resolve the mystery.

Night had already fallen when they reached the house. It was built of stone, badly neglected, full of cracks, with countless rooms, long corridors and arcades, all covered by a roof which had been wedged up where the rafters had caved in. In spite of her tiredness and her fear of the bats which flitted everywhere, Sofia made herself responsible for beds, sheets and blankets, had the wash-basins filled and mended torn mosquito-nets, promising them greater comfort for the following night.

Meanwhile, Victor had strangled two chickens by gripping them by the neck and whirling them in the air like little feathered windmills. Then he plunged them into boiling water, plucked them and cut them into small pieces, to make a quickly-prepared fricassee, into whose sauce he put much brandy and ground pepper—"pour réchauffer Messieurs les voyageurs." Discovering that there was fennel growing in the patio, he began to beat some eggs, announcing that he would make an omelette aux fines herbes.

Sofia was carrying things to the table, making a centre-piece of aubergines, lemons and colocynths. When Victor invited her to savour the smell of the fricassee, she noticed that he had put his arm round her waist, but this time with such a careless, fraternal gesture, without either pressure or insistence, that she did not take offence. Agreeing that the dish looked excellent, she freed herself with a pirouette and returned to the dining-room, showing no signs of annoyance.

They were gay at dinner, and even gayer after dinner, with the pleasant feeling of being comfortable and safe indoors, when the house was being lashed by a more insistent rain, which was drumming on the arums as if they were sheets of parchment, and knocking pomegranates and rose-apples off the trees in the garden. Victor's voice suddenly grew serious and he began to speak, unemphatically, of what had brought him to this country. Business, above all: Lyons silk had to pay a very high tax on its way through Spain to be shipped to Havana and Mexico; on the other hand, if it was exported through Bordeaux and sent to San Domingo, it could be brought here surreptitiously by North American ships on their way back from taking flour to the Antilles. Hundreds of bales of it had been introduced, by means of a contraband organisation set up by creole merchants with advanced ideas, abetted by certain harbour authorities, as a sort of revenge for the extortions of the Spanish monopoly. Working on his own for the mills of Jean-Baptiste Willermoz ("He must be a very important personage if you have to drop your voice as much as that to pronounce his name," thought Esteban), he had placed great quantities of Lyonnaise silk with different firms in the city.

"And is this business very honest?" asked Sofía, pointedly.

"It's a way of fighting the tyranny of monopolies," said Victor. "Tyranny must be fought in all its forms." One had to begin somewhere, because people here seemed to be asleep, inert, living in a timeless marginal world, suspended between tobacco and sugar. "Philanthropy" on the other hand was extremely powerful in San Domingo, where they were very much in touch with everything that was happening in the world. Since it was thought that the movement would become as widespread in this island as in Spain, he had been entrusted with the mission of making contact with local members and of going on to found a conventicle, as had been done elsewhere. But he had been deeply disappointed. The philanthropists of this rich city were few and timorous. They did not seem to appreciate the significance of social questions. They showed a certain sympathy towards a movement that was gaining world-wide power, but they were not active in any other way. Out of timidity, out of cowardice, they allowed legends to circulate about crucifixes being spat on, insults to Christ, sacrilege and blasphemy, which had been discredited elsewhere. (*"Nous avons autre chose à faire, croyez-moi."*) They had no conception of the world-wide significance of present developments in Europe.

"The Revolution is on the march and no one can stop it,"

said Ogé, with that imposing majesty of tone which he knew how to put into certain statements.

And this Revolution, thought Esteban, had been reduced to four lines of news about France, published in the local paper between a theatre programme and an advertisement for a sale of guitars. Even Victor recognised that since his arrival in Havana he had lost all contact with events which had been followed passionately in San Domingo.

"To start with," said Ogé, "there has been a recent decree authorising a man of my colour (and he pointed to his cheeks, which were darker than his forehead) to fill any public office there. This measure is of enormous importance. E-nor-mous."

And then, urging each other on, altering their pitch, taking the words out of each other's mouths, Victor and Ogé advanced by leaps and starts into an interesting but muddled exposition, out of which Esteban was able to gather a number of precise concepts in passing : "We have gone beyond the age of religion and metaphysics, we are now entering on an age of science"; "The stratification of the world into classes has no meaning"; "We must deprive the mercantile interest of their terrible power of unleashing wars"; "Humanity is divided into two classes, the oppressors and the oppressed. Habit, necessity, and lack of leisure prevent the majority of the oppressed from becoming aware of their condition; when they do become aware of it, civil war will break out." The terms *liberty, happiness, equality, human dignity,* and the very mysterious one of *class war,* coined by a Scottish economist, recurred continually in this reckless exposition, and were used to prove the imminence of a great conflagration, which to-night Esteban accepted as a necessary purification, as an Apocalypse which he longed to witness as soon as possible, so that he might start his life as a man in a new world. Yet the boy thought he could detect that Victor and Ogé, though united by the same words, were not in complete agreement over men, things and methods, as far as one aspect of these impending events was concerned.

The doctor was talking now about a certain Martinez de Pasqually, a famous philosopher, who had died a few years before in San Domingo, and whose teachings had left a deep impression on some people's minds.

"A humbug!" said Victor, and started talking ironically about a man who claimed that, at the time of solstices and equinoxes, he could establish mental communication over land and sea with his disciples, all alike kneeling on magic circles traced out in white chalk, and surrounded by lighted candles, cabalistic signs, aromatic smoke and other Asiatic paraphernalia.

"What we claim to do," said Ogé angrily, "is to release the transcendental powers dormant in man."

"Begin by snapping his chains," said Victor.

"Martinez de Pasqually," said the doctor violently, "explained that the evolution of humanity was collective, and that therefore any individual initiative necessarily implies the collective, social act; who *knows* most will *do* most for his fellow-beings."

This time Victor blandly agreed, accepting an idea which was not entirely at variance with his own convictions. Sofia expressed her confusion in the face of an ideological movement which took so many different and contradictory forms.

"Such complex questions cannot be approached as simply as that," said Ogé ambiguously, leaving her peering into the mists of a subterranean world, whose secrets remained shrouded in mystery.

Esteban suddenly felt that he had been living like a blind man on the fringe of the most exciting realities, and had failed to be aware of the one thing worth attention at that moment.

"That's because they keep us without news," said Victor.

"And we shall continue to go without news because the governments are frightened, terribly frightened, of the phantom that is stalking through Europe," concluded Ogé in a prophetic voice. "The time has come my friends, the time has come."

For two days they talked of nothing but revolutions, and Sofia was amazed at the passions which this new topic of conversation aroused. To talk revolutions, to imagine revolutions, to place oneself mentally in the midst of a revolution, is in some small degree to become master of the world. Those who talk of revolutions find themselves driven to making them. It is so obvious that such and such a privilege must be abolished that they proceed to abolish it; it is so true that such and such an oppression is detestable that measures are concerted against it; it is so apparent that such and such a person is a villain that he is unanimously condemned to death. Then, once the ground has been cleared, they proceed to build the City of the Future.

Esteban was in favour of the suppression of Catholicism and the institution of exemplary punishments for anyone worshipping "idols". In this he had the agreement of Victor, while Ogé was of a different opinion; since man had always manifested a tenacious aspiration towards something that might be called "the imitation of Christ", this feeling should be transformed into a desire to go even further—to elevate himself into a sort of archetype of human perfection. Little attracted by transcendental speculation, Sofia brought the others back to earth by expressing a concrete interest in the status of women and the education of children in the new society. And the debate became noisy over the question of whether the Spartan educational system was really satisfactory and adaptable to the times. "No," said Ogé. "Yes," said Victor.

On the third day, argument became so heated about the distribution of wealth in the new society that Carlos, reaching the finca after an exhausting ride, thought that the occupants of the house must be fighting. His appearance silenced their voices. He looked like the bearer of grave news, and it was grave indeed; the drive against the freemasons and suspicious foreigners had begun. Even though the Spanish government might have compromised with its liberal ministers at home, it was quite determined to extirpate progressive ideas in its colonies. Don Cosme had been overjoyed and had warned Carlos that he knew a warrant had been issued for the arrest of Ogé and Victor.

"Décidément il faut filer," said the trader, unperturbed. And fetching his portmanteau he took a map out of it, and indicated a point on the south coast of the island. "We've a long way to go," he said, and he told them that when he was at sea, he used to take sponges, coal and skins on board at this place, Surgidero, and knew people there.

Without another word the two of them went off to pack their things, leaving the others sunk in a grieved silence. They would never have believed that the departure of Victor, this stranger, this intruder, who had almost inexplicably entered their lives, could have affected them to such a degree. His arrival, to the accompaniment of a thunderous knocking, had had something diabolical about it—so had the cool way he had taken possession of the house, seating himself at the head of the table and moving the cupboards around. The apparatus of the physics laboratory had suddenly begun to work, the furniture had come out of its packing-cases, the sick had been cured, and the sluggish had been set in motion. And now they were to be left on their own, undefended, friendless, a prey to the machinations of a venal magistrature—vulnerable as they were through understanding so little about business and even less about the law. A lawyer had told Carlos that in cases where the probity of a guardian is in doubt, the Court proceeds to name a co-guardian, or advisory guardian, who is granted powers until the male issue reaches the age of twenty-one. But in any case they must take action, and apply to the Courts. Carlos had an ally under consideration in the person of a former book-keeper, recently dismissed by Don Cosme, who boasted of knowing a great deal about the latter's peculations. While this was going on it was likely that the persecution unleashed against the freemasons would die down. Such summer storms were common with the Spanish administration, but soon they would put their decrees back in the drawer and revert to their habitual torpor. The young people would remain in close touch with Victor. He would be able to return for a few weeks to look into matters in the warehouse, and to direct the business into new channels. He might even consider leaving his concerns in Port-au-Prince, which were less important than those here. He would be the manager they had dreamed of, and with his talent for figures he too might find it more profitable to establish himself in a city where there was such a large amount of trade. But now there was only one thing of immediate importance : Victor and Ogé must escape. Both were in danger of being seized and "expelled from the Dominions", as had happened to other Frenchmen, even those who had a long residence in Spain to their credit. Sofía and Esteban would accompany them as far as Surgidero.

They reached Surgidero without mishap three days later, thirsty, aching and stamping the dust from their feet. There was dust in their hair, dust inside their clothing, dust behind their ears, after an unpleasant journey past haciendas whose hospitality they had shunned, small sugar plantations where the year's milling was already finished, and sad villages, barely visible against a monotonous landscape of savannahs that were often under water.

The fishing village stretched along a dirty beach, covered with dead seaweed and patches of tar, where crabs swarmed between broken spars and decomposing ropes. A jetty of planks, damaged by the weight of some marble unloaded a few days previously, led down into a turgid, seemingly oil-covered sea, whose waves made no foam. In the midst of the sponge boats and coal hookers, a number of coastal schooners were visible, laden with wood and sacks. One boat, whose tall and slender masts stood out from the tree-trunks of the other vessels, put Victor in a good humour—for several hours he had been silent, brooding over his tiredness. "I know that ship," he said, "we must find out whether she's on her way out or on her way back."

And, suddenly impatient, he went into a sort of combined café, shop, ship-chandler's and tavern, and asked for rooms. All they had were some cells, each containing a wretched bed and a washstand, with whitewashed walls covered with inscriptions and more or less obscene graffiti. There was a rather better hotel but it was some distance from Surgidero, and Sofía was so tired that she preferred to remain here, where at least the floors were clean, a bit of breeze was blowing, and there were jugs of fresh water to wash the dust off.

While the travellers settled in as best they could, Victor went off to the jetty in search of information. Somewhat revived, Sofía, Ogé and Esteban met once more round a table where a supper of fish and French beans had been laid for them, while above their heads the insects flew into the glass of the lamp with a dry crepitation. They would have eaten with a good appetite but for the appearance of a plague of tiny flies, which had come in from the nearby swamps with the darkness. They got into their ears, their nostrils and their mouths, and crept down as far as their shoulders like cold grains of sand. Unaffected by the smoke from the dried coconuts which had been lit on the bars of a brazier to chase them away, the mosquitoes now arrived in swarms, in clouds, raising lumps on their faces, hands and legs.

"I can't stand any more!" shouted Sofía, and ran to her room where she crawled under her mosquito-net, after extinguishing the two candles on the stool which served as a bedside table. But she could hear them droning all round her. Her torments continued underneath the coarse netting, which had been eaten away by the damp and was full of holes. The tiny, shrill whistling moved from her temple to her shoulder, from her forehead to her chin, with pauses to alight on her skin. Sofia twisted and turned, beating herself, slapping herself, here, there and everywhere, on her thighs, between her shoulder-blades, behind her knees, on her sides. She could feel minute wings coming closer and closer to her temples with angry persistence. Finally she chose to curl up with a thick sheet, as coarse as sailcloth, pulled over her head. At last she fell asleep, bathed in sweat, on a bedspread soaked with sweat, her cheek buried in a lumpy pillow damp with sweat.

When she opened her eyes it was daylight; the shaved and spurred fighting-cocks from a cockpit were crowing; the plague of insects had vanished, but she was so tired that she thought she was ill. The thought of spending another day, another night, in that place, with its brackish water, its heat already apparent in the brilliance of the dawn, and its tormenting insects, was intolerable to her. Wrapping herself in a dressing-gown, she went down to the shop in search of vinegar to soothe the bites on her skin. She found Ogé, Esteban and Victor, already up and drinking cups of black coffee at last night's supper table, in the company of a ship's captain who, despite the earliness of the hour, had put on formal dress—blue broadcloth and gilt buttons—to come ashore. His clean-shaven cheeks bore the recent marks of an inefficient razor.

"Caleb Dexter," said Victor. And he added, lowering his voice : "Another philanthropist." Then, raising his voice again, he concluded peremptorily : "Get your things together. The *Arrow* sails at eight. We're all going to Port-au-Prince."

X

AND NOW, THE coolness of the water, and the huge shadow of the sails. After blowing across the land, the northerly breeze was gathering new impetus over the expanse of sea, and bringing with it those vegetal smells which the look-outs could scent high in the crow's nest, distinguishing the smell of Trinidad from that of Sierra Maestra or Cabo Cruz.

Sofia was hauling wonderful things up out of the water with a stick to which a small net had been attached: a bunch of sargasso, whose fruit she burst between her forefinger and thumb; the branch of a mangrove tree, still clad in soft oysters; a coconut the size of a walnut, so splendidly green that it seemed to have been recently painted. They were passing above banks of sponges which looked like dark walls in the limpid depths, or sailing between shoals of white sand, but always within sight of a hazy coastline which was becoming increasingly mountainous and rugged.

Suddenly delivered from the heat, the mosquitoes, and the prospect of a tedious return to a monotonous everyday life—more monotonous still in the absence of someone who had always had the power of transforming reality—Sofia had accepted this voyage delightedly, as if it had merely been an excursion on the waters of a Swiss lake, a *"promenade en bateau"* between romantic, pine-clad banks, unthought-of yesterday but which Victor had pulled from his sleeve like a conjurer at the critical moment. When there turned out to be room for them on board, with a little cabin below decks for her, their friend had offered them this sea-voyage, in return, as he said, for the affection and generosity which they had at all times shown him. They would be able to spend a few weeks in Port-au-Prince and come back on the same vessel—they did not need a safe-conduct, since they were travelling with a captain who was a "philanthropist"—when it returned from Surinam, whither its cargo was destined.

They had accepted it as an escapade, as something which took them back to the pleasant excesses of earlier days, and sent off a letter to Carlos, informing him of an adventure which seemed providential to Sofia after all her dreams of travelling, all those itineraries that had never got beyond paper, all those departures that had never been decided on. At least she was undertaking something new. Port-au-Prince was not London, or Vienna, or Paris; but it would mean a great change all the same. They would find themselves in a piece of France overseas, where people spoke a different language and breathed a different air. They would go to Cap Français, to the theatre in the Rue Vaudreuil, for a performance of *Le Légataire Universel* or *Zamire et Azor*. They would buy the latest music for Carlos' flute, and books, lots of books, dealing with the economic changes in Europe in the last hundred years, and with the revolution actually in progress.

The noise of voices distracted Sofia from the business of fishing —which had caused her to lie face downwards in the bows, with the sun drenching her skin. Victor and Ogé were on the poopdeck, dressed only in drawers, fighting with buckets of salt water —seeing who could let them down fastest to refill them again. The mulatto's torso was magnificently developed, with a narrow waist under broad, firm, glistening shoulders. Victor's chest was thicker, stockier, and the muscles stood out in firm relief; those on his back seemed to ripple over his bones each time he hauled up a bucket of water to empty it in the other's face.

"This is the first time I've felt really young," said Esteban.

"I wonder if we ever were young," said Sofia, returning to her fishing.

The water was now covered with iridescent jelly-fish, whose colours changed in time to the waves, except for an indigo blue, edged with red festoons, which remained constant. The *Arrow* was cleaving slowly through a vast migration of medusas, heading towards the shore. As she watched this multitude of ephemeral creatures, Sofia wondered at the continual destruction which was like a perpetual extravagance on the part of creation : the extravagance of multiplying only to suppress on a larger scale; the extravagance of engendering as much from the most elementary matrices as from the moulds which produced the men-gods, only to surrender the fruits to a world in a state of perpetual voracity. They came from the horizon in their lovely carnival costumes, these myriads of living things still suspended half-way between the vegetable and animal kingdoms—to be offered up in sacrifice to the sun. They would drift ashore on to the sand, where their glittering substance would gradually shrivel, and, as they shrank and lost their lustre, they would be reduced first to a glaucous remnant, then to a froth, and finally to a mere patch of damp, soon to be obliterated by the heat. A more complete annihilation could hardly be imagined, without trace or vestige, without anything to remind one even, of what had once been a living creature.

And after the jelly-fish came transparent molluscs, pink, yellow, striped, reflecting such a diversity of colours in the incandescent light of mid-day that the ship seemed to be cutting through a sea of jasper. With burning cheeks and hair loose in the breeze, Sofia revelled in a physical contentment she had never known before. She could sit for hours in the shade of a sail, watching the waves, her mind a blank, her whole body given up to a sort of voluptuousness, a soft laziness, her senses alert to any agreeable stimulus. Even her appetite had revived during the course of the voyage, because the Captain served food, drinks and fruit, in her honour, which surprised her palate with their new flavours—smoked oysters, the famous Boston biscuits, English cider, rhubarb tarts, which she was tasting for the first time, juicy medlars from Pensacola, which went on ripening during the voyage, melons from the orchards of New York.

Everything was so different, everything broke with what she was used to and helped to keep her in an atmosphere of unreality. When she asked the name of a certain oddly-shaped rock, or a little island, or a channel, her notions of geography, culled from Spanish maps, never coincided with the nomenclature of Caleb Dexter, for whom one was *Cayman Brac,* another *Northeast Cay,* another *Portland Rock.* The ship itself had something magical about it, with its "philanthropist" captain, who belonged to the secret world of Victor and Ogé, of Isis and Osiris, of Jacques de Molay and Frederick of Prussia, and who kept his apron, adorned with the Acacia, the Temple of the Seven Steps, the Twin Pillars, and the Sun and Moon, in a glass case next to his navigational instruments.

At night, under the little awning on the poop, Ogé would begin talking about the marvels of magnetism, or the collapse of traditional psychology, or the secret orders which flourished everywhere, under such names as the Asian Brotherhood, the Knights of the Black Eagle, Cohen's Chosen, the Philalethes, the Illuminati of Avignon, the Brotherhood of the True Light, the Philadelphians, the Rosicrucian Knights and the

Knights of the Temple. All pursued an ideal of equality and harmony, striving at the same time to perfect the individual, who was destined to ascend, by the aid of reason and enlightenment, into a paradise where humanity would find itself freed for ever from fears and doubts. All the same, Sofia noticed that Ogé was not an atheist like Victor, for whom the Christian priests were "mere clowns dressed in black and pulled by strings", while the Great Architect could be accepted as a temporary symbol, until the moment when science finished resolving the enigmas of creation. The half-breed often referred to the Bible—accepting some of the myths on which it was founded—just as he used terms taken from the Cabbala and from Platonism, frequently alluding to the Cathars, whose Princess Esclarmunda Sofia knew about from a charming novel she had read recently. According to Ogé, original sin was not perpetuated by the sexual act, but washed away by it each time. Making use of discreet euphemisms, he averred that the couple were realising a return to primal innocence, when out of the total and paradisiacal nakedness of their embrace there swam an appeasement of the senses, a jubilant and gentle calm, which was an eternally repeated intimation of the purity of Man and Woman before the Fall.

Victor and Caleb Dexter treated each other with the respect of colleagues and discussed the arts of navigation, arguing about a *Rocky Shoal,* mentioned in several treatises as being dangerously concealed at a depth of four fathoms, but which neither of them had ever seen in their journeyings along this coast. Mr. Erastus Jackson, the second mate on board the ship, joined the group to recount terrible tales of the sea, about Captain Anson, for instance, who lost his bearings and wandered for a whole month about the Pacific without being able to reach the island of Juan Fernandez; or about a schooner, found near the island of Grand Caicos, without a single member of the crew on board, but with the fires still alight in the galley, recently washed clothing hung out and not yet dry, and a still warm tureen of soup destined for the officers' dinner table.

The nights were superb. The Caribbean Sea was full of phosphorescence, drifting gently towards the shore, whose mountains could still be seen outlined in the faint light of a new moon. Sofia was absorbed by the sights which this surprising, improbable voyage offered to her eyes, in the way of floating vegetation, rare fish, green lightning, and prodigious sunsets building allegorical tableaux in a sky where each cloud could be read as a sculptural group—the battles of Titans, a Laocoön, a quadriga, or the fall of angels. She marvelled at the coralled depths; she discovered the snoring islands, with the deep bass voice of their caves full of perpetually shifting stones. She did not know whether to believe that sea-cucumbers swallowed sand, or whether it was true that whales came as far south as these latitudes. But on this voyage anything was becoming credible. One evening they pointed out to her a strange fish which they called a "sea-unicorn"; it took her mind back to Victor's first appearance at the House of the Knockers, when she had asked him mockingly whether there were sirens in the Caribbean Sea.

"They almost wrecked me one night," he said.

"I was on the point of doing so several times," said Sofia, picking up the ambiguity, but without confessing how painful this memory was to her now, whenever they brushed against each other in the narrow passages or on steep companion-ways, and she would check her pace, in the shameful expectation of feeling herself grasped once again. When all was said and done, *that*, in all its brutality, had been the one really important thing, the one private revolution, which had happened in her lifetime.

She went down to her cabin and threw herself on the bunk. Her wrinkled stockings were dripping with sweat, so were her breasts in her uncomfortably tight blouse, and her whole skin, chafed by the rough texture of the woollen blanket on her bed. At that moment she heard cries and running footsteps on deck. She tidied herself as best she could and went up to find out the cause of the excitement.

The ship was passing through a shoal of turtles; two sailors were trying to lasso the biggest of them from a boat that had just been lowered. But now sharks' fins appeared amongst the gorgeous carapaces and threatened to upset the boat. The fishermen returned, cursing and furious at all they had lost in the way of valuable tortoise-shell combs, book-markers and buckles, and striking out to right and left with their harpoons. As if the death of a handful of sharks could appease their wrath against the entire species, the sailors clutched the gunwales and hurled out fish-hooks on the ends of chains. The creatures snapped at them voraciously, and were caught on gaffs which came out through their eyes. Then they were hauled from the water, with ferocious jerks and terrible lashings of the tail, up on to the deck, where the sailors beat at them with sticks, poles, iron bars and even handspikes from the capstan. Blood oozed from the lacerated skin, dyeing the water, spattering the sails, running down into the bilges. "This is a good deed we're doing," shouted Ogé, lashing out with the rest, "these fish are horrible."

The entire crew was now on deck, some astride the yard-arms, others looking on in hopes of being able to deliver a blow, every one of them armed with a stick, a carpenter's tool, a saw or brace, blood-thirstily waiting his chance to strike and wound, and throwing out more chains and more hooks.

Sofia went down to her cabin to take off her blouse, which had been stained by some fish oil in the mêlée. In the mirror below the little window which let light into the cabin, she saw Victor come in : "It's me," he said, closing the door. Up above, the shouting and blaspheming continued.

XI

Que alboroto es este?
—Goya

WHEN THE SHIP entered the harbour of Santiago, Victor, who was leaning over the bows, made a gesture of surprise. There were *La Salamandre, La Vénus, La Vestale, La Méduse,* vessels which normally traded between Le Havre, Le Cap and Port-au-Prince, besides a multitude of smaller craft—hookers, schooners, sloops—which he knew belonged to traders in Léogane, Les Cayes and Saint Marc. "Have all the ships in San Domingo collected here?" he asked Ogé, who was equally unable to explain such an unaccustomed migration.

When the anchors had been dropped, they hurried ashore in search of information. The news they heard was alarming; three weeks before, a negro uprising had broken out in the northern regions. The revolt had become general and the authorities had been unable to control the situation. The town was full of refugee settlers. There was talk of terrible slaughter of white families, of conflagrations, savagery, and horrifying outrages—the slaves had flung themselves on the daughters of the whites and subjected them to extremes of cruelty. The country was given over to murder, pillage and lust.

Captain Dexter, who was carrying a small cargo for Port-au-Prince, decided to wait for a few days, in the hope of more peaceful news. If the disorders continued he would go to Puerto Rico and then to Surinam, without stopping in Haiti. Victor was very anxious about the fate of his business and did not know what to do. On the other hand Ogé appeared quite serene; the disturbances had no doubt been painted in exaggerated colours. It coincided too closely with other events, of universal import, to be merely a revolt of black incendiaries and violators of women. Some people had talked about crazed mobs, drunk with blood, after a certain July 14th, which was now in process of transforming the world. One of the most prominent . public officials in the colony was his brother Vincent, educated like him in France, a member of the Paris club of the Friends of the Negro, and a highly-enlightened philanthropist; he would have found a way to keep the rebels in check if they had not had some just reason for pouring into the streets and country-side. There were many men like Vincent here, imbued with philosophical ideas and perfectly aware of what the times demanded. The best course would be to wait for a bit; in a few days it would become clear exactly what had happened. If Dexter insisted on not calling at Port-au-Prince, the ships which had taken refuge in Santiago would soon be returning there, and they could travel pleasantly on board one of these to the neighbouring island.

Meanwhile they had to reckon with the heat—the heat that seemed to rise from the orlops, from the holds, from the hatches, from the very timbers themselves, all the time the *Arrow* remained anchored in the harbour with its sails furled—for this was Santiago harbour, and the month September. A universal smell of warm tar pervaded the cabins and companion-ways, but not sufficiently even so to rid the deck of a certain effluvium of potato peelings, rancid grease and dish-water, which was beginning to come up from the galley. And the worst of it was that there was no way of taking refuge ashore. There was no question of finding a lodging in the city, now that the refugees had filled all the inns, taverns and hotels, and were having to content themselves with spending the night on a billiard table or an armchair pushed up against the wall. The steps of the cathedral were covered with people who would fiercely defend the stretch of cool stone which served them as a bed.

Ogé and Esteban slept on the deck on the *Arrow*, waiting for the dawn, and then went ashore in the first tender, hoping to find some coolness in the streets of pink, orange and blue houses which, with their wooden grilles and nail-studded doors, evoked the early days of colonisation, when Hernán Cortés, still a humble *alcalde*, was sowing the first grapevines brought from Spain to the newly discovered Antilles. They breakfasted in a chop-house off whatever could be produced—for even food was scarce—and then sought shelter under some picturesque roofs of palm fronds, which some French actors had erected at the gates of Santiago as a sort of afternoon amusement park, thereby ingeniously taking advantage of an explosive situation.

Esteban was surprised that neither Victor nor Sofía wanted to go with them on their amusing expeditions to the town. In spite of the overwhelming heat, both preferred to remain on board the *Arrow*, which was left unmanned during these days of enforced immobility, since the sailors went ashore at the first opportunity, and returned in the ship's boats after dusk or at night, drunk and uproarious. Sofía explained that the temperature kept her awake until dawn, so that she only fell asleep from sheer exhaustion when the others were waking up. Victor, for his part, installed himself from dawn onwards on the fo'c'sle, facing the town, writing innumerable letters relating to his business affairs.

Several days went by in this way, with some on shore and others on board; some troubled by the unpleasant smells on the boat, others not noticing them, until one morning Dexter announced that a North American sailor, arrived the night before from Port-au-Prince, had told him that a state of open revolution prevailed there. He could not wait any longer; he would weigh anchor at mid-day and continue the voyage, leaving the island of San Domingo on his beam.

After collecting their belongings together and breakfasting off a Westphalia ham washed down with beer so warm that the froth would not come off the glasses, the travellers took their leave of the "philanthropist" captain and the men of the *Arrow*.

Sitting on their portmanteaux, in a doorway on the quay, they considered the situation. Ogé knew of a dilapidated Cuban schooner that would be leaving for Port-au-Prince next day, having been chartered by local tradesmen to look for refugees. The most sensible thing would be for Sofia to remain in Santiago, while the three men took the ship. If the situation was not as bad as it had been painted—and Ogé insisted that what was going on must amount to something more complex and heroic than mere looting—then Esteban would return aboard the same boat to fetch his cousin. Ogé was very confident moreover in the authority of his brother Vincent, of whom he had had no news for several months, but who occupied, he knew, a high administrative position in the colony. As for Victor there was no problem; he had a house, a business, and property in Port-au-Prince. Sofia became angry and asked them to take her with them, assuring them that she would not be a nuisance, that she did not need a cabin, that she was not afraid.

"It's not a question of being afraid," said Esteban, "but we can't expose you to what has happened to hundreds of other women there."

Victor agreed. If it was possible to stay on the island they would come and fetch her. If not, he would leave Ogé there as his agent, and return to Santiago to wait for the storm to subside. With so many French refugees in the town nobody was going to check whether the Victor Hugues here was the same one as had been denounced as a freemason in Havana. Santiago was now harbouring hundreds of members from the Lodges of Port-au-Prince, Le Cap and Léogane.

Accepting the men's decision, the girl remained alone with Victor in the middle of their scattered luggage, whilst Esteban and Ogé went off to resolve the difficult problem of finding respectable lodgings for her. On board the slim, proud *Arrow,* with its slightly raked masts, its delicate shrouds, its fluttering ensigns, the work of departure was beginning, and there was much movement of sailors about the deck.

The next morning an old, decrepit-looking Cuban bilander,

with patched sails, left Santiago harbour and set sail along a coastline which grew increasingly mountainous. The ship hardly seemed to progress at all, so often did it have to tack on its course in order to overcome the contrary currents.

An interminable day went past, and a night of such brilliant moonlight that Esteban, half-asleep in an uncomfortable position at the foot of the mast, thought twenty times that dawn had come. The bilander entered the mouth of the Gulf of Gonaïves, and before long came in sight of an island on which, according to Ogé, there were waterfalls whose water had the power of inducing a state of Orphic clairvoyance in women. Each year they made a pilgrimage to this bubbling altar to the Goddess of Fertility and of the Waters, and submerged themselves in the foam falling from the towering rocks. Some of them would begin to writhe and scream, possessed by a spirit which inspired them with prophecies—only too often fulfilled with terrifying accuracy.

"Fancy a doctor believing in that," said Victor.

"Doctor Mesmer," replied Ogé sarcastically, "has accomplished thousands of miraculous cures in your civilised Europe, by magnetising the water of wash bowls and inducing a state of trance in his patients, which the negroes have always known about. Only he made money from it. The gods of La Conâve do it for nothing. That's the only difference."

They continued to sail between hazy coastlines until nightfall. Victor, who had been excessively impatient throughout the day, slept heavily—as if anxious to restore his frayed nerves—after a meagre supper of herrings and biscuits. He was woken by Esteban a little before dawn. The bilander was drawing opposite Port-au-Prince. The highest part of the town was in flames. A gigantic conflagration reddened the sky, hurling up ashes towards the nearby mountains.

Victor insisted that a boat be lowered without delay, and shortly afterwards he was landing on the fishermen's quay. Followed by Ogé and Esteban, he traversed the streets, where some negroes were carrying clocks, pictures and furniture that had been rescued from the flames. The three of them reached a barren piece of ground where a few charred timbers still stood, smoking and scaly with ash, among some small fires. The trader stopped, trembling and twitching, the sweat running from his forehead, his temples, and the back of his neck.

"I'll do you the honours of the house," he said. "That was the bakery; the shop was here; my room behind." He picked up a half-burned oak plank : "It made a good counter."

His foot brushed against a scale-pan, blackened by the fire. He picked it up and looked at it for a long time. Suddenly he dashed it to the ground, with a noise like a gong, raising a flurry of soot. "I'm sorry," he said, and burst into sobs. Ogé went off in search of some particular friends living in the town.

The day was growing lighter, under low, smoke-laden clouds, which seemed to be compressed between the mountains enclosing the bay. Victor and Esteban, sitting on the oven from the bakery —the only identifiable object in all that chaos—watched the town recovering its normal rhythms, in the midst of the signs of its own annihilation. Peasants were coming in, bringing fruit, cheeses, cabbages and bundles of cane, to lay them out in a market which had ceased to be a market. From force of habit they took up their positions on the site of their non-existent stalls, setting out their wares in the open air, yet observing the alignment and the neatness of other days.

It seemed that after having set fire to everything the insurgents had vanished. The peacefulness of burnt charcoal, hot ashes, and live coals lying amid the debris, lent a bucolic appearance to the people who now arrived crying their wares : milk from their dappled goats, fragrant jasmine, delicious honey. The huge man standing at the end of the jetty, holding aloft the enormous squid he was trying to sell, was transformed into Cellini's Perseus. In the distance some monks were pulling the charred scaffolding out from a half-built church. Heavily laden donkeys went down streets that were no longer streets, following their usual route just the same, turning where they could now have crossed straight over, or pausing at an illusory corner where an innkeeper had reinstalled his flasks of brandy on planks mounted on bricks.

Victor's eyes returned again and again to the site of his annihilated office. Now that his anger had died down, he was oddly allured by this emancipating feeling of possessing nothing, of being left without property, without any furniture, a single contract or a book—without even a yellowing letter over whose handwriting he might grow sentimental. His life was reduced to a cypher, without promises to fulfil, without debts to pay, suspended between a past which had been destroyed and a future it was impossible to foresee. Fresh fires had broken out on the *mornes* : "For all that's left they might just as well burn the whole lot at once," he said. And he was still there when Ogé arrived at mid-day, beneath the white splendour of clouds which stretched from mountain-top to mountain-top.

Ogé's face was set, marked with new furrows which Esteban did not recognise. "It was well done," he said, his eyes sweeping over the fire. "You didn't deserve anything better." And in answer to Victor's furious, questioning look : "My brother Vincent was executed in the Place d'Armes at Cap Français; they smashed his body with iron bars. They say his bones sounded like nuts being cracked with hammers."

"The rebels?" asked Victor.

"No, you," replied the doctor, his eyes clouded and fixed, staring unseeingly. And in the midst of that desolation he recounted the terrible story of his younger brother. Appointed to fill an important administrative post, he had come up against the refusal of the French settlers to respect the decree of the National Assembly, by the terms of which negroes and half-breeds of sufficient education were authorised to fill public office in San Domingo. Tired of trying to establish his claim, Vincent took up arms, at the head of a band of malcontents who were also affected by the intransigence—the disobedience—of the whites, and, supported by another mulatto, Jean-Baptiste Chavannes, he marched on the town of Cap Français. Routed in the first encounter, Vincent and Jean-Baptiste sought refuge in the Spanish half of the island. But there they were seized by the authorities, placed in irons and sent back to Le Cap under escort. They were tied to the railings in a public square and exposed for several days to the general mockery, insulted and spat on by the passers-by, or even covered with garbage and filthy water. But the scaffold was already being erected, and the executioner was gripping his marlin-spike, ready to vent his fury on the legs, arms and thighs of the malefactors. After this came the axe. The heads of the young men were held on lances, and paraded as a warning along the road which leads to the Grande Rivière. As they passed, vultures swooped down and struck with their beaks at faces which had turned livid under torture and finally lost all human resemblance—they were mere sponges of flesh, with scarlet cavities, brandished by drunken guards who stopped at every tavern.

"There's plenty left to be burned," said Ogé. "To-night will be terrible! Get away as soon as you can!"

They went towards the wharfs, large stretches of whose planks had been burned, so that they were forced to walk on the supporting cross-pieces, which were made of fire-resistant quebracho. Below them floated corpses, being gnawed at by crabs. The Cuban bilander, laden with refugees, had been unable to wait any longer and had gone—so they learned from an old negro, who was stubbornly mending his nets, as if one break in the warp of the mesh were a problem of supreme importance, even in the midst of such widespread disaster. All the ships had abandoned the harbour except one, recently arrived, whose crew had only just heard what was happening in Port-au-Prince; it was a three-masted brig, with high gunwales, and an ever-increasing number of small craft were putting off towards it from the shore.

"That's your only chance," said Ogé. "Go on, before they cut you open."

The negro fishermen rowed them out in a boat so battered it had to be baled out with cups, but when they reached the *Borée* the captain, who was leaning over the side and spitting out insults, refused to allow them to come aboard. Victor then made an unusual sign—as if he were drawing something in the air—which silenced the sailor's imprecations. A rope ladder was let down for them and shortly afterwards they were on deck, beside the man who had understood the ruined trader's signal of abstract entreaty. The boat would be weighing anchor immediately and returning to France, packed tight with refugees—they were everywhere, sweating into already sweaty clothing, malodorous, ill with fever, insomnia or exhaustion, scratching at their first wounds or their first lice; one of them had been beaten, another wounded, another raped.

"There's no other solution," said Victor, when he saw that

Esteban was hesitating at the thought of this long, unplanned voyage.

"If you stay they'll kill you to-night," said Ogé.

"*Et vous?*" asked Victor.

"*Pas de danger*," replied the half-breed, pointing to his dark cheeks. They embraced, yet Esteban had the impression that the doctor was not as effusive as on other occasions. There was a stiffness, a new distance, a new seriousness, between their two bodies.

"I'm sorry for what's happened," Ogé said to Victor, as if he were suddenly assuming responsibility for a whole country. And making a slight gesture of farewell he returned to the boat, from whose side the fisherman was trying to thrust away the corpse of a horse with an oar.

Not long afterwards a thunderous sound of drumming broke over Port-au-Prince, reaching up to the peaks of the *mornes*. New fires were spreading into the red sunset sky. Esteban thought of Sofia, who would be waiting uselessly in Santiago—she had been lodged in the house of some respectable tradespeople, old suppliers of her father's. But it was better so. Ogé would arrange to let her know what had happened. Carlos would go and fetch her. The strange adventure which was now beginning was not suitable for women; from now on anyone on board who wanted to wash would have to do so in full view of everyone—and there were many other things which would have of necessity to be done in full view of everyone.

Esteban, torn between anxiety and remorse, yet happy that such incredible new things should be happening to him, felt more solid, more mature, more of a man, when he was with Victor Hugues. With his back to a city which seemed to be boasting of having buried its past beneath a mountain of ashes, the latter became more French than ever, now that he could speak French to Frenchmen, and learn the latest news from his country. This was interesting, unusual, extraordinary, to be sure. But none of it was so sensational or significant as the report of the King's flight and his arrest at Varennes. This was such a tremendous and new idea that the words "King" and "arrest" refused to be coupled together as an immediately acceptable possibility. A monarch arrested, put to shame, humiliated, and handed over to the custody of the people whom he claimed to govern, because he was now unfit to do so! The greatest Crown, the most illustrious Majesty, the most exalted Sceptre in the universe, dragged away between two gendarmes.

"And there was I haggling over contraband silk, when things like this were happening in the world," said Victor, raising his hands to his head. "Over there they are witnessing the birth of a new humanity."

The *Borée* sailed slowly with the night breeze, beneath a sky so brilliant with stars that the mountains to the East showed like intrusive shadows, cutting into the pure geometry of the constellations. The day's conflagrations lay astern. Towards the East the mind's eye could descry a Pillar of Fire, standing upright and magnificent, guiding the ship towards the Promised Land.

CHAPTER TWO

XII

Sanos y enfermos
—*Goya*

WHEN HE THOUGHT of his native city, made unreal and
strange by its remoteness, Esteban could only evoke it in the
colours of an aquatint, its shadows accentuated by the excessive
brightness of the light, its skies suddenly charged with thunder-
storms and huge menacing clouds, its narrow, muddy streets
full of negroes busy among the tar, tobacco and dried beef.
There was more charcoal than flaming colour in his picture of
the tropics, which, seen from here, had become static, oppressive,
monotonous, with their eternally repeated paroxysms of colour,
their too-short dusks, their nights dropping from the sky before
the lamps could be brought in—long nights made longer still by
the silence of those who fell asleep before they had heard the
voice of the nightwatchman chanting that it was ten o'clock by
Holy Mary, conceived without sin in the first instant of her
Natural Being.

Here, amidst the gorgeously variegated tints of early autumn
—a wonderful experience for someone coming from islands
where the trees underwent no change from green to blood-red or
sepia—it was all joyful banners, flourishing cockades and badges,
flowers for sale on street corners, and patriotic parades of shawls
and skirts lavishly decorated with red and blue. After living a
life given over to repetition and recollection for so long, Esteban
felt as if he had dropped into a huge carnival, whose characters
and costumes had been thought up by some great showman.
Everything was spinning around one, distracting and stupefying
one, in this constant tumult of gossiping women, coachmen calling to one another from their boxes, loitering foreigners, back-
biting footmen, loafers, procurers, commentators on the latest
happenings, newspaper-readers, and groups of men locked in

passionate argument. The spreader of baseless rumours was there, the man who knows better than anyone, the man who has it on good authority, the man who actually saw it, the man who was there and can describe it—not forgetting the very ardent patriot far gone in liquor, the journalist who has written three articles, the police spy feigning catarrh to excuse his muffler, the anti-patriot too patriotically arrayed for his costume not to reek of fancy dress—all of them were perpetually titillating this uncouth raree-show with some startling item of news.

The Revolution had infused new life into the streets—and the streets were of enormous importance to Esteban now that he lived in them, and watched the Revolution from them. "The joy and exuberance of a free people", he thought, listening and watching, proud of the title "Foreigner, friend of Liberty", which everyone bestowed on him. Some people might perhaps have grown quickly accustomed to all this; but, suddenly uprooted as he was from his drowsy tropics, he felt he was surrounded by exoticism—that was the word—a much more picturesque exoticism than that of his own country with its palm trees and sugar canes, where he had grown up without imagining that anyone could ever find it exotic. Here the flag-poles and streamers, the symbolic tableaux and the standards, seemed exotic—truly exotic—to him; and the wide-crouped horses looked as if they had come from some merry-go-round imagined by Paolo Uccello, so different were they from the nimble, bony nags—good Andalusians after all—of his own country.

Everything seemed to him worth stopping and looking at : the café with the Chinese décor and the tavern whose sign showed Silenus astride a barrel. The open-air funambulists, imitating the feats of famous acrobats; the dog's barber, who had set up shop on the banks of the river. Everything was strange, unforeseen, amusing : the clothes of the pedlar, with his tray of pins; the red-painted eggs; and the turkeys, described as "aristocratic" by the woman who was plucking them in the market. Every shop was a theatre to him, and its window display a stage-set; with shoulders of lamb set out on lace paper; or it might belong to the perfume seller, who was too pretty for one to believe that she made her living from the meagre articles she displayed; or the fan-maker; or that other woman, also pretty, who leaned her breasts on the counter and sold revolutionary emblems made of marzipan. Everything was striped, done up in ribbons, and decorated in the sugary colours of a Montgolfier balloon, or a lead soldier.

One seemed to be in the midst of a gigantic allegory of a revolution rather than a revolution itself, a metaphorical revolution, a revolution which had been made elsewhere, which revolved on a hidden axis, which had been elaborated in subterranean councils, invisible to those who wanted to know all about it. Esteban was unfamiliar with these new names, unknown yesterday and changing every day, and he could not discover who was responsible for the Revolution. Obscure men from the provinces suddenly arose to prominence: former lawyers, seminarists, barristers without briefs and even foreigners, and became of gigantic stature in a matter of weeks. He was dazzled, as it were, by the extraordinary proximity of events, and the innumerable faces which had recently appeared on the rostrums and in the clubs, where he would sometimes hear arguments in youthful voices belonging to people scarcely older than himself. He learned no more by attending meetings or mingling with the crowd, because he did not know the men concerned and was disconcerted by the torrential prodigality of words; but he marvelled at the orators, as a Laplander might if he were suddenly transported to the United States Congress. One man he liked for his quick, steely-hard delivery and his adolescent impetuosity; another because his eloquence was more caustic and incisive than that of the rest; another for the vulgar inflexions of his loud voice.

Victor Hugues was a poor informant at these times, because Esteban had so few opportunities of seeing him. They were both living in a modest lodging-house, badly lit and worse ventilated, where a reek of mutton, cabbage and leek soup prevailed at all hours, added to the smell of rancid butter which the threadbare carpets gave off of their own accord. At first they had been occupied in enjoying the life of the capital, and frequenting places of amusement and pleasure, where Esteban, by means of great extravagance and not a few violations of his purse, contrived to appease the traditional concupiscence of all foreigners who set foot on the banks of the Seine. But after some time Victor, ruined as he was, and with no money apart from what he had made in Cuba, began to think of the future; Esteban meanwhile was writing to Carlos, asking him for a letter of credit to be arranged through Messrs. Laffon of Bordeaux, who were agents for the Conde de Aranda's *garnacha* and muscatel wines. The Frenchman had resumed his habit of going out early, and would disappear until very late. Knowing him as he did, the young man forbore to question him. Victor was a man who only spoke about his successes after they had been achieved, by which time he was already aspiring to greater ones.

Thrown back on his own resources, Esteban allowed himself to be set in motion by the rhythm of each day—following the drums of a detachment of guardsmen, penetrating into a political club, or losing himself in an impromptu demonstration. He was more French than any of them, more revolutionary than those who were taking part in the Revolution, always clamouring for drastic measures, draconian punishments, exemplary penalties. He read extremist newspapers, and listened to the most implacable orators. Any rumour that spoke of a counter-revolutionary plot would fetch him into the street, armed with the first kitchen knife he had been able to lay hands on. To the great annoyance of the proprietress of the hotel, he had appeared one morning followed by all the children of the district, dragging the branch of a fir tree, which he planted in the courtyard, to represent a new Tree of Liberty. One day he took the floor in a Jacobin Club, and astonished those present with the suggestion that all they had to do to carry the Revolution into the New World was to inculcate the ideal of Liberty among the Jesuits who had been expelled from the Spanish dominions overseas and were now wandering in Italy and Poland.

The local booksellers dubbed him "The Huron", and, flattered by this nickname, combining the memory of Voltaire with a picture of America, he did all he could to combat the civilised customs of the *ancien régime*, by flaunting a frankness, a verbal brutality, a coarseness of sentiment, which at times distressed the revolutionaries themselves. "I glory in kicking a man that's down, or in talking about the noose in a hanged man's house," he said, taking a delight in his own insufferable crudity.

Thus he went on "huronading" from group to group, from meeting-place to meeting-place, as far as clubs where the Spaniards of Paris gathered—masons and philosophers, philanthropists and anti-clericals, who were actively conspiring to introduce the Revolution into the Peninsula. Here they were always running over the names of cuckolded Bourbons, licentious queens and cretinous princes, until Spain's backwardness was represented by a sombre picture of influential nuns, miracle-mongers, poverty, persecution and rags, and all that existed between the Pyrenees and Ceuta was plunged into the darkness of a conservative revival. This slumbering, tyrannised country, with its lack of progressive ideas, was contrasted with enlightened France, whose revolution had been welcomed, applauded and acclaimed by men like Jeremy Bentham, Schiller, Klopstock, Pestalozzi, Robert Bruce, Kant and Fichte.

"But it's not enough to take the Revolution to Spain, it must be taken to America too," said Esteban at these meetings, finding that in this he always met with the approval of one Feliciano Martinez de Ballesteros, from Bayonne, whom he soon grew to like for the witty anecdotes he told, and for the way he would sometimes start singing songs by Blas de Laserna, accompanying himself skilfully and spiritedly on an old clavichord which stood in the corner. It was marvellous to hear the Spaniards gathered round the keyboard, singing in parts :

> *"Cuando Majoma vivía*
> *Allá en la era pasada*
> *Era tanto lo que bebía*
> *Que del suelo se elevaba*
> *Con las monas que cogía*
> *Con las monas que cogía."*

They all flaunted waistcoats whose sale was prohibited by royal decree in Spain and her American dominions, with the word Liberty, worked in red silk, on the lining. Their nights were filled with talk of projects for an invasion, or uprisings in the provinces : plans for landings at Cadiz or on the Costa Brava, for the appointment of enlightened ministers, the founding of imaginary newspapers, the issue of proclamations; each of them enjoying the sound of his own babble, as the heads rolled and the crowns fell to the noisy accompaniment of pure-blooded words categorising all the members of the Iberian dynasty as cuckolds and harlots. Some of them bemoaned the fact that the Prussian, Anacharsis Clootz, the Apostle of the Universal Republic, had not included a single Spaniard amongst his retinue of English, Sicilians, Dutch, Russians, Poles, Mongols, Turks, Afghans and Chaldeans—all in their national costume—when he presented himself at the bar of the Constituent Assembly as the Ambassador of the Human Race, but had been content with some actor or other as a worthy representative of that neighbouring land, which groaned beneath the noose and the chains of despotism. As a result the voice of Spain had not been heard at that memorable ceremony, when even a Turk had spoken.

"They do right to despise us, because we are nothing yet," said Martinez de Ballesteros, shrugging his shoulders. "But our hour is coming." Meanwhile he knew some very brave men who were preparing to come to France and place themselves at the service of the Revolution. A certain young Abbé Marchena, amongst others, who seemed to be of superior intellect, to judge by the tone of his letters and by some translations of Latin poems which he had sent him.

But it was not everything, thought Esteban, to spend one's nights in animated conversation, and to wander like a booby in the street, gawping at march-pasts and civic celebrations. One memorable day he was initiated into the Foreigners' Lodge, and penetrated into that vast world of brotherly endeavour, of which Victor had only shown him glimpses. The lamps had been lit in the secret and resplendent Temple, through which he had to walk, trembling and dazzled by the flashing swords, towards the Pillars, Jachin and Boaz, the Delta and the Tetragrammaton, the Seal of Solomon and the Star of the Golden Number. There, arrayed in their aureoles and their emblems, stood the Kadosh Knights, and the Rosicrucian Knights, the Knights of the Brazen Serpent and the Knights of the Royal Ark, the Princes of the Tabernacle and the Princes of Libanus, the Princes of Jerusalem, the Grand Master Architect, and the Sublime Prince of the Royal Secret. It was towards these Degrees that one must begin to ascend, dumb with emotion, and feeling unworthy of such an honour—towards the mysteries of the Grail, of the Transformation of the Crude Stone into the Cubic Stone, of the Resurrection of the Sun in the Acacia, penetrating into the heart of a tradition which had been preserved and rediscovered, and which reached dizzily backwards into time, by way of Jacob Boehme, the Chemical Marriage of Christian Rosenkreuz and the Secret of the Templars, to the great initiation ceremonies of Ancient Egypt. Esteban had felt himself to be One with the All, illuminated and dazzled by the Ark which he must now build within his own being, in the likeness of the Temple built by the master Hiram Abif. He was at the centre of the Cosmos; above his head the Firmament was opening; his feet trod the road which leads from the Occident to the Orient. Emerging from the shadows of the Room of Reflection, his chest bared over his heart, his right leg bare, his left foot unshod, the Apprentice had replied to the three ritual questions as to what Man owes to God, to himself and to others. Afterwards enlightenment had dawned on him—the sublime enlightenment of a century towards whose prodigious events he had been moving blindly, gropingly, as if drawn by a will superior to his own, ever since the night of the great conflagration in Port-au-Prince. He now understood the exact significance of his bewildering voyage—like that of Percival in search of himself—to the Future City which, for once, had not been situated in America, like those of Thomas More and Campanella, but in the cradle of philosophy itself.

That night, unable to sleep, Esteban wandered till dawn through the old quarters of the town, with its houses filmed over with damp, and its tortuous, unfamiliar alleyways. Unexpected corners, topped with Gothic arches, suddenly loomed over him like the prows of gigantic ships, without either masts or sails, but covered with chimneys which were outlined against the sky in the fantastic postures of armed horsemen. Scaffolding, shop-signs, iron lettering and furled banners emerged from the darkness and the shadows, without revealing their exact shape. In one place there was a stack of market trolleys, in another a wheel was suspended above the contorted withies of half-woven baskets. A spectral cart-horse suddenly snorted in the depths of a yard, where a cart reared its shaft in a ray of moon-light, with the disquieting immobility of an insect preparing to eject its sting.

Following the old pilgrims' route to Santiago, Esteban stopped at the end of a street, where the sky seemed to be waiting for whoever climbed the hill, to gladden him with the scent of the harvest, a promise of clover, and the warm, moist breath of the wine-press. The young man knew that it was mere illusion, that there were other houses beyond, and many more in the network of suburbs. All the same, having stopped where he had to stop if he were not to forego the privilege of this majestic view of the heavens, he contemplated what for centuries had been contemplated by men singing canticles, men with pilgrim's badges, staffs and cloaks, men whose sandals had shuffled this road so often, feeling closer here to the Gates of Glory, knowing that a few short days away were the Hôpital Saint-Hilaire at Poitiers, the resinous Landes, and the rest-days at Bayonne, all culminating in the fusion of the four Pilgrims' Ways at the Bridge of the Queen of the Valley at Aspe. All through the years generation after generation had passed this way, impelled by an unquenchable fervour, walking towards the sublime handiwork of the Master Matthew, who had surely—there could be no doubt about it—been a mason, like Brunelleschi, Bramante, Juan de Herrera and Erwin Steinbach, architect of the Cathedral at Strasbourg. When he thought about his initiation Esteban felt ignorant and frivolous. To perfect himself he must get to know a whole literature of which he was as yet ignorant. To-morrow he would buy the books that would be useful to him, and enrich the elementary instruction he had so far received, by his own efforts.

Thus he became less aware than before of the revolutionary frenzy that convulsed the streets at all hours, and began to spend long nights in study, finding out more about the secret but sure passage of the Triad through the Ages.

One morning about seven o'clock Victor found him awake, dreaming about the Wormwood Star of the Apocalypse, having been absorbed in reading *The Coming of the Messiah* by Juan Josaphat Ben Ezra, an author whose name concealed, under its Arabic appearance, the identity of an active American revolutionary.

"Do you want to work for the Revolution?" the friendly voice asked him. Aroused from the depths of his meditations, and brought back to the excitement of a present reality which was nothing more or less than the first realisation of the Great Traditional Aspirations, Esteban answered yes, that he would be eager and proud to, and that he would never allow any doubts to be cast on his fervour, or his anxiety to work for Liberty.

"Ask for me at ten o'clock in Citizen Brissot's office," said Victor, who was wearing a brand-new suit of clothes, very well made, together with boots whose leather still creaked with newness. "Oh, and if the subject should arise, no nonsense about masonry. If you want to join us, never set foot inside a Lodge again. We've already wasted too much time on those cowards." Noticing Esteban's surprised expression he added: "Freemasonry is counter-revolutionary. There's no more to be said. The only morality now is Jacobin morality." And picking up the *Apprentice's Catechism* which was on the table, he broke it across the spine and threw it into the waste paper basket.

XIII

BY HALF PAST ten Esteban had been received by Brissot, and by eleven o'clock he had settled on a route which followed one of the old roads to Santiago, as far as the Spanish frontier. "Liberty must provide me with sandals, and a scallop-shell for my badge," said the young man, when he learned what was expected of him, much pleased with this impromptu piece of rhetoric. At this time they needed men of firm convictions, who could write good Spanish and translate documents out of French, to prepare the revolutionary literature for Spain; they were already beginning to print it in Bayonne, and anywhere else where presses were available, in the neighbourhood of the Pyrenees.

Brissot had been much influenced by the Abbé José Marchena, whose abilities and Voltairian wit had been highly praised, and who advised a rapid propagandist penetration of the Peninsula, so as to kindle a revolution that could not be long in starting there, just as its outbreak was imminent in other countries which were anxious to sunder the opprobrious fetters of the past. According to Marchena, Bayonne was "the most suitable place to assemble the Spanish patriots who want to work for the regeneration of their country"—not that this meant under-estimating Perpignan—but they would have to depend on intelligent men, capable of understanding that "the language of regenerated and republican France could not yet be used in Spain". They must "go on preparing gradually", respecting for some time to come "certain ultramontane prejudices, which are incompatible with liberty, but which are too deeply rooted to be extirpated at a single blow".

"Is that clear?" Victor had asked Esteban, as if to take responsibility for his protégé in front of Brissot. Clutching his staff, the young man replied with a short but sincere speech, seasoned with Spanish quotations, to show that he not only agreed with Marchena, but was also as well able to express him-self correctly in the French language as in his own.

Nevertheless, reconsidering his lot a few hours later, he thought that the mission entrusted to him was far from being an enviable one; to leave Paris at a moment like this would be to lose sight of the greatest drama in the world and isolate oneself in a remote province.

"This is not the time to complain," Victor said to him severely, when he learned of his hesitation. "I shall soon be going to Rochefort for some time. I should like to stay here too. But everyone must go where he is sent."

There followed three days of revelry, of costly meals and adventures with women, which renewed the bonds of friendship between the two men. Unburdening himself to Victor, Esteban could not hide from him that, although he had followed his advice as far as forgetting about freemasonry was concerned, his time at the Foreigners' Lodge had left him with a host of pleasant memories. They had called him a "Young American Brother", and had given him a manly toga to wear at his initiation. Moreover it could not be said that a healthy demo-cratic atmosphere did not reign there, when Charles Constantine of Hesse-Rothenburg could mix familiarly with a coloured patriot from Martinique, a former Jesuit from Paraguay, homesick for his mission-station, a Flemish typographer, expelled from his country for printing propaganda, or an exiled Spaniard, a pedlar by day and an orator by night, who claimed that free-masonry had already been active in Avila in the sixteenth century, as was proved by certain designs of compasses, set squares and mallets, recently discovered—according to him—in the Church of Our Lady of the Assumption, built by the famous Jewish architect Mosén Rubí de Braquemonte.

There too he had heard a lot of music by an inspired masonic composer, called Mosar or Motzarth, or some such name, because a Viennese baritone had sung some of his hymns at the initiation ceremonies, enriching the melodies of "Oh Holy Brotherhood of the Faithful", and of the invocation "You who give honour to the Creator under the name of Jehovah, God, Fu or Brahma", with florid cadenzas.

There he had lived in contact with the most interesting people, for whom the Revolution was a victory both political and material, which would lead to a total victory of Man-over-himself. Esteban had been reminded of Ogé when some Danish and Swedish brothers had talked about the wonderful court of the Prince of Hesse—and the aristocratic Charles Constantine had confirmed this—where people in a state of somnambulism had been questioned about the Fall of the Angels, the Building of the Temple, or the chemical composition of aqua Tofana. At the Schleswig court miraculous cures had been wrought by means of magnetism : a birch tree, a walnut tree and a fir tree had even been turned into springs of healing waters. The doors which hid the future had been thrown open, by comparing the omens yielded by eighty-five traditional forms of divination, including bibliomancy, crystalomancy, gyromancy and xylomancy. Extremes of subtlety had been attained in the interpretation of dreams, and, by means of automatic writing, they had held converse with the basic "ego", conscious of previous existences, which lies concealed within every one of us. Thus they learned that the Grand Duchess of Darmstadt had wept at the foot of the Cross on Golgotha, and that the Grand Duchess of Weimar had wit-nessed the judgement of Our Lord in Pilate's palace—just as the scientist Lavater had for years had a distinct awareness of having been Joseph of Arimathea. Some nights, in the magic castle of Gottorp—wreathed in mists which saturated the bandages of its Egyptian mummies—spiders descended on the tables where a Count Bernsdorf who had once been the Apostle Thomas, Louis of Hesse who could remember himself as John the Evangelist, and Christian of Hesse who had previously been the Apostle Bartholomew, were playing cards with aristocratic calm. Prince Charles frequently absented himself from these soirées; he preferred to shut himself away and *work*, fixing his gaze so intensely on a piece of metal which the Greeks used to call Electronum that small clouds formed in front of his eyes— clouds whose shapes could be interpreted as warnings and messages from the Other Shore.

"Rubbish!" exclaimed Victor, irritated by all this talk of prodigies. "When there are so many *real* things to think about, to waste time talking about that sort of filth is tantamount to a counter-revolutionary activity. We saw just in time what was hidden behind all those Salomonic masquerades—a treacherous desire to turn their backs on the times, and to distract people from their immediate responsibilities. Moreover, in the name of brotherhood the masons preach a criminal moderation. We must look on all moderates as enemies."

By piecing the fragments together, Esteban had been elucidating the mystery of Victor's own former connection with masonry. Jean-Baptiste Willermoz (who had supplied him with silk), High Chancellor of the Gallic Conventicle, and a man highly regarded by the Prince of Hesse, was also the head of an order which had drifted into mysticism and Orphism under the influence of Martinez de Pasqually, one of the Illuminati, who had died in San Domingo. This mysterious Portuguese Jew had founded chapters in Port-au-Prince and Léogane, winning over the minds of men like Ogé, who were given to esoteric speculation, but using his hermetic disciplines to deceive those who, like the former trader, were more attracted by an ideal of political subversion. Victor, who respected Willermoz' immense prestige as a philanthropist and industrialist—he had thousands of men working for him in his factories in Lyons—accepted the fundamentals of his doctrine, and had himself initiated according to the rite of the Grand Orient, but he refused (and from this had sprung his quarrels with Ogé), to accept the spiritualist practices advocated by Martinez de Pasqually, who boasted of being able to enter into mental communication with his disciples in Europe.

"All these magicians and mystics are a bunch of *emmerdeurs*," said Victor, who now prided himself on having both feet set firmly on the ground. He often spoke at the Jacobin Club, where he had the opportunity of rubbing shoulders with Billaud-Varenne and Collot d'Herbois, and where he had once managed to get close to Maximilien Robespierre, whom he considered superior to all the other revolutionary orators, worshipping him so passionately that Esteban, listening to extravagant praise of his eloquence, his ideas, his nobility, and even his unusual sartorial elegance in assemblies characterised by slovenliness and untidiness, finally said in a joking tone : "I can see that he's a sort of Don Juan for men." Victor, who disliked jokes of this sort, replied with an outrageous obscenity and laid his hand on the seam of his breeches.

After a long, bumpy journey, along muddy roads where the pine cones crackled under the wheels of the carriage, Esteban at last reached Bayonne, where he put himself at the disposal of the men who were working to foment a revolution in Spain : the ex-sailor Rubín de Celis, the *alcalde* Bastarreche, and the journalist Guzmán, a friend of Marat and a collaborator on *L'Ami du Peuple*. He got the discouraging impression that his new face and his desire for immediate action made him unwelcome here, where many of them had settled into a Jacobinism made rather dilatory by their scruples about Spain. They were still virulent about anything which concerned France, but as soon as their eyes turned towards Bidasoa they became tame and cautious.

The young man was soon sent off to Saint-Jean-de-Luz, now called Chauvin-Dragon, in honour of a heroic soldier of the Republic who had been a native of the place. Here there was a small but extremely active printing-press, to which had been entrusted numerous leaflets and revolutionary primers, selected by the Abbé Marchena, an astute agitator, always ready to move his pen in time to events, but who now travelled little in the frontier zone, preferring to spend most of his time in Paris, where Brissot granted him frequent audiences.

Esteban was unaware that he had any friends along that

coast, but he was fortunate enough to meet a solitary fisherman on the banks of the Untzin one evening, whom he greeted with delight; it was the witty Feliciano Martinez de Ballesteros, now no longer a mason and the proud possessor of the rank of colonel, having formed a corps of riflemen, the "Mountain Rifles", who were to engage the Spanish troops in the case of aggression, and to incite them to pass over to the side of the Republic. "We must be prepared," he said. "In our country the arch-whore is running amok; you need only look at our Godoys and Bourbon Messalinas."

Esteban went for long walks with this amusing Logronese, to villages which had recently changed their names: Itxasson was now called "Union"; Arbonne, "Constante"; Ustarritz, "Marat-sur-Nive"; Baigorry, "Thermopylae". During these first weeks the young man marvelled at the crude Basque churches, with their squat, war-like bell-towers, and their churchyards surrounded by stone slabs set into the ground; he would pause to watch a team of oxen pass, steered by a goad, and with a sheepskin stretched over the yoke; he climbed over hump-backed bridges, beneath whose arches torrents of snow-water raced, snatching at the orange fungus hidden in the cracks of the stone-work. He liked the architecture of the houses, with their indigo blue rafters, their gently sloping roofs, and the wrought iron anchors embedded in the hewn stone of the façades. The mountains of Carlovingian romance—with their sheer, crumbling spurs, traversed by paths on which, rounding a large rock which the Paladin Roland might once have set eyes on, one might suddenly meet a flock of bleating, milling sheep—and especially the pastures, the soft, moist, bright apple-green pastures, each one of them exactly like the next—led him to conceive the possibility that rustic bliss might be restored to all mankind by the principles of the Revolution.

But he had been rather disappointed by the people, as he got to know them better; these Basques, with their measured movements, their bull-necks and their equine profiles (great stone-masons, great hewers of trees, and navigators worthy of rubbing shoulders with the men who searched for the sea-route to Iceland, and had been the first to set eyes on a sea congealed into pack-ice), were tenacious in the preservation of their traditions. There was no one to equal them at finding ways and means of hearing a clandestine Mass, carrying wafers in their berets, hiding bells in barns and lime kilns, and erecting altars on the sly—in a barn, in the back room of an eating-house, or in a cave guarded by sheep-dogs—wherever it was least expected. A few hooligans might have smashed the idols in Bayonne Cathedral, but the Bishop had found men ready to help him cross into Spain, with his monstrances, cinguli and other baggage. A girl had to be shot for taking Communion at Villa de Vera. The inhabitants of several frontier villages had been convicted of sheltering and protecting refractory priests, and had been deported *en masse* to the Landes. Chauvin-Dragon went on being Saint-Jean-de-Luz to its fishermen, just as Baigorry was still dedicated to Saint Stephen as far as the peasants there were concerned. La Soule remained so attached to its Midsummer bonfires and mediaeval dances that nobody would have dared denounce anyone there for telling his rosary in his house, or for crossing himself when he talked about the witches of Zagarramurdi.

Esteban had been two months in this world, and found it increasingly alien, artificial and unstable—he would never succeed in understanding the Basque language, nor could he ever guess what they were saying from their faces—when the tremendous news broke that they were at war with Spain. But he could not yet cross into the Peninsula to witness the birth of a new nation, as he had liked to imagine himself doing when he listened to Martinez de Ballesteros optimistically forecasting an imminent uprising in Madrid. He was still a prisoner in a France blockaded on the Atlantic seaboard by English squadrons, and from which there was no means of returning to his own country. Up till now he had not thought about going back to Havana, anxious as he was to play his part, however small it might be, in a revolution that was destined to transform the world. But it was enough that he should find himself prevented from doing so for an almost painful nostalgia for his home and his own people, for a different culture and the flavour of a different world, to make him loathe his present employment, which was no more, after all, than a tedious bureaucratic chore. It had not been worth coming so far to see a revolution, and then not to see it, but to remain an eavesdropper, listening from a nearby park to the fortissimi swelling from an opera house to which he had not been able to gain admittance.

Several months went by, during which Esteban attempted to make himself indispensable by performing monotonous tasks. Nothing of what they had hoped for was happening in Spain. Even the war, in this part of France, was becoming languid and perfunctory; they were merely keeping a defensive watch on the strong forces deployed along the frontier by General Ventura Caro, who was just as determined not to move from his positions, despite the numerical superiority of his army. At night shots would be heard in the mountains, but it never went beyond a skirmish, or a fleeting encounter between reconnaissance patrols.

The long, sunny, peaceful summer passed; the autumn winds returned; the cattle were rounded up into their barns as soon as the cold winter winds made an appearance. As time went by Esteban noticed that his exile from Paris was resulting in such a confusion of mind that he finally felt unable to understand the developments of a political scene which was contradictory, spasmodic, in constant flux, self-devouring, entangled in committees and political machinery that could only be indistinctly seen from this distance. Unexpected reports kept arriving about the rise to power of unknowns, or the noisy fall of the famous, who, only yesterday, had been compared to the greatest figures of antiquity. It rained regulations, laws and decrees, which had already been abrogated or cancelled by emergency measures when the provinces still believed them to be in force. The weeks now had ten days; the New Year had been removed from January; the months were called "Brumaire", "Germinal" and "Fructidor", but they did not coincide with the old months; weights and measures were changed, upsetting the habits of people who instinctively used hands, arms and pecks. Nobody along that coast could say what was really happening, nor who were the men to trust, when the Basque-French identified themselves more closely with the Navarrese-Spanish than with the functionaries who suddenly dropped on them out of the remote North, to impose strange calendars, or change the names of the towns. The war that was now raging would be a long war, because it was not a war like the others, waged to satisfy the ambitions of a prince or to appropriate foreign territories. "The kings know," one could hear them shout on the Jacobin rostrums, "that no Pyrenees stand in the way of philosophical ideas; millions of men are on the march to change the face of the world."

And now it was March—it went on being March for Esteban, although he liked the sound of the "Nivose" and "Pluviose" of the new calendar—an ashen March, punctuated by rainstorms which swathed the hills of Ciboure as with gauze, and gave a ghostly look to the boats returning to harbour, from fishing on a rough, melancholy, grey-green sea, which dissolved in the distance without definite horizon into a misty, whitish, wintry sky.

From the window of the room where the young man did his translating and proof-reading, there was a distant view of deserted beaches, bristling with posts, where the ocean brought its deposits of dead seaweed, broken timbers and shreds of canvas, after the nocturnal storms which moaned in the interstices of the shutters and rattled the creaking weather-vanes eaten away by verdigris. And over there, in the Place Louis XVI, now the Place de la Liberté, stood the guillotine. Far from its more important setting, far from the square that had been spattered with a monarch's blood, where it had taken part in a transcendent tragedy, this rain-soaked machine—which was not terrible, but ugly; not ominous, but damp and gloomy—wore, when in use, the pitiful look of one of those provincial theatres where a second-rate company is trying to imitate the grand style of the actors of the capital. At the prospect of an execution a few fishermen carrying their baskets would stop; next, three or four passers-by, wearing enigmatic expressions and spitting out tobacco-stained saliva from between their teeth; finally a child, an alpargata seller, a squid vendor. And as soon as some person's blood had begun to flow from his trunk, like wine from the neck of a wineskin, they would proceed unhurriedly on their way.

It was March—an ashen March, punctuated by rainstorms, which made the straw in the barns swell, covered the goats' skins with mud, and introduced clouds of acrid smoke into the kitchens, with their tall chimneys and their smell of garlic and cheap olive oil. Esteban had had no news of Victor for some months now. He knew that he was carrying out, and with terrible severity, the functions of Public Prosecutor, before the Revolutionary Tribunal in Rochefort. He had even asked—and Esteban had approved of this—that the guillotine should be installed in the courtroom, so that no time should be wasted between a sentence and its execution. Deprived of Victor's ardour, energy and dash, and the glamour of his direct contacts with Billaud or Collot—or with any other exalted personage of the Times-in-which-we-live, an appellation which did not apply down here—Esteban felt himself to be shrinking, diminishing, losing all individuality; he felt that he was being swallowed by Events, to which his own very humble contribution was irredeemably anonymous. He felt so unimportant that he wanted to weep. In his distress he longed to lay his head in Sofía's firm lap, as he had done so many times, in search of that soothing, maternal strength which had flowed from her virgin womb, as if she had really been his mother.

And he was beginning to weep in earnest, thinking of his loneliness, of his uselessness, when he saw Colonel Martínez de Ballesteros come into his office-bedroom. The Commander of the Mountain Rifles was agitated and ruffled, his hands sweaty and trembling. He was obviously disturbed by something he had just heard.

XIV

"I've had enough of these Frenchies!" cried the Spaniard, dropping on to Esteban's bed. "More than enough! They can go to the Devil!" He buried his face in his hands and remained silent for a long time. The young man handed him a bowl of wine, which he drained at one gulp, asking for more. Then he began to pace from wall to wall, talking rapidly about what had made him angry. He had just been deprived of his military command, dismissed—"dis-mis-sed"—by some commissar from Paris, who had been sent down with unlimited powers to reorganise the troops in this sector. His disgrace was the consequence of a drive against foreigners, which had begun in Paris and was now reaching this frontier area : "They've discredited the masons, and now they're turning on the best friends the Revolution has got." It was rumoured that the Abbé Marchena was in hiding and being hunted, and might be guillotined at any moment : "A man who has done so much for Liberty." And now the French had taken control of the Bayonne committee, and eliminated the Spaniards—one for being a moderate, another because he had been a mason, another as a suspicious character. "Go carefully, my friend, because you are a foreigner too. A few months from now it will be a crime in France to be a foreigner."

Martinez de Ballesteros continued his agitated monologue : "While they were amusing themselves in Paris, dressing up whores as the Goddess of Reason, down here they were losing a golden opportunity of taking the Revolution into Spain by their inefficiency and jealousy. Now they can just sit down and wait ! . . . So much for their ideas of making the Revolution universal anyway; they're only thinking about the French Revolution now. And the rest . . . they can rot ! Everything here is coming to mean its opposite. They make us translate a *Declaration of the Rights of Man* into Spanish, and out of its seventeen principles they violate twelve every day. They took the Bastille, just to set free four forgers, two madmen, and a sodomite, yet they found a prison in Cayenne which is far worse than any Bastille."

Afraid that a neighbour might overhear him, Esteban led his visitor out into the street, on the pretext of having to buy some writing paper. Passing the former Casa Haranader, they went to the Libraire de la Trinité, which had now opportunely changed its name to "de la Fraternité". It was a badly-lit shop with a low ceiling, and from the rafters hung a lamp which was burning even in the middle of the morning. Esteban used to spend long hours here, browsing through the new books, in an atmosphere which reminded him rather of the back room in their warehouse in Havana, what with the piles of dust-covered articles, whence emerged armillary spheres, planispheres, nautical telescopes and physics apparatus.

Martinez de Ballesteros shrugged his shoulders at some recently arrived engravings which recalled great moments in the history of Greece and Rome : "These days every jackanapes thinks he's made of the same stuff as the Gracchi, Cato and Brutus," he murmured. And going up to a battered piano, he began to thumb through the latest songs by François Girouet, published by Frère, which were being sung everywhere to a guitar accompaniment, and were written in a code that was easy to decipher. He showed Esteban the titles : "The Tree of Liberty", "Hymn to Reason", "Despotism Cast Down", "The Republican Nursemaid", "Hymn to Gunpowder", "The Awakening of the Patriots", "Song of the Thousand Blacksmiths in the Arsenal".

"Even music has been rationalised," he said. "They've come to believe that anyone who writes a sonata is failing in his duty to the Revolution. Grétry himself springs the Carmagnole on us at the end of his ballets, so that he can lay claim to patriotism." And in order to register some sort of protest against the productions of François Girouet, he attacked the allegro of a sonata with diabolical energy, working off his wrath on the keyboard of the instrument. "One shouldn't play music by a mason like Mossar," he said, when he had finished the piece, "there might be an informer hidden inside the piano."

Esteban bought his paper and left the shop, followed by the Spaniard, who did not want to be left alone with his troubles. In spite of the freezing rain which was beginning to fall, an executioner in a beret was uncovering the guillotine, in anticipation of some condemned prisoner, who would lose his head without anyone to see him, except the guards already posted at the foot of the scaffold.

"Scarify them, go on, scarify them," muttered Martinez de Ballesteros : "Exterminations in Nantes, exterminations in Lyons, exterminations in Paris."

"Humanity will emerge regenerated from this blood-bath," said Esteban.

"Don't quote other people's sayings at me, and above all don't give me Saint-Just's Red Sea (he could never do better than 'Sen-Ju'), because that's just inferior rhetoric," said the other.

They passed the usual cart, in which a priest with his hands tied was being taken to the scaffold, and proceeding on down to the quay, they stopped opposite a small boat, on whose deck sardines and tunny-fish were floundering round a tawny skate straight out of a Flemish still-life. Martinez de Ballesteros seized an iron key which he wore attached to his watch-chain and threw it into the water with an angry gesture: "A key to the Bastille," he said. "It was false anyway. There are rascally locksmiths who manufacture them by the thousand. They've filled the world with such talismans. We've got more keys to the Bastille now than pieces of the True Cross."

Looking towards Ciboure, Esteban observed an unusual amount of movement on the road to Hendaye. Soldiers of the regiment of Pyrenean Rifles were arriving in disorder, in isolated groups, a few singing but most of them so tired—so eager to clamber up into some cart or other, so as to get a little further on their way without having to walk—that those who were singing could only be doing so because they were drunk. They looked like an army in disarray, not knowing where to go, neglected by their mounted officers, who had now reached the edge of the bay and were dismounting in front of an eating-house, to dry their wet clothes by the fire.

Esteban felt sick with fear at the thought that these troops might have been defeated, were being pursued perhaps by the enemy forces commanded by the Marquis de Saint-Simon, the leader of a band of *émigrés* from whom a bold offensive had been expected for some time. But from close to, these new arrivals looked as if they had been drenched by rain and mud rather than routed in battle. While the cold and the sick sought the protection of the overhanging roofs, and walls sheltered from the drizzle, the rest set up camp, and passed round the brandy, herrings and army bread. The sutlers were already setting up their grid-irons, producing a thick smoke from the damp wood, as Martinez de Ballesteros approached an artillery-man carrying a string of garlic over his shoulder, to find out the cause of this unexpected troop-movement.

"We're going to America," said the soldier, and as he uttered the word it suddenly shone with a solar brilliance in Esteban's mind. Trembling and anxious, with the almost angry expectancy of someone who finds himself excluded from a party given on his own property, the young man went with the dismissed colonel into the tavern where the officers were resting. They soon learned that the regiment was destined for the Antilles, and that more would be arriving, to form part of an armada assembling at Rochefort. They would be moved there in successive journeys, aboard small transport ships, but they would have to go carefully and keep well in-shore, because of the English blockade. Two of the Convention's commissars would be sailing in the ships, Chrétien and a certain Victor Hugues, an old sailor, so they said, who was familiar with the Caribbean waters, where a powerful English fleet was operating at the moment.

Esteban went out into the square, so afraid of losing this opportunity of escaping from a place where he felt threatened— for he knew that the uselessness of the work he was doing would soon be apparent to those who still paid him—that he sat down on a stone step, without being aware of the icy wind which tightened the skin on his cheeks.

"Since you're a friend of Hugues, do all you can to get him to take you. Hugues has become an important man since he's been able to count on the support of Dalbarade, whom we all knew when he was a pirate in Biarritz. You're mouldering away here. The stuff you translate is left piled up in a cellar. And you're a *foreigner*, remember that."

Esteban squeezed his hand: "And what will you do now?"

The other man answered with a gesture of resignation: "In spite of everything I shall go on the same. When you've worked at making a revolution, it's difficult to go back to what you did before."

After writing Victor Hugues a long letter—which he copied out, so that he could send it at the same time to the Navy Department, the Revolutionary Tribunal at Rochefort, and a former fellow-mason—whom he advised to find the addressee, wherever he might be—Esteban awaited the results of his petition. He had painted himself in clear terms as the victim of administrative indifference and discord amongst Spanish republicans, and he attributed the scant success of his activities to the mediocrity of the men who had succeeded one another in command. He complained of the climate, insinuating that it might induce a recrudescence of his old illness. On a more friendly note, he evoked memories of Sofía, and of the far-off house "where we all lived like brothers". He ended with a detailed enumeration of his talents, which could be of service to the revolutionary cause in America. "What is more," he ended up, "to be classed as a foreigner is not particularly desirable these days, as you know"; and then, thinking of the people who might intercept the letter, he added: "Some Spaniards in Bayonne have, it seems, fallen into deplorable counter-revolutionary errors. This has necessarily led to the imposition of a purge, in which, alas, the just may have to pay for the sinners."

There followed an anxious wait of several weeks, during which a constant fear made him avoid Martinez de Ballesteros or anyone else who might have made dangerous remarks about a recent event in the presence of a third party. Some people said that the Abbé Marchena, whose whereabouts were unknown, had been guillotined. A great fear began to disturb the nights of people living along that coast. Many eyes watched the streets out of round peep-holes in the darkened houses. So as to get the better of his fears, Esteban used to leave his inn shortly before dawn, making his way on foot, in the rain, to the nearby villages, where he drank cheap wine in some tavern or poor shop—one of those which sell buttons by the dozen, a few pins, a cow-bell, an oddment of material, or preserves in a box lined with wood-shavings. He used to return after dark, apprehensive of having received a visit from a stranger, or of finding himself summoned to the Old Castle of Bayonne, now transformed into a prison and commissariat, to answer for some mysterious "affair which concerns you". He was so disgusted by this hermetic, silent country, now full of dangers, that he found everything ugly which might have been thought attractive: the walnut trees and holm oaks, the houses of the old nobility, the flight of the kites, the cemeteries full of strange crosses bearing solar symbols.

When he saw the policeman enter, bringing him a letter, his trembling fingers would not open the envelope. He had to break the sealing wax with his teeth—they at least responded to his will. He knew the writing well, it was Victor Hugues', giving him precise instructions, urging him to come to Rochefort at once, and offering him a post as clerk in the fleet which would soon be leaving from the Island of Aix. With this piece of paper as a safe-conduct, Esteban could leave Saint-Jean-de-Luz with one of the regiments of Basque Rifles who were going to join the expedition—a risky expedition, which would have problems to solve along the way, because they did not know (no news having come) whether the English had occupied the French possessions in the Antilles. The theoretical destination of their voyage was the island of Guadeloupe, from where, in the event of being unable to land, the fleet would go on to San Domingo.

Victor embraced the young man coldly, when they met again after their long separation. He had lost weight, and the firm contours of his face reflected an energy which had been increased by command. Surrounded by officers, he was toiling away at the final preparations, studying maps and dictating letters in a room full of weapons, surgical instruments, drums and furled banners.

"We'll talk later," he said, turning his back on Esteban to read a despatch : "Go . . ."—then corrected *va* to *allez* : "Go to the Intendant's office and wait for my orders."

Although the familiar form of address was at that time held to be a symbol of the revolutionary spirit, he had used it deliberately. Esteban realised that Victor had imposed on himself the first discipline required for the office of Leader of Men : that of having no friends.

XV

Fuerte cosa es
—*Goya*

ON THE FOURTH of Floréal in the Year Two, the little squadron weighed anchor, without any shouting or fanfares. It was composed of two frigates, *La Pique* and *La Thétis,* the brig *L'Espérance,* and five troop transports, carrying one company of artillery, two of infantry and the battalion of Pyrenean Rifles with which Esteban had come to Rochefort. Behind them they left the Island of Aix, its fortress bristling with watchtowers, and a prison ship—*Les Deux Associés*—in which more than seven hundred prisoners were awaiting deportation to Cayenne, herded in holds where they had no room to lie down, restless with sleep or sickness, sharing their sores, epidemics and purulence.

The voyage began unpropitiously. The latest reports from Paris were not calculated to excite enthusiasm in Chrétien or Victor Hugues: the islands of Tobago and St. Lucia had fallen into the hands of the English; Rochambeau had had to surrender in Martinique. As for Guadeloupe, it was being subjected to continuous attacks, which were draining the military governor's resources. Everyone knew, of course, that the settlers in the French Antilles were monarchist scum; since the execution of the King and Queen they had been openly opposed to the Republic, and were now anxious for a definitive British occupation, and abetting the enemy's designs. The squadron was sailing into the unknown, and if it was to get quickly away from Europe, must evade the blockade off the French coast. Very strict orders had been issued to this end; it was forbidden to show a light after sunset, and the soldiers must retire early to their hammocks. They lived constantly on the alert, their weapons beside them, ready for a likely encounter. The weather, however, favoured their design, by bringing down friendly fogs over a docile sea. Laden with artillery and provisions, the ships were crammed with boxes, casks, bundles and piles of clothing, and the men had to share the cramped space which remained on deck with the horses, which ate their hay out of battered ship's boats instead of mangers. They were carrying sheep, too, whose pitiful bleating arose from the holds at all hours, while in boxes of earth, mounted on benches, grew radishes and vegetables destined for the officers' dinner table.

Esteban had had no opportunity of speaking to Victor Hugues since they left, but spent his time in the company of two typographers—the Loeuillets, father and son—who were travelling with the fleet, with a small printing-press intended for the printing of notices and propaganda.

As the ships left the mainland astern, the Revolution began to simplify itself in people's minds; freed from the uproar and rhetoric of street meetings, the Event was reduced to its basic elements and pared of contradictions. The recent condemnation and death of Danton became a mere incident on the road to a distant future which each man saw in the light of his own hopes. It needed an effort, of course, to admit the sudden infamy of tribunes who had only the day before been popular idols, acclaimed orators, the movers of masses. But soon it would lead to something which would please everyone, once they had ridden out the storms : the immediate future would be less irreligious, thought the Basque who had brought his scapularies on board; less antimasonic, thought the man who longed for his Lodges; more egalitarian, more communalistic, felt the man who dreamed of the final abolition of inequality, which could not survive the last privileges. For the present they were travelling towards a task which would be undertaken by Frenchmen against the English; the old doubts vanished now that they were far from taverns and popular gossip.

Esteban was still troubled by a single mental reservation : when he thought of Marchena—and he must have fallen, for he had been hand in glove with the Girondins—he deplored the fact that many foreigners, who were friends of freedom and threatened with death in their own country for being so, should be sacrificed for the sole crime of having trusted too much in the proselytising vigour of the Revolution. Too much trust was put, in such cases, in the confidences and accusations of nonentities. Robespierre himself, in a speech before the Society of the Friends of Liberty and Equality, had condemned these thoughtless accusations, denouncing them as tricks devised by the enemies of the Republic in order to discredit its best men. Esteban reflected that he had escaped just in time, since he was certainly amongst those who had fallen into disgrace. And yet he still hankered after the illusion of toiling in a greater dimension, of taking part in Something Big, which had so inspired him when Brissot sent him to the Pyrenees, assuring him that he would be contributing to the preparation of Mighty Events. These mighty events had now halted at the foot of the Pyrenees, behind which Death, true to its mediaeval practices, would continue to be inflicted by means of the theological symbols of the Flemish paintings which Philip II had hung on the walls of the Escorial.

At times like these Esteban would have liked to approach Victor, to confide his doubts in him. But the Commissar seldom put in an appearance, and when he did it was unexpectedly, surprisingly, in order to impose discipline. One night, coming on to a lower deck, he surprised four soldiers playing cards by the light of a candle stuffed into a cone of rag-paper. He drove them up on deck with the point of his sword pricking their buttocks, and made them throw the cards into the sea. "Next time, you yourselves will be the kings of that pack," he told them. He used to glide about underneath the sleeping men in their hammocks, feeling the material to see if it betrayed the hard shape of a stolen bottle. "Lend me your musket," he would say to a rifleman, as if impatient to have a shot at some fins outlined against the water. Then, forgetting the target, he would inspect the weapon and find that it was dirty and badly greased. "You swine!" he would shout, throwing the musket to the ground. Next day all the weapons would be gleaming as if they had just been taken from the armoury. Sometimes at night he clambered up to the crow's nest, his boots gripping the rungs of the rigging, or swinging out into the void when he missed his footing, until finally he stood erect, beside the look-out, plumed and magnificent, guessed-at rather than seen in the shadows, like an albatross which had folded its wings and settled above the ship. "Histrionics", thought Esteban, but they were histrionics which held him, as they did the other spectators, and revealed the potentialities of a man who could aspire to such roles.

The blowing of the reveille at full blast by the ships' buglers all together informed the soldiers one morning that they had left the danger zone. The first mate reversed his hour-glass and put away the pistols which up till now had been holding down his maps. Celebrating the start of a normal voyage with a swig of brandy, the men turned to their daily tasks with a boisterous joy, which suddenly broke through the tensions, alarms and frowns of the last few days. The men sang as they shovelled horse manure over the side, while the horses burrowed their heads into their boat-mangers. The men sang as they polished their weapons; the slaughtermen sang, as they sharpened the knives with which, to-morrow, they would begin to slaughter the sheep. The iron and the grindstone sang, the paint-brush and the saw, the curry-comb on the gleaming croup of a horse; and the anvil, installed to leeward, made a rhythm out of its bellows and hammers.

The last mists of Europe were dissolving under a sun which was still veiled, still too white, but already warm, and which glinted on the buckles of the uniforms, the gold of the galloons, the patent leather, the bayonets, and the saddle-trees that had been brought out into the daylight, from bow to stern. The pieces of artillery were uncovered, not yet with the intention of loading them, but merely to put the swabs down their throats and polish up their brass. On the poop deck the regimental band of the Pyrenean Rifles was rehearsing a march by Gossec, to which they had added a trio for the Basque *"túntún"* and fife, which proved so superior to the music on the scores that the troops jeered the rest as being harsh and discordant. Every man was busy at his appointed task, scanning the horizon without apprehension, singing and laughing in a general good humour which extended from the crow's nest to the orlops, when Victor appeared, in the full dress uniform of a commissar, and no more approachable than he had been before, in spite of the fact that he was smiling. He walked the deck, stopping to watch how they repaired the carriage of a cannon, or what the carpenter was doing further on; he patted the neck of a horse, and tapped the head of a drum with his finger; he showed interest in the health of an artillery man who was wearing his arm in a sling. Esteban noticed that when they saw him the men suddenly fell silent. The Commissar inspired fear. With slow steps he ascended the companion-ladder which led to the fo'c'sle. There, on the highest part of the ship's waist, casks had been stowed, side by side, under a voluminous canvas fixed to the sides with ropes. Victor gave instructions to an officer, who ordered the immediate removal of the casks to another part of the ship. Then a be-flagged long-boat was lowered into the water; the Commissar, on this first day of peace and prosperity, was going to take lunch with Captain de Leyssegues, the Commander of the fleet, aboard *La Thétis*. Chrétien, who had been sea-sick ever since they sailed, remained shut up in his cabin.

When Hugues' plumed hat disappeared behind *L'Espérance*, which was now sailing between the two frigates, joy reigned once more on board *La Pique*. The officers themselves, freed from their cares, shared in the good humour and singing of the sailors, as well as their taunts of the band, who had given up their Basque tunes and virtuosities on the fife, and could not even produce a decent Marseillaise. "This is our first rehearsal together," shouted the conductor to excuse himself, amidst hooting. But the men laughed at him as they would have laughed at anything at all; the vital necessity was to laugh, especially now, when the salvoes of *La Thétis* were welcoming the Commissar of the National Convention and raising him to a different and distant orbit. The Plenipotentiary was feared. Perhaps he enjoyed knowing that he was feared.

XVI

THREE MORE DAYS passed. Each time the first mate reversed his hour-glass, the sun seemed to grow rounder, and the sea was beginning to speak to Esteban with all its smells. One night, to get relief from the heat which was still increasing in the holds and lower decks, the young man went up on deck to contemplate the vastness of the first completely clear, cloudless sky they had met with during the crossing. A hand was placed on his shoulder. Behind him was Victor, shirt open, without his dress-coat, and smiling his smile of the old days: "We need women. Don't you agree?" And, as if driven by a nostalgic necessity, he began to recall those places they had both known in Paris, soon after they arrived, where there were so many attractive and willing women to be found. He had not forgotten Rosamund, of course, the German girl of the Palais Royal; or Zaïre, of the Voltairian name; or Dorina, with her pink muslin dresses; or that entresol where, for a payment of two *louis* one was offered in succession the variegated skills of Angélique, Zephire, Zoé, Esther and Zilia, who each embodied a different feminine type, and who comported themselves—in strict observance of a dramatic ritual which accorded magnificently with the character of their beauty —as frightened virgins, dissolute bourgeoises, fallen ballet-dancers, a Mauritian Venus (this was Esther) or a drunken Bacchante (that was Zilia). After having been the object of the expert attentions of each of these feminine archetypes, the visitor was finally thrown into the firm lap of Aglaé, she of the high, pointed breasts and the chin of a queen of antiquity, whose person always quenched, in peerless manner, the ascending scale of one's desires.

At another time Esteban would have laughed at these comic recollections. But he still felt ill at ease in conversation—Victor had paid no attention to him since their meeting in Rochefort—and he had soon exhausted his repertoire of monosyllables, in response to this unexpected loquacity.

"You're like a Haitian," said Victor. "They just answer 'oh, oh' to everything there, and you never find out what the other person's thinking. Let's go to my cabin."

The first thing to be seen there, between the nails where Hugues' hat and dress-coat were hanging, was a large portrait of the Incorruptible, with a lamp burning like a votive light beneath it. The Commissar set a bottle of brandy on the table and filled two glasses. "Your health!" Then he gave Esteban a rather sly look. He apologised, in a merely polite tone, for not having sent for him since they left the Island of Aix: responsibilities, duties, obligations, and so on—and their situation was not altogether clear yet. They had tricked the English blockade certainly, but they did not know what the ships would have to face when they arrived. Their main objective was to re-establish the authority of the Republic in the French colonies in America, and to combat separatist tendencies by every means possible, reconquering, if it proved necessary, territories which were perhaps being lost at that very moment.

Long silences punctuated his monologue, broken only by that half growled, half muttered *"Oui!"* which Esteban knew so well. He praised the lofty tone of patriotism which he had remarked in the boy's letter, and which had decided him to make use of his services: "Anyone who is disloyal to the Jacobins is being disloyal to the Republic and to the cause of liberty," he said. But Esteban made a slight gesture of irritation, not because of the phrase itself, but because it was one which Collot d'Herbois often used, and an ex-actor, grown increasingly fond of the bottle, seemed to him the last man to be dictating the norms of revolutionary morality. Incapable of suppressing this objection, he uttered it without raising his eyes.

"You may be right," said Victor, "Collot does drink too much, but he's a good patriot."

Emboldened by two glasses of brandy, Esteban pointed to the portrait of the Incorruptible : "How can a giant like that put so much trust in a drunkard? Collot's speeches reek of wine." The Revolution had produced illustrious men certainly, but it had also lent wings to a whole crowd of failed and resentful ones, exploiters of the Terror who, to give proof of their lofty patriotism, had had copies of the Constitution bound in human skin. These were not just fables. He had seen these horrible books, covered with a dark grey, over-porous leather—suggesting faded petals, rag-paper, chamois leather, or lizard-skin—which one's disgusted hands refused to touch.

"Regrettable, I know," said Victor with a frown, "but we can't be everywhere."

Esteban felt obliged to make a profession of faith which would leave no doubts about his loyalty to the Revolution; but he was annoyed by the absurdity of certain patriotic ceremonies, by certain unwarranted investitures, and by the abilities which superior men claimed to find in so many mediocrities. It was easy to get a stupid play produced if the dénouement included a Phrygian cap; patriotic epilogues had been written for *Le Misanthrope*, and in the Comédie Française's rejuvenated *Britannicus* Agrippina was referred to as "Citizeness"; many classical tragedies had been banned, yet the State subsidized a theatre where, in one inept production, Pope Pius VI could be seen fighting with Catherine II, using sceptres and tiaras, and a King of Spain fell over in a squabble and lost his enormous cardboard nose. Moreover they had for some time now been encouraging a sort of contempt for intelligence. In more than one committee the barbaric cry of "Don't trust anyone who has written a book" had been heard. All the literary clubs of Nantes—he knew this for a fact—had been closed down by Carrier. And that ignoramus Henriot had even gone so far as to ask that the Bibliothèque Nationale should be burned down—while the Committee of Public Safety was sending famous surgeons, eminent chemists, scholars, poets and astronomers to the scaffold.

Esteban stopped, seeing that the other man was showing signs of impatience. "What's the use of arguments," said Victor finally, "you talk as they must talk in Coblenz. And you wonder why the literary meetings in Nantes were stopped?" He thumped the table with his fist : "We are changing the face of the world, yet the only thing which worries you is the poor quality of a play. We are transforming men's lives and yet you lament because a few writers can't meet to read idylls and other rubbish. You would be capable of sparing the life of a traitor, of an enemy of the people, just because he'd written some pretty verses !"

From the deck came the sound of wood being dragged about. The carpenters, taking advantage of the fact that paths had been cleared between the bales, were carrying planks up into the bows, followed by sailors laden with large, oblong crates. When one of these was opened, a steely, triangular shape glinted in the moonlight, which the young man shuddered to see. These men, silhouetted against the sea, seemed to be performing some bloody and mysterious rite, as they laid the bascule and the uprights out flat on the deck, following a sequence determined by the sheets of instructions, which they consulted in silence by the light of a lantern. What was being set out there was a geometrical projection from the vertical, a false perspective, a configuration in two dimensions of what would soon take on height, breadth and a terrible depth. With something of the air of Aztec immolators, the dark figures toiled at their nocturnal joinery, taking parts, runners and hinges from the coffin-like crates; they were coffins too long for human beings, yet wide enough to grip their sides, for the stock and quadrate which they contained were intended to circumscribe a circle whose diameter was based on the average distance between a human being's shoulders. Hammers began to sound, beating out a sinister rhythm over the vast and restless sea, where the sargasso was already starting to appear.

"So that was travelling with us too !" exclaimed Esteban.

"Inevitably," said Victor Hugues, turning back to his cabin. "That and the printing-press are the most essential things we've got on board, apart from the cannon."

"Words and blood go together," said Esteban.

"Don't start using Spanish proverbs on me," said Victor, refilling the glasses. Then he fixed his interlocutor with a meaningful stare, and fetching a calfskin letter-case, he opened it slowly and took out a sheaf of sealed documents, which he threw on the table. "Yes, we're taking the guillotine with us. But do you know what I shall be giving the men of the New

World?" He paused, then added, stressing each word: "The Decree of the 16th Pluviose of the Year Two, by which slavery is abolished. From this time forward, all men domiciled in our colonies are declared to be French citizens, without distinction of race and with an absolute equality of rights."

He leaned out of the door of the cabin, watching the carpenters at work. Then he went on holding forth, with his back to the other, but certain of being heard: "For the first time a fleet is advancing towards America without bearing crosses aloft. Columbus' ships had them painted on their sails. They were the symbol of the servitude about to be imposed on the men of the New World in the name of a Redeemer who had died—so the chaplains probably said—to save men, to comfort the poor and to confound the rich." He turned round suddenly and pointed to the decree. "We, the cross-less, the redeemer-less, the god-less, are going there, in ships without chaplains, to abolish privilege and to establish equality. Ogé's brother is avenged."

Esteban lowered his head, ashamed of the objections he had raised so eagerly earlier on, as if to relieve his own intolerable doubts. He laid his hand on the decree, and felt the paper with its thick seals. "All the same," he said, "I would rather it were accomplished without our having to use the guillotine."

"That will depend on the people," said Victor, "the people there and our people as well. Don't imagine that I trust everyone who's travelling with us. We shall need to watch how more than one of them behaves when he finds himself ashore."

"Do you mean me?" asked Esteban.

"You or anyone else. I'm obliged by my position not to trust anybody. Some argue too much. Others reason too much. Some still have scapularies hidden away. Some say that life was better in that brothel they call the *ancien régime*. And there are soldiers who get together and plan to discredit the commissars the moment they've drawn their swords. But I know everything that is said, or thought, or done, on board these filthy ships. Be careful what you say. It will be repeated to me at once."

"Do you suspect me?" asked Esteban, with a bitter smile.

"Everyone is suspect," said Victor.

"Why don't you let the guillotine make its début on me to-night?"

"The carpenters would have to hurry to get it up; too much work for too ineffective a warning."

Victor began to remove his shirt. "Go to bed." He gave Esteban his hand, openly and cordially, as in the old days. Looking at him the boy was surprised by the likeness there was between the Incorruptible, as seen in the portrait in the cabin, and Victor's present appearance, seemingly remodelled in flagrant imitation of the carriage of the head, the fixed gaze and the courteous yet ruthless expression of the portrait. This glimpse of a trace of weakness, of Victor's eagerness to look physically like the man whom he admired above all others, was like a small but compensatory victory for Esteban. The man who, in the past, had so often dressed up as Lycurgus and Themistocles during their games at the house in Havana, now that he was vested with authority and had achieved his greatest ambition, was trying to imitate another man whose superiority he accepted. For the first time Victor Hugues' pride had bowed—perhaps unconsciously—before a master.

XVII

THE GUILLOTINE REMAINED shrouded in the bows, gaunt as a figure in a theorem, reduced to one horizontal and one vertical plane, as the squadron entered the warm seas, and the nearness of land was announced by the presence of tree-trunks, swept out by the currents, or bamboo roots, mangrove branches and fronds of coco-palms, floating in water made pale-green here and there by the sandy bottom. An encounter with British ships again became a possibility, and their ignorance of what might have happened in Guadeloupe, since the last news they had received on sailing, kept everyone in a state of expectancy which was only increased by each day of the voyage that passed without incident.

If it proved impossible to land in Guadeloupe the ships would go on to San Domingo. But the English might also have taken possession of San Domingo. In that event Chrétien and Victor

Hugues had orders to make for the shores of the United States, by any course they could, and to place themselves under the protection of that friendly nation. Esteban, although angry with himself and disgusted by what, viewed dispassionately, seemed an unpardonable piece of selfishness, could not stop his heart leaping when they talked of the possibility of the fleet putting in at Baltimore or New York. That would mean the end of an adventure which had already been absurdly prolonged; useless thereafter to the French ships, he would ask for his freedom—or would take it, which amounted to the same thing—and return, laden with history and stories, to somewhere where they would listen to him in amazement, as if he had been a pilgrim returning from the Holy Land.

Though his desire for action had been frustrated he had gained much experience, and his first foray into the great whirl of the world had constituted a preliminary initiation for future enterprises. For the present he must do something that would give meaning to his life. He would like to write, to discover, by means of writing and the disciplines which it imposes, the conclusions that were perhaps waiting to be drawn from what he had seen. He was not clear as to what this work would be. Something important at all costs, something which the age needed, something perhaps—and he revelled in the idea—which would displease Victor Hugues. A new theory of the State maybe, or a new version of *L'Esprit des Lois*. Perhaps a study of the errors of the Revolution. "Just what some swine of an *émigré* might write," he said to himself, abandoning this project forthwith.

During these last years Esteban had witnessed the development within himself of a critical propensity—annoying at times, inasmuch as it deprived him of the pleasure of certain spontaneous enthusiasms, shared by the majority—which refused to allow itself to be guided by any general criterion. When the Revolution was offered to him as a sublime event, without blemish or fault, the Revolution thereby became warped and vulnerable. Yet to a monarchist he would have defended it with the same arguments which exasperated him when they came from the lips of Collot d'Herbois. He abominated the outrageous demagogy of the "Père Duchesne" as much as he did the apocalyptic ravings of the *émigrés*. When he was with anti-clericals he became a priest, and with priests he became anti-clerical; he was a monarchist when he was told that all kings—James of Scotland, Henry the Fourth, Charles of Sweden forsooth!—had been degenerate, and an anti-monarchist, when he heard some of the Spanish Bourbons being praised. "I'm too fond of arguing," he admitted, remembering what Victor had said to him a few days before, "but I argue with myself, which is worse."

Hearing from the Loeuillets, whose tongues had gradually been loosened, of the terror which the Public Prosecutor had unleashed in Rochefort, he now viewed Victor with a mixture of rancour and uneasiness, tenderness and envy; rancour at finding himself excluded from his company; uneasiness after learning of his ferocity at the Tribunal; an almost feminine tenderness, which made him grateful in advance for any sign of friendship Victor might agree to show him; envy at his possession of a decree that was going to confer historical importance on this baker's son, born amongst ovens and flour-bowls. Esteban spent days conducting an interior debate with an absent Victor, giving him advice, demanding explanations, shouting at him, in mental preparation for a conversation which might never take place, and which, if it ever did take place, would modify the character of these preconceived speeches by substituting sensibility and even tears for reproaches, allegations, categorical questions and threats of a rupture, formulated in whispers.

During these days of waiting and uncertainty, Victor had himself rowed across early each day to *La Thétis*, in the be-flagged long-boat, to exchange impressions with de Leyssegues, both of them poring over maps, gazing at the reefs and shallows between which the squadron was now steering. Esteban hung about in his path as he left or returned, pretending to be absorbed in some task or other as he passed. But Victor never addressed him when he was surrounded by his captains and aides. This group, with its dazzling plumes and braid, made up a world to which he had no access. Watching him move away, Esteban would gaze with a mixture of anger and a kind of fascination at those powerful shoulders tightly encased in the sweat-stained cloth of his dress-coat; they were the shoulders of a man who knew the most intimate secrets of his home, of a man who had intervened in his life like fate itself, and driven it into ever more uncertain paths. "Don't waste kisses on frozen statues," the boy said to himself, quoting Epictetus with a sad smile, as he measured the distance which now separated him from his companion of old. Yet he had seen this frozen statue enjoying himself with women who were veterans of love's wars —chosen indeed because they were veterans—during the many escapades they had undertaken without any object beyond the quest for pleasure, when they first arrived in Paris. That naked Victor Hugues, parading his muscles in front of his lover for the night, fond of good wine and cynical jokes, had had an openness about him not to be seen in the frowning face of this resplendent man, proud of his revolutionary insignia, who to-day controlled the destinies of the fleet, having usurped the functions of admiral with an aplomb that had even intimidated de Leyssegues. "Your uniform has gone to your head," thought Esteban. "Mind you don't get drunk on uniforms; nothing could be worse than that."

At dawn one day two pelicans settled on the boom of *La Pique*. The breeze smelled of pasture-land, molasses and wood-smoke. The squadron sailed slowly on, taking soundings, since they were nearing the dreaded reefs of La Désirade. The men had all been on the alert since midnight, and now, crowding the sides, they gazed at the sullen profile of the island which had been there since dawn, like an enormous shadow stretching between the sea and a mass of very low clouds, stationary over the land. It was early June, and the water was so placid that the plunge of a flying-fish could be heard in the distance, and so limpid that the needle-fish could be seen flickering below the surface. The ships came to a standstill opposite a precipitous coastline which bore no trace of cultivation or habitation. A long-boat containing several sailors pulled away from *La Thétis*, rowing hard towards the land. At the same time Captain de Leyssegues and Generals Cartier and Rouger came on board *La Pique,* to wait for news with Chrétien and Victor Hugues.

After two hours, by which time the expectancy had risen to its height, the long-boat was seen to reappear. "What news?" the Commissar shouted to the sailors, when he thought that they were within range of his voice.

"The English are in Guadeloupe and St. Lucia," yelled one of them, giving rise to a whole witches' Sabbath of cursing on the decks of the ships : "They took the islands when we were leaving France."

Bitterness succeeded to tension. They would be back in the uncertainty of previous days; another dangerous voyage would now begin, through seas swarming with enemy ships, probably to find San Domingo also occupied by forces that could count on the support of the rich settlers, all monarchists, who would have gone over to the English with their hordes of negroes. And they could escape the British peril only by deviating so much from their course to avoid the Spanish peril that the fleet would end up in the area of the Bahamas at the worst possible time of year—Esteban recalled some lines from the *Tempest,* which spoke of the hurricanes in the Bermudas. The crew gave way to defeatism. Now that nothing could be done in Guadeloupe, the best course was to make off as quickly as possible. And some of them grew annoyed by the obstinacy of Victor Hugues, who made the men that had brought the information repeat the story of their brief expedition ashore over and over again. There was no room for doubt. The report had come from various people : a negro fisherman, a peasant, the waiter at a tavern; and then they had talked to the look-out posted at a small fort. They had all seen the squadron in the distance, although they had assumed them to be Admiral Jervis' ships, which either had sailed, would be sailing, or were sailing at that very moment, from Pointe-à-Pitre on their way to St. Kitts. The place where they were was surrounded by reefs and dangerous in the extreme. "I don't think we should wait any longer," said Cartier, "if they catch us here they'll destroy us."

Rouger was of the same opinion, but Victor would not give way. Soon the diapason of voices rose in anger. The Commanders and Commissars argued, with a great flurry of sabres, galloons, sashes and cockades, calling on Themistocles and Leonidas and swearing as only Frenchmen of the Year Two knew how.

Suddenly Victor Hugues silenced the rest with a barbed remark : "In a Republic the military do not argue, they obey. To Guadeloupe we were sent, and to Guadeloupe we shall go."

The others lowered their heads, as if cowed by the whip of a lion tamer. The Commissar gave orders to weigh anchor without delay, and to make for Les Salines in Grande-Terre.

Soon Marie Galante came in sight, wreathed in an opalescent mist, and the decks were cleared for action. And as the noise of preparations and hasty organisation grew—of rumbling gun-carriages, creaking cables and pulleys, shouts and the whinnying of the horses which could already scent the nearby land and its fresh pastures—Victor Hugues asked the typographers for several hundred posters printed during the crossing, and displaying in bold, black characters the text of the Decree of the 16th Pluviose, whereby the abolition of slavery was proclaimed, and equality of rights granted to all inhabitants of the island, without distinction of race or condition. Then he strode decisively across the deck, and, going up to the guillotine, he tore off the tarpaulin sheath which covered it, revealing it to the sunlight for the first time, its finely-tempered blade gleaming.

With all the insignia of his authority sparkling, Victor Hugues stood motionless, turned to stone, his right hand resting on the upright of the Machine, suddenly transformed into a symbolic figure. Together with Liberty, the first guillotine was arriving in the New World.

XVIII

CHRETIEN AND VICTOR HUGUES went in one of the first boats, perhaps to show the army that they were as fearless as the military in time of action. After the troops had landed, scattered shots were heard, followed by a brief interchange of fire, which died away into the distance. Night fell, and there was silence on board the ships, where a section of Marines was left, together with two companies of the Pyrenean Rifles, all under the command of Captain de Leyssegues.

Three days went by, during which nothing happened, nothing was heard, nothing was learned. To overcome his anxiety Esteban amused himself by fishing, in the company of the two typographers, who had nothing to do at moments like this. There was so much free space aboard the ships, now that the bulk of the army had gone, that the decks made one think of the stage of a theatre after the end of a spectacular production. There were pieces of clothing hanging up, abandoned bundles and empty crates lying about. One could move around as one liked, doze in the shade of the sails, carry one's bowl of soup to wherever seemed pleasantest, delouse oneself in the open air, or play cards, with one's eyes going constantly to the horizon between staking, in case the sail of an enemy ship should suddenly appear in the distance. This would have had all the features of a pleasant holiday in the Windward Islands, if the absence of news had not vexed so many of their minds. It was no good searching the shore with one's eyes. Nothing was happening there : a child picking clams out of the sand; a few dogs romping about with the water up to their teats; a family of negroes going by with enormous bundles on their heads, as if in everlasting migration.

Some people were beginning to fear the worst when, early on the morning of the fourth day, a messenger went aboard *La Thétis,* carrying orders for the fleet to move to Pointe-à-Pitre. The Republican army had been victorious. Following a skirmish soon after they landed, the French had advanced cautiously, without meeting the resistance they anticipated. Victor Hugues attributed the constant withdrawal of the English troops to the terror of the monarchist settlers at seeing men charging against their own infamous white flags with tricolours unfurled. The crews of the merchant ships which had been surprised in the harbour, had shown more spirit, and organised their resistance behind seventeen pieces of artillery in the fort of Fleur d'Epée. The night before, Cartier and Rouger had climbed to the assault of this redoubt, defended by nine hundred men, and had taken it by surprise at the point of their bayonets. Chrétien, setting too gallant an example, had fallen with his face to the enemy. Demoralised by this victory, the English were now entrenched in Basse-Terre behind the Rivière Salée, a tiny channel of water encroached on by mangrove trees, which, in spite of being so narrow, divided Guadeloupe into two distinct halves. Victor Hugues had been in Pointe-à-Pitre since midnight, setting up his government. Eighty-seven merchant ships, abandoned in the harbour, had passed into French hands. The shops were full of merchandise The squadron was expected there without delay.

Preparations began while the boats used for the landing were still returning to their ships. A great, a profound, an almost visceral joy animated the men, from the crow's nest down to the holds, as they clambered, ran, pushed on handspikes, hoisted, unreefed, reefed and took bearings. Victory, that was good. But, better than that, to-night there would be fresh hams, studded with cloves of garlic; plenty of wine, and beef with new carrots—a great deal of wine and the best rum; coffee of the sort that stains the cup, and women maybe—ruddy ones, copper-coloured ones, pale ones and dark ones; women who wore high-heeled shoes under the lace of their petticoats, women who smelt of frangipani, lemon water, vetiver, and—best of all —of women.

And with songs and shouts, and cries of "Long live the Republic", which rose from the quays and were taken up by the ships, the squadron entered the harbour of Pointe-à-Pitre on that day of Prairial in the Year Two, the guillotine borne erect in the bows of *La Pique*, shining like new, and completely unveiled so that all should see it clearly and recognise it. Victor and de Leyssegues embraced each other, and together they went to the former Seneschalship building—where the Commissar was installing his departments and offices—to stand before the body of Chrétien, lying with sash and cockade on a black catafalque decorated with red carnations, white tuberoses and blue plumbago.

Esteban was despatched to the Foreign Corn Exchange. To-day he would start to perform his functions in earnest, by opening a register of booty—within sight of the ships which had been left behind by the enemy. Everywhere posters were to be seen, proclaiming the abolition of slavery. Patriots who had been imprisoned by the "Big Whites" were set free. A motley, jubilant crowd wandered through the streets, acclaiming the new arrivals. To add to their delight it was learned that General Dundas, the British Governor of Guadeloupe, had died in Basse-Terre on the eve of the French landing. Luck was favouring the Army of the Republic. But the spree which the sailors

133

had all promised themselves that evening was realised only in imagination; shortly after mid-day Captain de Leyssegues began the work of fortifying and defending the port, sinking several old ships across the harbour bar to block the entrance, and installing cannon along the quays with their mouths facing out to sea.

But four days later their luck suddenly turned. A battery stationed on the Morne Saint-Jean, beyond the Rivière Salée, began a systematic bombardment of Pointe-à-Pitre. After landing his army at Le Gosier, Admiral Jervis laid siege to the town. The population was seized with terror as the projectiles fell haphazardly out of the sky at all hours, staving in roofs, piercing floors, causing tiles to fly off in an avalanche of red clay, ricocheting from the stonework, the paving stones and the posts at street corners, before rolling with a noise like thunder towards something they could knock down—a pillar, a railing or a man stupefied by the speed with which they descended upon him. A dry, ashy smell of old lime wrapped the town in an atmosphere of demolition, parching people's throats and inflaming their eyes. A cannon ball, striking a stone wall, would rebound off among the wooden houses, and hurtle down the stairs to strike a sideboard full of bottles, or a china cabinet, or to enter a cellar, where it came to a stop, scattering broken staves over the mangled body of a parturient mother. Detached by the impact, a bell would fall with such a tremendous clang that even the enemy gunners were made aware of it. This town of window-blinds, screens, flimsy balconies, wooden grilles, cleats and lathes was poorly protected against iron; everything had been made to take advantage of the slightest breath of wind. Each round was like a hammer striking against a wicker cage, and left corpses beneath the walnut-wood table where a family had taken shelter.

Soon there came a terrible new development : a battery equipped with ovens, stationed on the Morne Savon, started bombarding the town with red-hot shot. What was still left standing now began to burn. Fire succeeded to lime. They had not finished extinguishing one fire before another would break out somewhere else, in the baker's, the sawyer's, or the rum depot, which, once ablaze, poured out a sluggish river of blue flames into the street, to stream along the pavements towards the nearest incline. Since many of the poor houses had roofs of palm fronds and plaited fibre, a single red-hot projectile was sufficient to destroy a whole area of the town. And to cap it all, the lack of water meant that the fires must be fought with axes, saws, or machetes, so that to the destruction which fell from the sky was now added the deliberate destruction wrought by children, women and old men. A dense black smoke, rising from where a lot of old and dirty things were burning, caused a sudden darkness to fall on the town in broad daylight. And all this, which would have been intolerable, impossible to bear for a single hour, was prolonged day and night, amidst a perpetual uproar, in which the collapse of buildings merged with shouts, and the crackling of flames with the ground-level thunder of things rolling, colliding, rebounding and then striking like a battering-ram.

They were living through a catastrophe, and just when its climax seemed to have been reached, news arrived which made things even worse. Three attempts to silence the death-dealing batteries had failed. General Cartier had just died, worn out by insomnia, fatigue, and the unaccustomed climate. General Rouger had been wounded by a projectile, and was dying in a room of the building that had been turned into a military hospital. Some Dominican friars had mysteriously appeared, emerging from their hiding-places to stand at the heads of the patients' beds with a potion or a tisane in their hands. At a moment like this no one concerned themselves with their habits, but accepted the immediate relief given by their help, though it was soon followed by a reappearance of crucifixes and holy oil. This contraband faith insinuated itself wherever there were most wounds and gangrene, and not a few men, feeling death so close, threw away their cockades and asked for the Sacraments.

To their countless torments was now added that of thirst. Since corpses had fallen into the reservoirs, the water in them was poisoned and undrinkable. The soldiers boiled up sea water, confecting a salty coffee which they sweetened with enormous quantities of sugar, and then added alcohol to it. The water carriers, who had always supplied the town from their barrels, carried on boats or carts, were unable to reach the nearby streams because of the enemy fire. Rats swarmed in the streets, running about in the debris, invading everywhere; and as if one plague were not enough, grey scorpions appeared out of the old beams, thrusting their stings downwards wherever they got a chance. Several ships in the harbour had been reduced to drifting heaps of charred planks. *La Thétis*, mortally wounded perhaps, was heeling over amidst a panorama of broken masts and skeleton hulls.

On the twentieth day of the siege, colic made its appearance. People emptied themselves within a matter of hours, ejecting their lives through their intestines. As it was impossible to give them Christian burial, the bodies were interred wherever it was feasible : at the foot of a tree, or in some hole or other beside the latrines.

The cannon balls which had fallen into the Old Cemetery had disinterred bones and strewn them amongst the shattered gravestones and uprooted crosses. Victor Hugues had taken the last military leaders who were left to him, and his best troops, and entrenched himself on the Morne du Gouvernement, an eminence dominating the town, and offering, within its perimeter, the protection of a stone church.

Dazed, overwhelmed, incapable of thought, in the midst of this cataclysm which had now lasted for almost four weeks, Esteban passed the time lying in a sort of cave, or horizontal grave, which he had hollowed out amongst the sacks of sugar in the harbour warehouse, where the bombardment had surprised him while he he was taking an inventory. Opposite him the Loeuillets, father and son, had followed his example, and were sheltering in another cave amongst the sacks—a more spacious one, where they had stored part of the equipment for their press, notably the type cases, which out here were the most irreplaceable things of all. They did not suffer from thirst because there were several barrels of wine stored in the place, and, either from fear or the mere need to drink something, they would drain jars of this luke-warm liquid, which was growing increasingly bitter and left a dark crust on their lips. At a terrible time like this old Loeuillet, the son of a *camisard*, was not afraid to bring out the family Bible, which he had been carrying hidden in a box of paper. When a cannon-ball landed nearby, he would be emboldened by the great quantities he had drunk to declaim, from the depths of his cave, some verse or other from the

Apocalypse. And nothing could have been more applicable to reality than these sentences taken from the prophetic delirium of St. John the Divine : "The first Angel sounded; there followed hail and fire, mingled with blood, and they were cast upon the earth; and the third part of trees was burnt up and all green grass was burnt up."

"All this impiety," whined the typographer, "has brought us to the End of Time." At such moments Jervis' batteries became identified with the exemplary wrath of the Mighty Gods of Old.

XIX

ONE MORNING THE batteries fell silent. Men relaxed, animals laid back their ears; everything prone and inert remained prone and inert, but without any sudden alarms. One could hear the splash of the waves in the harbour, and a last tinkle of glass from a window, broken by a child's stone, startled people accustomed to an excess of noise. The survivors came out of their holes, their caves and their pigsties, covered in soot, muck and excrement, with filthy bandages dangling loosely from their wounds. Then they learned of the miracle : Victor Hugues, hearing two nights before that the English were wiping out the men in his advance positions and beginning to enter the town, had taken the desperate step of coming down from the Morne du Gouvernement with such vigour that the enemy had been repulsed several times and finally pursued across the Rivière Salée, to fall back on the entrenched camp of Berville in Basse-Terre. The French were victorious in this half of the island.

At noon a first convoy of water-carriers appeared, and were set upon by a ragged crowd, armed with saucepans, buckets, jugs and wash-bowls. Whole families threw themselves down to drink, jostled by the snouts and muzzles of their animals, burying their heads in the receptacles, fighting, lapping, vomiting out what had been drunk too quickly, stealing one another's pitchers, in a turmoil which had to be quelled with musket stocks. Their thirst slaked, they began to clean the main streets, pulling corpses out from under the wreckage. An enemy projectile still landed from time to time, knocking down a passer-by, dislodging a grille, chipping an altarpiece; but no one took any notice of such trivialities now, after what they had endured for four terrible weeks.

It was next learned that General Aubert, the last survivor amongst the expedition's Staff Officers, was dying of yellow fever; Victor Hugues was left sole master of the island of Grande-Terre. Summoning the Loeuillets to his office, with its broken windows and its half-burned curtains hanging like cheap festoons, he dictated to them, for immediate printing, the text of an edict in which a state of siege was proclaimed, and the formation, by compulsory conscription, of a militia of two thousand coloured men fit to bear arms. Any inhabitant who spread false rumours, who showed himself to be an enemy of Liberty, or who tried to cross over into Basse-Terre, would be summarily executed, and good patriots were urged to inform against all traitors. Captain Pélardy was promoted by decree to Divisional General, with Supreme Command of the Armed Forces, and Commander Boudet to Brigadier, with responsibility for training and disciplining the local levies.

Esteban marvelled at the energy the Commissar had shown ever since the day they landed at Les Salines. He had extraordinary powers of command, and unparalleled good luck into the bargain. Nothing could have been more providential for him at this time than the successive deaths of Chrétien, Cartier, Rouger and Aubert. With them had vanished the only men who could have opposed him. The tension which had existed between the military command and the civil authority was now effectually abolished. Victor Hugues, who had had several acrimonious arguments with the expedition's generals—so proud of their gold braid, their plumes and their campaigns—now relied on two henchmen who were devoted to him, and who knew moreover that it depended on him whether the Convention confirmed them in their new ranks.

That night wine flowed in the town, and, where energy remained for it, the soldiers found means to relieve themselves after their prolonged abstinence from women. The Commissar was jovial, witty and talkative at an officers' banquet, also attended by Esteban and the two Loeuillets. The mulattas brought glasses of rum punch round on trays, without getting annoyed if they felt themselves being seized round the waist or pinched under their skirts. Between toasts Victor Hugues announced that the name of the Morne du Gouvernement would be changed to Morne de la Victoire, and that the Place Sartines —which opened so prettily on to the harbour—would receive the name of Place de la Victoire. As for Pointe-à-Pitre, that would henceforth be known as Port-de-la-Liberté. ("They'll go on calling it Pointe-à-Pitre," thought Esteban, "just as Chauvin-Dragon will go on being Saint-Jean-de-Luz.") When the dessert finally arrived—sometime in the early hours of the morning— the young man heard, from the lips of one of the servants who was invited to sing, the nostalgic verses written by the Marquis de Bouillé, a cousin of Lafayette, who had been Governor of Guadeloupe as a very young man. Summoned to France twenty years before, he had taken leave of the island by writing a lament in the local dialect, which had haunted everyone's minds ever since:

"Adieu foulard, adieu madras,
Adieu grains d'or, adieu collier-chou,
Doudou an moin i ka pati
Hélas, hélas, cé pou toujou.

Bonjou Missié le Gouveneu,
Moin vini faire en ti pétition
Pou mandé ou autorisation,
Laissé Doudou au moin ban moin.

Mademoiselle c'est bien trop ta
Doudou a ou ja embaqué
Bâtiment la ja su la boué
Bientot i ke apareillé."

Intoxicated by the large quantities of punch he had drunk, Esteban felt compelled to rise from his seat, call for a toast to the *Doudou* who had such a nice voice, and ask that the terms *"Missié"* and *"Mademoiselle"* should be suppressed from the song, as offending against the democratic spirit, and should be replaced by *"Citoyen Gouverneur"* and *"Citoyenne"*. Victor Hugues frowned at the boy, and cut short the applause which had greeted this excessively republican proposal. But everyone was now beginning to sing in chorus : *"J'ai tout perdu et je m'en fous"*, François Girouet's latest song, which accorded splendidly with the implications of their recent victory :

> *"J'avais jadis sur ma table*
> *Bons poulets et chapons gras,*
> *Du pain comme on en voit pas,*
> *Du pain comme on en voit pas.*
>
> *Depuis la durée de la Guerre*
> *Je fais assez maigre chère,*
> *Mais je chante de bon coeur*
> *Georges tyran d'Angleterre*
> *Bois l'opprobre et nous l'honneur,*
> *Bois l'opprobre et nous l'honneur."*

By dawn they were all asleep in arm-chairs, surrounded by half-drained glasses, trays of fruit and the remains of the roasts, while the Commissar was taking a sponge bath in the open window of his room and chatting to the barber who was already sharpening his razor. Shortly afterwards reveille sounded, and at about eight o'clock, to a hailstorm of hammering, flag-poles, banderoles, garlands and symbolic tableaux began to go up in the former Place Sartines, while the band of the Pyrenean Rifles, in full-dress uniform, launched into revolutionary tunes with a shattering din of drums and a Turkish orchestra. Carpenters were erecting the platform from which the authorities would preside over the civic ceremony that had been decreed. Leaving their ruined homes, the people flocked into the square, attracted by this unusual early-morning music.

Esteban went to the Foreign Corn Exchange, where he had his bed, to relieve his headache with vinegar compresses, and take a spoonful of rhubarb to clear his liver. There he dozed for a time, waiting for what was always late in starting—as he knew from having lived in revolutionary Paris. It was about ten o'clock when he returned to the square, now full of a picturesque, tumultuous mob, which had forgotten its recent sufferings. The civil and military mandatories were already appearing on the platform, headed by Victor Hugues, Generals Pélardy and

Boudet, and Captain de Leyssegues. The people pressed around their new leaders, whom they were seeing for the first time in ceremonial dress, and a silence fell, broken by the fluttering of doves in a nearby patio.

After sweeping the concourse slowly with his eyes the Commissar of the Convention began his speech. He congratulated yesterday's slaves on having risen to the rank of free citizens. He eulogised the fortitude with which the population had endured the fateful days of the bombardment, and rendered homage to the victims, ending this first flight of words with an impassioned funeral oration to the memories of Chrétien, Cartier, Rouger and Aubert—this last had died barely half an hour before, in the building which was used as the military Hospital—and signifying with an angry gesture that Death always seized upon the best men. Then he talked of Christopher Columbus, who had discovered this island, peopled by happy, simple folk, living the healthy lives which are the human being's natural state, during his third voyage to America, and had given it the name of the ship in which he was sailing. But with the Discoverer had come the Christian priests, agents of that fanaticism and ignorance which had afflicted the world like a curse ever since Saint Paul propagated the false teachings of a Jewish prophet, the son of a Roman legionary called Pantherus—for Joseph and the manger were mere legends, discredited by the philosophers. He raised his arm towards the Morne du Gouvernement, announcing that the church which stood there was to be demolished so that all trace of idolatry should be destroyed, and that the priests still hiding, so he had been informed, in the neighbourhood of Le Moule and Sainte-Anne, would have to swear an oath to the Constitution.

Esteban was very attentive to the gestures of a mulatta, whose three-pointed madras proclaimed "I've still got room for you", in that knotted-headdress language which was understood by all the inhabitants of the island. Indeed he was too much engrossed watching grimaces, fingers playing with bracelets, and shoulders being shrugged above delicately-outlined vertebrae, to pay as much attention as he ought to the speaker, who was at that moment baptising the Place Sartines with the name of Place de la Victoire. Victor's clear, metallic voice reached him in waves, a witty phrase, a definition of liberty or a classical quotation standing out from the rest by its emphatic tone. For all his eloquence and vigour the Word failed to harmonise with the mood of these people, who had congregated here in a festive spirit, and were amusing themselves with games or brushing against the opposite sex, and making small effort to understand a language which differed greatly—especially with that southern accent which Victor flaunted like a coat of arms—from their homely local patois. But now the Commissar was coming to an end, after having indicted the India Company and the "Big Whites" of Guadeloupe by announcing that the struggle was not yet over : that the English in Basse-Terre still had to be eliminated, that very soon the final offensive would be launched and peace restored to these lands, now forever freed from slavery.

The speech had been lucid and well-developed, without excessive rhetoric, and the audience was just applauding the peroration—and its final quotation from Tacitus—when de Leyssegues noticed that a ship had forced the harbour bar, and was steering towards the nearby quay. But there could be no cause for alarm in such a miserable-looking craft; it was an old bilander with sails made out of badly-sewn sacks, so bare, so scratched and so dirty that it looked like some spectral skiff taken from the story of a ship-wrecked mariner. The bilander made fast and there was a commotion in the crowd; towards the Commissar's rostrum were advancing several toothless, lame men with shapeless hands and ears, and skin that was silvered by squamous blotches. They were lepers from La Désirade, come to swear allegiance to the Republic. With opportunistic aplomb Victor Hugues accorded them the honours due to infirm citizens, handing them a tricolour sash, and assuring them that he would soon be going to their island, to see what they needed and remedy their poverty.

This unexpected event served to enhance his growing popularity, and he was saluted with shouts and applause which brought him back on to the platform several times; he afterwards withdrew to his office, followed by the military leaders.

Up above, an ill-aimed round from the enemy batteries traversed the cloudless sky and finished harmlessly in the waters of the bay. In the town a stench of carrion prevailed, but as evening came on the lemon trees began to flower. It was like an Epiphany of the Trees, after so many Offices for the Dead.

XX

Extraña devoción
—Goya

IN SPITE OF having announced an early offensive against Basse-Terre, Victor Hugues hesitated to undertake it. He may have been deterred by the shortage of arms; he was afraid that the coloured militia were not sufficiently trained, and he was waiting, with evident impatience, for the reinforcements from France which he had asked for the moment the siege of Pointe-à-Pitre began.

Several weeks passed, during which the enemy fire occasionally vented its spite on the town. But after what they had been through, the people put up with these trifles, relieving their feelings with a mild shrug of the shoulders, a blasphemy, or an obscene gesture into the sky. By a wise precaution the guillotine had not been taken from the locked room where, already assembled and oiled, it was waiting for Monsieur Anse, former executioner of the Tribunal at Rochefort—he was a mulatto, educated in Paris, a man of exquisite manners and a tolerable violinist, whose pockets were always full of sweets for the children—to come and work the trusty mechanism, which had been invented by an agent for clavichords. The Commissar knew how much an over-hasty application of the Machine had cost France, during her occupation of frontier areas. He did not want Guadeloupe to turn into another Belgium. Besides he had no complaints about the populace, who had grown accustomed, during the long vicissitudes of their history, to living amicably with the master of the moment. For the present he was supported by the great manumitted masses, revelling in the delights of their brand-new citizenship, although their very joy provided him with an initial problem of government : convinced that they no longer had a master whom they need obey, the former slaves were reluctant to cultivate the fields. The arable land was being over-run by weeds, because they were in no position yet to punish men too rigorously who found patriotic excuses for refusing to bend their backs over the ploughed fields, or to be herded together again in the furrows, picking up useless bits of wood and endless thorns, under a sun which favoured the growth of all species impartially without recognising human preferences.

It was now that *La Bayonnaise* appeared, bringing them arms, stores, and a few infantrymen—although a far smaller number than the military authorities had asked for. The Convention was short of men, and could not release large forces to defend a remote colony. Esteban, summoned to Victor Hugues' office for something connected with his work, noticed that the Commissar was busy reading what he had been most eager to receive after the official despatches—the Paris newspapers, in which his name was occasionally mentioned. Glancing through the papers which the other had already read, Esteban was amazed to learn of the celebration of the Festival of the Supreme Being, and, what was even more disconcerting, of the condemnation of atheism as an immoral attitude, and consequently both aristocratic and counter-revolutionary. Atheists had suddenly come to be looked on as enemies of the Republic. The French people now recognised the existence of a Supreme Being and the immortality of the soul. The Incorruptible had said that even if the existence of God and the immortality of the soul had only been dreams, they would still have been the most sublime conceptions of the human spirit. Men without God were now qualified as "abandoned monsters".

Esteban began to laugh so heartily that Victor looked at him over his opened newspaper, frowning, and asked, "What's the joke?"

"It wasn't worth ordering them to pull down the chapel on the Morne du Gouvernement, just to be told this," said Esteban, who had, these last few days, recovered the natural good humour of his race and something of his old personality in this environment, with the taste of its fruit, the smells of the sea and the look of some of its trees.

"It seems perfectly all right to me," said Victor, not answering him directly. "A man like that can't be wrong. If He thought it was necessary to do it, then it was well done."

"And for having done it they're praising him in the language of Te Deums, Lauds and Magnificats," said Esteban.

"Which befits his stature," said Victor.

"It's just that I don't see what difference there is between Jehovah, the Great Architect and the Supreme Being," said Esteban. And he reminded the Commissar of his impieties in the past, of his sarcasms directed at the masons' "Salomonic masquerades". But Victor was not listening.

"There was still too much Judaism in the Lodges. And the God of the Catholics, associated through his priests with the worst agents of inquisition and tyranny, has nothing to do with acknowledging the existence of a Supreme Being, infinite and eternal, whom we should worship in a reasonable and dignified way, as befits free men. We're not invoking the God of Torquemada, but the God of the philosophers."

Esteban felt disconcerted by the incredible servility of a vigorous and lively mind, which could yet be so completely given over to politics that it shied away from a critical examination of the facts, and refused to acknowledge the most flagrant contradictions; faithful to the verge of fanaticism—for this could indeed be classed as fanaticism—to the pronouncements of the men who had invested him with his authority. "And if they open the churches to-morrow, will the bishops stop being 'mitred bipeds', and will the saints and virgins come out in procession through the streets of Paris?" the young man asked.

"He must have some good reason for doing it."

"But you . . . do you believe in God?" cried Esteban, hoping to drive him into a corner.

"That is a purely personal question and in no way affects my obedience to the Revolution," replied Victor.

"For you the Revolution is infallible."

"The Revolution," said Victor slowly, looking towards the harbour, where they were working to right the listing shell of *La Thétis,* "the Revolution has given meaning to my life. I have been assigned a role in the great task of our times. I shall attempt to perform it to the very best of my ability."

There was a pause which lent an added resonance to the shouts of the sailors heaving on ropes in time to sea-shanties.

"And are you going to establish the worship of the Supreme Being here?" asked Esteban, for whom the possibility of seeing God enthroned once more seemed the final recantation.

"No," replied the Commissar, after a slight hesitation. "They still haven't finished demolishing the church on the Morne du Gouvernement. It would be too soon. We must go about it more slowly. If I were to start talking now about a Supreme Being it wouldn't be long before the people here were showing him nailed to a cross, with a crown of thorns and a wound in his side; that wouldn't get us anywhere. We're not in the same latitude here as the Champ de Mars."

At that moment Esteban had the malicious satisfaction of hearing from Victor Hugues' lips what Martinez de Ballesteros might have said. Yet *over there* many Spaniards had been persecuted and guillotined for stating that the methods laid down in Paris were inapplicable to countries strongly attached to certain of their national traditions. "You mustn't enter Spain preaching atheism," they had advised. The lovely breasts of some Mademoiselle Aubry, dressed up as the Goddess of Reason, could not be exhibited in Saragossa Cathedral, as they had been in Notre-Dame—which shortly afterwards was offered for sale, though no one could be persuaded to buy such a monumental, Gothic and inhospitable building for his own private use.

"I dreamed of such a different revolution," murmured Esteban.

"And who authorised you to believe in what didn't exist?" Victor asked him. "Anyway all this is just empty talk. The English are still in Basse-Terre, that's the only thing which need concern us." And he added in a cutting tone : "A revolution is not argued about, it's done."

"And when I think," said Esteban, "that the altar on the Morne du Gouvernement would have been saved if the mail from Paris had reached us sooner. If a better wind had been blowing on the Atlantic, God would still have been in his house. Who knows who is doing what here?"

"Get back to your work!" said Victor, pushing him towards the door with a heavy hand planted between his shoulder blades. The door closed so noisily that the mulatta who had been singing as she busily polished the banisters asked slyly : "*Monsieur*

Victor fâché?" And Esteban crossed the dining-room, followed by the chirruping of the girl's laughter.

The Loeuillets' press was working feverishly, printing pamphlets destined for the French peasants who lived on the neutral islands, promising them work and lands if they took refuge with the revolutionary government. In this way the available forces were growing, although weeks went by without the men on the Rivière Salée making up their minds to force a passage across it.

The situation was still unchanged at the end of September, when the Commissar learned that yellow fever was ravaging the British ranks, and that General Grey, afraid of the cyclones which lashed the Windward Isles at this time of the year, had taken the bulk of his fleet to Fort-Royal in Martinique, where the harbour offered better protection against hurricanes. They deliberated about the best way of taking advantage of the situation. Finally it was decided that the French Army should be divided into three columns, under de Leyssegues, Pélardy and Boudet, and try its luck with a triple landing on Basse-Terre. Canoes, skiffs, fishing dories and even Indian pirogues, were commandeered, and the attack was launched at night. Two days later the French held Lamentin and Petit-Bourg. And early in the morning of the 6th of October, they began the siege of the entrenched camp of Berville.

In Pointe-à-Pitre they lived in a state of hourly expectancy. Some were of the opinion that the siege would be a long one, since the English had had enough time to fortify their positions. Others said that General Graham had been demoralised by the support shown for the revolutionary government in Grande-Terre, where people seemed to laugh at the broadsides he was still firing over the town, purely out of anger, from the Morne du Savon.

During these days Esteban was often with Monsieur Anse, the custodian and operator of the guillotine, who was collecting a regular curiosity shop, of sea-fans, lumps of mineral, embalmed moon-fish, roots shaped like animals and bright-coloured snails. They would often relax at the magnificent cove of Le Gosier, with its little island shining like a chalcedony heart. After placing bottles of wine to cool in the sandy shallows, Monsieur Anse would take an old violin from its case and, with his back to the sea, start playing a pretty pastorale by Philidor, which he embellished with variations of his own. He was an excellent companion on an excursion, ever ready to marvel at a piece of sulphur, a butterfly with Egyptian markings, or some unknown flower which had appeared in their path.

At mid-day on the 6th of October, Monsieur Anse received orders to load the guillotine on a cart and leave hurriedly for Berville. The place had been taken. Without even having had to order the assault, Victor Hugues had given General Graham four hours to capitulate. And when the Commissar entered the entrenched camp, littered with equipment left behind in the flight, he found twelve hundred English soldiers who could not speak English : in his retreat Graham had only taken with him twenty-two of the monarchist settlers who had been particularly loyal to him, and had abandoned the rest where they stood. Stunned by this act of extreme treachery on the part of the man who had been their leader, the Frenchmen who had fought under the British flag were gathered in pathetic groups, without even having had the time to take off their uniforms.

"Some things are impossible," said Monsieur Anse as he left, making an ambiguous gesture towards the cart, where the guillotine was hidden under its tarpaulin, because the wind carried the scent of rain—it was already falling on Marie Galante, which had suddenly gone from pale green to lead grey, as a thunder-cloud swept across it.

"Some things are impossible," Monsieur Anse repeated, when he returned the following morning, drenched and chilled. And, somewhat drunk, having tried to warm his body with rum at wayside taverns, he told Esteban that the guillotine could not be used for mass executions, that the work had its own tempo and rhythm, and that he could not conceive how the Commissar, who knew the machine well, could imagine it possible for eight hundred and sixty-five men to pass under the blade. He had done all that was humanly possible to accelerate the proceedings, but by midnight only thirty of the prisoners had been punished for their treachery. "That's enough!" the Commissar had shouted, and the rest had been shot in groups of ten or twenty, as the cart returned to Pointe-à-Pitre, trying to avoid the bad roads. In the case of the handful of English soldiers who had been cut off in Berville, Victor Hugues had proved magnanimous, and, after disarming them, had allowed them to rejoin their routed army. And to a young British captain who was slow to leave, he had said : "It's my duty to be here, but who's asking you to look at the French blood I find myself obliged to shed?"

The era of the "Big Whites" was over in Guadeloupe. The news had been proclaimed, with a great rolling of drums, in the Place de la Victoire.

"Some things are impossible," repeated Monsieur Anse, grieved by this first professional failure. "There were eight hundred and sixty-five of them. A Herculean task." And Esteban listened to his story again and again, as if he were hearing of some volcanic eruption in a far-off country. For him Berville was simply a name. And as for the rest, eight hundred and sixty-five faces were too many for him to be able to picture any one of them in particular.

XXI

A FEW CENTRES OF resistance still remained in Basse-Terre. But the remainder of the men betrayed by Graham slipped through their fingers, by contriving to seize a bilander and escape to a neighbouring island. When Fort Saint-Charles fell, the campaign was as good as over. La Désirade and Marie Galante—whose Governor, a former member of the Constituent Assembly, had gone over to the English, and preferred to commit suicide rather than fight—were in French hands. Victor Hugues was master of Guadeloupe and could tell everyone that they would now be able to work in peace. And in order to support his words with a symbolic gesture, he planted some trees, which would give shade in future to the Place de la Victoire.

Then something happened which they had all been awaiting for some time, with impatient curiosity : the guillotine began to function in public. The day it made its début—on the persons of two monarchist chaplains, surprised in a barn where arms and ammunition were hidden—the entire town herded into the market-place, where a sturdy platform had been erected with steps at the side, supported, as in Paris, by four cedar-wood stanchions. And since Republican fashions had already found their way into the colony, the mestizos appeared dressed in short blue jackets and white trousers with a red stripe, while the mulattas displayed new headdresses in the colours of the day. It would be hard to imagine a more joyful or ebullient crowd, with the splashes of indigo and strawberry which seemed to ripple in time to the flags in the limpid morning sunlight. The servants from the Commissariat were leaning out of the windows, shouting and laughing—and laughing still louder when the trembling hand of an officer slid up over their hams. Many children had clambered up on to the roofs of the buildings to get a better view. Smoke came from the fried-food stalls, fruit juice and *garapiña* was flowing from pitchers, and spirits were soaring from white rum drunk so early in the morning.

When Monsieur Anse showed himself on top of the scaffold in his best ceremonial clothes—the excellent shave the barber had given him showed how seriously he took his work—he received a prolonged ovation. Pointe-à-Pitre was not Cap Français, where, for some time past, there had existed an excellent theatre, supplied with new shows given by companies of actors on their way to New Orleans. Here they had nothing of that sort; they had never seen a theatre open to all, and, for this reason, the people were now discovering the essence of Tragedy. Fate was present among them, its blade waiting, with inexorable punctuality, for those who had been ill-advised enough to turn their arms against the town. And the spirit of the Chorus was active in every spectator, as strophes and anti-strophes, occurrences and apostrophes were bandied across the stage.

Suddenly a Messenger appeared, the Guards fell back, and the tumbril made its entry on to the bedecked expanse of the public square, bearing the two condemned men, their hands joined by the same rosary tied round their wrists. Solemn rolls on the drum were heard, the bascule took the weight of a fairly corpulent man, and the knife fell in a clamour of expectation.

Minutes later the first two executions had been performed. But the crowd did not disperse, perhaps temporarily disappointed that the spectacle had been so brief—the liquid blood was still draining away through the cracks in the stage. The merrymaking must continue longer, on this new holiday and day of rest. They must show off their new clothes. And as figure-dances were best for displaying costumes, and for swirling many-coloured carmagnole skirts, they all began to form in quadrilles, advancing and retiring in line, changing partners, holding each other round the waist, bowing, and ignoring the self-appointed leaders of the dance, who tried in vain to maintain some discipline amongst the files and groups. Such was the din in the end, and so great was the desire to dance and jump and laugh and shout, that they all joined together in an enormous wheel, soon to be broken up into a chain which, after circling round the guillotine, swept into the surrounding streets, and came and went, invading patios and gardens until nightfall.

That day marked the inauguration of the Great Terror on the island. The guillotine functioned ceaselessly now in the Place de la Victoire; the tempo of its blade increased. And since the desire to witness executions was kept alive in a place where everyone knew everyone else, at least by sight, if not from business dealings—one man harboured a grudge against another, who, in his turn, had not forgotten some humiliation he had suffered—the guillotine became the centre of the life of the town. The crowds from the Market migrated to the pretty harbour square, with its shop windows and its braziers, its corner-men and its open-air stalls, where—as heads fell which yesterday had been respected and adored—fritters and peppers, corozo nuts and puff pastry, custard apples and fresh porgies were offered for sale at all hours of the day. And since it was now a very good place for doing business, the square became a running exchange for bric-à-brac and things abandoned by their owners; one could buy a grille, a mechanical bird, or the remains of a dinner service at cut prices. Harness was bartered for cooking-pots, playing cards for firewood, fashionable watches for Margarita pearls. A vegetable stall went up on the same day that a pedlar's stand was erected, which came under the heading of a mixed shop—tremendously mixed—where one could observe kitchen utensils, gravy dishes engraved with coats of arms, silver plates, chess men, tapestries and miniatures. The scaffold had become the hub of an exchange, of a forum, of a perpetual auction sale. The executions no longer even interrupted the haggling, importuning and arguing. The guillotine had begun to form part of normal everyday life. Amongst the parsley and the marjoram, miniature guillotines were sold as ornaments, and many people took them home. Children exerted their ingenuity to construct little machines for decapitating cats. A beautiful mulatta who was fancied by one of de Leyssegues' lieutenants offered her guests liqueurs in wooden flasks made in the shape of people; when placed on a bascule they ejected their corks—which naturally had prettily painted faces—as a toy knife came down on them, operated by a tiny automatic executioner.

But in spite of the many novelties and amusements that were being introduced into the pastoral, cloistered life of the island, some people could see that the Terror was beginning to descend the rungs of the social ladder, and was now scything at ground level. When he learned that numerous negroes in the Les Abymes district were refusing to work on fincas which had been expropriated, declaring that they were free men, Victor Hugues had the most troublesome of them arrested and condemned to the guillotine. In fact Esteban noticed with some surprise that the Commissar, after talking so much about the sublime Decree of the 16th Pluviose of the Year Two, was not showing any great sympathy towards the negroes; "It's enough for them that we should look on them as French citizens," he was wont to say, in a harsh voice. Some racial prejudice remained in him from his long residence in San Domingo, where the settlers had treated the slaves particularly severely—always castigating them as idlers, idiots, thieves, gallows-birds and good-for-nothings, while making them work from sunrise to sunset. Besides which, the soldiers of the Republic were very partial to dark skin where women were concerned, and they lost no chance of beating or whipping black men on the slightest pretext, although they acknowledged that some of them—a corpulent leper called Vulcan for instance—were turning out to be first-rate gunners. Brothers while the war lasted, black and white were divided by the peace.

For the present Victor Hugues decreed that work was compulsory. Any negro accused of being lazy or disobedient, argumentative or troublesome, was condemned to death. And since the whole island must learn its lesson, the guillotine was removed from the Place de la Victoire, and began to travel, to go on journeys and excursions : on Monday it arrived soon after dawn in Le Moule; on Tuesday it was working in Le Gosier, where someone had been convicted of idleness; on Wednesday it despatched six monarchists, who had been hiding in the former parish church of Sainte-Anne. It was taken from village to village, stopping at taverns on the way. By means of drinks and bribes the executioner and his assistants could then be persuaded to make it work in the void, so that everyone could learn about its mechanism. And since the escort of drums which served to drown any last screams from the victims in Pointe-à-Pitre could not be taken on these jaunts, a large bass drum was carried in the cart, and lent a festive air to the demonstrations. The peasants put banana stalks on the bascule to test the strength of the machine—nothing looks more like a human neck than a banana stalk, with its cross-section of moist, porous ducts—to see whether they would be severed. And to settle an argument they even went so far as to demonstrate that a bunch of six sugar canes would not resist the knife. Then the delighted visitors would go on to their destination, smoking and singing in time to the drum, wearing their Phrygian caps, which had turned from red to chestnut with sweat. On its return the bascule would be laden with such quantities of fruit that it seemed to be borne on a Car of Plenty.

At the beginning of the Year Three, Victor Hugues found himself at the peak of his success. Enthusiastic over the reports it had received, the Convention ratified all his military promotions, approved his appointments and decrees, congratulated him in panegyrical prose, and announced that they were sending him reinforcements of men, arms and ammunition. But the Commissar no longer needed them; his compulsory levy had created an army of ten thousand adequately trained men. He was proceeding to build fortifications at all vulnerable points along the coastline. The confiscation of property had filled his coffers, and the shops were well-stocked with all essentials.

During his trip to the other half of the island, Victor Hugues —who remembered having been there many years before—had been moved by the beauty of the town of Basse-Terre, full of the noise of the running water in the public fountains, which gave a delicious coolness to the avenues of tamarind trees. It was a nobler, more thoroughbred town than Pointe-à-Pitre, with its paved streets, its shady mole, and its stone houses reminiscent of certain corners of Rochefort, Nantes or La Rochelle. The Commissar would willingly have transferred his residence to the quiet and friendly parish of Saint-François; but the harbour, which was adequate for unloading a flock of sheep from the neighbouring islands—they were thrown overboard when they arrived and allowed to swim ashore—offered scant protection for his fleet.

Continuing his triumphal progress, he was acclaimed by the lepers of La Désirade, the "Small Whites" of Marie Galante, and even by the Carib Indians of that island, who asked, through their chief, for the honour of being accorded the benefits of French citizenship. Knowing that these men were magnificent seamen, well acquainted with an archipelago they had been sailing with their swift boats long before the ships of Ferdinand and Isabella's High Admiral appeared in these waters, he distributed cockades and promised them what they asked. Victor Hugues showed more sympathy towards the Caribs than towards the negroes : he liked them for their pride, their aggressiveness, and their haughty motto "The Caribs are the only race", especially now that they wore tricolour cockades in the fastening of their loin-cloths.

During his visit to Marie Galante, the Commissar asked to be shown the beach where these would-be conquerors of the Caribbean had many years before impaled some French buccaneers who had tried to steal their wives. Skeletons, bones and skulls still remained on the stakes, planted close to the sea; pierced by the wood, like insects transfixed by a naturalist's pins, the corpses had attracted such an enormous number of vultures that for several days the shore, seen from a distance, seemed to be covered with bubbling lava.

Though he was overwhelmed with kindness and acclamations, the Commissar had not forgotten that the English were patrolling these waters in the attempt to exercise a sort of blockade. Victor would shut himself up at nights in the company of de

Leyssegues—who now displayed the galloons of a rear-admiral —to draw up plans for a naval action that would embrace the whole of the Caribbean. The project was kept very secret, and they were working on it one day when Esteban entered the Commissar's office, and found him sweating and dishevelled, his face convulsed with anger. He was circling the large council table, pausing behind the officials, who had abandoned their task and were arguing over the pages of some newspapers which had just arrived.

"Have you heard?" he shouted at the boy, pointing to a news report with a trembling hand. There was printed the incredible chronicle of what had taken place in Paris on the 9th Thermidor. "Swine!" Victor was yelling. "They've wiped out all the best men!"

The sheer magnitude of the event stupefied Esteban. Moreover everything stood out in doubly dramatic relief because of its remoteness. Like someone who carries a mental picture of an object which he has long contemplated, and assumes it to exist even after it has been lost to sight, so they had talked in this very room (as though he were present and would survive into the future) of a man who had ceased to exist several months earlier. While they had been arguing here about the cult of the Supreme Being, its founder had already uttered, at the foot of the scaffold, the terrible cry torn from him by the pain of his broken jaw, as the executioner brutally snatched away the bandage.

For Victor Hugues the deed was doubly atrocious, for its implications set his mind forming conjectures. It was not only that the giant had fallen, whose portrait was still securely hanging there, for all to see, just as it had done during the days of his greatness; it was not only that the Commissar had been deprived of the man who had placed his trust in him, and given him power and authority—but he would now have to wait weeks and weeks, perhaps even months, to learn what turn events were taking in France. It was probable that the reaction would take the form of ruthless revenge. Perhaps there was already a new government, which would overturn all that its predecessor had done. New Plenipotentiaries would appear in Guadeloupe, with sullen faces, making gestures of refusal and entrusted with mysterious orders. The report about the massacre at Berville, which Victor Hugues had sent to the Convention, might go against him. Perhaps he had already been dismissed, or charged with an indictment which could mean the end of his career, or the end of his life. He read and re-read the names of those who had fallen on the 9th Thermidor, as if from them he might decipher the key to his own fate.

Some of those present were suggesting quietly that now they would be entering on a period of leniency, indulgence and the re-establishment of religion. "Or a restoration of the monarchy," thought Esteban, whose response to this idea, because of the contradictory predispositions of his mind, included a feeling of relief that peace should have returned after so many storms, a hope that freedom of movement would be restored everywhere, and a rejection and execration of the monarchy. If men had striven so hard, if so many people had prophesied, suffered, acclaimed and fallen, amidst the conflagrations and triumphal arches of a vast, apocalyptic dream, then it was at least essential that the hands of the clock should not be put back. The blood which had been shed must not find itself bartered for the oils of an anointed monarchy. It was still possible that a just man would arise, perhaps more just than the man who had lapsed from justice so many times, through being too prone to talk in abstract terms—this had been one of the evils of the times. They could hope for a Liberty which would be more enjoyed and less proclaimed; an Equality which would be imposed by law rather than dissipated in words; a Fraternity which would pay less heed to informers, and would show itself in the reinstitution of proper courts of law, once more provided with juries.

Victor was still pacing up and down the room, more calmly now, his hands behind his back. Finally he halted in front of the portrait of the Incorruptible. "Well, here everything will go on as before," he said at last. "I shall ignore this news. I don't accept it. I shall continue to recognise no other morality except Jacobin morality. No one is going to move me from here. And if the Revolution must perish in France, it will continue in America. The time has come for us to occupy the Mainland." And, turning to Esteban: "Go at once and translate *The Declaration of the Rights of Man and of the Citizen* into Spanish, and the text of the Constitution as well."

"Of '91 or '93?" asked the lad.

" '93. I don't know of any other. The ideas that are going to stir up Spanish America have got to come from this island. If we had followers and allies in Spain then we will have them on the Mainland here too. Even more of them perhaps, because discontent flourishes more in colonies than in the mother country."

XXII

WHEN THE OLD *camisard* Loeuillet learned that he would have to print texts in Spanish, he realised to his horror that he had not brought any "ñ"s in his type cases. "Who'd have thought you made that sound by dressing up a letter?" he said, furious with himself. "Do they think a noble and majestic word like '*cygne*' can be written 'cine'?" The fact that he had not been warned was further proof of the state of disorder and disorganisation among these men who aspired to rule the whole world. "Didn't it occur to them that tildes are used in Spanish?" he shouted. "Ignoramuses." He finally decided that the tildes would be replaced with circumflex accents, cut from other letters, which would considerably complicate the work of typesetting.

But the *Declaración de Derechos del Hombre y del Cuidadano* was soon printed, and the copies handed over in the Commissar's office, where a leaden atmosphere of anxiety and disagreement reigned. The wind of Thermidor was blowing through many minds. The criticisms which some of them had previously kept to themselves now began to be expressed in secretive conclaves, suspicious of anyone who approached too close. When Esteban took his Spanish version of the 1793 Constitution to Loeuillet, the typographer remarked on the speciousness of propaganda which claimed to be putting ideals into practice so as to create an illusion of achievement where in fact there was none and this in a field where up till now even the best intentions had suffered terrible rebuffs. Perhaps the Americans would now try to apply some of the principles which

157

the Terror had trampled on so completely, only to violate them later, impelled by the political contingencies of the moment. "They don't mention the knife or the prison ships here," said the *camisard,* alluding to the hulks which still filled the Atlantic ports of France, with their groaning cargoes of prisoners—like the *Bonhomme Richard,* whose name, recalling as it did Benjamin Franklin's Almanach, sounded like a piece of irony.

"Let's get back to our printing," said Esteban. For the present he had a daily task to perform, which he fulfilled conscientiously, finding a sort of relaxation, of relief from his doubts, in translating to the best of his ability; he became painstaking, almost pedantic, in his search for the exact phrase, the best synonym or the right punctuation, and was distressed that contemporary Spanish should be so loath to accept the concise locutions of modern French. He found a sort of aesthetic pleasure in translating well, even when the meaning of the words was indifferent to him. He spent days polishing up his version of a report from Billaud-Varenne, about "The Theory of Democratic Government, and the need for instilling a love of the patriotic virtues by means of public entertainments and moral education" although the incoherent prose of a writer who was continually invoking the ghosts of the Tarquins, Cato and Catiline, seemed to him as dated, as false, and as far removed from reality, as the words of the masonic hymns they had taught him to sing in the Foreigners' Lodge.

The Loeuillets, father and son, often had recourse to his superior knowledge in order to accomplish their difficult task of setting up texts in an unknown language, asking him for the explanation of some orthographical symbol, or for advice about the correct division of a word at the end of a line. The old *camisard* bestowed the loving care of a good craftsman on the lay-out of his pages, lamenting the lack of a colophon or an allegorical vignette to adorn the end of the text. Neither the editor-translator nor the typographers believed very much in the words which would be multiplied and propagated as a result of their labours; but if the task were to be done it must be done correctly, without maltreating the language, and without neglecting anything which was part of the job.

They were proceeding now to the printing of an "American

Carmagnole"—a variation on another, earlier one, written in
Bayonne—intended for the peoples of the New Continent:

Verse : *"Yo que soy un sin camisa*
Un baile tengo que dar
Y en lugar de guitarras
Cañones sonarán,
Cañones sonarán,
Cañones sonarán.

Refrain: *Bailen los sin camisas*
Y viva el són y viva el són,
Bailen los sin camisas
Y viva el són del cañon.

Verse: *Si alguno quisiera saber*
Porque estoy descamisado,
Resulta que con los tributos,
El Rey me ha desnudado,
El Rey me ha desnudado,
El Rey me ha desnudado.

Refrain: *Bailen los sin camisas . . .*

Verse: *Todos los Reyes del Mundo*
Son igualmente tiranos,
Y uno de los mayores
Es el infame Carlos,
Es el infame Carlos,
Es el infame Carlos.

Refrain : *Bailen los sin camisas . . ."*

In the verses which followed, the anonymous author showed his
perfect understanding of the situation in America by giving their
deserts to the Governors, Magistrates and Mayors; to the Judges
in the Courtrooms, and to the Intendants and Administrators,
who were the accomplices of the Crown. Nor did the balladist
ignore the cult of the Supreme Being, because he wrote further

on: "God defends our cause, He directs our arm, and the King with his crimes has angered his Judge." "Long live love of one's country," he concluded, "and long live Liberty. May tyrants and royal despotism perish!"

This was exactly the way the Spanish conspirators in Bayonne used to express themselves—and Esteban had had confused tidings of them. It was quite certain though that Marat's friend, Guzmán, had been guillotined. Of the Abbé Marchena it was said that he might have escaped the purge of Girondins—but it was not certain. As for the worthy Martinez de Ballesteros, he would still be searching for a reason to go on living—to survive—at the same time lending his services to a Revolution completely different from the one which had aroused his early enthusiasm.

At this time an acquired velocity and momentum still kept many men working in a world very different from the one they had wanted to forge; they were disillusioned and embittered, but, like the Loeuillets, incapable of not performing their appointed daily task properly. They no longer held opinions; the main thing was to be alive, working at something which allowed them to return each morning to the tranquil practice of a trade. They lived for the day, thinking of their reward: a glass of wine in the evening, a cold bath, the breeze which would get up at sunset, the flowering of the lemon blossom, or the girl, perhaps, who would be coming to make love with them that night. In the midst of events of such magnitude that they swamped the ordinary man's powers of assimilation, criticism or evaluation, it had suddenly become astonishingly entertaining to watch the transformations of some mimetic insect, the nuptial manoeuvres of a black beetle, a sudden multiplication of butterflies. Esteban had never been so consciously interested in very small things— the twinkling tadpoles in a barrel of water, the germination of a fungus, ants nibbling at the leaves of a lemon tree and leaving it like lace—as in these times dedicated to universality and excess.

A pretty mulatta had come into his room one day, on the futile pretext of asking him for pen and ink, glittering with bangles and wearing well-ironed skirts over rustling petticoats that smelled of vetiver. Half an hour after their bodies had come together in a delectable intimacy, the woman had introduced herself with a graceful curtsey, without even a belt to cover herself with, as *"Mademoiselle Athalie Bajazet, coiffeuse pour dames"*.

"What a marvellous country!" the young man exclaimed, forgetting all his cares.

Since then Mademoiselle Athalie Bajazet had slept with him every night. "Every time she takes her skirts off she presents me with two tragedies by Racine," said Esteban to the Loeuillets, amidst loud laughter.

The demands of his accountancy—he had to take inventories of certain of the cargoes arriving in the island's ports—sometimes took the lad to Basse-Terre, riding down uneven paths where the vegetation was particularly luxuriant, because of the many streams and torrents which came down from the mist and vapour always enveloping the Mornes. During these expeditions he discovered a vegetation similar to that of his native island—a proper knowledge of which had put an end to his illness—and this rediscovery filled a gap which had lasted throughout the latter part of his adolescence. He breathed in with delight the delicate fragrance of the anonas, the grey acidity of the tamarinds, the fleshy softness of all these fruits, with their red and purple pulp, concealing in their most recondite folds sumptuous seeds with the texture of tortoise-shell, ebony or polished mahogany. He buried his face in the white coolness of the corozos; he tore at the amaranthine star-apple, searching with avid lips for the crystalline droplets secreted in the depths of its pulp.

One day, while his unsaddled horse frisked about in the waters of a stream, its four hooves in the air, Esteban embarked on the adventure of climbing a tree. And after passing the first test, which meant reaching the inaccessible lower branches, he began to ascend towards the crown of the tree, up a sort of spiral staircase of increasingly slender and more serried branches supporting the great cloak of foliage, the green beehive, the sumptuous roof, which he was seeing from inside for the first time. A rare, profound and inexplicable exaltation overcame Esteban, when at last he was able to rest, astride the crest of this trembling structure of wood and leaves. Climbing a tree is an intimate experience which can perhaps never be conveyed. A man who embraces the tall breasts of a tree-trunk is realising a sort of nuptial act, deflowering a secret world, never before seen by man. His glance suddenly takes in all the beauties and imperfections of the Tree. He discovers the two tender branches, which part like a woman's thighs and conceal at their juncture a handful of green moss; he discovers the circular wounds left behind by the fall of withered shoots; he discovers the splendid ogives of the crown, as well as the strange bifurcations where all the sap has flowed into a favoured branch leaving the other a wretched sarment, ripe for the flames. As he climbed to his vantage-point, Esteban understood the secret relationship so often established between the Mast, the Plough, the Tree and the Cross. He remembered a text from Saint Hippolytus : "This wood belongs to me. I nourish myself on it, I sustain myself with it; I dwell in its roots, I rest in its branches; I give myself up to its breathing as I give myself up to the wind. Here is my strait gate, here is my narrow path; a Jacob's Ladder, at whose summit is the Lord." The great symbols of the Tau, the Cross of Saint Andrew, the Brazen Serpent, the Anchor and the Ladder, were implicit in every tree; the Created anticipated the Constructed, providing patterns for the future Builder of Arks.

The evening shadows surprised Esteban swaying on a tall tree-trunk, rapt in a somnolent voluptuousness, which might have lasted indefinitely. Now some of the vegetable life below was taking on new shapes; the papaws, their udders hanging from their necks, seemed to be coming alive, ready to start out for the smoky distances of La Soufrière; the *ceiba*—the "mother of all trees" according to some negroes—was becoming more like an obelisk, more columnar, more monumental, as it towered against the dusky sky. A dead mangrove turned into a tangle of snakes, arrested in the act of striking; another, alive and brimming over with sap which oozed through its mottled bark, suddenly blossomed in a blaze of yellow.

Esteban followed the life-cycle of these growths with the interest he would have felt in any form of zoological evolution. First the fruit appeared in the form of seeds like green beads— whose bitter juice had the taste of iced almonds. Then the developing organism took on form and contour, stretching downwards and fashioning a profile ending in a witch's chin. Colours came out on its face. It passed from mossy green to saffron and ripened into a ceramic splendour—Cretan, Mediterranean, yet always Antillan—before the first signs of decay appeared : small black circles, which began to eat into the pulp fragrant with tannin and iodine. Then one night it became detached, and fell with a muffled sound into the grass below, damp with dew, announcing the imminent death of the fruit, for its flaws would grow wider and deeper, until they opened into wounds infested by flies. Like the corpse of a prelate in some edifying *Danse Macabre,* the fallen fruit continued to shed its skin and its viscera, until it was left a skeleton, a striped and colourless seed, wrapped in a shroud of ravelled cotton. But here, in this world which knew no winter deaths or spring resurrections, the cycle of life was endlessly renewed; weeks later the recumbent seed, like a miniature Asiatic tree, was sprouting a shoot, with pink leaves so like human skin in their smoothness that one's hands were afraid to touch them.

At times Esteban was caught in a heavy shower on his journeys through the foliage, and then he used to compare, in his auditory memory, the difference between the rains of the Tropics and the monotonous drizzle of the Old World. Here a vast, powerful noise, in maestoso tempo and as protracted as the introduction to a symphony, heralded the advance of the storm from a long way off, and the vultures would fly lower and lower, in ever-tightening circles, and then vanish. A delectable smell, of damp trees, of earth full of humus and sap, spread everywhere, making birds puff out their ruffs and horses lay back their ears, and inspiring the young man with a rare feeling of physical desire, a vague anxiety to share his longings by embracing another body. The rapid fading of the light was accompanied by a sharp tapping in the topmost branches, and then, suddenly, there was a cold, joyful cascade, producing a different note from each substance it struck—the melody from the climbers and banana trees, the accompaniment from the membranous leaves, the percussive bass from the largest leaves of all. The water was intercepted high up, by the crowns of the palm trees, which scattered it, like cathedral gargoyles, to beat a stately tattoo on the fronds of the smaller palms; then the drops rebounded from these tender green drum-skins and fell on to a foliage so dense that, by the time they reached the level of the arums— as taut as the skin of a tambourine—they had been divided, subdivided and vaporised a thousand times, at each successive storey of the vegetal mass, to be gleefully received at ground level by the couch grass and esparto. The wind set the tempo for this vast symphony, which quickly turned the streams into freshets, noisy with avalanches of dislodged pebbles, and then into tumultuous cascades, which overflowed their banks and carried down rocks, dead tree-trunks, many-clawed branches, and roots so entwined with purls and threads that when they reached the slime lower down they were held fast like becalmed ships. And then the sky grew calm, the clouds vanished, the sunset took fire, and Esteban continued his journey, on a wet and frisky horse, under showers of spray from trees each distinguishable by its individual contribution to the great Magnificat of scents.

When he returned to Pointe-à-Pitre after these excursions, Esteban felt a stranger to the times he lived in : a stranger in a remote and bloody world, where everything seemed absurd. The churches were still closed here, though they had perhaps reopened in France. The negroes had been declared free citizens, but those who had not been forced to become soldiers or sailors were bending their backs from sunrise to sunset, as they had done before, under the whips of their overseers, behind whom, for good measure, they could now see the implacable azimuth of the guillotine. New-born children were now being called Cincinnatus, Leonidas or Lycurgus, and were being taught to recite a Revolutionary Catechism which no longer corresponded with reality—just as at the recently formed Jacobin Club they continued to talk about the Incorruptible as if he were still alive. The ravening flies swarmed over the greasy planks of the scaffold, while Victor Hugues and his army commanders were getting uneasily used to taking long siestas under mosquito-nets —watched over by mulattas, who fanned them with palm fronds.

XXIII

WITH ALMOST FEMININE susceptibility Esteban grieved over Victor Hugues' increasing loneliness. The Commissar continued to carry out his functions with ruthless severity, speeding up the tribunals, allowing the guillotine no respite, re-affirming old sophistries, dictating, issuing edicts, legislating, judging. He was in the thick of everything, but those who knew him well realised that his excessive activity was motivated by a secret desire to numb himself. He knew that even among his most obedient subordinates there were many who dreamed of seeing the sealed document arrive, copied by the hand of some faithful amanuensis, which announced his dismissal. At a time like this the young man would have liked to be at his side, to be a companion to him, to comfort him. But the Commissar had become increasingly elusive, and would shut himself up to read until the early hours of the morning, or go off to the cove at Le Gosier in the evening in a carriage, which he would only share occasionally with de Leyssegues. There, clad in nothing but a pair of linen drawers, he would set out to row to the uninhabited island, whence he only returned when the plague of nocturnal insects emerged from the mangrove plantations along the coast. He perused the works of classical orators, perhaps preparing an eloquent defence. His orders became hasty and contradictory. He was subject to unpredictable outbursts of anger, leading to the sudden dismissal of an associate, or the enforcement of a death sentence which everyone assumed to have been commuted.

One ill-fated morning he ordered that the remains of General Dundas, the former British Governor of the island, should be disinterred and scattered in the public thoroughfare. For hours on end dogs fought together as they tore at the tastiest pieces of carrion and carried from street to street the unspeakable human remains still adhering to the dress uniform in which the enemy leader had been buried.

Esteban would have liked to have been able to soothe this troubled spirit, who was on his guard the moment an unexpected sail showed on the horizon, and whose loneliness grew as he increased in historical stature. Swift and relentless, endowed with military genius, fearless as few men are, Victor had had, in this island, a success which by far exceeded other achievements of the Revolution. And yet a remote political upheaval, far away —where they now knew that a White Terror had been unloosed to follow the Red Terror—had set in motion unknown forces which would probably hand the colony over to people incapable of governing it. To make matters worse it was also known that Dalbarade, his protector, who had been so vigorously defended by Robespierre when accused of having protected one of Danton's friends, had gone over to the Thermidor faction. Disgusted by such events and in constant anxious expectation of news which never came, the Commissar began to expedite preparations for an undertaking which he had been elaborating with Rear-Admiral de Leyssegues for some months past. "To hell with the lot of them," he shouted one day, thinking of the men who would be examining his situation in Paris. "By the time they arrive here with their arse-paper, I shall be so powerful I'll be able to rub their own faces in it."

And one morning an unusual amount of activity was observed in the harbour. Several light ships, bilanders for the most part, were drawn up on shore and shored up for careening. Aboard the larger ships, carpenters, caulkers and men with paint-brushes, saws and hammers were toiling in rowdy concert, as gunners transferred light cannon aboard, sculling them out in rowing boats. Leaning from a window in the old Foreign Corn Exchange Esteban could see that one of their lesser tasks was to change the names of the vessels. *La Calypso* had suddenly turned into *La Tyrannicide*; *La Sémillante* into *La Carmagnole*; *L'Hirondelle* into *La Marie-Tapage*; *Le Lutin* into *Le Vengeur*. Other new names were coming to light, painted in very visible letters against the old timbers which had served the King for so long: *La Tintamarre, La Cruelle, Ca-ira, La Sans-jupe, L'Athénienne, Le Poignard, La Guillotine, L'ami du Peuple, Le Terroriste, La Bande Joyeuse*; while *La Thétis*, cured of the wounds she had received during the bombardment of Pointe-à-Pitre, was on the way to becoming *L'Incorruptible,* surely at the behest of a certain Victor Hugues, who knew how to juggle with the generic neutrality of certain words.

Esteban was just asking himself the reason for all this preparation, when Mademoiselle Athalie Bajazet informed him that he was wanted immediately in the leader's office. The punch-glasses which one of his serving-women was carrying out showed that the Commissar had been drinking—although he still preserved that surprising sureness of movement and thought, which was usually reinforced rather than diminished in him by liquor. "Are you particularly anxious to stay here?" he said to Esteban, with a smile.

The question was so unexpected that Esteban leaned against the wall, an agitated hand ruffling his hair. Until now the impossibility of leaving Guadeloupe had been so obvious that it had never even occurred to him to think about it. "Are you particularly anxious to stay in Pointe-à-Pitre?" Victor insisted.

In Esteban's imagination a providential ship hove in sight, a shining ship destined for escape, with sails turned orange by the splendour of the sunset. Perhaps the Commissar had received a threatening letter, and yielding to his personal anxieties had decided to renounce his authority and remove to some Dutch port, whence he would be able to sail freely to wherever he liked. It was known that the ambition of many of the Robespierrists who were now disbanding was to get to New York, where there were French printing presses ready to publish memoirs and philippics. Nor was there any lack in the Colonies, either, of men who dreamed of New York.

Esteban talked frankly about himself; he could no longer see what useful purpose he would be serving in this island when it was ruled by persons unknown. It was obvious that the reaction would sweep away all the present officials. (He looked at the trunks and portmanteaux that were already arriving at the office on the backs of porters, to be stored in the corners to which Victor assigned them.) Moreover he was not a Frenchman. And for that very reason he would be treated as political factions usually treated foreigners who have joined another party. He would perhaps go the same way as Guzmán or Marchena. If he were given the means of leaving, he would leave without hesitation.

Victor's expression had hardened perceptibly during this confession. By the time Esteban noticed it, it was too late: "You poor fool!" shouted the other. "So you think I've already been beaten, thrown out, annihilated, by that Thermidor rabble? So you're one of those who'd be secretly overjoyed to see me hauled off to Paris between two guards? Your mulatta mistress was right when she told me you spent your time in defeatist discussions with that old son of a bitch, Loeuillet! I paid the whore good money to tell me that! So you want to get away before it all comes to an end? Well . . . It's not going to end, d'you hear me? It's not going to end!"

"How vile!" cried Esteban, exasperated with himself for having been frank with a man who had laid a trap for him after having him watched by the woman who shared his bed.

Victor said in a tone of command: "You will take your records, your writing materials, your arms, and your baggage, and you will go on board *L'Ami du Peuple* to-day. There you'll be able to get away for a time from what you, I know, would hypocritically call my 'unavoidable cruelties'. I am not cruel. I do what I have to do, and that's not the same thing."

He softened his voice, as if he were chatting casually with one of his lieutenants, and, looking over towards the trees on the Place de la Victoire, whose sturdy young shoots were already covered with new leaves, he explained to Esteban that the British threat still hung heavily over the island, that an enemy fleet was to be assembled in Barbados, and that it was essential to anticipate events. From the point of view of naval strategy, only privateering—privateering in the grand, authentic, classical manner—had given results in Caribbean waters, by using light, mobile ships, which could easily take refuge in shallow inlets and manoeuvre in places bristling with coral reefs. This had always worked against the heavy Spanish galleons of the old days, and it would work to-day, against the over-heavily armed British ships. The Privateer Fleet of the French Republic would operate in small squadrons, with complete autonomy of action, in a zone bounded by the Mainland and including the waters of all English and Spanish possessions in the Antilles, without any restriction in latitude, though they would take care not to molest the Dutch. Of course a ship might fall into the hands of the enemy, to the great delight of those who were disloyal to the Revolution. ("There are some, there are some," said Victor, stroking a thick bundle of confidential reports, amongst which a denunciation scrawled on rag-paper lay next to a subtle indictment faultlessly written by an anonymous hand on watermarked bond paper.) Deserters enjoyed the greatest indulgence if they threw away their Phrygian caps at the right moment. They were presented to the journalists as victims of an intolerable régime, especially if they were French. They were made to talk of their disillusionment and their sufferings under a tyranny worse than any previously known, and the way was made easy for them to return to their homes where they would penitently recount their misfortunes amongst the pitfalls of unattainable Utopias.

Esteban was indignant at the intentions that were being attributed to him : "If you think that I'm capable of lending myself to that sort of thing, why are you putting me on one of your ships?"

The other butted him in the face with his nose, like someone giving a real-life imitation of a quarrel between marionettes : "Because you are an excellent clerk and we need one with each squadron, to draw up a record of captures, and to make inventories quickly, before some miscreant lays his hands on what belongs to the Republic." And, taking a pen and a ruler, the Commissar drew up six columns on a broad sheet of paper. "Come here," he said, "and stop looking so obstinate. You'll keep the booty book like this : first column, GROSS PROFITS; second column, PROFITS FROM SALES AND AUCTION— (if there are any); third column, FIVE PER CENT FOR SICK MEN ON BOARD; fourth column, 15 CENTS FOR SICK MEN'S POOL; fifth column, DUE TO PRIVATEER CAPTAINS; sixth column, LEGITIMATE EXPENSES INCURRED IN DESPATCHING LIQUID ASSETS (if for any reason they have to be sent through another squadron). Is that clear?"

At that moment Victor Hugues looked like a worthy provincial shop-keeper, involved in the drudgery of balancing his books at the end of the year. Even in the way he held the pen there remained something of the former trader and baker from Port-au-Prince.

CHAPTER THREE

XXIV

Se aprovechan
—*Goya*

WITH A JUBILANT display of artillery salvoes, tricolours and revolutionary songs, the little squadrons began to leave the harbour of Pointe-à-Pitre. After making love to Mademoiselle Athalie Bajazet for the last time, and biting her breasts with a ferocity which owed much to the grudge he bore her, Esteban had beaten her buttocks black and blue—her body was too beautiful for him to be able to hit her anywhere else—as an informer and a police spy, and left her groaning, remorseful, and, perhaps for the first time, genuinely enamoured of him. She had helped him to dress, calling him *"Mon doux Seigneur"*, and now, from the poop of the brig, which was already leaving the little Ilet à Cochons astern, the young man gazed at the distant town with a delightful feeling of relief. The squadron of two small ships and one larger one, in which he was sailing, seemed in truth far too frail and humble to challenge the powerful English luggers, or their dangerously mobile and narrow cutters. But this was preferable to remaining in an increasingly demoniac world, where Victor Hugues was set on increasing his own stature to fit the hypostatic dimensions of the title he had already been given by the American newspapers : "The Robespierre of the Isles".

Esteban took in a deep breath, as if wanting to rid his lungs of some mephitic exhalation. Now they were headed for the open sea, and beyond that for the mighty ocean of Odysseys and Anabases. As the shore receded, the sea was taking on a deeper blue, and they entered on a life dictated by its rhythms. A marine bureaucracy was established on board, as each man went about his duties : the steward nosed about in the store-room; the carpenter set to work changing the tholes on a pinnace; one man caulked, another regulated the clocks, watched anxiously by the cook, who had guaranteed that a hake they had been given would be served at six o'clock in the officers' ward-room—while the great soup of leeks, cabbages and potatoes had to be in the bowls on the men's tables before the sky was tinged by the sunset.

That night everyone felt as if he had returned to a normal existence, to a leisurely daily time-table far removed from the fearful scansion of the guillotine, as if he had emerged from a chaotic temporality, to enter something immutable and eternal. Now they would live without newspapers from Paris, without reading of accusations or inquisitions, without hearing loud contradictory voices; they could live with their faces turned to the sun, engaged in a duologue with the stars, questioning the almacantar and the Pole Star.

L'Ami du Peuple had hardly entered the open sea before a whale was spotted, spouting water with the gracefulness of a fountain, but it soon submerged in fear of being attacked by one of the bilanders. And on the surface of the sea, almost violet now in the dusk, Esteban could make out the silhouette of the enormous fish, in water made even darker by its shadow—like some modern analogue to a creature from another century, strayed into unknown latitudes from perhaps four or five hundred years ago.

For several days the little squadron—comprising *La Décade* and *La Tintamarre*, in addition to the brig—sighted no other shipping, and seemed to be engaged on a pleasure cruise, rather than bound on a mission of aggression. They dropped anchor in a cove, furled the sails, and the sailors went ashore, some for firewood, others for clams—which were so numerous that they could be found three inches down in the sand—and took advantage of the occasion to lounge about amongst the *uvero* trees on the beach, or to bathe in a creek. The clarity, transparency and coolness of the water, so early in the day, produced in Esteban an exaltation very like a state of lucid intoxication. Floundering about within his depth, he learned to swim, and could never bring himself to return to the shore when it was time to do so; he felt so happy, so enveloped and saturated by the light, that sometimes, back on dry land, he had the dazed, tottering gait of a drunken man. He called this his "water-drunkenness", and afterwards offered his naked body to the ascending sun, lying on his stomach in the sand, or face upwards, arms and legs splayed as if crucified, with such an expression of joy on his face that he looked like some fortunate mystic, favoured with an ineffable vision.

On occasions, inspired by the fresh energy which this life had infused in him, he undertook prolonged explorations of the steep cliffs, clambering, jumping, paddling—and marvelling at the things he discovered among the rocks. There were the pulpy leaves of the madrepore; the speckled, pitcher-shaped apples of the cowries; the slender cathedral architecture of certain snails, which, with their winged and needle-pointed shells, could only be seen in terms of the Gothic; the beaded whorls of the sea-periwinkles, the Pythagorean convolutions of the spindle-shell, the simulation with which many shells concealed in their depths the splendours of an ornate palace, under the humble plaster of their exterior. At his approach the sea-urchin proffered its black spines, the timid oyster closed, the star-fish shrank, and the sponges, attached to some submerged rock, swayed amidst rippling reflections. In this prodigious Island Sea, even the pebbles of the ocean bed had style and elegance; some were so perfectly rounded that they looked as if they had been turned on a lapidary's lathe; others were abstract in shape, but seemed to dance with excitement, to be lifted, lengthened, turned into arrows, by a sort of impulse springing from the matter itself. There was translucent rock, with the clarity of alabaster; rock like violet-coloured marble; granite, across which the light danced under the water; and humble rocks, bristling with sea-snails, whose seaweed-flavoured flesh the young man extracted from their tiny green-black shells with a cactus spine.

The most prodigious cacti mounted guard over the flanks of these nameless Hesperides where the ships put in on their adventurous course : tall candelabra, panoplies with green helms, green pheasants' tails, green swords, green hummocks, hostile-looking water-melons, trailing quinces with spines hidden beneath their deceptive smoothness. This was a distrustful world, ever ready to inflict pain, but prodigally giving birth to some red or yellow flower, which it offered the young man at the cost of a prick, along with the treacherous gift of an Indian fig or a prickly pear, only yielding its flesh when the last palisade of eager spines was overcome.

In contrast to this vegetation armed with spikes, which prevented him from climbing up to certain of the hill-tops crowned with ripe anonas, there was the Cambrian world down below : infinite and multifarious forests of coral, with its texture of flesh, lace and wool, its blazing, auriferous, transmuted trees : alchemical trees out of some book of spells or hermetic treatise; nettles whose undersides one could not touch; flamboyant ivy, twined in counterpoints and rhythms so ambiguous that all delimitation between the inert and the palpitant, the vegetal and the animal, was abolished. Amidst a growing economy of zoological forms, the coral forests preserved the earliest baroque of Creation, its first luxuriance and extravagance, hiding their treasures where, in order to see them, the young man had to imitate the fish he had once been, before he was shaped by the womb—regretting the gills and tail which would have enabled him to choose these gorgeous landscapes as his permanent dwelling-place. In these coral forests Esteban saw a tangible image, a ready—and yet so inaccessible—configuration, of a Paradise Lost, where the trees, barely named as yet by the torpid, hesitant tongue of the Man-child, would be endowed with the apparent immortality of this sumptuous flora, this ostensory, this burning bush, where autumn and spring could be detected only in a variation in the colours, or a slight shifting of the shadows.

Going from surprise to surprise, Esteban discovered a plurality of beaches, where the sea, three centuries after the Discovery, was beginning to deposit its first pieces of polished glass—glass invented in Europe and strange to America; glass from bottles, from flasks, from demijohns, in shapes hitherto unknown on the New Continent; green glass, with opacities and bubbles; delicate glass, destined for embryonic cathedrals, whose hagiography had been effaced by the water; glass fallen from ships or saved from shipwrecks, polished by the waves with the skill of a turner or a goldsmith till the light was restored to its extenuated colours, and cast up as a mysterious novelty on this ocean shore.

There were black beaches, formed of slate and pulverised marble, where the sunlight formed sparkling furrows; yellow beaches, with shifting slopes where each flux left behind the trace of its arabesque, constantly smoothing it away before returning to inscribe another; white beaches, so white, so dazzlingly white, that on them sand would have showed as an imperfection, for they were vast cemeteries of broken shells—tossed, tumbled, triturated shells, reduced to a powder so fine it escaped through one's fingers like water.

It was wonderful, amidst this multiplicity of Oceanides, to find Life everywhere, stuttering, budding, creeping, on eroded rocks and floating tree-trunks alike, in a perpetual mingling of the animal and the plant kingdoms, of that which floated, and was carried or brought, and that which moved of its own volition. Here some of the reefs had forged their own growth; the rock was maturing; for millennia past the submerged stone had been engaged in the task of completing its own sculpture in a world of vegetable-fish, mushroom jelly-fish, fleshy star-fish, floating plants, and ferns which took on tints of saffron, indigo or purple, according to the time of the day. A white dusting of flour would suddenly appear against the submerged trunks of the mangroves. Then this flour became sheets of parchment; the parchment swelled and hardened, and turned into scales, which adhered to the trunk with suckers, until, one fine morning, oysters had formed on the trunk of the tree and were cloaking it with their grey shells. And it was a branch of oysters which the sailors brought in, after detaching a limb of the tree with their machetes : a plant made of shell-fish, with a root, a branch and a handful of leaves, and the salty enamel of the shells, which offered the rarest and least definable of foodstuffs to the human palate.

No symbol conformed better to the Idea of the Sea than that of the amphibious women of the ancient myths, whose flesh had been present to men's hands in the pink cavity of the strombs, to which for centuries the mariners of the Archipelago had pressed their mouths to produce from them the raucous sound of a trombone, of a Neptunian bull, of some solar creature, bellowing out across an immensity dedicated to the Sun.

Carried into a world of symbiosis, standing up to his neck in pools whose water was kept perpetually foaming by cascading waves, and was broken, torn, shattered, by the hungry bite of jagged rocks, Esteban marvelled to realise how the language of these islands had made use of agglutination, verbal amalgams and metaphors to convey the formal ambiguity of things which participated in several essences at once. Just as certain trees were called "acacia-bracelets", "pineapple-porcelain", "wood-rib", "ten o'clock broom", "cousin clover", "pitcher-pine-kernel", "tisane-cloud", and "iguana-stick", many marine creatures had received names which established verbal equivocations in order to describe them accurately. Thus a fantastic bestiary had arisen of dog-fish, oxen-fish, tiger-fish, snorers, blowers, flying fish; of striped, tattooed and tawny fish, fish with their mouths on top of their heads, or their gills in the middle of their stomachs; white-bellies, swordfish and mackerel; a fish which bit off testicles—cases had been known—another that was herbivorous; the red-speckled sand-eel; a fish which became poisonous after eating manchineel apples—not forgetting the vieja-fish, the captain-fish, with its gleaming throat of golden scales; or the woman-fish —the mysterious and elusive manatees, glimpsed in the mouths of rivers where the salt water mingled with the fresh, with their feminine profiles and their siren's breasts, playing joyful nuptial pranks on one another in their watery meadows.

But for joyfulness, for eurhythmy, for grace of movement, nothing could compare with the games of the dolphins, leaping from the water in twos, threes and twenties, or underlining the arabesque of a wave with their own flitting shapes. In twos, threes or twenties, the dolphins would spiral in concert, integrating themselves into the wave's very existence, their lively movements, as they paused, leapt, fell back and rested, so closely indentified with it, that they seemed to bear the wave on their bodies, to lend it their own rhythms and measure, their own tempo and sequence. And then they would disappear, vanish in search of new adventures, until their next encounter with a ship again disturbed these dancers of the sea, who knew only how to perform pirouettes and triton leaps, in illustration of their own legends.

Sometimes a great silence foreshadowing an Event would fall over the water, and then some enormous, belated, obsolete fish would appear, a fish from another epoch, its face placed at the extreme end of its massive body, living in a perpetual fear at its own slowness, its hide covered with vegetation and parasites like an uncareened hull. The huge back emerged amidst a swirl of remoras, with the solemnity of a raised galleon, as this patriarch of the depths, this Leviathan, ejecting sea-foam, emerged into the light of day, for what might perhaps be only the second time since the astrolabe was brought into these seas. The monster opened its pachyderm's eyes, and, discovering a battered sardine-boat sailing nearby, submerged once more, anxious and afraid, down towards the solitude of the depths, to await some other century before it returned again to a world full of perils.

The Event concluded, the sea went back to its business. The hippocampi ran aground on the sand among empty sea-urchins, divested of their quills, which, as they dried, turned into geometrical apples, so neatly arranged that they could have formed part of Dürer's "Melancholy". The colours of the parrot-fish were kindled, as the angel-fish, the devil-fish, the cock-fish and the St. Peter-fish merged their entities in the sacramental drama which was being played out in this great theatre of Universal Voracity, this fluid unity, where like was eaten by like, consubstantiated and imbricated before its time.

If the island was narrow, Esteban would try to forget the times he lived in by walking alone over to the other side, where he felt himself master of everything; the snail-shells were his, and their music at high-tide; so were the turtles in their topaz armour, hiding their eggs in holes which they then filled in and brushed over with their scaly flippers; and the dazzling blue stones, sparkling on a shoal of virgin sand, never trodden by human feet. His too were the pelicans, who had little fear of man because they knew too little about him; they would fly in the lap of the waves with pouched cheeks, then suddenly rise and drop almost vertically, their beaks driven by the whole weight of their bodies, their wings folded to accelerate their fall. Then the bird would lift its head with triumphant pride, the body of its prey would pass down its throat, and there would be a joyful shaking of the caudal feathers as a token of satisfaction, an act of thanksgiving, before it rose in a low and undulating flight, as parallel to the movement of the sea above the surface as was the vertiginous course of the dolphins below it.

Stretched out on sand so fine that even the tiniest insect left the marks of its passage behind, naked and alone in the world, Esteban watched the luminous, motionless clouds, so slow to change their formations that sometimes a whole day was not enough to erase a triumphal arch or the head of a prophet. Total happiness, outside time and space. *Te deum*. Or else, with the point of his chin resting on the cool leaves of an *uvero*, he became absorbed in the contemplation of a snail—a single snail—which stood like a monument, level with his eyes, blotting out the horizon. This snail was the mediator between evanescent, fugitive, lawless, measureless fluidity, and the land, with its crystallisations, its structures, its morphology, where everything could be grasped and weighed. Out of a sea at the mercy of lunar cycles—fickle, furious or generous, curling and dilating, forever ignorant of modules, theorems and equations—there appeared these surprising shells, symbolising in number and proportion exactly what the Mother lacked, concrete examples of linear development, of the laws of convolution, of a wonderfully precise conical architecture, of masses in equilibrium, of tangible arabesques which hinted at all the baroquisms to come. Contemplating a snail—a single snail—Esteban reflected on how, for millennium upon millennium, the spiral had been present to the everyday gaze of maritime races, who were still incapable of understanding it, or of even grasping the reality of its presence. He meditated on the prickly husk of the sea-urchin, the helix of the mollusc, the fluting of the Jacobean scallop-shell, astonished by this science of form which had been exhibited for so long to a humanity that still lacked eyes to appreciate it. What is there round about me which is already complete, recorded, real, yet which I cannot understand? What sign, what message, what warning is there, in the curling leaves of the endive, the alphabet of moss, the geometry of the rose-apple? Contemplate a snail—a single snail. *Te deum*.

XXV

Esteban had been very frightened during their first skirmish, and taken cover in the very bottom of the ship—his indispensable status of clerk entitled him to do so—but he soon came to realise that the life of a privateer, as understood by Captain Barthélémy, the commander of the squadron, normally contained few alarms. When they met a powerful, heavily-armed ship, they held on their course without breaking the Republican flag. If they met with a possible prize, the lighter ships headed it off, while the brig loosed off a warning shot. The enemy flag was struck without resistance, in token of surrender. The ships grappled, and the Frenchmen leaped on board to inspect the cargo. If it was of little value they took anything that might be useful—including the intimidated crew's money and personal possessions—and transferred it to *L'Ami du Peuple*. Then the ship was handed back to its humiliated captain, who either pursued his voyage, or returned to his port of departure to report his misfortune. If the cargo was important and valuable, they had orders to seize it, ship and all—especially if the ship was a good one—and take it to Pointe-à-Pitre, together with her crew. But this eventuality had not yet arisen for Barthélémy's squadron, whose ledgers Esteban kept with bureaucratic scrupulousness.

There were normally more bilanders and junks to be found in these waters than real merchantmen, and they seldom carried cargoes of interest. They had certainly not left Guadeloupe to look for sugar, coffee and rum, which abounded there. Yet even in the most battered and sorry-looking ships the Frenchmen found things to lay their hands on; a new anchor, arms, gunpowder, carpenters' tools, cables, a recent chart, with information useful for coasting along the Mainland. And apart from these there was what could be ferreted out from sea-chests and dark corners. One man would find two good shirts and a pair of nankeen breeches; another an enamelled tobacco-box, or the jewelled chalice of a monk from Cartagena, whom they threatened to throw overboard if he did not surrender the "whole Mass"—the cross and ostensory, which might well be gold. These were a matter of individual spoils, which necessarily escaped Esteban's accounting, and which Barthélémy pretended to ignore, so as not to make himself unpopular with his men; for he knew that in these days ships' captains always came off worst in disputes with their Republican crews, especially if, like him, they had previously served under the King.

Thus on the poop-deck of *L'Ami du Peuple* a sort of exchange and mart had been established, of articles displayed on chests or hung from the rigging. The sailors from *La Décade* and *La Tintamarre* used to visit it when they moored in some creek or other to cut firewood, and they, in their turn, brought over what they wished to trade. Among clothes, caps, belts and kerchiefs, the oddest things used to appear : reliquaries made out of a turtle's shell; Havanese dressing-gowns that were a froth of lace; nut-shells containing a whole wedding procession of fleas in Mexican costume; embalmed fish with tongues of crimson satin; small caymans stuffed with straw; wrought-iron imps; boxes of snails; birds made out of sugar-candy; three-stringed guitars from Cuba or Venezuela; aphrodisiac potions made from *Garañon* grass or the famous *bejuco* of San Domingo; together with all kinds of trophies which could be associated with thoughts of women : ear-rings, bead necklaces, petticoats, loin-cloths, locks of hair tied with ribbon, nude drawings, pornographic engravings, and, to cap them all, a shepherdess doll concealing beneath her skirts silky and well-provided sexual organs, so perfectly executed on a minute scale that they were wonderful to see. Since the owner of the figurine asked an exorbitant price for it, and was treated as a robber by those who could not afford to purchase it, Barthélémy, fearing a scuffle, had the object bought by the purser of the brig, with the intention of presenting it to Victor Hugues, who, since the 9th Thermidor, had been openly given to reading pornographic books, perhaps so that he could boast that Paris politics no longer interested him.

The ships' crews were delighted one day when, having given chase to a Portuguese ship, they discovered that the *Andorinha* was fully laden with red, white and Madeira wine, in such quantity that the holds smelled like a wine-press. Esteban hastened to make an inventory of the casks, which would need to be safeguarded from the over-thirty sailors—they had already taken possession of several barrels, and despatched their contents in long draughts. Alone and safe from interference or competition in a shady hold that was more like a wine-cellar, the clerk helped himself out of an ample mahogany bowl, in which the taste of the must was combined with the scent of the thick, cool wood, that had a fleshy feel against the lips.

Esteban had learned in France to appreciate the noble juice of the vine, which had nourished the proud and turbulent civilisation of the Mediterranean, now spread into this Caribbean Mediterranean, where the blending of characteristics had for many thousands of years been in progress within the ambit of the peoples of the sea. Here, after long being scattered, the descendants of the lost tribes had met again, to mingle their accents and their lineaments, to produce new strains, mixing and commixing, degenerating and regenerating, a temporary enlightenment followed by a leap backwards into the darkness, in an interminable proliferation of new profiles, new accents and proportions. In their turn they had been reached by the wine which had passed from the Phoenician ships, the warehouses of Cadiz, and the amphorae of Maarkos Sestos, into the caravels of the Discovery, along with the guitar and the glazed tile, and had landed on these shores so propitious to the transcendental encounter of the Olive with the Maize.

Sniffing the damp bowl, Esteban remembered, with sudden emotion, the old, patriarchal casks in the warehouse in Havana —so distant and remote from his present life—where the isochronous dripping of the taps had produced the same sound as he was listening to here. Suddenly, the absurdity of his present existence became so clear to him—he was in a theatre of the absurd—that he leaned, dazed, against the side of the ship, his eyes staring in amazement, as if he had seen his own face appear on a stage. Lately the sea, the life of the body and the vicissitudes of the voyage had enabled him to forget himself, to indulge in the purely animal satisfaction of feeling himself growing increasingly strong and healthy. But now he could see himself against this background of a ship's hold full of wine, of which he had known nothing yesterday; and he asked himself what he was doing in such a place. He had been searching for a path which was closed to him. He had been awaiting an opportunity which did not come. A bourgeois by birth, he was working as a privateers' clerk—there was absurdity in the mere mention of such a profession. In reality he was a prisoner, because his present fate bound him to a nation of men who were at war with the whole world. Nothing could have been more like a nightmare than this stage on which he could watch himself, dreaming yet awake, both judge and protagonist, participant and spectator; surrounded by islands which resembled the one island he could not reach; condemned, perhaps for a lifetime, to smell the smells of his childhood, to find tokens of his adolescence in trees, houses, tricks of the light (Oh, the smears of orange paint, the blue doors, the pomegranates hanging over the mud walls!), but without having what was his—what had belonged to him since childhood and adolescence—restored to him. One evening the door-knocker of the house had sounded, setting in motion the diabolical process which had begun by over-turning three lives united until that moment, and had continued with games that brought Lycurgus and Mucius Scaevola out of their graves, before it finally embraced a city of bloody tribunals, and an island, several islands, a whole sea of islands, where the will of one man, the posthumous agent of another silent will, weighed upon all other lives. Since Victor Hugues had appeared —the first thing that he had known about him was that he carried a green umbrella—the Ego which he had seen against the background of casks and barrels had ceased to belong to itself; his present and his future were controlled by the will of another. Better to drink, and blur this unwanted lucidity, which was so exasperating at the moment that he wanted to scream. Esteban held the bowl under a faucet and filled it to the brim. Above him the crew were rendering "The Three Gunners from Auvergne".

The following day they landed on a deserted, wooded coast, where the first mate of *L'Ami du Peuple*—a mixture of Carib and negro, born on Marie Galante, who derived real authority from his knowledge of the Antilles—knew that there were wild boars, and also how to make a *boucan* fit to go with the wines which they would put to cool in the mouths of the streams. The hunt was soon organised, and the animals that were brought in, still with that angry contraction of the snout which wild boars get when cornered, were handed over to the cooks. After cleaning off the bristles from the black hides with fish-scaling knives, they laid the bodies on gridirons over red-hot embers, their chines to the heat, their bellies held open by thin pieces of wood. On to the flesh a fine rain began to fall, of lemon juice, bitter oranges, salt, pepper, marjoram and garlic, whilst a litter of green guava leaves, laid over the embers, sent a white, unripe-smelling smoke swirling up round the skins— sprinkled from above, sprinkled from below—which were taking on the colour of tortoise-shell as they grilled. From time to time, with a dry, crackling sound, a great cleft opened to release the fat, provoking a fountain of sparks from the bottom of the trench, where even the earth now smelled of scorched boar. When the pigs were almost cooked, their yawning bellies were filled with quails, wild pigeons, grouse and other recently plucked birds. Then the sticks which had kept the entrails exposed were removed and the ribs closed over the wildfowl, acting as a flexible oven which held them tightly in, consubstantiating the flavour of the dark, lean meat with that of the light, fat meat, to produce a *boucan* which, as Esteban said, was a *Boucan of Boucans*—a Song of Songs. The wine flowed into the drinking vessels in time to the gormandizing. In their drunkenness they smashed barrels with axes; they hurled barrels down the gravel slopes, to break their staves open against a sharp boulder; they broke barrels by rolling them from group to group in a long drawn-out battle; barrels were shattered, holed with gunshots, and danced on by a bad flamenco dancer, a half-Spanish homosexual, who was taken on board *La Décade* as galley-boy, because he was a friend of Liberty. At last the crews fell asleep, gorged and slaked, at the foot of the *uvero* trees, or on sand which was still warm from the sun.

Waking heavily at dawn, Esteban noticed that many of the sailors had gone down to the shore, and were staring over towards the ships, of which there were now five, including the *Andorinha*. The new arrival was so antiquated and unusual in appearance, with its half-broken figurehead, and its dirty faded fo'c'sle, that it seemed to have sailed out of another century—a boat manned by men who still believed that the Atlantic ended in a Sea of Darkness. A caique soon set off from its battered sides, and was urged towards the beach by several almost naked negroes, who paddled standing up, to a barbaric river-boatman's chanty. The man who seemed to be the leader jumped ashore, making genuflexions that were interpreted as gestures of friendship, and addressed one of the cooks in a dialect which the latter, born perhaps in Calabar, seemed half to understand. After a discussion full of gesticulations, the interpreter explained that the old boat was a Spanish slave-trader, and that its crew had been thrown overboard by the mutinied slaves, who were now placing themselves under the protection of the French. All along the African coast they knew that the Republic had abolished slavery in its American colonies, and that the negroes there were now free citizens. Captain Barthélémy shook the leader by the hand, and presented him with a tricolour cockade, which was received with shouts of delight by the members of his band and passed from hand to hand. Then the caique began to bring more negroes ashore, and more still, while the impatient ones were swimming ashore in order to find out what was happening. And suddenly, unable to contain themselves, they threw themselves on the remains of the *boucan,* gnawing bones, devouring dried viscera, sucking the cold fat, to assuage themselves after weeks of hunger.

"Poor fellows," said Barthélémy, his eyes misty. "This is quite enough to absolve us from a great many sins." Esteban was much moved, and filling his bowl with wine offered it to these erstwhile slaves, who kissed his hands. The supercargo from *L'Ami du Peuple,* who had been over to examine the surrendered ship, now arrived with the news that there were women aboard, many women, hidden below decks, shaking with misery and fear, and ignorant of what was happening ashore. Barthélémy wisely gave the order that they should not be disembarked. A boat took meat, ships' biscuits, bananas and wine out to them, while the men resumed the activities of the night before, and went off hunting more wild pigs. To-morrow they would have to return to Pointe-à-Pitre with the Portuguese ship, the various merchandise they had taken one way or another, the cargo of wine, and these negroes, who would make a useful addition to the coloured militia—always in need of extra hands for the arduous tasks of fortification by means of which Victor Hugues was securing his position.

Towards nightfall, the orgy of the previous day began again, but in a very different atmosphere. As the wine went to their heads, the men seemed to become increasingly preoccupied by the presence of the women, whose cooking-stoves glowed against the sunset, and whose laughter could be heard from the shore. The sailors from the slaver were asked for details about them. Some of them were very young, handsome, well set-up—the traders did not accept old women, because they were an unmarketable commodity. And as they grew more heated with drink, more detailed descriptions began to flow: "There are some with buttocks like this . . . some of them are stark naked . . . there's one in particular . . ."

Suddenly ten, twenty, thirty men ran to the boats and began to row out to the old ship, ignoring the shouts of Barthélémy, who was trying to restrain them. The negroes had stopped eating, and stood up gesticulating anxiously. Soon the first black women arrived, to be ringed by an aggressive concupiscence; tearful, supplicant, perhaps genuinely frightened, they nevertheless submitted to the men, who hauled them off towards the nearby thickets. Nobody paid any attention to the officers, although they had unsheathed their swords. And in the midst of the disorder more and more negresses were arriving, who began to run about the beach, pursued by the sailors. Thinking to help Barthélémy, who was screaming insults, threats and orders which no one could hear, the negroes threw themselves on the whites, armed with sticks. There was a violent mêlée, with bodies being hurled on to the sand, trodden on and kicked; bodies being raised into the air and dashed on to the rocks; men falling into the sea, locked together, one trying to drown the other by holding his head under water. Finally the negroes were driven into a cave in the rocks, while chains and bilboes were brought from their ship to shackle them.

Barthélémy returned to *L'Ami du Peuple*, in great disgust, leaving his men to their violence and their orgies. Taking care to provide himself with a piece of damp canvas to lie on—he knew the drawbacks of lying on sand—Esteban took one of the slave girls to a sort of cradle, carpeted with dry lichen, which he had discovered amongst the rocks. She was very young and submitted docilely, preferring this to other, worse brutalities, and unwound the torn stuff she was wearing. She offered the young man the tense smoothness of her adolescent breasts, the nipples liberally smeared with ochre, and her firm, fleshy thighs, which were ready to clasp, to arch, or bend till her knees touched her chest.

From all over the island there rose a muffled concert of laughter, exclamations, whispers, and sometimes over them all an indistinct bellowing, like the lament of some sick animal, hidden in a nearby lair. From time to time the noise of a quarrel broke out, perhaps over the possession of a woman. Esteban was renewing his memories of the smell, the textures, the rhythms, and the panting of Someone who had, long ago, in a house in the Arsenal quarter of Havana, revealed to him the paroxysms of his own flesh. Only one thing mattered that night—Sex. Sex, engaged in its own rituals, multiplied into a sort of collective liturgy, recognising no restraint, no authority, no law.

Dawn broke amidst a fanfare of reveilles, and Barthélémy, determined to exert his authority, ordered the crews to return to their ships immediately. Anyone who remained on the island would be left behind there. There were further altercations with sailors who wanted to keep their black women as a legitimate personal prize. The Captain of the squadron appeased them with a formal promise that the women would be handed over to them when they reached Pointe-à-Pitre. Their manumission would take place there, after they had complied with the legal requirements of naming and registering, which turned former slaves into French citizens. The negroes and negresses returned to their ship, and the squadron set sail for home.

But shortly after they had got under way, Esteban, whose sense of direction had become much keener lately—he had in addition acquired some knowledge of navigation—thought he could recognise that the course which the ships were on was not exactly designed to take them to Guadeloupe. Barthélémy frowned when the clerk remarked on this. "Keep it a secret," he said. "You know very well I can't keep the promise I made those scoundrels. It would be a fatal precedent. The Commissar wouldn't tolerate it. We're going to a Dutch island, where we shall sell the shipload of blacks."

Esteban looked at him in astonishment and quoted the Decree of the Abolition of Slavery. The Captain took from his despatch-box a letter of instructions, signed and sealed by Victor Hugues:

"By virtue of her democratic principles France may not operate in the slave trade. But the captains of privateers are authorised, if they should deem it convenient or necessary, to sell the slaves they have captured from ships belonging to the English, Spanish or other enemies of the Republic in Dutch ports."

"But that's outrageous!" exclaimed Esteban. "Have we aboiished the slave trade just so that we can act as slavers between other countries?"

"I'm only carrying out what's written here," said Barthélémy drily. Then, thinking that he was obliged to justify an inadmissible ordinance: "We live in an illogical world. Before the Revolution a slave-trader sailed these seas, owned by a *philosophe* and a friend of Jean-Jacques. And do you know what she was called? The *Contrat Social.*"

XXVII

WITHIN A FEW months, revolutionary privateering had become a fabulously successful business venture. Encouraged by their triumphs and their profits, and eager for greater pickings still, the Pointe-à-Pitre Captains grew increasingly bold in their sorties, and ventured farther afield, as far as the Mainland, Barbados, and the Virgin Islands—nor were they afraid to show themselves in the vicinity of islands from which a fierce-looking squadron might well put out to engage them. As the days passed they perfected their techniques. They resurrected the traditions of the corsairs of old, and chose to sail in squadrons composed of small ships—bilanders, cutters and lithe schooners, which were easy to manoeuvre and hide, quick to make a getaway, and could press home an attack—rather than bigger, slower ships, that provided an easy target for the enemy's guns, the British in particular, the tactics of whose gunners differed from those of the French in that they tried not to dismast the ships but to hit the timbers of the hull as the mouths of the cannon fell with the waves and made their aim more certain.

As a result of all this the harbour at Pointe-à-Pitre was full of new shipping, and the warehouses no longer had room for so much merchandise and so many different things; in order to store what continued to arrive daily, it had proved necessary to erect sheds on the edge of the mangrove plantations which bordered the town. Victor Hugues had grown a little fatter, but even if his body had begun to stretch the stuff of his frock-coat, he displayed just as much energy as ever. Contrary to many people's hopes, the remote and overworked Directory had recognised the Commissar's efficiency in recovering the colony and defending it against the Spanish threat, and had just confirmed him in his authority. And the Mandatory had succeeded in forming himself into a sort of autonomous, independent, one-man government in this part of the globe, thus realising, to an alarming extent, his unconfessed ambition of identifying himself with the Incorruptible. He had wanted to *be* Robespierre, and now, in his way, he *was* Robespierre. Just as Robespierre had once talked about *his* government, *his* army and *his* fleet, so Victor Hugues now talked about *his* government, *his* army and *his* fleet.

The Plenipotentiary was just as arrogant as he had been in the early days, and when the chess-boards and the playing-cards came out he would claim for himself the role of sole Continuer of the Revolution. He boasted that he no longer read the Paris papers, because "their lies nauseated him". Esteban noticed all the same that Victor Hugues was very proud of the island's prosperity, and of the money which he was continually sending to France; he was recovering the outlook of the well-to-do tradesman, calculating his wealth with a smiling face. When his ships returned with a good haul the Commissar attended the unloading, and priced the bales, casks, household goods and arms with a trained eye. Through an agent, he had opened a mixed shop in the vicinity of the Place de la Victoire, where he held a monopoly in certain articles—they could only be bought there, at arbitrarily fixed prices. At the end of the evening Victor never failed to call in on the business to compare the books, in the shadows of an office which smelled of vanilla, and whose arched doors, with their fine ornamental ironwork, opened on to two conjoining streets.

The guillotine too had become bourgeois, and was smoothly

operated one day out of five by the assistants of Monsieur Anse, who now devoted the greater part of his time to completing his collection for his curiosity shop, already rich in coleoptera and lepidoptera which had been ennobled with impressive Latin names. Everything was very expensive, yet there was always money enough to pay for it in this world with its closed economy, where prices rose constantly and the currency returned again and again into the same pockets, to be quoted at a higher rate, even though it might come back debased, its metal content reduced by filings and raspings which could be detected by the fingers.

During one of his furloughs in Pointe-à-Pitre, Esteban—whose face was so tanned that he looked like a mulatto—was delighted to learn, albeit very belatedly, of the peace treaty between France and Spain. He thought that communications would now be restored with the Mainland, Puerto Rico and Havana. But he was deeply disappointed when he heard that Victor Hugues refused to acknowledge what had been agreed at Basle. He was determined to go on seizing Spanish ships, and to hold them, as being "suspected of supplying military contraband to the English", and he gave his Captains authority to "requisition" them, and to provide their own definitions of what was to be understood by "military contraband". Esteban would have to go on carrying out his duties with Barthélémy's squadron; he watched his opportunity recede, of escaping from a world which the timeless life at sea, recognising no law but that of the winds, had made increasingly alien to him.

As the months passed he became resigned to living each day as it came—he never reckoned them up but was content to enjoy the modicum of pleasure which he might derive from spending the time quietly or sitting fishing. He had grown to like some of his companions on the ship : Barthélémy, who still had the manners of an officer of the *ancien régime* and paid great attention to the appearance of his clothes at moments of stress; Noël, the surgeon, endlessly working on a confused thesis about the vampires of Prague, the devils of Loudun, and the epileptics of the Saint-Médard cemetery; the slaughterman Achilles, a negro from the island of Tobago, who played frightful sonatas on different-sized kettle-drums; and Citizen Gilbert, the master caulker, who recited long extracts from classical tragedies with such a Southern accent that the lines always gained a few extra syllables and failed to conform to the alexandrine metre, as Brutus turned into Brutusse, or Epaminondas into Epaminondasse.

Besides which, the young man was fascinated by the world of the Antilles, and the perpetual iridescence of light that played on its manifold forms, prodigiously varied yet unified by a common climate and vegetation. He loved mountainous Dominica, with its deep greens, and its villages called Bataille and Massacre in memory of spine-chilling events of which history had little to tell. He grew to know the clouds of Nevis, reclining so gently on the hills that the High Admiral, when he saw them, took them to be impossible snowcaps. He dreamed of one day climbing to the top of the sharp peak of St. Lucia, whose mass, set in the sea, looked from a distance like a light-house, built by unknown engineers, in anticipation of the ships which would one day bring the Tree of the Cross, in the inter-section of their yard-arms. Placid and friendly to whoever approached them from the south, the islands of this inaccessible archipelago were steep, rugged, and eroded by the high waves that broke in sheets of spray on the side which towered up against the north winds. A whole mythology of shipwrecks, of sunken treasure, buried without epitaph, of treacherous lights burning on stormy nights, of portentous births—of Madame de Maintenon, a Sephardic miracle-worker, and an Amazon who finally became Queen of Constantinople—was associated with these islands, whose names Esteban would repeat to himself in a whisper, delighting in the euphony of the sounds: Tórtola, Santa Ursula, the Fat Virgin, Anegada, the Grenadines, Jerusalem Caida.

Some mornings the sea dawned so calm and silent, that the isochronous creaking of the ropes—higher-pitched when they had been taken in, deeper if they were let out—combined in such a way that anacruses and fortissimi, appogiaturas and grace notes were heard from stem to stern, added to by a high-pitched brass section when a harp of taut cables was suddenly plucked by a puff of wind.

But to-day, as they sailed along, the light winds had suddenly increased, and were driving taller, denser waves ahead of them.

The pale-green sea had become the colour of ivy, opaque and ever more turbulent, and then changed from inky-green to smoky-green. The old salts sniffed the gusts, knowing there would be a different smell about them from the dark shadows bearing quickly down on the ship and the abrupt lulls, broken by warm showers, whose drops were so heavy that they seemed to be made of mercury. Towards dusk the moving column of a waterspout came in sight, and the ships went from crest to crest as if held in the palm of a hand, and were scattered in the darkness, their navigation lights lost to view. They were running now across the frenzied ebulliency of a sea stirred up of its own free-will, which struck at them head-on and from the beam, hurling itself broadside against the hull; and even by rapid straightening of the helm they could not avoid the onslaughts, which swept the deck from side to side once they were no longer head-on to the seas. Barthélémy ordered safety-lines to be brought up, to aid the working of the ship : "We've caught the full force of it," he said, as the classic October storm rose, giving unmistakable warning that it would reach its climacteric after midnight. Seeing that there was no way to escape the ordeal of facing the storm, Esteban locked himself in his cabin and tried to sleep. But it was impossible to go to sleep when one could feel one's viscera moving from side to side the moment one's body was stretched out. They had entered into a vast region of roaring wind, reaching from horizon to horizon, and causing every timber, every plank, in the ship's frame to groan. The hours passed, while the men kept up their struggle on deck. The brig seemed to be sailing at an inadmissible speed; to be picked up, dropped, dashed aside, tilted over, penetrating ever deeper into the eye of the hurricane. Esteban had given up any attempt at self-control and was leaning against his bunk, sea-sick, terror-stricken, waiting for the water to come spilling down the hatchways, filling the holds and breaking in the doors.

Then, suddenly, a little before dawn, it seemed to him that the howling in the sky had diminished, and that the waves' onsets were becoming less frequent. Up above, on deck, the sailors had joined in a great chorus, and were shouting a canticle at the tops of their voices to the Virgin of Perpetual Help, the seaman's intercessor with the Divine Wrath. Opportunely renewing an old French tradition in their time of need, the Privateers of the Republic called on the Mother of the Redeemer to placate the waves and still the wind. Voices that had so often harmonised in lewd songs now prayed to the One Conceived Without Sin, in the language of the liturgy. Esteban crossed himself and went up on deck. The danger was past; they had no news of the other ships—gone astray perhaps, or perhaps foundered —but *L'Ami du Peuple* was sailing alone into a gulf full of islands.

Full of islands, but with the incredible difference that these islands were very small, mere designs or ideas for islands, which had accumulated here just as models, sketches and empty casts accumulate in a sculptor's studio. Not one of these islands resembled its neighbour, nor were any two constituted of the same material. Some seemed to be made of white marble, and were perfectly sterile, monolithic and smooth, rather like Roman busts, buried up to their shoulders in the water; others were piles of schist, in parallel striations, to whose desolate upper terraces two or three trees, with very old, withered branches, grappled with their multiple roots—or sometimes there was only one tree, infinitely lonely, its trunk turned white by the salt, looking like a huge varech. Some had been so hollowed out by the action of the waves that they seemed to float without any visible point of support; others had been eaten away by thistles, or crumbled by landslides. Caves yawned in their sides, from whose roofs giant cacti hung head downwards, their red and yellow flowers extended in festoons like curious theatrical chandeliers, serving as a sanctuary for some strange and enigmatic geometrical shape, isolated and mounted on a plinth—a cylinder, a pyramid, or a polyhedron—like a mysterious object of veneration, a Stone of Mecca, a Pythagorean symbol, the materialisation of an abstract cult.

As the brig penetrated deeper into this strange world, which the pilot had never seen before and was unable to locate after the terrible deviations of the night, Esteban felt compelled to give expression to his astonishment at these *things* which had been placed here, and to invent names for them : that could only be Angel Island, with those outspread Byzantine wings outlined in the sheer rock; this was Gorgon Island, with its head wreathed in green snakes; and next to it were the Truncated Sphere, the Anvil Incarnate, and Soft Island, so completely covered with guano and the excrement of pelicans that it looked like an insubstantial light-coloured mass being swept along by the current. From the Staircase of Candles, they moved on to the Headland-which-seems-to-be-watching; from the Newly-launched Galleon to the Fortress, crested with foam from the waves which were driven into channels too narrow for them and transformed into huge plumes as they broke upwards against the vertical headlands. After Frowning Rock came the Horse's Skull—with awful shadows for its eyes and nostrils—then the Ragged Islands, rocks so old, so poor, so humble, that they looked like beggars covered in rags alongside the other fresh, gleaming, eburneous islands, apparently thousands of years younger. From Temple-Cave, consecrated to the adoration of a diorite Triangle, they passed on to the Condemned Isle, disintegrated by the roots of the sea-fig trees, which had inserted their limbs in amongst the rocks—like ship's ropes, which swell more and more each year, until they finally bring about a collapse. Esteban marvelled when he realised that this Magic Gulf was like an earlier version of the Antilles, a blueprint which contained, in miniature, everything that could be seen on a larger scale in the Archipelago. There were volcanoes set down amongst the waves here too, but fifty seagulls were enough to provide them with a snowcap. There were Fat Virgins and Thin Virgins here also, but ten sea-fans, growing side by side, would have sufficed to span their bodies.

After sailing slowly forward for several hours, with the leadsman constantly on the alert, the brig found itself opposite a grey beach, bristling with posts, on which voluminous nets were hung out to dry. They could see a fishing village—seven houses thatched with leaves, with communal sheds to protect the boats—dominated by a watch-tower of pebbles, where a stubborn-looking sentinel was waiting for a shoal of fish to appear, his conch within reach. In the distance, on top of a spur, could be seen an embattled castle of sombre, cyclopean aspect, standing on a wall of violet-coloured rock. "Las Salinas de Araya", said the mate to Barthélémy, who gave orders to turn about, so as to escape from the proximity of that terrible fortress—the work of the Antonellis, Philip II's military architects—which had stood on guard for centuries over the Spanish exchequer. Picking its way between the reefs with all sails set, the ship left what they now knew to be the Gulf of Santa Fé.

XXVII

SEVERAL MONTHS PASSED in these same concerns and activities. Barthélémy, who always went after what was safe and boardable, without seeking to become the scourge of the seas, had a providential flair for finding the prizes that were best laden and worst defended. Apart from an ugly encounter with a Danish ship from Altona, whose crew defended themselves spiritedly, refusing to haul down their colours and sailing straight at the ships which stood in their path, the little squadron led a peaceful and prosperous life. Their clerk was not of the stuff of heroes, but spent much of his time absorbed in reading, and the rest jokingly invited him to hide himself in the hold each time they spotted a fishing dory.

But by now *L'Ami du Peuple* was showing signs of wear, from being kept in action continually, returning one day only to sail again the next—her Captain, stimulated by the sight of so many colleagues grown suddenly rich, had been possessed by the demon of gain. The slightest bad weather and the ship became feminine and complaining, heavy and sluggish. She creaked in every timber. The paint had swelled up in blisters on the masts and along the sides, and her gunwales showed dirty and battered. She had to go for repairs, which suddenly cast Esteban ashore, in a Guadeloupe whose changes he had had no chance of registering properly during the short stays he had been making there recently.

Pointe-à-Pitre was now certainly the richest town in America. It was hard to believe that even Mexico, of which so many wonderful things were told, with its goldsmiths and silversmiths, its mines at Taxco, and its vast spinning mills, had ever achieved a similar prosperity. Here gold glittered in the sun, in a reckless stream of *louis,* quadruples, British guineas, and Portuguese *"moëdas"*, stamped with the effigies of John V, Queen Mary and Pedro III; while for silver one could finger escudos worth six pounds, Philippine and Mexican piastres, and at least eight different coinages made of base metal, which had been notched, holed and milled to suit each person's convenience. The small shopkeepers of past days had been gripped by the fever, and had become outfitters to privateers, some on their own account, others associated in companies and partnerships. The old India Companies, with their coffers and jewel cases, were being revived here in this remote extremity of the Caribbean Sea, where the Revolution was making many people happy in a very real sense. The folios of the register of captures had been swelled by the inscription of five hundred and eighty ships, of all types and ports of embarkation, which had been boarded, sacked and towed back by the squadrons.

At such a time they felt little interest in what might be happening in France. Guadeloupe was self-sufficient, and was now viewed sympathetically and even enviously by some of the Spaniards on the Mainland, who received its propaganda through the Dutch possessions. And it was a prodigious sight to see the adventurers land after returning from some lucky foray. They disembarked from the ships and passed in a glittering cavalcade through the streets, brandishing samples of calico, green and orange muslins, Mazulipatan silks, Madras turbans, Manila shawls and whatever other precious materials they could find to flutter in the faces of the women. They wore an astonishing costume, which had now become established as local usage, and consisted of bare feet—or stockings worn without shoes—beneath a whole kaleidoscope of braided dress-coats, shirts trimmed with fur and ribbons at the collar, and as a crowning glory—this was a point of honour with them—a felt hat, its brim half turned down, adorned with feathers that had been dyed in the colours of the Republic. The negro Vulcan hid his leprosy beneath such finery that he looked like an emperor being led in triumph. The Englishman Joseph Murphy, mounted on stilts, clashed his cymbals together on a level with the balconies. And after they had landed from the ships, they all made their way to the Morne-à-Cail district, escorted by the huzzas of the crowd, where a disabled comrade had opened a café—*Au Rendez-vous des Sans-Culottes*—with a cage of toucans next to the bar, and walls covered with symbolic caricatures and obscene drawings done in charcoal. The festivities soon got going, and for two or three days there would be a wild spree with women and brandy, while the shipowners watched over the unloading of the cargo, appraising the goods as they appeared on the tables which had been placed beside the ships.

One evening Esteban was surprised to meet Victor Hugues in the café in the Morne-à-Cail, surrounded by ships' captains, all talking seriously—an unusual thing in this place. "Sit down and order, boy . . ." said the Agent of the Directory—he had been raised to this rank some time before—who, to judge by the speech he was making, in a voice over-eager to gain assent, had not got them all on his side. Emphasising details and figures, and quoting fragments of more or less official reports, he was accusing the North Americans of selling arms and ships to the English in the hope of driving France out of her American colonies, and of forgetting what the latter had done for them. "The very name of American," he vociferated, repeating what he had written in a recent propaganda sheet, "inspries only scorn and horror here. The Americans have become reactionary, the enemies of every ideal of liberty, after fooling the world with their Quaker play-acting. The United States are encased in a proud nationalism, hostile to anything that might challenge their authority. The same men who achieved independence are now denying everything which made them great. We shall have to remind this treacherous nation that but for us, who squandered our blood and our money to give them that independence, George Washington would have been hung as a traitor."

The Agent boasted of having written to the Directory urging them to declare war on the United States. But their replies had revealed a lamentable ignorance of realities, and been full of invitations to caution which had soon turned into cries of alarm and calls to order. It was the regular soldiers who were to blame, said Victor, like Pélardy, whom he had driven from the colony, after violent differences of opinion, for meddling in what did not concern him; now they were intriguing against him in Paris. He invoked the success of his own schemes, the clearing of the island, and its present prosperity. "As for me, I shall go on being hostile to the United States. The interests of France demand it," he concluded, with the aggressive firmness of a man who intends to silence any objections in advance.

It was obvious, thought Esteban, that this man, who until now had governed with absolute authority, was beginning to sense all around him the powerful presence of those whose importance had been enormously increased by success and wealth. Antonio Fuët, a sailor from Narbonne, to whom Victor had entrusted the command of a spanking new ship, with an American rig and mahogany gunwales sheathed in copper, had become a figure of epic stature, acclaimed by the crowds, after firing on a Portuguese ship with guns loaded with gold coins, for want of any other form of projectile. Later the surgeons from the *Sans-Pareil* had worked on the dead and wounded, and recovered the money embedded in their bodies and entrails with the points of their scalpels. And it was the same Antonio Fuët—now known as "Captain Moëda"—who had had the audacity to deny the Agent (as a civil and not a military authority) admittance to the club jokingly called the "Palais Royal", which the wealthy Captains had opened in a church, with gardens and out-buildings covering a whole block in the town.

Esteban was thunderstruck to learn that freemasonry had been reborn, and was both powerful and active amongst the privateers. They had a Lodge in the Palais Royal, where the Jachin and Boaz columns rose once more. After the short-lived interlude with the Supreme Being, they had reverted to the Great Architect, the Acacia and Hiram Abif's mallet. Captains Laffitte, Pierre Gros, Mathieu Goy, Christophe Chollet, the renegade Joseph Murphy, Peg-leg Langlois, and even a half-breed called Petréas-the-Mulatto officiated as masters and knights, true to a Tradition that had been restored through the zeal of the brothers Modesto and Antonio Fuët. So it was not the muskets with their sawn-off barrels, used for boarding the enemy, which sounded during the initiation ceremonies, but the noble ceremonial swords, wielded by hands which had probed the flesh of corpses to rescue coins blackened by too-adhesive blood.

"All this confusion," thought Esteban, "is because they regret the Crucifix. You can't be a bull-fighter or a privateer unless you have a Temple, where you can give thanks to Someone for taking the weight of your life on his shoulders. We shall soon be seeing ex-voto offerings to the Virgin of Perpetual Help." And he rejoiced inwardly when he realised that subterranean forces were beginning to undermine Victor Hugues' authority. That reverse process of the affections was working in him, which makes us long for the humiliation and downfall of people whom we used to admire, when they became too proud or arrogant. He looked towards the platform of the guillotine, still standing in its old position, and, to his own disgust, succumbed to the temptation of thinking that the Machine—it was less active now, and often left covered for weeks on end—was waiting for the Plenipotentiary. Such cases had occurred. "I'm a swine," he said to himself. "If I were a Christian I would go to confession."

A few days later there was a great hubbub in the harbour quarter, which was virtually the entire town. Captain Christophe Chollet, of whom nothing had been heard for two months, was returning with his men amid thunderous salvoes, followed by nine ships captured after a naval engagement off Barbados. They flew the flags of Spain, England and North America, and one of the last to come in carried the unusual cargo of an opera company, complete with musicians, scores and scenery. The troupe in question was that of Monsieur Faucompré, a powerful tenor, who had for years been taking Grétry's *Richard Coeur-de-Lion* from Cap Français to Havana, and from Havana to New Orleans, as part of a repertoire which also included *Zémire et Azor*, *La Serva Padrona*, *La Belle Arsène*, and other spectacular productions, often embellished with virtuoso stage-craft—magic mirrors and storm scenes. But now their plan to take the lyric art to Carácas and other American cities, where the smaller companies, whose travelling expenses were low, were beginning to realise great profits, had ended in Pointe-à-Pitre, a town without a theatre. But Monsieur Faucompré, a shrewd impresario as well as an artist, having heard of the colony's new-found wealth, was delighted to find himself there, after the alarming experience of being boarded, during which he had had the presence of mind to assist his compatriots by giving useful directions from the shelter of a hatchway. His company was French, he found himself now amongst Frenchmen, and the tenor, accustomed as he was to encouraging the Royalist settlers with the aria *"Oh, Richard! Oh, mon Roi!"*, now went over to the revolutionary camp, and gave "The Nation awakes" from the Rear-Admiral's quarter-deck, delighting the sailors with top notes which made the glasses ring in the officers' ward-room— so the steward declared.

With Faucompré there arrived Madame Villeneuve (whose versatile talents could be adapted, if need be, to the role of simple shepherdess as well as those of the Mother of the Gracchi, and the Luckless Queen) and Mesdemoiselles Montmousset and Jeandevert, both blonde and talkative, who excelled in anything light by Paisiello or Cimarosa.

The ships that had been captured in this bizarre engagement were soon forgotten when the company came ashore, the women ostentatiously dressed in the latest fashions—fashions still strange to Guadeloupe, where they knew little as yet about veiled hats, Greek sandals, or almost transparent tunics with waistlines directly below the bosom, which clung closely to the body and showed its contours off to good advantage. With them came trunks full of costumes as showy as they were sweat-stained; pillars and thrones were carried on shoulders, and the concert clavichord was taken to Government House in a mule cart, with all the care which might have been shown in moving the Ark of the Covenant. The Theatre had come to a town without theatres, and as a theatre would have to be created, they took advantage of a heaven-sent opportunity.

Since its platform would make a good stage, the guillotine was moved to a nearby yard, where it was taken over by hens, who roosted on top of the uprights. The boards were brushed and scrubbed to remove all traces of blood-stains, an awning was stretched between the trees, and rehearsals began of the work which was the most popular of their whole repertoire, as much because of its world-wide fame as because some of its couplets had provided a foretaste of the revolutionary spirit—*The Village Soothsayer*, by Jean-Jacques. Since the musicians whom Monsieur Faucompré had brought with him were few in number, it was agreed that they should be augmented by instrumentalists borrowed from the band of the Pyrenean Rifles. But, faced with the lack of science of men who insisted on playing their parts with gusto but five beats behind, the company's conductor chose to dispense with their services, and to entrust the accompaniment for the singers to a piano, a few wind instruments and the indispensable violins, whom Monsieur Anse had undertaken to train.

And so, one night, there was a gala performance in the Place de la Victoire. It was a formal occasion, and every revolutionary *noueau riche* in the colony turned out. When the lower orders had expanded to the boundaries of the space reserved for the upper classes—separated from the plebs by ropes sheathed in blue velvet, with red, white and blue knots—the Captains appeared, smothered with braid, medals, sashes and cockades, accompanied by their bedecked and bedizened *doudous,* glittering with good and indifferent jewellery, and displaying Mexican silver and Margarita pearls wherever it was possible to display them. Esteban arrived with a sparkling, transformed Mademoiselle Athalie Bajazet, flashing spangles, and stark naked under a Greek tunic in the very latest fashion.

Victor Hugues and his officials were in the front row, surrounded by solicitously chirping women, and being served with trays containing punch and wine; but they did not look round at the back rows where the mothers of the lucky concubines had been stowed—big, fat, heavy-breasted women, quite unfit to be seen, wearing dresses that were out of fashion and had been laboriously altered and let out to accommodate their luxuriant persons. Esteban noticed that Victor frowned when Antonio Fuët's arrival was greeted with an ovation, but the overture began at this moment, and Madame Villeneuve silenced the applause before launching into Colette's aria :

> *"J'ai perdu tout mon bonheur,*
> *J'ai perdu mon serviteur,*
> *Colin me délaisse . . ."*

The Soothsayer appeared, with a guttural Strasbourg accent, and the action continued, in the midst of general enjoyment, which remembered nothing of that other enjoyment aroused not long since in these same surroundings, by the novel mechanism of the guillotine. Quick to seize on any passing allusion, the audience managed to applaud all the verses expressing revolutionary sentiment, to which Colin, played by Monsieur Faucompré, eagerly drew attention by winks directed at the Agent of the Directory, the officials, the Captains, and their lady-friends. .

> *"Je vais revoir ma charmante maîtresse,*
> *Adieu châteaux, grandeur, richesse . . ."*

> *"Que de seigneurs d'importance*
> *Voudraient avoir sa foi;*
> *Malgré toute leur puissance*
> *Ils sont moins heureux que moi."*

There were shouts of enthusiasm when the Finale was reached, and it had to be repeated five times, to appease the insatiable demands of the audience :

> *"A la ville on fait bien plus de fracas*
> *Mais sont-ils aussi gais dans leurs ébats?*
> *Toujours contents,*
> *Toujours chantants,*
> *Beauté sans fard,*
> *Plaisir sans arts,*
> *Tous leurs concerts valent-ils nos musettes?"*

And for a grand finale there were revolutionary hymns, sung at the top of his voice by Monsieur Faucompré, dressed as a *sans-culotte,* followed by a great party in Government House, where toasts were drunk in the best vintage wines. Victor Hugues ignored the assiduous attentions of Madame Villeneuve, whose mature beauty was reminiscent of some luxurious Leda in a Flemish painting, and was engaged in an intimate conversation with a Martiniquan half-caste, Marie-Anne Angélique Jacquin, to whom he seemed to have become greatly attached, perhaps because, sensing himself to be surrounded by intrigue, he felt a need for some human warmth, which, as Mandatory, he would have liked to despise. To-night the man without friends was friendly towards everyone. When he passed behind Esteban, he laid his hand on his shoulder with a fatherly gesture. Shortly before daybreak, he retired to his bedroom, while

Modesto Fuët and the deputy Lebas—the Agent's confidant, thought by some, perhaps baselessly, to be a Directory spy— went off into the country in the company of the singers Montmousset and Jeandever.

The young clerk, who had drunk a great deal, returned through the dark streets to his inn, amused to watch how Mademoiselle Athalie Bajazet, after taking off her classical-style sandals, pulled her Greek tunic up to her thighs in order to wade through the puddles left by the previous day's rain. Finally, increasingly alarmed at the risk of being splashed with mud, she pulled the dress right up over her head, and left it rolled up on her shoulders. "It's hot to-night," she said, by way of an excuse, swatting the mosquitoes which were attacking her buttocks. Behind them sounded the hammers of the men who were finishing dismantling the scenery of the opera.

XXVIII

ON THE 7th of July 1798—there were certain events for which the chronology of the Revolutionary calendar was not adequate —the United States declared war on France in American waters. The news resounded through all the Chancellories of Europe like a thunder-clap. But for a long time the prosperous, voluptuous, blood-stained island of Our Lady of Guadalupe knew nothing of an item of news which had to cross the Atlantic twice in order to reach it. Everyone went about his own affairs, complaining daily of a summer which had proved particularly hot that year. A herd of cattle died from an epidemic; there was an eclipse of the moon; the band of the Pyrenean Rifles beat retreat; fires broke out in the countryside because the sun had dried up the esparto.

Victor Hugues knew that the vindictive General Pélardy was doing all he could to discredit him with the Directory, but the Agent, whose earlier anxiety had faded, considered that he was irreplaceable in his present situation. "As long as I can continue to send these gentlemen their ration of gold, they'll leave me alone," he said. The gossips of Pointe-à-Pitre claimed that his personal fortune amounted to more than a million pounds. There was talk of a possible marriage with Marie-Anne Angélique Jacquin.

It was at this point that, urged on by an increasing appetite for money, he formed an agency by which he ensured for himself control of the property of the *émigrés*, the public finances, the equipment of the privateers, and a monopoly of the customs dues. Great was the storm which this move provoked, since it directly affected a large number of people who had profited from his régime up till now. The arbitrariness of the step received so much adverse criticism in the streets and public squares that the guillotine had to be brought out into the open once more, and a fresh, though brief, reign of terror instituted, as a timely warning. The *nouveaux riches*, the favourites, dishonest officials and usufructuaries of property abandoned by its owners, all had to swallow their protests. Behemoth had become a business-man, surrounded by balances, weights and measures, which were constantly in use evaluating the wealth swallowed up by his warehouses. When they learned that the United States had declared war, the same men who had been plundering North American schooners now threw the blame on Victor Hugues for what they saw as a disaster whose consequences might prove catastrophic for the colony. Since the news had been a long time in reaching them, it was very possible that the island was already surrounded by hostile ships and might be attacked to-day, that very evening, or to-morrow. There was talk of a powerful fleet having left Boston, of troops having landed in Basse-Terre, of an imminent blockade.

Such was the atmosphere of apprehension and alarm, when, one evening, the carriage which Victor Hugues used for his excursions into the surrounding country-side stopped outside the Loeuillets' printing office, where Esteban was at work correcting proofs. "Leave that," the Agent shouted through a window, "and come with me to Le Gosier."

During the journey they talked of trivialities. When they reached the cove the Agent made the young man get into a boat and then, taking off his frock-coat, rowed out to the island. There he stretched himself full length on the beach, uncorked a bottle of English cider, and began to talk in measured tones. "They're throwing me out, that's the only way of putting it, they're throwing me out. The gentlemen of the Directory want me to go to Paris and give them an account of my administration. And that's not all: some boot-licking General Desfourneaux is coming out to replace me, while that scum of a Pélardy is going to return in triumph as Commander-in-Chief of the Armed Forces."

He lay back on the sand, and looked up at the sky, which was already growing dark: "All they're waiting for now is for me to hand over the power. But some of the men are still on my side."

"Are you going to declare war on France?" asked Esteban, who considered Victor capable of any effrontery after what had happened with the United States.

"On France, no. But on its swinish government, maybe yes."

There was a long silence, during which the young man wondered why the Agent, who was so little given to confidences, should have chosen him as the recipient of a piece of news still generally unknown—and a piece of news so catastrophic for a man who had not yet experienced a single serious reverse in his whole career.

Victor's voice was heard again: "There's no reason why you should stay in Guadeloupe. I'll give you a safe-conduct for Cayenne. From there you can get to Paramaribo. There are Spanish and North American ships there—you'll be all right on one of them."

Esteban contained his delight, afraid of falling into a trap, as had happened once before. But this time everything was above board. The defeated man explained that for a long time he had been helping more than one exile in Sinnamary and Kourou, by sending them money, medicine and provisions. Esteban knew that some of the most important protagonists of the Revolution had been confined in Guiana, but he knew it only in a vague and general way, because in many cases names quoted as those of "deportees" had later appeared signing articles in the Paris newspapers. He knew nothing of the fate of Collot d'Herbois in America; he had heard that Billaud-Varenne was raising parrots somewhere near Cayenne.

"I've just found out that that swinish Directory have forbidden anything to be sent to Billaud from France. They want him to die of hunger and misery," said Victor.

"Wasn't Billaud one of the ones who betrayed the Incorruptible?" asked Esteban.

The other man rolled up his sleeve and scratched the red rash on his forearm: "This isn't the time to criticise a man who was a great revolutionary. Billaud made mistakes, but they were the mistakes of a patriot. I'm not going to let them starve him to death."

Nevertheless, in his present circumstances, it did not suit him to be looked on as the protector of this member of the Committee of Public Safety. What he asked from the young man, in exchange for his liberty, was that he should embark next day on *La Vénus de Médicis*, a schooner bound for Cayenne with a cargo of wine and flour, and convey a large sum of money to this unfortunate friend. "Be careful with Jeannet, the Agent of the Directory there. He's morbidly jealous of me. He tries to copy me in everything, but he's just a caricature. A cretin. I was on the point of declaring war on him."

Esteban noticed that although Victor still looked healthy, he had an unpleasant yellow tinge to his skin, and his stomach protruded too far under his carelessly buttoned shirt.

"Well, *petiot*," he said with sudden kindness. "I'll put this Desfourneaux in prison the moment he arrives, then we'll see what happens. For you the great adventure is over. You can go back home, to your father's warehouse. It's a good business; look after it. I don't know what conclusions you'll come to about me, that I'm a monster perhaps. But remember that there are times when it's no use being soft."

He picked up some sand and poured it from one hand to another, as if they had been the bulbs of an hour-glass. "The Revolution is breaking up. I've got nothing left to cling to. I don't believe in anything."

Darkness was falling. They returned across the bay, got into the carriage, and went back to Government House. Victor picked up some envelopes, and some sealed packages: "This is the safe-conduct, and some money for you. This is for Billaud. This letter is for Sofia. *Bon voyage . . . émigré.*"

Esteban embraced the Agent with sudden affection. "Why did you get mixed up in politics?" he asked, recalling the days before Victor had bartered his freedom for the exercise of an authority which had in the end become a tragic servitude.

"Maybe because I was born a baker," said Victor. "Probably if the blacks hadn't burned my bakery that night, the United States Congress wouldn't have met to declare war on France. If Cleopatra's nose . . . Who said that?"

When he found himself in the street once more, on the way back to his inn, Esteban had that feeling of living in the future which the proximity of some great change induces. He felt curiously detached from his environment. All these familiar and habitual things were growing remote from his real existence. He stopped in front of the Privateers' Lodge, knowing that he was seeing it for the last time.

He entered a tavern in order to take leave of his life in this town, alone, over a glass of brandy laced with lemon and nutmeg. The counter, the barrels, the chatter of the mulatta serving-women belonged to the past. The links were being snapped. This tropical region of which he had been a part for so long began to seem exotic once more. In the Place de la Victoire, Monsieur Anse's assistants were busy dismantling the guillotine. The Machine had concluded its fearful task in the island. The gleaming steel triangle, which the Plenipotentiary had suspended between its uprights, was returned to its box. The Narrow Gate was taken down, through which so many men had passed out of the daylight into that darkness whence there is no return. The Instrument, the only one to have reached America as the secular arm of Liberty, would now gather rust amongst the scrap metal in some warehouse. On the eve of staking his all, Victor Hugues was spiriting away the contrivance which he himself had elevated into a primordial necessity, along with the printing-press and the guns, preferring to die himself, perhaps, in such a way that he could contemplate his own death with the utmost pride.

CHAPTER FOUR

XXIX

Las camas de la muerte
—*Goya*

When he was tired of wandering from the Porte de Remire to the Place d'Armes, and from the Rue du Port to the Porte de Remire, Esteban sat down on a post at a street corner; he felt discouraged by what he had seen and had the impression that he had plunged into the lunatic asylum in the "Rake's Progress". Everything in this island city of Cayenne seemed improbable, disjointed, out of place. One thing he had been told on board *La Vénus de Médicis* was true. The nuns of Saint-Paul-de-Chartres, who were in charge of the hospital, went about the streets in the habits of their order, as if nothing had happened in France, and ministered to the health of revolutionaries who could not have dispensed with their services. The grenadiers—he wondered why—were all Alsatians, with doughy voices, who had failed so completely to adapt themselves to the climate that their faces were covered in large eruptions and boils the whole year round. Several negroes, now supposedly free, were exposed on a platform with their ankles fettered to an iron bar, as a punishment for laziness. Although there was a leper colony on the island of Le Malingre, many moribund sufferers wandered about as they liked, displaying their nightmarish afflictions to procure alms. The coloured militia was a sample-book of rags; the people looked somehow oily; all the whites of any standing seemed bad-tempered.

Having grown accustomed to the graceful costumes of the Guadeloupan women, Esteban was continually amazed by the shamelessness of the black women here, who went about everywhere naked from the waist up—an unattractive sight in the case of the old women, whose cheeks puffed out as they chewed their tobacco. And there was a new element here too: wild-looking Indians, who came to the town in their *piraguas,* to sell guavas, medicinal lianas, orchids and culinary herbs. Some brought their women-folk, in order to hire out their bodies in the moat of the fort, the shadows of the powder magazine, or behind the cloistered church of Saint-Sauveur. One saw faces that had been tattooed or daubed with extraordinary colours. Yet the oddest thing of all was that, despite a sun which got into one's eyes and heightened the exotic quality of the scene, this multi-coloured world, picturesque enough to look at, was in reality a sad, exhausted world, where everything seemed to have been toned down to the sombre shades of an etching. A Tree of Liberty, planted opposite the ugly, peeling building which served as Government House, had withered for want of irrigation. A Political Club, founded by the Colony's officials, had been installed in a large house of many corridors; but they lacked the energy these days to keep up the speech-making of the past, and the place had been turned into a permanent gaming-house, where the cards were dealt under a fly-blown portrait of the Incorruptible, which no one could be bothered to take down, even at the Agent of the Directory's request, because the corners of the frame were nailed firmly to the wall.

Those who enjoyed property or an administrative sinecure had no other distractions apart from eating and drinking, and met at interminable blow-outs, which began at mid-day and continued into the night. But everywhere one missed the animation, the rainbow skirts and the new fashions which had so enlivened the streets of Point-à-Pitre. The men wore striped suits inherited from the *ancien régime,* and sweated so profusely in their thick coats that their backs and armpits were always soaking wet. Their wives wore skirts and dresses just like those of the chorus of village women in a Paris opera. There was not a single attractive house, an amusing tavern, or a place to stay. Everything was mediocre and uniform. Where it looked as though there had once been a Botanical Garden, all that could be seen now was a stinking shrubbery, rubbish-dump and public urinal, where mangy dogs scavenged.

Looking over towards the Mainland one became aware of the closeness of a dense, hostile vegetation, far more impassable than the walls of a prison. Esteban felt a sort of dizziness when he realised that the forest which began there was the same one which extended, unbroken and unrelieved, right to the banks of the Orinoco and the Amazon; to Spanish Venezuela; to the Laguna de Parima; to far-off Peru. Everything that had seemed friendly in tropical Guadeloupe, became aggressive, inpenetrable, matted and hard here, with these overgrown trees which devoured each other, were imprisoned by lianas and eaten away by parasites. For someone who had come from places with such pretty names as Lamentin, Le Moule or Pigeon, there was something unpleasant and corrosive about the very sound of Maroni, Oyapoc and Approuague, which suggested swamps, a brutal fecundity, an implacable proliferation.

Esteban went with the officers from *La Vénus de Médicis* to pay his respects to Jeannet, and handed over Victor Hugues' letter, which was read with an almost ostentatious reluctance. The Directory's Private Agent in Guiana—to look at him one would never have believed that he was Danton's cousin—was a repulsive figure, with his greenish complexion, caused by a liver complaint, and his lack of a left arm, which had had to be amputated as the result of a bite from a wild boar. Esteban learned that Billaud-Varenne had been banished to Sinnamary and, like the majority of the French deportees—many of them confined in Kourou or Counamama—was forbidden to enter the town. There, said Jeannet, they had abundant arable land, and everything they needed to pay the full penalties imposed on them by various Revolutionary governments.

"Are there many refractory priests?" asked Esteban.

"There are all sorts," replied the Agent with studied indifference: "Deputies, *émigrés*, journalists, magistrates, scholars, poets, French priests and Belgian priests."

Esteban did not think the time ripe to show curiosity as to the exact whereabouts of particular people. The Captain of *La Vénus de Médicis* had advised him to get the money to Billaud-Varenne through intermediaries, and it was in the hopes of achieving this that he took a room in the hotel of a certain Hauguard, the best in Cayenne, where one could get good wine and a passable meal.

"We haven't had the guillotine here," said Hauguard, as the negresses, Angesse and Scholastique, collected up the plates and went out for a bottle of rum. "But our fate may be even worse, because it's better to die by one clean stroke than bit by bit." And he explained to Esteban what was to be understood by the "arable land", which Jeannet had made out to be the saving of the deportees. It might be possible in Sinnamary, where Billaud was, to eke out a miserable existence, somewhat mitigated by the presence near by of a sugar plantation and a few quite prosperous haciendas; but the very names of Kourou, Couamama and Iracoubo were synonymous with a lingering death. Confined in areas which had been arbitrarily chosen, and unauthorized to move from them, the exiles were herded nine or ten at a time into filthy huts, the healthy and the sick together as in prison ships, on land that was liable to flood and unsuited to any form of cultivation. They were hungry and penniless, and deprived of even the most indispensable medicines unless some doctor, sent on an official tour of inspection by the Agent of the Directory, gave them some brandy as a sort of sovereign and solitary panacea. "They call it the dry guillotine," said Hauguard.

"Miserable enough, certainly," said Esteban. "But a lot of killers from Lyons, public prosecutors and political assassins have been sent here, people who used to arrange the guillotined bodies in obscene positions at the foot of the scaffold."

"The righteous and the sinners are mixed up together," said Hauguard, fanning away the flies.

The young man was on the point of asking about Billaud, when a tattered old man approached the table in a nimbus of brandy fumes, shouting that whatever calamities assailed the French it was no more than they deserved. "Leave the gentleman alone," said the inn-keeper, showing a certain amount of respect to the corpulent old man, whose appearance, for all its penury, did not lack a certain majesty.

"We were like Biblical patriarchs, surrounded by our progeny and our flocks, masters of granaries and threshing floors," said the intruder, with an archaic, rather ponderous and halting accent, which Esteban was hearing for the first time. "Ours were the lands of Pré-des-Bourques, Pont-à-Buot, Port Royal, and many more which were unequalled anywhere in the world, because our piety—our great piety—had brought down the blessing of God upon them."

He slowly crossed himself, with a movement that was so unusual in these times that Esteban found it the height of originality.

"We were the dwellers in Acadia, the Nova Scotians, such faithful subjects of the French King that for forty whole years we refused to sign an infamous document by which we were to recognise as our Sovereigns the fat cow Anne Stuart, and a certain King George whom the Evil One will receive in his fiery mansions. And this was why the Great Disturbance came upon us. One day the English soldiers drove us from our houses, took our horses and our cattle, plundered our coffers, and deported us to Boston or, what was worse, to South Carolina or Virginia, where we were worse treated than the negroes. And in spite of our wretchedness, and the animosity of the Protestants, and the odium of all those who watched us walking the streets like beggars, we continued to give praise to our lords : to Him who reigns in Heaven, and to him who reigns on earth, son succeeding father. And since Acadia could never again be what it had been when our tillage was blessed by the Most High, we were offered restitution of our lands and our granaries a hundred times, in exchange for our submission to the British Crown. And we refused a hundred times, sir. Finally, after having been decimated, after scratching ourselves with Job's potsherd and sitting amongst the ashes, we were rescued by the navies of France. And we arrived in our distant country, sir, assured of salvation. But they scattered us on the unproductive lands, and would not heed our complaints. And we said : 'The blame does not lie with the good King, who is perhaps ignorant of our present misery, and cannot imagine what our fathers' Acadia was like.' And some, like myself, were brought here to Guiana, where the soil speaks an unknown tongue. Men of the spruce tree and the maple, of the holm oak and the birch, we found ourselves here, where nothing germinates or puts forth but malign growths, where the day's ploughing is undone in the night by the agency of the Devil. Here, sir, the Devil's presence is manifested in the impossibility of establishing order. What is made to be straight becomes curved, what should be curved becomes straight. After the thaws of spring, the sun, which was life and joy in our Acadia, became a curse on the banks of the Maroni. What served there to fatten the ears of corn, here became the scourge which chokes and corrupts the ears of corn. But still I had my pride at not having abjured my loyalty to the King of France. I was amongst Frenchmen, who at least looked on me with respect as having belonged to a people that had been free like no other, and which had nevertheless chosen ruin, exile and death rather than fail in their loyalty . . . Ours, sir, were the lands of Pré-des-Bourques, Pont-à-Buot and Grand Pré. And then one day it was you Frenchmen (and the drunkard hammered the table with gnarled fists), who dared to behead our King, and brought to pass the second Great Disturbance, that was to strip us of our dignity and our honour. I found myself treated as a 'suspect', as an enemy of I know not what, as being against I know not what, I, a man of more than sixty summers, suffering because I did not want to be anything but French; I, who lost my inheritance, and watched my wife die, rent asunder in childbirth, in the hold of a prison ship, because I would not deny my country or my faith. The only Frenchmen left in the world, sir, are the Acadians. The rest have become anarchists, obeying neither God nor man, who think only of becoming like the Lapps, Moors and Tartars."

The old man reached for a bottle of rum and, pouring an enormous measure down his throat, went over and collapsed on to a pile of sacks of flour, where he went to sleep face downwards, muttering about the trees which would not grow in this country.

"They were great Frenchmen, certainly," said Hauguard. "The trouble is they've survived into an age which is not theirs. They're like people from another world."

And Esteban thought how absurd it was that these Acadians, convinced of the immutable grandeur of a régime which they saw as all pomp, allegory, imagery and symbols should, here in Guiana, have fallen in with other men who had immediately recognised the weaknesses of this same régime and devoted their lives to the task of destroying it. Distance had its martyrs, who would never understand those who were martyred for being too close. Men who had never looked on a Throne conceived of it as monumental and flawless. Those who had seen one with their own eyes knew how fissured and tarnished it was.

"What will the angels in Heaven think?" said Esteban, a question which must have seemed to reach the height of incoherence to Hauguard.

"That you are a solemn young fellow," replied the other, laughing. "Although in the last days of his life Collot d'Herbois did nothing but implore their help."

And Esteban then learned of the lamentable end of the killer from Lyons. On arriving in Cayenne, he had been lodged with Billaud in the nuns' hospital, and by a cruel chance had occupied a cell called the "Room of Saint Louis"—he, who had demanded that the last Louis should be condemned immediately, without formalities. From the start he had given himself up to wild drinking bouts, scribbling down, in the taverns, disconnected fragments of a True History of the Revolution. On nights when he was drunk, he wept over his misfortunes and his loneliness in this hellish place, with histrionic gesticulations and outbursts which infuriated the austere Billaud : "You're not on the stage," he shouted at him. "You might at least preserve your dignity and remember that you've done your duty, like me."

The backwash from the Thermidorian reaction arrived belatedly in the colony, and excited the negroes against the former members of the Committee of Public Safety. They could not venture into the streets without being subjected to jeers and insults. "If I had to begin over again," Billaud would say between his teeth, "I wouldn't waste freedom on men who don't know at what cost it was achieved. I would revoke the Decree of the 16th Pluviose of the Year Two." (Bringing it to America had been Victor's proudest hour, thought Esteban.)

Jeannet made Collot leave the town, and confined him in Kourou. There, far gone in drink, the Good Father Gerard wandered about the streets, his coat torn and his pockets full of dirty sheets of paper, imploring passers-by for help, tumbling into ditches to sleep, and starting quarrels in the taverns which denied him credit. One night, thinking perhaps that it was brandy, he drank a bottle of medicine. He was sent to Cayenne by a medical officer in a half-poisoned condition. But the negroes responsible for his transfer abandoned him by the roadside, saying that he had murdered God and men. Prostrated by sunstroke, he was finally taken to the nuns' hospital of Saint-Paul-de-Chartres, where for the second time he chanced to be put into the "Room of Saint Louis". He began to shout and invoke God and the Virgin, imploring forgiveness for his sins. Such was the din that an Alsatian guard, infuriated by this belated repentance, reminded him that a month before he had still been ready to blaspheme against the holy name of the Mother of God, and had said moreover that the story of Saint Odile was pure humbug, invented to degrade the masses. But now, convulsed with sobs, Collot asked for a confessor, immediately, as soon as possible, groaning that his bowels were on fire, that the fever was devouring him, that there could no longer be any salvation for him. Finally he fell to the ground, where he lay in a pool of vomited blood. Jeannet learned of his death while he was playing billiards with some officials. "Let them bury him. He doesn't deserve any more honours than a dog," he said, without even letting go of his cue, which was lined up for an easy cannon.

But on the day of the burial a joyful rolling of drums filled the city. Well aware that something had changed in France, the negroes had the belated idea of celebrating their Carnival of the Epiphany, which had lapsed during the years of official atheism. From early morning they had been dressing up as African kings and queens, as devils, wizards, generals and clowns, and pouring into the streets with gourds, timbrels and anything else which could be beaten or rattled in honour of Melchior, Caspar and Balthazar. The grave-diggers, their feet tapping impatiently in time to the distant music, hollowed out a narrow grave as fast as they could, and pushed the cracked coffin into it with its lid half-unfastened.

At mid-day, when dancing was going on everywhere, several lead-coloured, hairless, long-eared pigs appeared, of the variety which have pointed snouts and are always hungry. Inserting their noses into the grave, they found some good meat behind the wood, which had already collapsed under the weight of earth. And the abominable rout began to stir, prod and poke at the body in their greed. One of them carried off a hand, and devoured it with a sound like the crunching of acorns. Others vented their fury on the face, the neck and the loins. The vultures, already waiting, perched on the mud walls of the cemetery, would take care of the rest. Thus the story of Jean-Marie Collot d'Herbois ended, beneath the Guianese sun.

"A fitting death for carrion like him," said the old Acadian, who had been listening to the end of the story, sitting on a sack of flour and scratching his sores.

XXX

A FEW DAYS were sufficient for Esteban to realise that Victor Hugues had been over-optimistic in telling him that to get from Cayenne to Paramaribo would be a simple matter at a time like this. Jeannet, jealous of the prosperity of Guadeloupe, also had his privateers: rapacious young skippers, with none of the presence or stature of Antonio Fuët, who fell on all strayed and solitary ships, thus justifying the epithet of "Brigands' War" which the Americans were now bestowing on the French naval operations in the Caribbean. In order to provide himself with money, Jeannet sold what these men brought him for any price at all in Surinam. For this reason he only gave safe conducts to land on Dutch soil to men whom he trusted or to his business associates. He excused his strictness on this point by stating that in this way he avoided deportees escaping—some had got away a few months before, thanks to the connivance of some enemy of the régime.

New faces were not welcome in Cayenne. Any stranger was immediately seen as a possible Directory spy. If Esteban had not attracted much attention it was because he was taken to be merely another member of the crew of *La Vénus de Médicis,* which remained at anchor, awaiting a cargo. But the day must come when she would sail, and with it the inevitable return to Pointe-à-Pitre, where a civil war might have flared up, or where the inquisitorial machinery of the White Terror might have been set in motion. The mere thought gave the young man a sinking feeling. His pulse gave a dull thump, and something seemed to fall inside his chest, leaving him unable to breathe. He was incapable of sleeping right through the night. He would wake up shortly after going to bed, with the sensation that everything was pressing down on him; the walls were there to fence him in, the low ceiling to rarefy the air he breathed; the house was a dungeon, the island a prison, the sea and the jungle were walls of an immeasurable thickness. The light of dawn brought him a certain relief. He got up full of hope, thinking that to-day something would happen, some unforeseen event would open the way for him. But as a day without incident passed he was invaded by a despondency which by dusk had deprived him of all hope and strength. He collapsed on to his bed, remaining so still—turned to stone and incapable of making a movement, as if his body were immensely heavy—that the negress Angesse, thinking that he was suffering from an attack of intermittent fever, poured spoonfuls of a quinine mixture into his mouth to revive him. Then he would be overcome by the terror of being alone, and go down to the dining-room of the hotel, begging anyone at all to keep him company—Hauguard, some jovial drinker, the Acadian with his Biblical recollections—so that he might stupefy himself with talking.

At this juncture it was learned that Jeannet had been dismissed by the Directory in favour of a new Agent, Burnel, who, it was rumoured, thought very highly of Billaud-Varenne. This news was received with alarm by the functionaries of the colony. Afraid that the prisoners in Sinnamary would denounce the ill-treatment and depredations they had suffered, they sent medicine and supplies to the more active and influential amongst them, whose accusations might come to the ears of the new Mandatory. And an odd situation arose, in which the last Jacobins, who had been persecuted in France, were able to raise their heads in America, where they were inexplicably favoured with power and official positions.

An active traffic was suddenly established between Cayenne, Kourou and Sinnamary, and Esteban thought he might take the opportunity of using it to dispose of the packets and letters entrusted to him by Victor Hugues. There was nothing to prevent him destroying the contents of the packages, which were sewn up in canvas, or purloining the valuables from the locked and sealed boxes which formed the rest of his charge. In this way he would be rid of a burden which was bound to be compromising at a time when a police search was a distinct possibility, nor would he have to account for this heinous act—less heinous now that the situation of the Most Important Exile had changed. Moreover, Billaud-Varenne was a person who inspired a strong aversion in him.

But as a result of frequenting revolutionary circles Esteban had become supremely superstitious. He believed that to boast about one's health or happiness was to court illness or misfortune. He believed that fate was always hard on those who showed too much confidence in their luck. And he believed above all that the non-fulfilment of an obligation, or, in some cases, the mere fact of someone's not exerting himself to help an unfortunate, could produce a paralysis of the forces or influences favourable to that person, who had been convicted of egoism or neglect by some unknown power that weighs up our actions.

When he realised that he could never have found a way, however far-fetched, of reaching Paramaribo, he thought that circumstances might favour him again if he took steps to carry out Victor Hugues' commission. For lack of any other confidant, he unburdened himself to Hauguard, a man accustomed to finding himself in this position with all sorts of different people, and who moved between his saucepans and his black women without ever losing any sleep over politics. From him he learned that whereas Collot d'Herbois had been the object of general contempt because of his alcoholism, his histrionic weeping, and his cowardice at the end, Billaud knew himself to be surrounded by hatred; and although this was far from intimidating him, it had the effect of arousing a pride which astonished the very men who had suffered the rigours of deportation because of some indirect or forgotten order he himself had given. Among so many who were disheartened and repentant, enfeebled and embittered, the ruthless man of old seemed to be hewn from solid rock, and refused to weaken on account of isolation or solitude, declaring that if History were to take a leap backwards and set him down once more face to face with the contingencies he had lived through, he would act exactly as before. True, he raised parrots and cockatoos, but that was so that he could say sarcastically that his birds, like nations, repeated everything you felt inclined to teach them.

Esteban would have liked to get out of travelling to Sinnamary, and to consign what he was looking after to some trustworthy person of the inn-keeper's acquaintance. To his great surprise Hauguard advised him to go and speak to the Mother Superior of the nuns of Saint-Paul-de-Chartres, whom Billaud esteemed very highly, and had addressed as "most worthy sister" ever since she had attended him during a grave illness contracted shortly after his arrival in the colony.

The following day the young man was shown into a narrow room in the hospital, where he stopped, astonished, in front of a huge crucifix, hanging opposite a window which opened on to the sea. Between four white-washed walls, in a room whose only furniture was two stools, one made of shaggy hide, the other of horse-hair—one from the Ox, the other from the Ass—the dialogue between the Ocean and the Figure took on a sustained, everlasting pathos, outside of time or place. Everything that could be said about Man and his World, all that might be contained in the notions of Light, Birth and Darkness, was said —said for all eternity—in what passed between the stark geometry of the black wood and the fluid immensity of the universal womb, through that intermediary body at the crucial hour of his death and rebirth.

It was so long since Esteban had confronted a Christ that he had the impression of committing an act of fraudulent intimacy as he looked at him now, standing very close, like someone meeting an old acquaintance who had returned without permission from the authorities to the common fatherland from which he had been exiled. This individual had for a time been the witness and the confidant of his childhood; he was still present above every bed in the far-off family house, where he would be awaiting the return of the Wanderer.

And then he remembered so many things with which they were both familiar. Words were not lacking in which to talk about a certain flight into Egypt and a famous night in a stable, with all the Kings and Shepherds (and now I remember the musical-box with its shepherdesses, brought to my room by those Kings one Epiphany which was particularly melancholy because I was ill); and the merchants selling trinkets at the doors of the temple; and the fishermen by the lake (I always imagined them like the tattered, bearded men who sold fresh squid in my city); and the storms that were stilled, and the green palms of a certain Sunday (Sofia used to bring me the ones the Clares gave her; they were soft and bitter, made from king-palm leaves, and they stayed moist for several days, plaited round the iron bars of my bed); and the great trial too, and the sentence, and the fixing of the nails. "How long could I have borne it?" Esteban used to ask himself as a child, thinking that a few nails piercing the centre of one's hands could not have hurt so very much. And he had tried a hundred times, driving in a pencil, a needle, the spout of an oil-can, forcing them in without overmuch pain. With the feet the ordeal would be worse no doubt, because of their thickness. Nevertheless it was possible that crucifixion was not the worst torture which man had invented. But the Cross was an Anchor and a Tree, and it was necessary that the Son of God should suffer his agony on the shape which symbolised both Earth and Water—the wood and the sea, whose eternal dialogue Esteban had surprised that morning in the narrow room of the hospital.

Aroused from these timeless reflections by the blast of a bugle sounding from the top of the fortress, it suddenly occurred to him that the weakness of a revolution which had so stunned the world with the clamour of a new *Dies Irae* lay in its lack of convincing gods. The Supreme Being was a god without a past. No Moses had arisen of sufficient stature to hear the words in the Burning Bush, nor to arrange a treaty between the Eternal and the Chosen People. He had not been made flesh, nor had he lived among us. There was nothing sacramental about the ceremonies celebrated in his honour; the singleness of purpose was lacking, the steadfastness in the face of the contingent and immediate, whose curve had been plotted through the centuries by the stoned man in Jerusalem, and the forty legionaries of Sebastes; by Sebastian the Archer, Irenaeus the Pastor, the Doctors Augustine, Anselm and Thomas; together with Felipe de Jesús, the modern martyr of the Philippines, in whose honour several sanctuaries in Mexico had been adorned with Chinese Christs, made of sugar-cane fibre, with such a fleshy texture that

223

the hand recoiled when it touched them, under the illusion that life still throbbed in the spear-wound in their sides—no other spear had ever been reddened in such a way. As an unbeliever, Esteban had no need to pray, but he was enjoying the company of the Crucified, and he felt that he had been restored to a familiar atmosphere. This God belonged to him by hereditary right; he could reject him or not, but in either case he formed part of the patrimony of his race. "Good morning," he said to him amiably, in a low voice.

"Good morning," answered the calm voice of the Mother Superior behind him. Without further preamble, Esteban explained the object of his visit.

"Go to Surinam as our emissary," the nun said to him, "and find the Abbé Brottier. You can trust him with your commission, he is the only sure friend Monsieur Billaud-Varenne has in this colony."

"Very odd things happen here," thought Esteban, "there's no question about that."

XXXI

As a result of the deportations, Sinnamary had certainly become a very strange place, with something unreal and fantastic about it, for all the sordid reality of its poverty and purulence. It was a sort of Ancient State, set amidst vegetation which belonged to the world's beginnings, ravaged by pestilence and constantly traversed by burial parties; the men here—Hogarthian figures—lived out a perpetual caricature of their duties and functions. There were the Priests with their once forbidden missals again in evidence, celebrating Mass now in the Cathedral of the Forest—the Indian community's house, whose common hall had the look of a Gothic nave, with its soaring rafters supporting a tall roof of palm fronds. There were the Deputies, still divided, argumentative, schismatic, invoking History and quoting classical texts; their Forum was the back-yard of an inn, surrounded by pens where the pigs stuck their snouts through the railings when the discussions got too heated. The Army was there, represented by the incredible Pichegru—Pichegru was a character whom Esteban could not manage to integrate into the Guianese scene—who gave orders to an army of phantoms, forgetting that an ocean lay between him and his soldiers.

And there in the midst of them all, taciturn and abhorred like one of the Atrides, was the former Tyrant, whom no one would speak to, but who was deaf, unmindful, indifferent, to the hatred which his presence provoked. Children paused when the ex-President of the Jacobins, the ex-President of the Convention, the ex-member of the Committee of Public Safety, went by, the man who had approved the killings in Lyons, Nantes and Arras, who had signed the Laws of Prairial, who had advised Fouquier-Tinville, who had not hesitated to demand the deaths of Saint-Just, Couthon and Robespierre himself, having already pushed Danton towards the scaffold—all of which meant little to the negroes in Cayenne, however, compared with his matricide, for that was what, in fact, the beheading of the Queen of such a vast place as Europe had signified for them. And oddly enough these tragic events, enacted on the greatest stage in the world, conferred a sort of chilling majesty on Billaud-Varenne—a power of fascination over those who hated him most.

While others who might have been held to be his accomplices shunned him ostentatiously, he would be visited, on the oddest pretexts, by a ragged Breton priest, a former Girondin, a landowner ruined by the freeing of the slaves, or a subtle abbé with encyclopaedist leanings—like this Brottier, at whose door Esteban was now knocking, after a tedious voyage in a schooner along a low-lying coast covered with swamps and mangrove plantations. The man who came out to receive him was a Swiss planter called Sieger, with the scarlet nose of a white-wine drinker. He was waiting for the Abbé : "He's attending to some of the dying," he said. "Just when that swine Jeannet decides to send them medicine, chick-peas and anise, the exiles start kicking the bucket at the rate of ten or twelve a day. When Burnel gets here it'll be nothing but a huge cemetery, as Iracoubo is already."

Esteban then learned that Billaud was so confident of the new Agent of the Directory's protection that he was already preparing to occupy an important post in the colony, and was drawing up—in anticipation—a programme of administrative reforms. Frowning and imperturbable, this Orestes would pace the confines of Sinnamary in the gathering dusk, preserving a sartorial correctness which contrasted strangely with the growing neglect of the other exiles, whose months of suffering could have been reckoned up at sight, simply from the degree of slovenliness or penury in their dress.

Recent arrivals wore their dignity like a suit of armour, and were made into giants by their clothes, in this world of bent and naked beings. Surrounded by a vanquished and supplicant crowd, the Magistrate held his head high, and promised that they would soon be seeing him in Paris, confounding and chastising his enemies; the disgraced Army Commander, resplendent in his gold braid, talked about "his" officers, "his" infantry, "his" guns. The man who had ceased to be People's Representative once and for all still saw himself as such; the forgotten Author, whom even his relations thought to be dead, composed satirical plays and hymns of hate. All of them took to writing Memoirs, Apologias, Histories of the Revolution, and countless Theories of the State, whose sheets were read in groups, in the shade of a carob tree or a clump of bamboos. This exhibition of pride, hatred and vindictiveness, in the midst of the tropical undergrowth, had turned into a new *Danse Macabre*, in which everyone flourished their rank and titles, as they were summoned by hunger, sickness and death. One man had put his trust in the friendship of someone in high places, another in the pertinacity of a lawyer, yet another in the imminent revision of his "case". But back in their huts they again became aware that their feet were being eaten away by insects which burrowed under the toenails; while each morning their bodies emerged from sleep with fresh wounds, fresh sores, fresh abscesses.

It was always the same to begin with : as long as the members of a new batch of *émigrés* still preserved some energy they formed themselves into Rousseauesque communities, sharing out the tasks, and imposing time-tables and rules—and quoting the *Georgics* to give themselves courage. The hut which had been left vacant by the death of its previous occupants was repaired; some went for firewood and water, while others devoted themselves to the tasks of tree-felling, tilling and sowing. With help from what they could shoot or catch, they reckoned to survive until the first harvest. And since the Magistrate could not get his only frock-coat dirty, nor the Army Commander soil his uniform, they took to wearing tunics made of coarse cloth, which were soon stained with resins and vegetal saps as effective as any dye. They all began to look like peasants in a Le Nain painting, with their bristly chins, and their eyes sinking ever deeper into their sockets. Death was already industriously at work on the scene of their labours, helping them to clear the ground, turn the soil, or scatter the seeds into the furrow. One man was beginning to suffer from fever; another to vomit greenish bile; a third complained of an upset and swollen stomach.

Meanwhile the wild plants again and again invaded the areas that had been cleared, and the seedlings were eaten away as soon as they had begun to grow by a hundred different species of animals. Those who still persevered in trying to wrest something from the soil had become emaciated beggars by the time the rains broke—in so solid and pitiless a downpour that they woke up in their huts one morning with the water up to their knees, and surrounded by overflowing rivers, and fields which could not absorb any more.

This was the moment which the blacks chose to cast their spells on these improvised colonists, whom they considered as intruders, arbitrarily installed on land whose ownership they ultimately claimed for themselves. Each time they awoke, the Magistrate, the Army Commander and the People's Representative found themselves menaced by strange objects, as terrifying as they were indecipherable : the skull of an ox, its horns painted red, planted opposite the hut; gourds full of small bones, grains of maize and iron filings; or stones, shaped like faces, with shells for eyes and teeth. There were pebbles wrapped in blood-stained cloths; black hens hung head downwards from the lintel; or nooses of human hair, fixed to the door with a nail—a nail no one knew anything about, in a place where every nail had its price, and which had just been inserted without any sound of hammering. An atmosphere of malevolence surrounded the exiles, under the black clouds which seemed to press down on the roofs. Some of them tried to keep calm by remembering the witches of Brittany and the malicious hobgoblins of Poitou, but still they could not sleep in peace, knowing that they were surrounded, watched and visited by nocturnal agents who never left any trace but used mysterious signals to announce their presence.

Riddled by invisible moths, the Army Commander's uniform, the Magistrate's frock-coat and the Tribune's last shirt came to pieces in their hands one fine morning, and to make matters worse a rattlesnake, hidden in the undergrowth, struck swiftly and ruthlessly, like a spring uncoiling, impelled by a powerful thrust from its tail. Within a few months the proud Magistrate, the vain Army Commander, the former Tribune, the People's Representative, the Refractory Priest, the Public Prosecutor, the Police Spy, the Man-who-used-to-have-influence, the Licence-fee-lawyer, the Renegade Monarchist, and the Babouviste who was set on abolishing private property had all become pitiful objects, swathed in rags, dragging themselves towards a grave in the cold clay, whose cross and epitaph would be erased off the face of the earth when the next rains broke. And then, as if all this were not enough, rapacious flocks of abject colonial officials swooped down on these fields of destruction; and (in exchange for the dispatch of a letter, a promise to fetch a doctor or procure a palliative, some rum or food) carried off a wedding ring, an amulet or a family medallion—some personal possession that had been defended until exhaustion-point as a last pretext for going on living.

Night was already falling when Sieger, tired of waiting, suggested to Esteban that they should go to the Public Enemy's house, where it was probable that they would find the Abbé Brottier. Up till now the young man had felt no interest in seeing this too-famous exile, but the news that he would soon be enjoying a certain authority in Cayenne decided him to accept Sieger's proposal.

So, with a mixture of curiosity and fear, he entered the dilapidated but extraordinarily well-kept house, where Billaud was sitting in an arm-chair that had been eaten away by woodborers, reading old newspapers, his eyes reflecting months of boredom.

XXXII

Fiero mon struo
—Goya

THERE WAS SOMETHING of the dignity of a de-throned monarch in the rather distant condescension with which the former Terrorist received Victor's consignment. He did not seem greatly interested in finding out what the packages and the sealed boxes contained, but offered Esteban a place at his table and a bed for the night—which he cautiously described as "Laconian". Then he asked whether they had had any news in Guadeloupe that had not reached this "world's sewer" which was Cayenne. When he heard that Victor Hugues had been summoned to Paris to give an account of his administration, he stood up in a sudden rage: "That's the limit! Now the cretins are going to destroy the man who prevented the island from becoming a British colony again. They're going to lose Guadeloupe, while they wait for perfidious Albion to grab Guiana." (His language has not changed much, thought Esteban, remembering having translated a famous speech in which Billaud had inveighed against "perfidious Albion", who was hoping to achieve control of the seas "by covering the Ocean with her floating fortresses".)

At this point the Abbé Brottier arrived, very agitated at something he had just witnessed: in order to bury the day's dead more quickly, the black soldiers of the Sinnamary garrison had dug scandalously inadequate graves for them and jumped on the stomachs of the corpses so as to force them into holes barely large enough for a sheep. Elsewhere they had not even taken the trouble to carry the corpses, but had dragged them along to the burial-ground by the legs. "They left five of them unburied, tied up in their hammocks and already stinking, because they said they were tired after carrying so much carrion. The dead and the living will be together to-night in the houses of Sinnamary." (Esteban could not but remember another paragraph from that same speech of Billaud's, given four years earlier: "Death is a summons to equality, which a free people should consecrate by a public act, to remind themselves unceasingly of this necessary warning. A Funeral Ceremony is a consolatory act of homage, which obliterates even the horrid imprint of Death; it is Nature's final farewell.")

"And to think that we've given liberty to people like that!" said Billaud, returning to an idea which had been obsessing him ever since he arrived in Cayenne.

"Nor must we be too anxious to see the Pluviose Decree as the noble error of revolutionary humanitarianism," observed Brottier ironically, in the bold tones of a man who allowed himself the liberty of arguing very freely with the Terrorist. "When Sonthonax thought that the Spanish were going to attack San Domingo, he took it on himself to proclaim the freedom of the negroes. This took place a whole year before you all wept with enthusiasm in the Convention, and declared that equality was established between all the inhabitants of French possessions overseas. In Haiti they did it to get the Spaniards off their backs, in Guadeloupe to make sure of chasing out the English, here to give a death blow to the rich land-owners and the old Acadians, who were very ready to ally themselves with the Dutch or the British, if that would stop the Pointe-à-Pitre guillotine from being brought to Cayenne. Colonial politics—that's all!"

"And with the worst possible results," said Sieger, who had been left without workmen because of the decree : "Sonthonax fled to Havana, and now the blacks in Haiti want their independence."

"Just as they want it here," said Brottier, reminding them that two conspiracies had already been suppressed in the Guianas, the initiative for the second having been attributed, perhaps fancifully, to Collot d'Herbois. (Esteban could not repress a laugh, inexplicable to the others, when he reflected that Collot might have wanted to create a sort of black Coblenz in these parts.)

"I can still remember that ridiculous proclamation which Jeannet had stuck up on the walls in Cayenne, when he announced the Great Event," said Sieger. His voice grew solemn : "Masters and slaves no longer exist. The citizens hitherto known under the name of black maroons may return to their brothers, who will afford them security, protection, and the happiness which enjoyment of a man's rights inspires. Those who were slaves may deal as equals with their former masters, when undertaking or completing work."

Then, lowering his voice: "All the French Revolution has achieved in America is to legalise the Great Escape which has been going on since the sixteenth century. The blacks didn't wait for you, they've proclaimed themselves free a countless number of times."

And with a knowledge of American history rare in a Frenchman (but Esteban suddenly remembered that he was Swiss), the planter began to enumerate the black uprisings which had taken place in that Continent with terrible regularity.

The cycle had opened to the thunder of drums in Venezuela, when the negro Miguel had rebelled with the miners of Buria, and founded his kingdom in a landscape so dazzlingly white that it seemed to be made of ground glass. And then had come the sound not of organ pipes but of pipes of bamboo, striking rhythmically on the ground, as a Congo or Yoruba Archbishop, unknown at Rome yet possessing both crozier and mitre, performed the ceremony of consecration by placing a royal garland about the brow of the negress Guiomar, the wife of the first African King of America; Guiomar had become as important as Miguel.

And already the drums were sounding in the Valley of the Negroes in Mexico, and along the coast of Veracruz, where the Viceroy Martín Enriquez, as a warning to the runaways, had ordered all fugitives to be castrated, "without further investigation of their crimes or excesses".

But if these attempts had been ephemeral, the Palisade of Palm Trees established in the heart of the Brazilian jungle by the high chief Ganga-Zumba was to last sixty-five years; against this pliant fortification of wood and fibre more than twenty military expeditions, both Dutch and Portuguese, were dashed to pieces, their artillery useless against a strategy which resurrected old tricks from the Numidian wars, and sometimes used animals to strike panic into the white men's hearts. Field-Marshal Zumbi, the nephew of King Zumba, was invulnerable to bullets, and his men could travel across the roof of the jungle, dropping on to the enemy columns like ripe fruit.

And this War of the Palm Trees still had forty years to run when the maroons of Jamaica took to the mountains and created an independent state which was to last almost a century.

The British Crown was forced to approach these mountain-dwellers and deal with them as government to government, promising their chieftain, a powerful hunchback called Old Cudjoe, the manumission of all his men and the cession of fifteen hundred acres of land.

Ten years later the drums were beating in Haiti; in the Cap region the Muslim Mackandal, a one-armed man to whom lycanthropic powers were attributed, began a Revolution-by-Poison, laying down unknown poisons in houses and pastures, which proved fatal to men and domestic animals. And scarcely had he been burned in the market-place, before Holland was forced to assemble an army of European mercenaries to fight in the Surinam jungle against the terrible maroon troops of three popular chieftains, Zan-Zan, Boston and Araby, who were threatening to destroy the colony. Four exhausted companies were quite unable to deal with these men from a secret world, who understood the language of wood, fur and fibre, and vanished into settlements hidden amongst inaccessible crags, where they had resumed the worship of ancestral gods.

Only seven years ago, just when it seemed that White Supremacy had been re-established on the continent, another black Mohammedan, Bouckman, had risen in the Bosque Caimán in San Domingo, burning houses and devastating the countryside. And it was no more than three years ago that the negroes in Jamaica had rebelled again, to avenge the condemnation of two thieves who had been tortured in Trelawney Town. To quell this latest uprising it had proved necessary to mobilise the troops in Port Royal and transport packs of Cuban hunting dogs to Montego Bay.

And now, at this very moment, more drums were sounding, amongst the coloured people of Bahía—the drums of the "Tailors' Revolt", demanding the privileges of Equality and Fraternity to the rhythm of a *macumba,* and so introducing the djuka-drum into the French Revolution itself.

"You can see," concluded Sieger, "that the famous Pluviose Decree didn't bring anything new into this continent; it was just one more reason for proceeding with the everlasting Great Escape."

"It's amazing to think," said Brottier, after a pause, "that the blacks in Haiti refused to accept the guillotine. Sonthonax only managed to erect it once. The blacks arrived *en masse* to see how you beheaded a man with it. When they had grasped the mechanism they got angry, hurled themselves on it, and smashed it into little pieces." The Abbé had loosed his arrow, knowing where it would wound.

"Did they have to show great severity to restore order in Guadeloupe?" asked Billaud, who must have known very well what had happened there.

"Especially at the beginning," said the young man, "when the guillotine was in the Place de la Victoire."

"A harsh reality, which pardons neither man nor woman," said Sieger ambiguously.

"Although I don't remember any women being guillotined there," said Esteban, immediately realising what an unfortunate remark this was.

The Abbé, over-anxious to steer the conversation in a different direction, became enmeshed in banalities : "That's because only the whites subject women to the most extreme penalties of the law. The blacks split people open, rape them, and disembowel them, but they would be incapable of executing a woman in cold blood. At least I've never heard of a case."

"To them a woman is a belly," said Esteban.

"To us she is a head," said Sieger. "To have a belly between your hips is pure fate; to have a head on your shoulders is a responsibility."

Billaud shrugged to signify that the epigram lacked wit. "Let's get back to the subject," he said, with a slight smile, which barely disturbed a face so impassive that one could never tell whether he was absorbed in his own reflections or listening to the conversation.

The planter returned to his inventory of escapes : "All I know is that Bartolomé de las Casas was one of the worst criminals in history. Almost three centuries ago he created a problem so great that it is even more far-reaching than an event like the Revolution. Our grandsons will look back on these horrors in Sinnamary, Kourou, Counamama and Iracoubo as trivial episodes in the story of human suffering, while the problem of the negro will still be paramount. Now they're legalising their escape on

San Domingo and driving us from the island. Next they'll be claiming to live on a completely equal footing with the whites."

"They'll never achieve that," shouted Billaud.

"Why not?" asked Brottier.

"Because we're *different*. I've done with such philanthropic daydreams, Father. A Numidian has a long way to go before he becomes a Roman. A Garamantine isn't an Athenian. This Euxine Sea that we've been banished to is not the Mediterranean."

At this point Brigitte, Billaud's young servant girl, appeared. During her comings and goings between the kitchen and the untidy room which served as a dining-room, she had attracted Esteban's attention by a delicacy of feature unusual in a woman without a trace of the mulatta or the octaroon. She might have been thirteen, but her slim body was perfectly formed, and her full breasts swelled the coarse cloth of her dress. In a respectful voice she announced that supper was ready—an ample stew of sweet potatoes, bananas and dried beef. Billaud went for a bottle of wine, a rare luxury which he had been enjoying for barely three days, and the four of them sat down facing one another, without Esteban being able to understand by what unusual combination of circumstances such a curious friendship could have sprung up between the Public Enemy, an Abbé (who perhaps owed his deportation to the latter) and a Calvinist planter who had been ruined because of the ideas which the master of the house represented.

They were all talking politics. It was rumoured that Hoche had been poisoned, that Buonaparte's popularity was growing daily, that amongst the Incorruptible's papers several revealing letters had come to light, according to which, when he had been overthrown by the events of Thermidor, he had been preparing to go abroad, where he had private assets securely hidden away. This everlasting gossip about present aspirants to and past wielders of power had long bored Esteban. These days every conversation followed the same course. The young man had come to long for a quiet discussion about the city of God, the life of the beaver, or the wonders of electricity.

It was not yet eight o'clock when, feeling himself being overcome by sleep, he apologised for nodding so often, and asked permission to lie down on the straw bed which Billaud had offered him. He took up a book which had been left on a stool. It was a novel by Ann Radcliffe—*The Italian, or the Confessional of the Black Penitents.* He felt a personal allusion in a sentence which he came on by chance : "Alas, I no longer have a home, a circle to smile welcome upon me. I have no longer even one friend to support, or retain me ! I am a miserable wanderer on a distant shore."

He awoke shortly after midnight; Billaud-Varenne was writing by the light of a candle in the next room, having taken off his shirt because of the heat. From time to time he would kill some insect which had settled on his shoulders or the back of his neck with a powerful smack. Beside him the young Brigitte lay naked on a bed, fanning her breasts and thighs with an old copy of *La Décade Philosophique.*

XXXIII

THAT OCTOBER—AN October of cyclones, violent nocturnal rain-storms, intolerable heat in the mornings, and sudden downpours at mid-day, which only made it more oppressive still as they evaporated with a smell of mud, bricks and wet ashes— was a month of constant moral crisis for Esteban. He was deeply shocked by the death of the Abbé Brottier, struck down on a short visit to Cayenne by some pestilence he had brought with him from Sinnamary. The young man had set his hopes of getting to Surinam on the possible influence of this active and uninhibited priest. But now, left without anyone whom he could trust, Esteban was a prisoner, with a whole town, a whole country, as his prison. And this country was bounded by such a dense jungle on the landward side that its only gateway was the sea, a gateway that was locked with enormous keys of paper, which were the worst ones of all. They were currently experiencing a universal proliferation, a multiplication of pieces of paper, covered in seals, stamps, signatures and counter-signatures, whose titles exhausted all possible synonyms for "leave", "safe-conduct", "passport", and any other terms which might have been taken to signify authorisation to move from one country to another. The tax-gatherers, tithers, excisemen, revenue men and customs officials of old now seemed to have been no more than the colourful precursors of this legal and political retinue who were busy everywhere—some out of fear of the Revolution, others out of fear of the Counter-Revolution—circumscribing man's freedom, in so far as it concerned his primordial, fertile and creative potentiality of moving about the surface of the planet it had fallen to his lot to inhabit. Esteban grew quite exasperated and stamped with rage when he reflected that a human being, denied his ancestral nomadism, had now to subordinate his sovereign desire for mobility to a *piece of paper*. "I certainly wasn't born to be a good citizen as they understand the words these days," he thought.

During this month all was sound, fury and chaos in Cayenne. Jeannet, angered by his dismissal, used the black militia against the Alsatian troops who were claiming several months' back pay. Then, alarmed by what he had done, he announced an imminent blockade of the colony by North American ships, and evoked visions of possible famine, which caused terrified queues to form at the doors of the food shops. "This way he'll manage to sell all the stuff he's got stored away before the next one grabs it," said Hauguard, who had seen much double-dealing in the colony in his time.

November began, and the tension eased when Burnel arrived on board the frigate *L'Insurgente,* to be greeted by salvoes from the batteries in the fort. As soon as he was installed in Government House, the new Agent of the Directory ignored the men who flocked into the ante-rooms with all sorts of things to "tell him", and sent for Billaud-Varenne from Sinnamary, embracing him ostentatiously, much to the alarm of those who thought that the former Terrorist had been forgotten. The news spread round Cayenne that the two men had been closeted for three whole days in an office—even the snacks of wine and cheese they ate between meals had been carried in to them—examining a series of local political problems. They may also have discussed the situation of the deportees, for some of the sick at Kourou were unexpectedly transferred to Sinnamary. "A bit late," muttered

Hauguard. "The death rate in Kourou, Counamama and Ira-coubo in a good month is about thirty per cent. I know of one batch of fifty-eight prisoners, brought in by *La Bayonnaise* a year ago, of whom only two are still alive. There was a scholar amongst the last lot of dead : Havelange, the Rector of the University of Louvain."

The innkeeper was right : exile had over-reached itself in these fields of death, littered with black vultures, bones and tombstones. Four great Guianese rivers had given their Indian names to these vast graveyards of white men—many of whom had died because they had remained faithful to a religion which the white man had been striving to inculcate into the American Indians for almost three hundred years.

The Swiss, Sieger, who had come to the town to negotiate discreetly for the purchase of a finca for Billaud-Varenne, made a surprising confidence to Esteban, which showed to what an extent the spirit of the Jacobins, the *"cordeliers"* and the *"enragés"*, now predominated amongst the rulers of Cayenne. Surreptitiously backed by the Directory, Burnel planned to send secret agents into Surinam, who were to use the Decree of Pluviose of the Year Two to promote a general uprising amongst the slaves there, so that the colony could then be annexed—a felony which became all the more reprehensible when it was remembered that Holland was now the only faithful ally whom France had in those parts.

That night Esteban invited the Swiss to his room, so that he could ply him with the hotel's best wines, in the company of Angesse and Scholastique—who needed little persuading to remove their skirts and blouses once Hauguard had gone off to bed, in no way scandalised by his guests' whims. After the fun had subsided, the young man talked frankly to Sieger, and begged him to use his influence to procure him a passport for Surinam. "I could be supremely useful there as a propagandist or an agitator," he stated, with a gesture of complicity.

"You're doing the right thing in trying to get away," said the other man. "Only speculators and friends of the Governor can be interested in this country now. You've got to be either a politician or a dummy. Billaud-Varenne liked you. We'll try and get the document you need."

A week later *La Diomède*, now called *L'Italie Conquise*, weighed anchor for the neighbouring colony, where it was to attempt to sell, this time for Burnel's benefit, a cargo of merchandise which Jeannet's captains had captured on the high seas.

When Esteban found himself in the streets of Paramaribo, after an anxious wait in the depressing and sordid surroundings of Cayenne—a world whose whole history had been nothing but a succession of rapes, plagues, murders, banishments, and collective death agonies—he felt that he had arrived in a town painted and furbished for a great fiesta, a town which had a little of the Flemish kermesse about it, and a lot of the tropical Jauja. A cornucopia from some still life seemed to have spilled out into the avenues of orange trees, tamarinds and lemon trees, with their pretty wooden houses, three or four storeys high, whose windows had gauze curtains but no glass. The interiors were adorned with huge well-stocked cupboards, and under high, tulle mosquito nets there rocked spacious flounced hammocks.

The girandoles and chandeliers, the lustrous mirrors and glass shutters of Esteban's childhood had reappeared. Barrels were being rolled along the wharves; geese cackled in the backyards; the fifes of the garrison started playing; and on top of the Fort Zeelandia, a guardsman marked each hour as it passed on the sundial by striking a bell with whirling arms like a toy figure. In a food shop, next door to a butcher's where turtle meat was displayed alongside a shoulder of lamb studded with cloves of garlic, Esteban once more saw wonders he had quite forgotten—bottles of porter, thick Westphalia hams, smoked eels and red mullet, anchovies pickled in capers and bay-leaves, and potent Durham mustard. Along the river cruised boats with gilded prows and lamps on the poops, their negro oarsmen wearing white loin-cloths, and paddling amidst awnings and canopies of bright silks or Genoa velvet. They had reached such a pitch of refinement in this overseas Holland that the mahogany floors were rubbed every day with bitter oranges, whose juice, absorbed by the wood, gave off a delicous aromatic perfume.

The Catholic church, the Protestant church, the Lutheran church, the Portuguese synagogue and the German synagogue, with their texts, liturgies, gold candles, luminaries and sumptuous Hanukkah-Menorah lamps; their bells, organs, canticles, hymns and psalms ringing out on Sundays and Feast Days, at Christmas and at Yom-Kippur, at the Jewish Passover and on Holy Saturday—all appeared to Esteban's eyes as symbols of a tolerance which, in some parts of the world, men had persevered in attaining and defending, without weakening in the face of religious or political inquisition.

While *L'Italie Conquise* was engaged in unloading and selling her cargo, the young man disported himself on the banks of the Surinam, which was a sort of public bathing-place for the town; here he learned that North American ships were frequent visitors, amongst them a slender schooner called the *Arrow*. Although not daring to hope that his stay in Paramaribo might coincide with the appearance of Captain Dexter's ship—moreover it might easily have changed masters in six years—Esteban felt that he had reached the final stage of his adventures. When the French schooner sailed he would remain here in Paramaribo as the Cayenne government's "commercial agent", responsible for distributing, wherever they would be most effective, several hundred printed copies of the Decree of Pluviose of the Year Two, translated into Dutch, and accompanied by a call to revolt. Esteban had already chosen the spot where he would throw the leaflets, well weighted down with large stones, so that they would disappear for ever into the depths of the river. Then he would wait until a Yankee ship arrived, one of those which called at Santiago de Cuba or Havana on their way back to Baltimore or Boston.

Meanwhile he would endeavour to enjoy himself with one of these soft, luxuriant Dutch blondes, who could be seen leaning out of their windows after supper to breathe the night air, their bodies almost golden against the lace which swathed them. Some of them sang, accompanying themselves on a lute; others, as a pretext for an unannounced visit, took their embroidery from door to door, displaying nostalgic views of a street in Delft, the façade of a famous town-hall reconstructed from memory, or a colourful confusion of escutcheons and tulips. Esteban had been told that these friendly souls particularly favoured foreigners, knowing as they did that their husbands kept dusky mistresses in their haciendas in the country, where they only too frequently remained to sleep. *Nigra sum, sed formosa, filiae Ierusalem.*

Nolite me considerare quod fusca sum quia decoloravit me sol.

But this underground conflict was not peculiar to the region. Many white men, having overcome their first scruples, grew so attached to the warmth of black flesh that they seemed to have been put under a spell. Stories were current of infusions, drugs, and mysterious liquids, surreptitiously administered to a pale-skinned lover in order to "bind" him, to hold him, and to alienate his will to such an extent that he ended by becoming indifferent to the women of his own race. The Master enjoyed playing the roles of the Bull, the Swan and the Shower of God, in which the gift of his noble seed was accompanied by others, of bracelets, handkerchiefs, silk chemises, and floral essences brought from Paris. The white man, whose aberrations in dependent territories were viewed with indulgence, lost nothing of his prestige by making love to a black woman. And if a brood of quadroon, octaroon, or mulatto children resulted, this proliferation gained him an enviable reputation as a fertile patriarch. The white woman, on the other hand, who lay with a coloured man—cases were very few and far between—was looked on with abomination. There was no worse role one could play, between the lands of the Natchez and the shores of the Mar del Plata, than that of colonial Desdemona.

Esteban's stay in Paramaribo—after the departure of *L'Italie Conquise*—ended with the arrival of the *Amazon*, a merchantman from Baltimore, returning from the River Plate. During the interval of waiting he had enjoyed the favours of a mature lady, who read novels which she considered to be still contemporary, such as Richardson's *Clarissa Harlowe* and *Pamela*, but whose body was cool and sweet-smelling, and always smothered with rice powder, which she applied with magnificent prodigality. She entertained him with Portuguese wines, while her husband slept out at his hacienda "Egmont", for reasons already established.

Two hours before carrying his baggage aboard the *Amazon*, Esteban went to the hospital in the town, to get the senior physician, Greuber, to confirm that a certain small swelling under the left arm, which was troubling him, was benign. After an emollient had been applied to the painful spot, the worthy doctor took leave of him in an ante-room, where nine negroes under armed guard were quietly smoking a bitter, fermented tobacco smelling of vinegar, in clay pipes whose stems were so eroded that the bowls touched their teeth. The young man learned with horror that these slaves, convicted of attempted flight and desertion, had been condemned by the Courts of Justice in Surinam to have their left legs amputated. And since the sentence must be cleanly and scientifically carried out, without resort to archaic methods belonging to the age of barbarism and which might cause excessive suffering or endanger the prisoners' lives, the nine slaves had been brought to the best surgeon in Paramaribo, so that he could carry out the court's verdict, saw in hand.

"They cut off arms as well," said Doctor Greuber, "when a slave lifts his hand against his master." And the surgeon turned to the men who were waiting : "Who's first?"

When he saw a tall negro with a determined forehead and powerful muscles stand up in silence, Esteban ran out to the nearest tavern, on the point of fainting, and shouted for brandy to overcome his horror. He looked at the façade of the hospital, unable to take his eyes off a certain closed window, or stop thinking of what was taking place behind it. "We're the worst monsters in all Creation," he repeated to himself angrily; he felt furious with himself, and capable of setting fire to the building, had he the means of doing so.

As the *Amazon* started downstream, in the central current of the Surinam, Esteban threw several packages over the gunwale, down into a fishing canoe rowed by black men. "Read these," he shouted to them. "Or if you can't read, then find someone who can read them for you." They were the Dutch versions of the Decree of Pluviose of the Year Two, and the young man was now congratulating himself on not having thrown them into the river, as he had previously intended.

XXXIV

THEY WERE OPPOSITE the Dragon's Mouths, on a night of innumerable stars, at the place where Ferdinand and Isabella's

High Admiral had seen the fresh water and the salt water locked in combat, as they had been ever since the days of the Creation. "The fresh water pushes so that the other shall not enter, the salt water so that the other shall not escape." But now, as then, the great tree-trunks that had come down from the interior, uprooted by the August freshets and battered by the rocks, were taking to the open sea, and escaping from the fresh water to be scattered over the immensity of the salt water. Esteban could see them, floating towards Trinidad, Tobago and the Grenadines, outlined in black against the seething phosphorescence, like the long, the very long, boats which, not so many centuries since, had followed the same course, in search of a Promised Land.

During that Stone Age—still so recent and so real for many—the men who had gathered round the fires at night had been obsessed by the Empire of the North. Yet they had known little about it. The fishermen got their news from the mouths of other fishermen, who had had it from other fishermen farther off to the north, who had had it in their turn from other fishermen even more distant. But the Objects had travelled, had been introduced as a result of barter and countless voyages. There they were, enigmatic and solemn, in all the mystery of their design. They were small stones—but what did size matter?—whose eloquence lay in their shape; they were stones which watched, challenged, laughed or contracted into strange grimaces, and which had come from the land where there were immense esplanades, virgins' baths, and unimaginable buildings.

Gradually, from talking so much about the Empire of the North, men began to acquire proprietary rights over it. Words handed on from generation to generation had created so many things that these *things* became a sort of collective patrimony. This distant world was a Land-in-Waiting, where the Chosen People would necessarily settle one day, once a celestial sign should have come for them to depart. In expectation of this, the human mass increased day by day, and the ant-swarms of people grew at the mouths of the Endless River, of the Mother-River, situated hundreds of days' journey to the south of the Dragon's Mouths. Some tribes had come down from their sierras, abandoning the villages where they had lived since time immemorial. Others had deserted the right bank; while the jungle dwellers emerged from the thickets at each new moon in exhausted groups, dazed from travelling for long months in a green shade, following the water-courses and skirting the swamps.

But the delay was prolonged. So vast was the undertaking, and so long the road they had to travel, that the chiefs could not make up their minds to start. Sons and grandsons grew up, and still they were all there, pullulating and inactive, talking always of the same thing, and contemplating the Objects, whose prestige had grown with the passage of time.

And then one night, as will always be remembered, a blazing shape crossed the sky with a mighty hiss, indicating the direction which men had established long before as leading to the Empire of the North. Then, divided into hundreds of fighting squadrons, the horde set out, and penetrated into foreign lands. All the males of other races were ruthlessly exterminated, and the women kept for the propagation of the conquering race. Thus there came to be two languages; that of the women, the language of the kitchen and of childbirth, and that of the men, the language of warriors, to know which was held to be a supreme privilege.

For more than a century the march went on, through forests, plains and defiles, until the invaders found themselves face to face with the Sea. They had heard reports that the people of other nations, learning of the terrible advance of the Men of the South, had removed to islands lying far—but not so very far —beyond the horizon. Fresh Objects, similar to those they already knew, indicated that the Road to the Islands was perhaps the most favourable for reaching the Empire of the North. And since it was not time that counted, but only their obsessional desire to reach the Land-in-Waiting some day, the men stopped, to learn the arts of navigation. The broken canoes abandoned on the beaches served as models for the first attempts of the invaders, made out of hollowed tree-trunks. But since they had long distances to cover, they began to make them ever bigger and longer, with high, pointed bows, capable of containing up to sixty men.

And one day the great-great-grandsons of the men who had begun the migration on land began the migration on water, sailing out in groups of boats in search of the islands. They found it an easy matter to overcome the currents and to cross the straits, and leapt forward from island to island, slaughtering the inhabitants—gentle farmers and fishermen, ignorant of the arts of war. From island to island the mariners advanced, growing increasingly skilled and bold, and already used to steering by the stars. As they pursued their course the towers, esplanades and buildings of the Empire of the North seemed to appear before their eyes. The islands were growing bigger, more mountainous and more fertile; they must surely be getting close. Three more islands, two more, or perhaps only one—they counted in islands —and they would reach the Land-in-Waiting. Their vanguard was already on the largest of them—the last stage of their journey perhaps. The wonders which were imminent would not be for the grandsons of the invaders; their own eyes would look upon them. And merely to think of it quickened the tempo of their chants, as the rows of oars dipped into the water, driven by eager hands.

But it was now that there began to loom on the horizon strange, unrecognised shapes, with hollows in their sides, and trees growing on top of them, bearing canvas which billowed and fluttered, and displayed unknown symbols. The invaders had encountered other unsuspected, unsuspectable invaders, come from no one knew where, just in time to destroy an age-old dream. The Great Migration would no longer have an objective, the Empire of the North would fall into the hands of these unexpected rivals. In their despair, their visceral fury, the Caribs hurled themselves against these enormous ships, terrifying the men who defended them by their recklessness. They clambered up the sides and attacked them with a savage desperation, which these new arrivals could not understand.

Two irreconcilable historical periods confronted one another in this struggle where no truce was possible. Totemic Man was opposed to Theological Man. For the disputed Archipelago had suddenly become a Theological Archipelago. The islands were changing their identity, and were being integrated into the great, all-embracing sacramental drama. The first island discovered by these invaders from a continent inconceivable to the islanders themselves had received the name of Christ, and the first cross, made of branches, was planted on its shore. For the second they had gone back to the Mother, and had called it Santa María de la Concepción. The Antilles were being transformed into an immense stained-glass window, flooded by sunlight. The Donors were already present in the shape of Ferdinand and Isabella; the Apostle Thomas, Saint John the Baptist, Saint Lucy, Saint Martin, Our Lady of Guadalupe and the supreme figures of the Trinity were set in their respective places; and the towns of Navidad, Santiago and Santo Domingo arose against a background of cerulean blue, whitened by the coralliferous labyrinth of the Eleven Thousand Virgins—as impossible to count as the stars in the *Campus Stellae*. With a leap of some thousands of years, this Mediterranean Sea had become the heir of the other Mediterranean, and received the Christian Laying on of Hands, together with wheat and Latin, wine and the Vulgate. The Caribs would never reach the Empire of the Mayas, but would remain a frustrated people who had been dealt a death wound just as their age-old design reached its climax. And all that remained from the failure of their Great Migration, begun perhaps on the left bank of the Amazon River in an age which the chronology of others designated as the thirteenth century, was the reality of the Carib petroglyphs on the beaches and the river-banks—indications of an unrecorded epic—with their human figures, inlaid in the rock, beneath a proud solar symbolism. . . .

At dawn, with the stars still shining, Esteban came to the Dragon's Mouths, the place where the High Admiral had seen the fresh water and the salt water locked in combat ever since the days of the Creation. "The fresh water pushes so that the other shall not enter, and the salt water so that the other shall not escape." But this fresh water was so copious that it could only come from an infinitely large continent or, what was more likely, for those who still believed in the existence of the monsters catalogued by San Isidoro of Seville, from the Earthly Paradise. This Earthly Paradise, with its fountain which fed the greatest rivers in the world, had been transplanted by the cartographers many times from Africa to Asia and back again. So many times that when he tried the water through which his ship was moving, the Admiral, finding it "increasingly fresh and palatable", conjectured that the river which had brought it down to the sea must have its source at the foot of the Tree of Life. This shining thought led him to doubt the classical texts: "I cannot find, nor have I ever found, any Latin or Greek author who states categorically where the Earthly Paradise is situated in this world, nor have I seen it marked on any map."

And since the Venerable Bede, Saint Ambrose and Duns Scotus had all located Paradise in the East, and these men from Europe thought that they had reached the East (having sailed with the sun and not against it), it became dazzlingly evident that this Spanish island, named after San Domingo, was Tarsis, Caethia, Ophir, Ophar and Cipango—in fact all the islands or regions cited by the ancients, and up till now wrongly located in a world enclosed by Spain, just as the entire peninsula had been by the efforts of its reconquerors. The "tardy years" foreseen by Seneca had arrived, "when the Oceanic sea will loosen the connections of things, and a great continent will emerge; and a new navigator, like the one who guided Jason, will discover a new world; then the Island of Thule will no longer be the last land".

The Discovery had suddenly taken on a gigantic theological dimension. This voyage to the Gulf of Pearls in the Land of Grace had been described glowingly and emphatically in the Book of the Prophet Isaiah. The Abbot Joaquín Calabrés' prophecy was confirmed, that out of Spain would come the man who was to rebuild the House of the Mount Sion. The world was shaped like a woman's breast, at the tip of whose nipple grew the Tree of Life. And now they knew that from this inexhaustible source, sufficient to quench the thirst of every living creature, there sprung not only the Ganges, the Tigris and the Euphrates, but also the Orinoco, the route for the great tree-trunks which came down to the sea, at whose head-waters the Earthly Paradise—now attainable, accessible and knowable in all its splendour—had finally been located, after so long a delay.

Here then at the Dragon's Mouths, where the water turned transparent in the rising sun, the Admiral could shout his exultation aloud, having understood the meaning of the age-old struggle between the fresh water and the salt water: "Let the King and the Queen, the Princes and all their Dominions, give thanks to Our Saviour Jesus Christ who has granted us this victory. Let there be processions; let solemn celebrations be held; let the churches be filled with palms and flowers; let Christ rejoice on Earth, as there is rejoicing in Heaven, to think that salvation is at hand for so many people hitherto consigned to damnation."

The abundant supplies of gold in these lands would put an end to the abject servitude to which Man had been subjected by the scarcity of gold in Europe. The prophecies of the Prophets had been fulfilled, the divinations of the ancients and the inspired intuitions of the theologians confirmed. The everlasting Battle of the Waters, in such a spot as this, proclaimed that they had finally reached the Promised Land, after an agonising wait of so many centuries.

So Esteban found himself by the Dragon's Mouths, which had devoured so many expeditions, after they had abandoned the salt water for the fresh, in search of that ever elusive and evanescent Promised Land—so elusive and evanescent that it had ended by concealing itself for ever behind the cold mirror of the Patagonian Lakes. And as he leaned over the side of the *Amazon*, opposite the broken, wooded coastline where nothing had changed since the day when Ferdinand and Isabella's High Admiral first set eyes on it, he reflected on the persistence of this myth of the Promised Land. It had changed in character to suit each successive century, responding to a constantly renewed hunger, and yet it was still the same. There was, there had to be, it was essential that at any given moment there should be, a Better World. The Caribs had conceived of this Better World in their own terms, just as in his turn Ferdinand and Isabella's High Admiral had imagined it, here by the seething Dragon's Mouths, where he had been enlightened and illumined by the taste of water from afar. The Portuguese had dreamed of the wonderful kingdom of Prester John, just as the children of the Castilian plain would one day dream of the Valley of Jauja after a supper of a crust of bread with olive oil and garlic. The Encyclopaedists had discovered a Better World in the society of the Ancient Incas, just as the United States had seemed to be a Better World, when they sent ambassadors to Europe without wigs, who wore buckled shoes, spoke clearly and simply, and bestowed blessings in the name of Freedom.

Esteban himself had set out for a Better World not so very long ago, dazzled by the great Pillar of Fire which seemed to stand over towards the East. And now he was returning from what had proved unattainable, in a state of great weariness, from which he vainly sought relief by recalling some agreeable experience. As the days of the voyage slipped by, what he had lived through came to seem like a long nightmare—a nightmare of fire, persecution and chastisement, as foreseen by Cazotte, with his camels vomiting up greyhounds, and by all the other augurs of the End of the World who had so proliferated during this century. The colours, sounds and words which still pursued him produced in him a profound discomfort, like that caused somewhere in the breast—where anxiety is expressed physically in the palpitations and asymmetry of the visceral rhythms— by the last after-effects of an illness which might have proved fatal. He saw what he had left behind him in terms of darkness and tumult, drums and death agonies, shouts and executions, and he associated it in his mind with the idea of an earthquake, a collective convulsion or a ritual fury.

"I have been living amongst barbarians," Esteban said to Sofia, when she opened the heavy door to him with a solemn creak of hinges—the door of the familiar house that still stood on its corner, still oddly decorated with those tall, white-painted grilles.

CHAPTER FIVE

XXXV

Con razón o sin ella
—*Goya*

"You!" Sofia had exclaimed when she saw him appear—a broader, taller Esteban, tanned by the sun, with rough, uncared-for hands, and his few possessions carried sailor-fashion in canvas bags slung over his shoulders : "You!" And she kissed him, on the mouth, on his badly-shaven cheeks, on his forehead, on the neck.

"You!" said Esteban, surprised, dumbfounded, by this woman now embracing him, who was so much a woman, so firm and mature, so different from the narrow-hipped girl whose picture he had carried with him in his mind—so different from someone who had been too much of a girl-mother to be a cousin, and too much of a girl to be a woman; so different from the sexless companion of his games, his comforter when he was ill—the Sofia of the old days.

He looked around him now, rediscovering everything, but with an undeniable feeling that he was a stranger. He had dreamed so often of the moment of his return, but he did not feel the expected emotions. Everything that he knew—knew only too well—seemed foreign to him, and he was unable to re-establish physical contact with these objects. There, at the foot of the tapestry, with its cockatoos, unicorns and greyhounds, was the old harp; there were the bevelled looking-glasses and the Venetian mirror with its misty flowers; there was the book-shelf, its volumes now neatly arranged.

Followed by Sofia, he went into the sitting-room with its broad cupboards and its blackened still-lives—hares and pheasants surrounded by friut. He went to the room next to the kitchens which had been his from childhood. "Wait while I go and get the key," said Sofia. (Esteban remembered that in these old Creole houses it was customary to leave the rooms of the dead permanently locked.) When the door was opened he found himself confronted by a dusty labyrinth of puppets and physics apparatus, tangled and twisted together on the ground and on the arm-chairs and the iron bedstead which had been for so long the scene of his torments. The discoloured Montgolfier balloon still hung from its string; the backcloth of the puppet theatre still showed a Mediterranean port, ideal for a performance of *Les Fourberies de Scapin*. Around the orchestra of monkeys lay broken Leyden jars, barometers and speaking tubes, from the old days.

This sudden collision with his childhood—or with a childish adolescence, which came to the same thing—made Esteban burst into tears. He wept for a long time, with his head in Sofia's lap, just as he had done as a sickly, unhappy child, when he had entrusted his sorrows to her for life. Some of the forgotten links of the chain were being reforged. Some of the objects were now beginning to speak to him. They returned to the drawing-room, and passed through the hall where the pictures were. The harlequins still pursued their lively carnivals and their journeys to Cytherea; the still-lives by some imitator of Chardin still displayed the timeless beauties of their cooking-pots, fruit baskets, two apples, a slice of bread, and a clove of garlic, beside the picture of the deserted, monumental square which, with its feeling of "airlessness"—the atmosphere lacked depth—was very much in the style of Jean-Antoine Caron. Hogarth's fantastic characters were still in their place, leading one on to "The Execution of Saint Dionysius", whose colours, far from having faded in the glare of the Tropics, seemed to have taken on an extraordinary brilliance. "We had it restored and varnished a short time ago," said Sofia.

"So I see," said Esteban. "The blood looks almost as though it were fresh."

But further on, where scenes of wheat and grape harvests had formerly hung, there were now new oil paintings to be seen, cold in style and sparing in their brushwork, which depicted edifying scenes from Ancient History, Tarquinades and Lycurgueries such as Esteban had so often suffered during his last years in France. "Is this sort of thing coming in here?" he asked.

"It's a style which is very popular nowadays," said Sofia. "It has something more than colour : it's got ideas, it offers a moral, it makes you think."

Esteban suddenly stopped, stirred to the very depths, in front of the "Explosion in a Cathedral" by the anonymous Neapolitan master. In it were prefigured, so to speak, so many of the events he had experienced that he felt bewildered by the multiplicity of interpretations to which this prophetic, anti-plastic, un-painterly canvas, brought to the house by some mysterious chance, lent itself. If, in accordance with the doctrines he had once been taught, the cathedral was a symbol—the ark and the tabernacle—for his own being, then an explosion had certainly occurred there, which, although tardy and slow, had destroyed altars, images, and objects of veneration. If the cathedral was the Age, then a formidable explosion had indeed overthrown its most solid walls, and perhaps buried the very men who had built the infernal machine beneath an avalanche of debris. If the cathedral was the Christian Church, then Esteban noticed that a row of sturdy pillars remained intact, opposite those which were shattering and falling in this apocalyptic painting, as if to prophesy resilience, endurance and a reconstruction, after the days of destruction and of stars foretelling disasters had passed.

"You always liked looking at that picture," said Sofia, "I think it's absurd and nasty."

"Nasty and absurd to the present generation," said Esteban. And suddenly remembering that he had a cousin, he asked after Carlos.

"He went off into the country early this morning, with my husband," said Sofia, "they'll be back later."

And she was astonished by the expression of stupefaction, of sorrowful surprise, which showed on Esteban's face. Adopting a light, casual tone of voice, and indulging in a verbal extravagance which was rare in her, the girl began to tell how, a year before, she had married the man who was now Carlos' partner in the business—and she pointed to the communicating door, still set in the wall, next to the bed out of which the trunks of the two palm trees rose, like columns in a different style of architecture from the rest. Carlos had got rid of Don Cosme as soon as the anti-freemason scare was over—in the end it proved no more than a threat—and had had the idea of finding a partner who, in exchange for an appreciable share of the profits, would supply a capacity for hard work, and above all the commercial knowledge which he himself lacked. He had hit on a man he had met at the

Lodge, who was capable and well versed in economic matters.

"The Lodge?" asked Esteban.

"Let me go on," said Sofia, and launched into a panegyric of the man who had completely set the business to rights soon after joining it, and who had taken advantage of the times of glittering prosperity which the country was now going through to triple and quintuple the profits from the warehouse. "You'll be rich now!" she cried to Esteban, her cheeks aflame with enthusiasm : "Really rich! And you owe it—we owe it—to Jorge. We were married a year ago. His ancestors were Irish, he's related to the O'Farrells."

Esteban was displeased that Sofia should stress this connection with one of the most powerful and influential families in the island : "I suppose you're always entertaining these days?" he asked peevishly.

"Don't be an idiot! Nothing has changed. Jorge is one of us. You'll get on very well with him." And she began to talk of her present contentment, of the happiness it gave her to make a man happy, of the security and comfort a woman feels who knows that she has a companion.

Then, as if seeking forgiveness for a betrayal : "You're a man. You'll want a home of your own. Don't look at me like that. I tell you everything is as it was."

But the young man was looking at her with an expression of great sadness. He would never have expected to hear such a succession of bourgeois commonplaces from Sofia's lips : "to make a man happy", "the security a woman feels who knows she has a companion". It was terrifying to realise that a second mind, situated in the womb, was now emitting its ideas through Sofia's mouth—Sofia, a name which defined the woman who bore it as possessing a "smiling wisdom". The name Sofia had always appeared in Esteban's imagination as shaded by the great Byzantine dome, wrapped in palms from the Tree of Life and surrounded by Archons in all the mystery of Intact Womanhood. And now the achievement of physical satisfaction, added perhaps to the still concealed joys of incipient pregnancy—whose warning came when the blood which had welled from its deep source since the days of puberty ceased to flow—had sufficed for the Elder Sister, the Young Mother, the pure feminine entelechy of other times, to have become a good, sensible, prudent wife,

254

whose mind was centred on her protected womb and on the
future well-being of its fruits, proud that her husband should
be related to an oligarchy which owed its wealth to the age-old
exploitation of vast numbers of negroes. Strange as he had felt—a
foreigner—entering *his* house once again, Esteban felt stranger
still—even more of a foreigner—confronted by this woman who
was too visibly the queen and mistress of that same house, where
everything was too neat, too clean for his taste, and too well-
protected against knocks or damage.

"Everything smells Irish here," thought Esteban, as he asked
permission (yes, "asked permission") to take a bath, a bath to
which he was accompanied as usual by Sofia, who stayed talking
to him until he had only his drawers left to take off.

"So much mystery about what I've seen so many times," she
said laughing, as she threw him a bar of Castile soap over the
top of the screen.

They lunched alone, after Esteban had been round to the
kitchen and the pantry, and embraced Rosaura and Remigio.
Both were excited and overjoyed, and looked exactly as they had
when he left them : Rosaura still attractive, Remigio in that
indeterminate middle-age of a negro destined to see his full
century of years out in the kingdom of this world. They spoke
little, or they spoke of trifles, looking at each other all the time,
with so many things to tell each other that they could not
express any of them. Esteban made vague allusions to the places
he had been to, but did not go into details. Once the atmosphere
of intimacy dissolved by his long absence had been restored, and
he began to talk, he would need hours, days even, to describe
his experiences during the convulsed and lawless years he had
just lived through. Now that he had left them behind these
years seemed short to him. Yet they had had the effect of
making certain things immensely older, certain books above all.
An encounter with the Abbé Raynal on the library shelves
made him want to laugh. The Baron d'Holbach, Marmontel,
with his comic opera Incas, Voltaire, whose tragedies had been so
contemporary—so subversively contemporary—barely ten years
before, now seemed quite remote and out of date—as out-moded
as a fourteenth-century treatise on Pharmacy would seem to-day.
But nothing was as out of place, as incredibly cracked, split open

255

and diminished by events, as *Le Contrat Social*. He opened the copy, whose pages were covered with admiring interjections, glosses and notes inscribed in his own hand—his hand of long ago.

"Do you remember?" said Sofia, leaning her head on his shoulder. "I didn't understand it before; now I understand it very well."

The two of them went up to the bedrooms. Esteban stopped, confronted by the evocation of an intimacy shared with an unknown man; he stared at the wide—yet too narrow—double bed; at the two tables at its head, with their books in different bindings; at the slippers of Cordoba leather, placed next to Sofia's. Again he felt that he was a stranger when he was offered the adjoining room, "which is supposed to be Jorge's study, but which Jorge never uses", Esteban went down to his old room, and after piling the physics apparatus, the musical boxes and the puppets in a corner, slung the hammock he had brought from the two rings fixed to the wall—the same ones that had once supported the sheet, rolled up like a rope, on which he had rested his head during his asthmatic attacks.

Sofia suddenly asked him about Victor Hugues. "Don't talk to me about Victor Hugues," said the young man, hunting in his sailor's kit-bags. "There's a letter from him for you. He has turned into a monster." And putting some money into his pocket, he went out into the street, impatient to breathe the air of a city which had struck him as greatly changed when he landed.

After walking for a short time he found himself in front of the newly-built cathedral; with its sober entablatures of stone from the seashore—already rich in the associations of age when it was entrusted to the masons—crowned with modest curlicues in a temperate baroque style, this church surrounded by handsome palaces with grilles and balconies represented an evolution of taste amongst those who controlled the architectural destinies of the city.

He wandered until it grew dark, through the Calle de los Oficios, the Calle del Inquisidor, and the Calle de Mercaderes, going from the Plaza del Cristo to the church of the Espiritu Santo, from the rejuvenated Alameda de Paula to the Plaza de Armas—beneath whose arcades noisy groups of idle passers-by were gathering to gossip in the twilight. A crowd of gapers had collected in front of a house from which emerged the novel sound of a pianoforte recently imported from Europe. The barbers strummed guitars on the doorsteps of their shops. In a courtyard a talking head was being fraudulently exhibited. Two flashily dressed slave girls solicited him as he passed, prostituting themselves for the benefit of a very honourable, Catholic lady— this was a common practice in the city. Esteban fingered the money he had brought with him, and accompanied the pair of them into the shadows of a dubious tavern.

It was dark when he returned to the house. Carlos hurried forward to embrace him. He had not changed much; he seemed a little maturer, a little more important, perhaps a little fatter. "We business-men lead a sedentary life," he laughed.

And then Sofia introduced her husband: he was a slim man, who might have been taken for twenty-five although his real age was thirty-three, whose face was made genuinely handsome by the delicacy and nobility of the features, by the wide, open forehead, and the sensual, if somewhat cold and disdainful mouth. Esteban had been afraid of seeing some vulgar, glib and superficial business-apprentice, and was favourably impressed by him, although he noticed that in his bearing, attitudes and dress he cultivated that style of condescending seriousness, distant deference and slight melancholy which, along with a preference for dark clothes, wide, limp collars and apparently unkempt hair styles, was characteristic of the young men who, for several years now, had been educated in Germany, or—as in this case—in England.

"You can't say he's not good-looking?" asked Sofia, looking at her husband with tender admiration.

The mistress of the house had put out a lavish display of candelabra and silverware that night, for the reunited family's first dinner together. "I can see that the fatted calf has been killed," said Esteban, when he saw the beautifully dressed birds appear, and the most subtly concocted sauces, on a procession of trays that reminded him of the dinners which the three adolescents had once served in this same dining-room, dreaming that they were in the Palace of Potsdam, the Baths at Carlsbad, or framed by some rococo palace on the outskirts of an imaginary Vienna. Sofia explained that the galantines, the pâtés, the truffle and garlic stuffing had been specially chosen for someone who had lived for so long in Europe and must have had his palate

257

immeasurably refined by the exquisite things he had tasted. But Esteban, casting his mind back, was forced to admit—it had never occurred to him before—that though he had been dazzled at first by an artificial cuisine that abounded in aromas, blends, subtle ways with oil, herbs and spices, and faint flavours of essences, it had not lasted for long. Having had to adjust himself for months on end to the red peppers, dried cod, and fried garlic of Basque cooking, Esteban had grown fond of country dishes and sea-food, and preferred the taste of the basic ingredients to what he called, with a pronounced scorn for sauces, "slimy food". He eulogised the clean, scented sweet potato, cooked under ashes; green bananas, fried in olive oil; the palm-cabbage, that amazing high-growing asparagus containing the goodness of a whole tree; turtle *boucan*, and *boucan* of wild pig; sea-urchins and mangrove-tree oysters; cold *gazpacho*, with army bread and young crabs, whose fried shells turned to powder in your teeth covering your lips with sea salt. And above all he remembered the sardines, taken still alive out of the nets at the end of a midnight fishing expedition, cooked over a brazier, and devoured on deck with raw onion and a loaf of black bread, with a hand stretched out between mouthfuls to a wineskin bulging with strong red wine.

"And I martyred myself the whole evening reading cookery books just for this," said Sofía, laughing.

Coffee was served in the big drawing-room, where Esteban missed the disorder of the past. It was obvious that the man whose ancestors had been Irish had imposed certain norms of respectability, as consort of the mistress of the house. Moreover, Sofía was too attentive to his every want, and came and went, bringing him a light for his pipe before she sat down on a little footstool beside his arm-chair. And from the husband's silence, the smiling expectancy of Carlos, and the excessive restlessness of Sofía, who had now gone for a cushion, it could be sensed that they were all waiting for the moment when, like the travellers of old—to these people, situated so far away from the events, he seemed like the Sir William Mandeville of the Revolution—Esteban should begin on the story of his adventures. He had difficulty in finding the first words, when he realised that they would bring so very many others in their train, and that

dawn would find him still sitting on the same divan, still talking.
"Tell us about Victor Hugues," said Carlos at last.

Then, realising that Ulysses would not be released that night
from the obligation of recounting his Odyssey, Esteban said to
Sofia : "Bring me a bottle of the cheapest wine there is, and put
another one to cool for later, because the story will be a long one."

XXXVI

> No hay que dar voces
> —*Goya*

HE HAD BEGUN his story light-heartedly, by recalling the
incongruous episode of the journey from Port-au-Prince to
France aboard a ship crammed with refugees, who had almost all
turned out to be masons and members of a very influential
Philadelphian Club in San Domingo. It had certainly been
curious to see all those philanthropists (friends of the Chinese,
the Persians and the Algonquins) promising themselves the
pleasure of inflicting the most fearful punishments after the
revolt of the blacks had been crushed, when they could proceed
to settle accounts with ungrateful servants who had been the first
to set lighted torches to the plantations on their haciendas.

Then Esteban recounted, in a jocular tone, his *"huronades"*
in Paris, his hopes and his dreams, his escapades and experiences,
illustrated by anecdotes : about the citizen who wanted to have
a colossal monument erected on the French frontier, of such a
terrifyingly aggressive symbolism—it was to include a bronze
giant whose face alone would be enough to inspire terror—that,
when they saw it, Tyrants would beat a hasty retreat, with their
intimidated armies; and about the man who had wasted the
Assembly's time at moments of national crisis by pointing out
that the title of "Citizeness", given to women, left one in doubt
on the agonising question of whether they were "Miss" or not. He
told how *Le Misanthrope* had been provided with a revolutionary dénouement, with Alceste coming back suddenly reconciled
with the human race; he made fun of the huge success in France,
after he left, of a novel that had reached him in Guadeloupe,
called *Petit Emile,* in which a poor child was taken to Versailles

and learned with surprise that the Dauphin also said "dadda".

He would have liked to continue in this jaunty mood, but gradually the deeds and sights which his words were recreating began to take on a more sombre hue. The red of the cockades became a darker crimson; the Age of the Scaffold had succeeded to the Age of the Tree of Liberty. At some imprecise, unascertainable, but awful moment, an exchange of souls had taken place; the man who had been gentle when he fell asleep awoke terrible, the man who had never gone beyond verbal rhetoric began to sign death warrants. And then had come the Great Delirium, a delirium all the more incomprehensible when one considered where it had broken out : in the very country where civilisation seemed to have achieved a perfect equilibrium, a country of serene architecture and incomparable craftsmanship, a country where Nature had been tamed, and where the language itself seemed to have been made to fit the measures of classical poetry. No race could have been more unsuited to a background of scaffolds than the French. Their inquisition had been mild compared with that of the Spanish. Their Saint Bartholomew's Day was a trifle beside the wholesale slaughter of Protestants ordered by King Philip. From this distance Billaud-Varenne seemed an absurd figure to Esteban, with the bloody, exotic features of an Aztec priest, raising the obsidian knife on high, against a background of majestic columns and Houdon statues, in a garden from which all vegetal exuberance was excluded.

The Revolution had certainly answered to some obscure millennial impulse, and developed into the human race's most ambitious adventure. But Esteban was appalled by the cost of the undertaking : "We forget the dead too easily." The dead of Paris, of Lyons, of Nantes and of Arras (and there were a growing number of towns like Orange, whose sufferings were only now coming to light); those who had died in the Atlantic prison ships, in the fields of Cayenne, and in so many other places; not forgetting those whose deaths could never be reckoned, who had been abducted or defenestrated, or who had vanished. To these must be added the living corpses, the men whose lives had been shattered, their vocations frustrated, their work cut short; who would now eke out the rest of their days in misery, if they could not summon up the necessary energy to kill themselves. He praised the unlucky *babouvistes,* whom he considered as the last of the pure revolutionaries, faithful to the most immaculate ideal of liberty, but tragically contemporary with men who were still preaching, in the colonies, a Liberty and a Fraternity which were mere political stratagems aimed at preserving old territories or annexing new ones. The old Jehovah, whose churches and cathedrals were now re-opening in all the places which had surrendered temporarily to atheism, had emerged victorious from his ordeal. His worshippers could now claim that what had taken place was in the last resort no more than the manifestation of His anger against all the philosophers who had dared to twist his beard during the century that was now entering its last weeks, had treated his Moses as an impostor, his Saint Paul as a bore, and had even insinuated—as Victor Hugues had once done in a speech which owed much to the Baron d'Holbach—that Jesus' real father was a Roman legionary.

And the narrator concluded bitterly, draining his last glass of wine : "This time the Revolution has failed. Perhaps the next will be the real one. But if they want to find me when it breaks out they'll have to hunt high and low. We must beware of too much fine talk, of Better Worlds created by words. Our Age is succumbing to a surfeit of words. The only Promised Land is that which a man can find within himself."

As he said this Esteban thought of Ogé, who had been so fond of quoting a sentence from his master Martinez de Pasqually : "A human being can only become enlightened if we awaken the divine faculties within him, kept dormant by the predominance of matter."

The first light of dawn was reflected in the windows and mirrors of the drawing-room. The first matin-bells were ringing on a Sunday which had been whipped by the north wind since the small hours. To the voices of the bells he had known since childhood was now added a gruff refrain from the new cathedral. The night had passed with strange swiftness, as in the happy days of topsy-turvydom. And now, in no hurry to go to bed, wrapped in blankets which they had fetched one by one to cover themselves in their arm-chairs, the four of them remained silent, as if absorbed in their own reflections.

"Well *we* don't agree," said Sofia suddenly, in a small bitter-sweet voice which always heralded an argument.

Esteban felt obliged to ask whom she meant by *we*.

"The three of us," replied Sofia, with a sweeping gesture which seemed to exclude him from the family circle.

Then, as if talking to herself, she entered on a monologue which found visible assent on the faces of Jorge and Carlos. One could not live without a political ideal; the happiness of a whole people could not be achieved at the first attempt; grave errors had been made certainly, but these errors would serve as a useful guide for the future; she realised that Esteban had been through certain painful experiences—and she sympathised with him very much—but perhaps he had been the victim of an exaggerated idealism; she admitted that the excesses of the Revolution were deplorable, but great human victories could not be achieved without pain and sacrifice. To sum up : nothing big could be done in this world without blood being shed.

"Saint-Just said that first," exclaimed Esteban.

"Because Saint-Just was young. Like us. What amazes me when I think of Saint-Just is how close he still was to a school desk." She knew all about everything her cousin had told her—as far as politics were concerned of course—knew more perhaps than he did, who had only been able to obtain a partial and limited view of events, a view sometimes marred by the proximity of ridiculous trifles, by the inevitable naïvetés, which in no way detracted from the greatness of a superhuman design.

"So descending into Hell was just a waste of time?" cried Esteban.

All she meant was that from a distance one got a more objective impression of things, a less emotional one. She deeply deplored the beautiful monasteries that had been destroyed, the fine churches that had been burned, the mutilated statues, the shattered stained-glass windows. But if Man's happiness demanded it, then Middle Gothic could be wiped from the face of the earth.

The word "happiness" had the effect of infuriating Esteban : "Be careful! It's the pious believers like you, the deluded, the devourers of humanitarian pamphlets, the Calvinists, who erect guillotines."

"I wish we could erect one at once in this cretinous and

corrupt city, in the Plaza de Armas," replied Sofia. She would have watched with pleasure the decapitation of all the inept officials, all the exploiters of slaves, all the self-satisfied rich, all the man in gold braid who inhabited this island, which had been cut off from all Knowledge, relegated to the world's end, reduced to the level of an illustration on a tobacco-box, by the most pitiful and immoral government in modern times.

"They need to guillotine a few people here," agreed Carlos.

"More than a few," decreed Jorge.

"I was prepared for anything," said Esteban, "except to find a Jacobin Club here."

Not quite, the others explained. Merely well-informed people (hearing this repeated infuriated Esteban), who were resolved to "do something". It was essential to have regard to the times, to possess an object in life, to take some part in the transformation of the world. This last year or two, Carlos had applied himself to founding a small Androgynous Lodge—Androgynous because they were too few in number to be able to do without educated and intelligent women—with the political aim of spreading the philosophical writings which had fostered the Revolution, as well as some of its basic texts : the *Declaration of the Rights of Man*, the French Constitution, important speeches, civic catechisms, etc. They brought him various loose sheets and leaflets, whose obsolete type-faces and clumsy lay-out proclaimed them as -the clandestine productions of the printing-presses of New Granada or Havana—or perhaps of the River Plate, or Los Angeles. Esteban knew these publications. He knew them so well that, from the idiosyncrasy of certain turns of phrase, the dexterity of certain transpositions, the presence of an adjective whose Castilian equivalent had cost him a great deal of trouble, he was able to identify his own translations, made at Victor Hugues' direction in Pointe-à-Pitre and set by the Loeuillets. And here were these same texts reappearing, having been multiplied on the presses of the Mainland. *"Vous m'emmerdez!"* he shouted as he ran out of the room, overturning a chair.

Crossing the patio he noticed that there was a key in the lock of the door leading to the warehouse. He was curious to visit this place which, in a way, belonged to him, and which would be empty, it being Sunday. The smell of brine, sprouting potatoes, dried beef and onions, which he had formerly found so unpleasant, now entered his nostrils like that of a rich, life-giving humus. It was the smell of ships' holds, of quayside granaries, of well-stocked cellars. The red wine dripped from the faucets; the rinds of the La Mancha cheeses were turning green; fats oozed through the earthenware of their pot-bellied jars. But there reigned an order unknown previously. Everything had been aligned, piled up, or left hanging, according to its constitutional requirements. Up above, hanging from the cedar-wood rafters, were hams and strings of garlic; cereals were heaped up to form walls; below were barrels of anchovies and pickled fish. And beyond, in the patio, which was now roofed over, were show-cases, protected by iron grilles, containing samples of goods which had been introduced to widen the scope of the business : salt cellars, reliquaries and candle snuffers of Mexican silver; delicate English porcelain; elegant *chinoiseries*, brought in through Acapulco; mechanical toys, Swiss watches, and wines and liqueurs from the former cellars of the Conde de Aranda.

Esteban went towards the office, where the books, inkwells, pen sharpeners, salvers, rulers and balances were all in their right-ful places, awaiting those who would be using them the next day. Noticing that the best office was occupied by two particularly imposing desks, the young man pictured a third, which would perhaps be assigned to him, over there against the mahogany-panelled wall, where was displayed an oil painting of the father of the family and founder of the firm, frowning, as he always did, and exuding probity, severity and a spirit of enterprise. He thought of himself here on radiant mornings to come, shut up amidst samples of rice and chick-peas, appraising, reckoning, arguing with some morose debtor, or some provincial retailer, while outside the sun sparkled on the waters of the bay, as a clipper passed, bound for New York or Cape Horn. He realised that *this* would never interest him sufficiently for him to devote the best years of his life to it. He had been corrupted by his sea-voyages, by living from day to day, by his habit of owning nothing. Although he saw himself as having been rescued from the pit, he did not feel that he was yet back in reality, in a recovered normality.

He went to his room. Sofia sat waiting for him, among the

puppets and physics apparatus, unable to resign herself to going to bed, her face reflecting a deep sorrow. "You're angry with us," she said, "because we have faith in something."

"Having faith in something which takes on a different aspect every day will involve you in great and terrible disappointments," said Esteban. "You know what you hate. That's all. That's why you are ready to put your trust and your hopes in anything else at all."

Sofia kissed him, as she used to when he was a child, and tucked him into the hammock: "Everyone can believe what they like, and we'll go back to being as we were before," she said, as she went out.

Left alone, Esteban realised that that was impossible. There are times made for decimating flocks, confounding tongues, and scattering tribes.

XXXVII

THE DAYS PASSED, but Esteban could not make up his mind to begin work in the warehouse. "To-morrow", he would say, as if apologising to people who had asked nothing of him. And the next day he would roam about the city, or cross the bay by boat and go to the town of Regla. There were strong cane-syrups and heady sangarees for sale there, on counters covered with roast piglets that reminded him of the *boucans* of the old days. Unserviceable schooners, rejected as being old and decrepit, lay mouldering in a backwater, huddled together like beggars on a winter night, and rocking ceaselessly in the gentle surge, as it lapped through their holed sides covered with barnacles and purple algae. At one place could be seen the ruined hulks in which the Jesuits expelled from the Spanish Dominions had been confined for months on end, after being brought by the Portobello route from their remote Andean monasteries. Sellers of prayers, ex-votos, and sorcerers' charms—magnets, jet, pieces of iron and coral—practised their trade openly. Here every Christian church had a maroon church behind its sacristy, dedicated to Obatalá, Ochum or Yemanyá, nor could any of the parish priests protest, since the freed negroes worshipped their old African gods in the form of the images standing on the altars of the Catholic churches. Sometimes, when he returned, Esteban went to the Coliseo Theatre, where a Spanish company brought to life a world of beaux and ruffians with its rhythmic *tonadillas,* to remind people of a Madrid cut off by the war.

Towards Christmas, Sofia, Carlos and Esteban were invited by some relations of Jorge's to spend the holiday on a finca, considered to be one of the most prosperous and flourishing on the island. Carlos and Jorge were too involved in the end of the year buying and selling to leave the warehouse, but they decided that Sofia should go on ahead with Esteban, while they completed their business in the city and followed a week later. This idea was not at all unacceptable to Esteban, who still felt estranged from Sofia by the presence of her husband; nor had he yet succeeded in re-establishing a real friendship with Carlos, who was too bound up in the business, often out at night at a masonic meeting, or too tired by his day's work to do anything more, after dinner, than doze in an arm-chair in the drawing-room, pretending to be listening to the chatter of the others.

"Now I shall find you again." Esteban said to Sofia, once they were alone together in the intimacy of the carriage, bumping towards Artemisa. Under the raised oilskin hood, they both felt as though they were jolting over the bad roads in a cradle. They ate at taverns and stages along the way, and amused themselves by ordering either the commonest or the most unusual things—boiled meat and vegetables in dark gravy, or grilled ring-doves—while Sofia, who never drank wine at the family dinners, discovered handsome-looking bottles amongst the cheap brandies and red wines. Her face grew flushed, she perspired at the temples, but she laughed the laugh of the old days, and was less of the lady, less of the mistress of the house, as if she had been delivered from a tolerated but persistent criticism.

On the way she pressed Esteban to talk about Victor Hugues. He asked Sofia about the letter he had brought for her.

"Nothing," she said. "I expected rather more. You know him : jokes that lose all their point when they're written down. And, deep down, sad. He says he has no friends."

"His loneliness is his punishment," said Esteban. "He thought that he had to renounce all friendships in order to become great. Even Robespierre didn't go that far."

"He was always given to asking too much from himself," the girl replied. "That's why, when he wanted to raise himself above his station, he showed that he wasn't up to it. He aspired to being a tragic hero, and he never got beyond a minor part. Moreover he played in the wrong theatres. Rochefort, Guadeloupe . . . The back stairs!"

"He's a small man. Many things show that." And Esteban searched his memory for anything that might deflate that too-proud figure : a stupid phrase he had overheard one day, a trivial expression, a sign of subservience or weakness—as when, on a famous occasion, he had remained silent, smiling unpleasantly, when Antonio Fuët threatened to horsewhip him if he presented himself uninvited at the Privateers' Lodge. And besides, there was his worship of Robespierre, which had degenerated into mimicry. He began to list the charges against his former friend, for the very reason that he had been fond of him, and his weaknesses were therefore all the more unpardonable. "I should like to speak well of him, but I can't. Too many things spoil his memory for me."

Sofía listened to him, marking her assent in her own particular way, with little grunts which could be interpreted as signs of surprise, disapproval, shock, or of horror at a piece of cruelty, a blunder, a pettiness, or an abuse of authority. "Let's forget Victor; he was the bad product of a great revolution."

"A product who finally made a fortune and married a rich woman," observed Esteban ironically. "Unless he's been locked up in Paris for his malversations. Or perhaps for the crime of insubordination. Not to mention what the magistrates of the New Terror may have been able to accuse him of."

"Let's forget Victor."

But after another few miles they again began to talk about Victor Hugues, in a fresh exchange of condemnatory commonplaces : "He's vulgar" . . . "I don't know how we could have found him so interesting" . . . "he's uneducated, his speeches are quoted from books he's just read" . . . "An adventurer" . . . "He was never anything more than an adventurer" . . . "He fascinated us because he came from a long way away, and had travelled a lot" . . . "There's no doubt he was brave" . . . "Reckless too" . . . "Fanatical to begin with, unless he was pretending to be, out of ambition" . . . "A political animal" . . . "Men like that bring discredit on a revolution".

Set in the midst of palm trees and coffee plantations, Jorge's relations' house was a sort of Roman palace, with tall, smooth, Doric columns set at intervals along the external galleries, which were decorated with china plates, ancient vases, Talavera mosaics, and jardinières overflowing with begonias. The drawing-rooms, the colonnades of the central patio and the dining-rooms could comfortably have accommodated a hundred people. The fires in the kitchens were always alight, and the days passed in a succession of breakfasts, light luncheons and cold collations; the supplies of food were inexhaustible, while a cup of chocolate or a glass of sherry was always within reach. The white marble statues adorning the garden made a wonderful picture against the pomegranates and bougainvillaea of a vegetation fenced in by creepers. Pomona and Diana the Huntress watched over a natural pond, carpeted with ferns and arums, hollowed out in the widened bed of a stream. Long avenues, shaded by almond trees, carobs and royal palms, faded into the green distance, where one could see a mysterious Italian pergola, covered with rambling roses, a small Greek temple, erected to shelter some goddess of mythology, or a maze of box trees, in which it was pleasant to lose oneself as the evening shadows lengthened.

The owners of the house were ever attentive to the welfare of their guests, but did not bother them. The old principles of Creole hospitality left everyone free to do as they fancied, and while some rode off down the paths on horseback, others went hunting or walking, and the remainder dispersed, one with a chess-board, another with a book, into the vast parklands. A bell hanging on a high tower set the tempo for their daily lives, summoning them to meals or to social gatherings, which were attended by those who felt like it. After the evening meal, which ended in the coolness of ten o'clock, garlands of lamps were lit on the great terrace behind the house, and a concert began, given by an orchestra of thirty black musicians, who had been trained by a German maestro, a former violinist with the Mannheim Orchestra. Then, under a starlit sky—so starlit that it seemed over-laden with stars—there would sound the stately introduction to a Haydn symphony, or else the instruments would break gaily into a dashing Allegro by Stamitz or Cannabich. On occasions, with the collaboration of some of the guests who had good singing voices, they gave short operas by Telemann, or Pergolesi's *La Serva Padrona*.

So the time passed, in these final days of a Century of Enlightenment which seemed to have lasted more than three hundred years, so very many were the things that had happened in it.

"A wonderful life certainly," said Sofia, "but behind those trees there is something unforgiveable." And she pointed towards the line of tall cypresses, towering like grey-green obelisks above the surrounding vegetation, behind which another world was hidden : the world of the slaves' huts, whence their drums sometimes sounded, like a distant hailstorm.

"I regret it as much as you do," replied Esteban, "but our efforts will never succeed in arranging things any differently. Other men failed in the attempt even when they were granted Full Powers."

On the evening of the 24th of December, whilst some of the party were eagerly completing the arrangements for Christmas Day, invading the kitchens at intervals to make sure that the turkeys were browning in the ovens, and that the sauces were beginning to give off their eloquent aroma, Esteban and Sofia went to the entrance of the finca, with its monumental iron gates, to wait for Carlos and Jorge who would soon be arriving. A sudden shower caused them to take shelter in one of the pergolas, ablaze with newly-opened poinsettias. The rain brought the scents out of the earth and drew a last breath of perfume from the fallen leaves on the paths. "The rain is over and gone; the flowers appear on the earth; the time of the singing of birds is come", murmured Esteban, quoting a Biblical text which he remembered having read as a child.

And then a dazzling light dawned on him. He felt as though he had been saved, restored to himself, by a joyous revelation : Now you understand everything. You know what has been ripening within you all these years. When you look at her face you understand the only thing you need to understand, you who were so eager to pursue truths which passed your understanding. She it was, the first woman you knew, whom you embraced as a mother in place of someone you never knew. She it was who revealed the wonderful tenderness of woman to you, watching over your sleeplessness, pitying your sufferings, soothing you with her caresses when dawn came. She is the sister who knew the successive changes in your body, as only some unimaginable lover, growing up beside you, could have known them.

Esteban leaned his head on a shoulder which seemed to have been formed from his own flesh and burst into such deep uncontrollable sobs that Sofia, full of astonishment, took him in her arms and drew him to her, kissing him on the forehead and cheeks. But it was an eager, thirsty, too-avid mouth which now sought hers. Removing his face from hers with her hands, she abruptly broke free, and remained standing in front of him, watching his reactions like someone who observes the movements of an enemy. Esteban looked at her, sadly, passively, but with such a fire in his eyes that Sofia, feeling herself being looked at as a woman, took a step backwards. And now the young man spoke to her—of what he had just understood, of what he had just discovered within himself. In a changed voice, he uttered unlooked-for, inadmissible words, which, far from moving her, sounded to her like hollow clichés. She did not know what to do, or what to say; she was almost ashamed of having to endure this monologue full of irritating confessions about trivial disappointments in bedrooms, desires that had never been satisfied, and obscure hopes which had brought the wanderer in arid lands back to his starting-point.

"That's enough!" shouted Sofia, her anger written on her face. Perhaps another woman would have heard him out with interest, but her refusal to accept them made his words ring false. And as their tempo increased, so did that of her own shouts of "That's enough!", until the diapason rose into a register that was final, conclusive, irrefutable.

There was an anguished silence. Both their hearts were pounding as if they had together made some enormous effort. "You've spoilt everything, you've destroyed everything," she said. And it was Sofia now who burst into tears, and began to run in the rain.

Night fell over a prostrate body. Henceforth nothing would be as it had been. What had burst from him in this moment of crisis would create a permanent barrier of mistrust, of reticent silences, of hard looks, which would be intolerable to him. The best thing to do would be to go away, he thought, to abandon the familiar surroundings, although he knew that he lacked the strength for it. The times had become so dangerous that a traveller started on his journey expecting the worst, as in the days of the Middle Ages. And Esteban knew, too, how much that was tedious could be contained in the word *adventure*.

The rain had stopped; the undergrowth was full of lights and fancy-dresses. Shepherds appeared, and millers with floury faces, negroes who were not negroes, old women aged twelve, men with beards, and men with cardboard crowns, all shaking maraccas, cow-bells, tambourines and timbrels. And girlish voices sang in chorus:

> *"Ya viene la vieja*
> *Con el aguinaldo.*
> *Le parece mucho.*
> *Nos parece poco.*
> *Pampanitos verdes,*
> *Limones en flor.*
> *Bendita la madre*
> *De nuestro Señor."*

Behind the clumps of bougainvillaea, the house was a blaze of candelabra, lamps and Venetian lustres. Now they would have to wait for midnight, surrounded by trays of punch. Twelve strokes would ring out from the tower, and everyone would have to gulp down the traditional twelve grapes. Then would ensue the interminable dinner, prolonged by a dessert of hazel-nuts and almonds broken open with the nutcrackers. And the negro orchestra would to-night give the first performance of some new waltzes, whose music they had only received the day before and had been rehearsing since morning.

Esteban did not know how to escape from the festivities, from the pestering children or the servants who summoned him by name to take part in a wine-tasting game, which was already beginning to make the laughter ring out louder under the illuminated colonnades.

At this moment the brisk trot of horses was heard. Remigio had appeared at the end of the avenue, sitting on the box of a mud-spattered carriage. But there was no one inside. Reining

271

up abruptly when he saw Esteban, he told him that Jorge had been suddenly taken ill, and was in bed, struck down by a new epidemic that was afflicting the city, and was attributed to the great slaughter on the battlefields of Europe, whose mephitic infection had been brought over by some Russian ships recently arrived to barter goods they had never seen before for the tropical fruits that were very popular with the rich gentlemen of St. Petersburg.

XXXVIII

THE HOUSE SMELLED of illness. The moment they entered it their throats were aware of the presence of mustard and linseed in the distant kitchens. There was a constant coming and going along corridors and up staircases, with tisanes, poultices, potions and camphorated oil, whilst marshmallow water and lily bulbs were brought up in buckets to cool the skin of the patient, who could not shake off a tenacious fever rising at times to a state of raving delirium.

After a melancholy journey, made at full speed, and during which they hardly spoke to each other, Sofia and Esteban had found Jorge in a very serious condition. Nor was it a question of one isolated case. Half the city had been prostrated by this new epidemic, which only too often had a fatal outcome. When his wife appeared, the sick man looked at her out of exhausted eyes, and seized her hands as if he might find in them some hope of salvation. Since the doors of the room were kept closed to avoid draughts, the atmosphere prevailing was thick and suffocating, full of the smell of medicinal fumes, rubbing alcohol, and the wax from the candles which were kept alight because Jorge had an oppressive conviction that if he fell asleep in the dark he would never wake up again. Sofia tucked him up, soothed him, and put a vinegar compress on his burning brow, before going to the warehouse to get from Carlos the details of the treatments recommended by the doctors—who had, in fact, little idea of how to combat a disease they had never met with before.

Thus they entered the new century, alternating between nights of insomnia or watchfulness, days of hope and days of discouragement, during which, as if summoned by mysterious voices, cassocks appeared against the glazed tiles of the hallway, offering to bring images and miraculous relics. There were prescriptions and bottles of medicine all over the upstairs furniture, together with the half-burned tapers that had been used to fix the cupping glasses. Sorrowful but serene, Sofia would not leave her husband's bedside, however repeatedly she was told that the disease was extremely contagious. With no other precautions beyond rubbing herself with aromatic lotions and always keeping a clove in her mouth, his wife attended the sick man with a solicitude and a tenderness which reminded Esteban of the days of his own asthmatic adolescence. Sofia's affection—an unconscious anticipation of maternal feelings perhaps—was centred on another man, and the evidence of this became all the more painful to him now that he had greater cause than ever to regret the days of a Paradise Lost—as lost now as it had been unappreciated then—when he should have been counting his blessings; instead, because they were habitual and everyday, he had accepted them as belonging to him by right.

Night after night Sofia sat unsleeping in her nurse's chair, or dozed so lightly that a sigh from Jorge was enough to wake her. Sometimes she would leave the room, a profound grief depicted on her face: "He's delirious," she would say, bursting into tears. But her courage returned when she saw that he had regained consciousness, and was hanging on to life with unexpected tenacity, making an incredible effort of will to stand up against the acute pains which bored into his sides, and shouting that death would not defeat him. During these moments of temporary improvement, he made plans for the future: no, he was not going to waste his youth between the walls of a business. A human being was not born for that. As soon as his convalescence was over they would both go off abroad, they would carry out the journeys they had always postponed. They would go to Spain, to Italy; he would finally get his health back in the mild climate of Sicily. They would leave this noxious island for ever, where people were always being exposed to epidemics like those that had afflicted Europe in the old days.

Esteban heard these projects, and felt a rending anguish at the thought that they could be realised, and that he would perhaps find himself deprived of a presence which was the sole justification for his present existence, empty as it was of ambitions, ideals or desires. He could measure the disillusionment with which his personal experiences had left him, when he had to receive people who came to the house at all hours to enquire after the patient. None of them interested him. Their conversation meant nothing to him, especially when the visitors were some of the latter-day philanthropists who flocked to the little Androgynous Lodge his family had founded, and which he had stubbornly refused to attend since his return to Havana. The *ideas* which he had left behind had now caught up with him, in an environment where everything seemed organised to neutralise them. The people who were pitying the lot of the slaves to-day had bought fresh negroes to work on their haciendas yesterday. The men who talked about the corruption of the colony's government had themselves prospered in the shade of that corruption, which had favoured their profiteering. The men who were beginning to talk about possible independence had been only too delighted to receive some title of nobility from the Royal Hand. The same state of mind that had led so many aristocrats in Europe to build their own scaffolds was becoming general among the rich here. Forty years too late, people were reading books in favour of revolution which that revolution itself, impelled into unforeseen channels, had made inappropriate.

After three weeks they began to have renewed hopes about the sick man's condition. Not because it had improved. But it seemed to have become stationary, though serious, after sufferings which in anyone else would have already ended in death. The doctors had learned something from having observed so many cases, and they opted to apply to their patients a treatment very similar to that used in combating pneumonia.

They were quite hopeful therefore when, one evening, a knocking was heard at the front door. Esteban and Sofía leaned over the balustrade in the patio to see who was knocking so loudly, and they saw Captain Caleb Dexter appear, in a blue frock-coat and ceremonial gloves. Not knowing that there was a sick man in the house, he had come round without warning, as on other occasions, the moment the *Arrow* dropped anchor in Havana harbour. Esteban joyfully embraced this man whose presence brought back such pleasant memories. When he learned the state of things, the North American expressed his deep regret, and insisted on fetching some fomentations, successfully used by the sailors on his ship, although Sofia tried to dissuade him, for Jorge's skin had by now been so inflamed by poultices that he could hardly bear even the least irritant of them. But Caleb Dexter, convinced of the merits of his fomentations, went to fetch them, returning as the lamps were being lit with various unguents and salves which smelled of corrosive acids.

Another place was laid at the table, and the appearance of a noble English soup-tureen inaugurated the first cheerful dinner that had been eaten under that roof for several weeks. Jorge was asleep, delivered into the care of a Clare nun, who had been sent for at Sofia's orders. "He will recover," said Carlos. "My heart tells me he's out of danger."

"May God hear you," said Sofia, using an expression which was not habitual with her and which, in her mouth, suddenly sounded like a propitiatory spell—although Esteban could not be sure whether the god invoked was the Jehovah of the Bible, the God of Voltaire, or the Great Architect of the masons, such was the multiplicity of the gods worshipped during the recently expired Century of Enlightenment.

It was inevitable that Esteban should recount his travels in the Caribbean again, but this time he did so with pleasure, good-humouredly even, since the sailor was acquainted with the scene of his great adventure.

"The state of war between France and the United States will surely not last much longer," said Caleb Dexter, "they're already opening negotiations for peace." As for Guadeloupe, chaos had reigned there ever since Victor Hugues had refused to surrender his authority to Pélardy and Desfourneaux, and was at last forcibly deported. Military uprisings were an everyday occurrence, while the Big Whites of yore, reborn from out of what had seemed to be their own ashes, were waging war against the new Big Whites, and winning back their former privileges. For the rest, there was a general tendency in the French colonies to return to the practices of the *ancien régime,* especially now that Victor Hugues had just taken up his resplendent post as Agent of the Directory in Cayenne. Had they not heard? said the sailor, noticing the stupefaction of the others, for whom Victor Hugues was a defeated man, whose career had been shattered, a prisoner perhaps, perhaps condemned to death. And now they learned that after winning his battle in Paris this man had returned to America in the guise of a conqueror, the possessor of a new cocked hat and invested with fresh authority. When they heard the news, said the Yankee, a wave of terror had swept through Guiana. People dashed into the streets shouting that now the most terrible misfortunes would come upon them. The exiles in Sinnamary, Kouron, Iracoubo and Counamàma, who had lost hope of surviving the epidemics, called loudly on the Most High, asking that they should be spared further suffering. There was a collective panic, such as might have resulted from the coming of an antichrist. Placards had to be posted on the walls in various parts of Cayenne, informing the inhabitants that times had changed, that what had occurred in Guadeloupe would not be repeated here, and that the new Agent was animated by a spirit of generosity and justice, and would do all that was possible to ensure the colony's happiness. ("*Sic*," said Esteban, recognising the rhetoric of old.)

And the tragi-comic feature of the case was that, to prove his good-will, Victor Hugues had arrived in Cayenne with a band of musicians ostentatiously installed in the bows of his ship, in the self-same spot where the guillotine had long ago stood, when he had brought it to Guadeloupe as a fearful warning to the population. But now noisy marches by Gossec, the latest songs from Paris and country-dances for fife and clarinet sounded from the place whence there had so often come, six years before, the sinister noise of the knife dropping down its uprights as it was tested by Monsieur Anse.

Victor Hugues had come alone, leaving his wife in France— or perhaps he had not married in the end, Caleb Dexter did not know for certain, because his news had come from Paramaribo, where they had been most concerned at the time at the proximity of the feared Agent of France.

But to everyone's astonishment, this Agent had shown himself to be magnanimous, had visited the exiles, and had somewhat improved their miserable lot, promising them that many of them would soon be returning to their homeland.

"The wolf is wearing sheep's clothing," said Esteban.

"Just a tool of the politicians, adjusting himself to the orders of the day," said Carlos.

"An extraordinary character all the same," said Sofia.

Caleb Dexter withdrew early, because his ship was due to sail shortly before dawn; they would have a longer talk in a month's time, when he would again be calling at Havana on his way south. Then they would celebrate the patient's recovery, in the very best wine. Esteban drove him to the quay in the carriage.

When he returned he met Carlos in the hallway of the house : "Run and fetch the doctor," he said, "Jorge is suffocating. I'm afraid he won't last the night."

XXXIX

THE SICK MAN went on fighting. One would never have believed that this pallid, fragile man, who looked like the last of his line, could have had such reserves of vitality. He was now in an almost continual state of asphyxia and devoured by fever, yet he still had strength enough to scream, during his delirium, that he refused to die. At various times Esteban had watched an Indian die, or a negro; with them things had happened very differently. They had lain down like wounded animals, unprotesting, increasingly remote from everything around them, increasingly anxious to be left alone, as if resigned in advance to their final disintegration. Jorge, on the other hand, twitched and complained and groaned, incapable of accepting what had already become obvious to the others. It was as though civilisation had robbed men of all courage in the face of death, despite all the arguments that had been forged throughout the centuries so that they might understand it lucidly, and accept it with serenity. And now that death grew inexorably closer with each tick of the clock, he must still convince himself that it was not an end but a passing, and that, beyond it, another life was awaiting him, which he would enter with certain guarantees provided on this side of the barrier. It was Jorge himself who asked for a priest, who accepted as a last confession what was no more than a babbling of disjointed phrases.

Realising that the doctors had admitted defeat, Rosaura persuaded Sofía to let her bring an old negro sorcerer to the house "Why not?" said the girl. "Ogé didn't despise sorcerers."

The necromancer proceeded to "clean" the room with aromatic water; he threw snails on the floor, to see whether they fell facing upwards or downwards; and ended by carrying in plants, brought from a herbalist who kept a shop near the market. However, they were forced to admit that his lore relieved the patient's sufferings, and revived a heart which at moments showed symptoms of mortal weakness.

But there was not much longer to wait. The sick man's physical mechanisms were failing, one after another. The negro's potions afforded only a temporary relief. The undertaker's men were drawn by an infallible instinct to prowl round the house at all hours. Esteban was not surprised when he saw Carlos' tailor appear with mourning clothes. Sofía had ordered hers from a *modiste,* in such quantity that they filled several large baskets, which had been set down anyhow in the back room that the girl had been using to dress and undress in since her husband's illness. Perhaps in obedience to some personal superstition, she had resolved not to open them. Esteban understood this perfectly; by ordering these black clothes to be made, she had performed a magic rite. To have taken them out before their time would have been to accept what she refused to accept. They must each pretend to believe that black would never again need to be worn under that roof.

But three days later, after a complete cardiac failure, black made its entry through the front door shortly after four o'clock in the afternoon; the black of monks' habits, the black of cassocks, the black of friends, of customers of the warehouse, of brother masons, of acquaintances and employees; the black of the undertakers with their catafalque and their paraphernalia; the black of the real blacks, remotely linked to the family for four generations by the chains of subservience, and who now issued forth, like forgotten shadows, from their distant quarters of the town, to form into mournful choruses under the arches of the patio. In this ruthlessly segregated society, the wake was the only ceremony which overthrew the barriers between races and classes; then it was permitted that the barber who had once shaved the deceased's cheeks should come and rub shoulders by his coffin with the Captain-General of the colony, the Rector of the Board of Physicians, the overseer from the Fresh-Water Wells, or the rich landowner who had recently been granted the title of Marquess by royal proclamation.

Sofía was thinner after her nights of vigil, numbed by that deep-seated grief which forbears from showing itself in tears or lamentation, and bewildered by the sight of hundreds of unknown faces—that night the whole business-world of Havana had foregathered in the house with the tall pillars—but she carried out her widow's role with a dignity and a self-control which Esteban himself marvelled at. She was pale and frowning, nauseated perhaps by the perfume of so many different flowers, whose mingled scents combined with those of the tapers and candles, and the lingering medicinal fumes, with their suggestions of mustard and camphor, to form a waxy smell. Yet, despite her graceless weeds, the girl preserved a beauty which triumphed over her physical imperfections. Her forehead was perhaps too self-willed; her eyebrows too thick; her eyes too slow to respond; her arms were long, her legs too weak maybe to support the fine architecture of her hips. But, even in these present painful circumstances, she shone with a light of integral womanhood, whose source was somewhere deep within her; Esteban saw this, and appreciated the secret reserves of her potent humanity.

He went out into the patio to escape the droning of prayers which filled the drawing-room where the body lay. He went to his room where—in contrast to the prevailing mood—the puppets looked like some monstrous inventions of Callot's. He threw himself into the hammock, unable to rid his mind of a persistent thought—tomorrow there would be one man fewer in the house. The projected travels that had so distressed him a few days ago would never take place. The tedious year of mourning would now run its course, with Masses in memory of the deceased, and obligatory visits to the cemetery. He had a whole year in front of him in which to convince the others of the need of a change of scene. It would be easy to return to a subject which had enlivened their discussions ever since the days of their adolescence. Carlos, who was too involved in the warehouse, would perhaps accompany them for two or three months. Then he would arrange to remain alone with Sofia, somewhere in Europe—and he thought of Spain, a country less menaced now by the French wars, which had leapt across the Mediterranean and landed up absurdly in Egypt. The vital thing was not to hurry, not to let oneself be carried away by momentary impulses. To take advantage of the inexhaustible resources of hypocrisy. To lie when it was useful. To play the role of Tartuffe conscientiously.

He went back to the blackness of the wake, shaking hands, and receiving condolatory embraces from the people who were still coming in through the front door and crowding the corridors. He looked at the coffin. The man who lay there was an intruder. An intruder who tomorrow would be carried out on men's shoulders, without Esteban even having committed the hidden crime of wishing for his physical elimination—the term the *philosophes* of the last century had pedantically used to describe some poor unfortunate's execution. By closing the house, and once more reducing the family circle to its rightful proportions, the mourning would re-create the atmosphere of the old days. Perhaps they would return to the old disorder, as if the clock had been put back. After the long night of the wake, after the funeral with its responses, cross-bearer, oblations, vestments, tapers, baize and flowers, obituary and requiem—and people would notice that one man had come in full-dress uniform, another had wept and groaned that we are as nothing—after the departure of the mourners, when they would have to shake a hundred sweaty hands, under a sun that tortured the eyes as it reflected off the marble headstones, then the natural links would be restored with what they had left behind them.

And when the exhausting obligations of the funeral had been fulfilled, they again gathered about the big table in the dining-room : Carlos, Esteban and Sofia, just as in the old days, in front of a meal which had been ordered from a nearby hotel, as it was Sunday. Remigio, who could not go to the market because he was at the cemetery, brought in trays covered with cloths, beneath which appeared porgies cooked with almonds, marzipan, young pigeons *à la crapaudine*, truffles and candies, ordered personally by Esteban, who told them they must send out for anything which they had not got, no matter what the price.

"What a coincidence," said Sofia, "I seem to remember that we ate almost the same things after the death of . . ." (her voice broke off, since their father was never mentioned in the house).

"Exactly the same," said Esteban, "the menus don't vary much in hotels."

And he noticed that his cousin was leaning with her elbows on the table, as if the slovenly manners of the old days were reappearing in her. She tried a little of everything, unsystematically, staring at the table-cloth and toying mechanically with the glasses. She withdrew early, exhausted by her nights of vigil. But it would have been pointless now to expose herself to a posthumous contagion, and she had the narrow bed of her girlhood brought out from an attic bedroom and set up in the room where some of the baskets of mourning clothes still remained unopened.

"Poor Sofia!" said Carlos, when the two men were left alone. "Fancy being left a widow at her age!"

"She'll soon marry again," said Esteban, fingering a grey seed, tied up with gold thread, which had been his personal talisman during his time at sea, to ward off storms and prevent misfortune.

During the days which followed, he tried to make himself useful by going regularly to the warehouse, where he occupied Jorge's office and pretended that he had suddenly begun to find business supremely interesting. He learnt surprising news from his daily contact with retailers from the market and men from the provinces. The whole island was in a state of hidden ferment. The wealthy landowners lived in a state of constant dread, for they believed there might be a conspiracy amongst the negroes, who might be inspired to do here what they had done in San Domingo. Rumours were current about a mulatto chieftain, whose name no one knew, whom no one ever saw, but who was roaming the countryside stirring up the workmen on the sugar plantations. The literature of those "accursed Frenchmen" was hidden in too many pockets. Threatening lampoons began to appear, posted on the walls of the city during the night by unknown hands, welcoming the Revolution in the name of "freedom of conscience", and announcing that the guillotine would soon be going up in the public squares. A subversive intent was attributed to any gesture of violence on the part of a negro—even if he was a madman or a drunkard. And apart from all this, ships were bringing reports of political unrest in Venezuela and New Granada. Everywhere the winds of conspiracy were blowing. It was said that the garrisons were at the ready, and that extra cannon had arrived from Spain to reinforce the batteries in the Castillo del Príncipe.

"Drivel," said Carlos, when they came to him with such reports, and he would prudently steer the conversation on to the subject of commerce. "In this overgrown village, people don't know what to talk about."

XL

Amarga presencia
—Goya

ONE NIGHT WHEN Carlos and Sofía were out attending some ceremony at the Androgynous Lodge, Esteban, who had a slight cold, settled down in the drawing-room, with a large glass of punch within reach, to read an old compilation of prognostications and prophecies published fifty years before by Torres y Villarroel, the Great Piscator of Salamanca. He was startled to find that this man, who boasted of being a Doctor of Alchemy, Magic, and Natural and Transmutatory Philosophy, in order to sell more almanachs, had announced the fall of the French monarchy, in terms of terrifying accuracy:

> "Cuando los mil contarás
> con los trescientos doblados
> y cincuenta duplicados
> con los nueve dieces más,
> entonces, tu lo verás,
> mísera Francia, te espera
> su calamidad postrera
> con tu Rey y tu Delfín,
> y tendrá entonces su fin
> tu mayor gloria primera."

He then moved on to read Villarroel's life story, and was much diverted by the picaresque life which had led the poet by intricate paths to be, in turn, a guide to blind hermits, a student, a bull-fighter, a quack, a ballet dancer, an executor, a mathematician, a soldier in Oporto, and a University professor, before finally finding peace in a monk's habit. Esteban had just reached the mysterious episode of the poltergeists who disturbed the peace of a Madrid house by knocking the pictures off the walls, when he noticed that what had earlier been a heavy shower was developing into a real downpour, driven by a gusty wind. He became absorbed in his reading again, and ignored an upstairs window that sounded as if it had been left open. He reflected that there was a nice coincidence in the fact that one of the windows in the house should begin to bang at the exact moment he reached the pages dealing with ghosts and apparitions. But when the noise continued, Esteban found it too disturbing, and went upstairs.

It was a French window in the room where Sofia now slept which was open, and it had been foolishly remiss of him not to have gone up to close it before, because the rain had been driving straight in, and looked as though it had been emptied over the floor in bucketfuls, soaking the carpet by the bed. A hollow in the tiles beside the wardrobe was turning into a lake. In this lake stood the baskets of mourning clothes, still unopened, their dry wickerwork greedily soaking up the water. Esteban put them on the table, but found they were so wet that he thought he should take out the garments inside. He opened the first one, and just when he was expecting to plunge his hands into a mass of pitch-black cloth, there came out to meet him a riot of bright materials, satins and silk dresses, showing a desire for display such as he would never have found in Sofia's wardrobes. He raised the lid of the next one; in it was a costly array of the finest cambric and Valenciennes lace, made up into exquisite chemises and other intimate garments.

Thunderstruck, and feeling as if he were guilty of having violated a secret, Esteban closed the baskets again, and left them where he had put them. He went down for some cloths to mop the floor. But all the time he was doing this he could not take his eyes from the wicker chests, which had come to the house, along with their contents, during the days when Jorge had been sweating out his last fever in the next room. His cousin had certainly worn new mourning clothes at the wake. But they had simply been three dresses, worn alternately, and Esteban had thought it odd at the time that Sofia should have chosen such drab and dowdy ones—he had interpreted it as a desire for self-mortification. But now he did not know how to reconcile this desire with the other, which he had just discovered, to accumulate all these expensive, useless and unsuitable clothes. Amongst them were dresses that would have attracted attention at balls or the theatre; stockings by the dozen; embroidered sandals; sumptuous finery intended both for worldly show and for the most premeditated intimacy.

He raised the lid of the basket he had not yet opened. The clothes it contained were more normal, more ordinary : clothes for the street and for daily wear, for informal occasions, together with bright, cheerful dressing-gowns, which advertised the quality of their satin and the subtle details of their workmanship. But the riddle remained; nowhere could he see the colour black, or anything that might correspond to mourning, or a demonstration of grief. Sofia knew of the speed with which feminine fashions changed, especially in these days, when the city was passing through a new wave of prosperity and all the women knew what was being worn in Europe. It was inexplicable therefore that the girl should have brought this sumptuous trousseau when she did, knowing that by the end of the year of mourning which she must necessarily observe—and even then she would have to keep the rules of half-mourning—these clothes would no longer be in fashion.

Esteban was still torturing himself with questions, pursuing the most heart-rending suppositions, one after another, and even thinking that his cousin might be leading a double life, unsuspected even by her brother, when he heard the noise of a carriage coming in through the gates. Sofia appeared in the doorway of the room, where she stopped in surprise. Esteban explained what had happened as he wrung a blanket out into a bucket. "The clothes must be soaked," he said, pointing to the baskets.

"I'll take them out myself. Leave me alone," said Sofia, pushing him towards the door. After wishing him goodnight she turned the key in the lock.

The following day Esteban was in the warehouse, unable to concentrate on his work, when he heard a commotion in the street. Windows were being closed, as the cry went up that the negroes had followed the example of those in Haiti and had risen in revolt. The street hawkers loaded up their goods, and fled precipitately back to their homes, some with hand-carts full of toys, others with sacks bulging with trinkets for altars. On every doorstep women stood gossiping about rape and murder, and the uproar around them grew louder when a coach took the corner too fast and overturned. People congregated in isolated groups and exchanged the most conflicting reports : two regiments had been sent to the city walls to repel the advance of a column of slaves; the darkies had tried to break into the powder magazine; some French agitators, brought by ship from Baltimore, were operating in the city; there were fires in the Arsenal district.

It was soon learned that all this commotion was due to a fight between some blackamoors and some American sailors, who had made the most of whatever was being offered in the way of women, liquor and cards in the famous cave of La Lola, and had then tried to escape without paying, after thrashing the croupier, kicking the proprietress, and breaking consoles and mirrors. The affair had culminated in a pitched battle, with the intervention of a band of Congolese, who were going to the Iglesia de Paula, lanterns held high, to pay their respects to a patron saint. There had been a scuffle with machetes and clubs, aggravated by a sudden charge from the watchmen, and several men had been left lying on the ground wounded.

An hour later order had been restored, but the quarter was still restless. The Governor took advantage of the occasion to put a stop to certain activities which were beginning to worry him, and made it known by public proclamation that severe measures would be taken against anyone suspected of spreading subversive ideas, sticking lampoons on the walls—this was a very common occurrence—advocating the abolition of slavery, or making insulting remarks about the Spanish monarchy.

"They're still playing at revolutions," said Esteban that evening, when he returned home.

"It's better to play at anything rather than nothing," Sofia replied bitterly.

"At least I've got no secrets to hide," said Esteban, looking her straight in the eyes. She shrugged and turned her back on him.

Her expression became hard and determined. During dinner she kept silent, and avoided questioning glances. Yet she did not do so with the embarrassment of someone who feels that they have been caught out in a reprehensible design, but rather with the haughty expression of a woman determined not to offer any explanations.

That night, while Esteban and Carlos amused themselves by pursuing a dull game of chess right up to checkmate, Sofia hid her face behind an enormous volume of astronomical maps.

"The *Arrow* arrived to-night," said Carlos suddenly, threatening Esteban's last knight with his black bishop: "The Yankee will be here to eat to-morrow."

"I'm glad you remembered," said Sofia from the distant world of her constellations. "We'll lay another place at the table."

And it was at dinner time the next day that Esteban arrived home, expecting to find all the lights burning. But when he entered the drawing-room, he realised that something untoward was happening. Dexter was pacing nervously from one wall to another, making curious excuses to Carlos, who had collapsed in tears, and whose incipient obesity made a caricature of him as he sat huddled in grief.

"I can't do anything," the American was shouting, his arms flung wide. "She's a widow and of age. To me she's just another passenger. I've spoken to her. She won't listen to reason. Even if she were my own daughter I couldn't do anything."

And he went into details : she had bought her passage through Muralla and Co., paying for it with cash. Her papers had been procured for her by a fellow mason, and displayed the necessary stamps. She would go as far as Barbados, and there leave the *Arrow,* to take one of the Dutch ships going to Cayenne.

"Cayenne," said Carlos, as if stunned. "Cayenne, do you say ! Instead of Madrid, London or Naples !"

Then, becoming aware of Esteban's presence, he said to him as if he were already in the know : "She's like a mad woman. She says she's tired of the house, and tired of this town. She was going to set off just like that, without any warning and without saying good-bye. She's been on board the ship for the last two hours, with her baggage and everything."

He had been down to try and dissuade her : "You might as well talk to the wall. I couldn't drag her off. She wants to go."

Then he turned to Dexter : "You, as Captain, have the right to refuse a passenger. Don't tell me you haven't."

Irritated by an insistence which cast doubts on his integrity, the Captain raised his voice : "There's no legal or moral reason why I should. Let her do as she wishes. No one can stop her going to Cayenne. If she doesn't sail this time, she will the next. And if you lock the doors, she'll get through the window."

"But why?" the others shouted, refusing to give in. Dexter pushed them firmly away with his large hands.

"Kindly understand once and for all that she knows very well why she wants to go to Cayenne—to Cayenne and nowhere else." And, wagging his forefinger like a preacher, he quoted a Biblical proverb : "The words of a tale-bearer are as wounds and they go down into the innermost parts of the belly."

This quotation, with the vulgarity of its last word, acted on Esteban like a counter-irritant. Taking the sailor by the lapels of his frock-coat, he asked for a clear, firm, explanation, with no beating about the bush.

Dexter replied with a brutal phrase which made everything clear : "While you and Ogé went off whoring along the wharfs in Santiago, she stayed on board with *him*. My sailors told me about it. I was so disgusted I set sail as quickly as I could."

Esteban had no need to ask anything more. Everything fell into place. He now knew why those luxurious clothes had been ordered, the moment it was known that Someone had again become all-powerful in a neighbouring part of America; he understood the hidden intention behind a hundred interrogations he had undergone, when, in return for a few disparaging epithets about *him*, she had contrived to learn everything she wanted to know about his life, his triumphs, his mistakes. She had agreed hypocritically that he was a monster, an abominable person, brutalized by politics, so that, bit by bit, with little quick tugs, she could extract more and more about the gestures, desires and actions of this disgraced and reinstated Plenipotentiary. And this silent, repressed longing had continued to work industriously away, until it broke out into a hunger which not even the presence of a dying man had been able to restrain.

In all this there was a sickening incongruity between the flowers and candles of the funeral and her troubled thoughts, which had become only too manifest in the purchase of intimate garments, fashioned to mould themselves to the contours of her naked body. Sofia suddenly revealed herself to Esteban in the ignoble, unthinkable light of a woman who lies submissive, acquiescent and happy under the weight of a man who has experienced the resistance of her unbroken flesh. Remembering the disgust she had felt one night at the world of the prostitutes, who were no more than subservient protagonists—perhaps the most *disinterested*—in the act of human copulation, Esteban was unable to reconcile the two personalities inhabiting the same body : that of the girl who had blushed with indignation and anger at an act which her religious upbringing had made unclean, and the other, who had so soon afterwards succumbed to desire, and involved herself in the expedients of dissimulation and complicity.

"It's your fault, for marrying her to a cretin," shouted Esteban, seeking someone to blame for what he held to be a monstrous defection.

"It was never a good marriage," said Dexter, smoothing down his wrinkled lapels in front of a mirror. "When a husband and a wife understand each other in bed, they're all right, even if they fight. It was a complete farce in this case. *Something* was missing. You only had to look at his hands, they were the hands of a Catholic nun, with soft fingers that couldn't get hold of things."

And Esteban recalled the excessive care which Sofia had taken —even beside the grave—to play the role of faithful spouse, acting all the time with a submissiveness, solicitude and propriety foreign to her independent and erratic tastes. He was almost pleased that she had not come a virgin to that marriage, which he considered as a quite unforgivable capitulation to the usages of a despised society. But this very fact again evoked that powerful presence who still, even from that distance, made his weight felt in the house.

Observing that Carlos did nothing, but was still dazed and tearful, he got up : "I'll fetch her somehow," he said.

"You won't get anywhere by making a scandal," said Dexter. "She has the right to go."

"Go and make one last attempt," said Carlos.

Esteban slammed the door and set out for the quays. When he

arrived at the pier where the *Arrow* was moored, he felt choked by the smell of recently landed fish; he was walking between baskets of porgies, goatfish and sardines, whose scales glistened in the light of torches. From time to time a fisherman would plunge his hand under a jute cover, pull out a handful of squids, and throw them on the scales.

Sofia was standing in the bows, on the side nearest the shore, still dressed in her mourning clothes, a tall dark figure, seemingly insensible to the smell of fish-scales, octopus-ink and blood which drifted up to her. There was something about her of the impassivity of a mythological heroine contemplating the offerings brought to her habitation by some seafaring race. Esteban's violence abated when he saw this motionless woman, who watched him approach without making any movement, and stared at him with disarming steadiness.

And suddenly he was afraid. He felt defenceless against the possibility of hearing certain words which, from her lips, would sound with a deafening eloquence. He did not dare go on board. He looked at her in silence. "Come," he said finally.

She turned towards the harbour, and leaned her back against the gunwale. On the other shore gleamed the lights of districts she had never been to; beyond, mingling together, were the lights of the vast baroque chandelier which was the city, with its red, green and orange glass shining amongst the arcades. To the left lay the dark channel that led to the blackness of the open sea, the sea of adventures, of hazardous voyages, of the endless wars and conflicts that had stained this many-islanded Mediterranean red with blood.

She was going to the man who had made her conscious of her own being, and who, in a letter brought by someone that now stood grieving beneath her, had spoken of feeling lonely in the midst of his triumphs. There was much to be done where he was; a man of his temperament could not help elaborating great enterprises; projects in which both of them would be able to achieve their true stature.

"Come," the voice below repeated. "You think you are too strong."

To return would be to doubt this strength, to consummate a second defeat. She had known too many nights when her body had been cold, when she had pretended to a joy she did not feel. "Come."

Behind lay the ancestral house, clinging to her body like a shell; out there was the dawn, the radiance of the open spaces, far from street cries and bells. Here, the parish church, the poor-box, tedium and uneventfulness; out there, an epic world, inhabited by Titans.

"Come," the voice repeated. Sofia withdrew from the ship's side and was hidden by the shadows on the deck. Esteban went on talking to her, raising his voice. But his monologue was drowned by the noise of the fishermen, as the gusts of words rose towards her, telling of a house which they had all built together and which would henceforth lie in ruins.

"As if real houses could be built by brothers and sisters," she thought. Esteban clung to the hull of the ship, and went on talking unheeded. This enormous wooden body, smelling of salt, seaweed and marine vegetation, was soft, almost feminine, in the way it gently surrendered its moist flanks to him. Above him a figurehead, with a chalky white woman's face and eyes ringed by a thick blue line, had taken the place of the other woman, who would be sailing back into the world of desire at dawn, laden with rich and beautiful things and delivered from the black clothes that had detracted from her beauty and interfered with her pleasures. She would be leaving the family circle, to profane its secrets, to divulge them to another who was perhaps already waiting for her. The young man felt miserable and naked—naked with a nakedness she had known too well to see in terms of nakedness—when he reflected that his desire for violence had not gone beyond entreaty.

The woman above him was waiting for the wind to fill the sails. She was bearing the furrow of her loins towards another's seed; she would be the cup and the ark, like the woman in Genesis who had to abandon the home of her fathers in order to go with her man.

People were beginning to look at him, and to cup their ears, laughing, to hear better what they thought he was saying. He backed away from the ship, and amongst the fishermen's baskets he met Captain Dexter.

"Is everything clear now?" asked the sailor.

"Perfectly clear," replied Esteban. "I wish you all *bon voyage.*"

XLI

HE WAS STANDING now at a corner near the quay, undecided and ashamed of his defeat. He muttered over all the things he should have said, but which had not passed his lips. The ship was still there, close by him, surrounded by torches, and with something maleficent about her in the darkness. The mermaid on the prow, with the twin strands of her hair attached to the gunwales, emerged from the shadows from time to time, when a lantern illuminated the death mask of her face, as if she had been exhumed from a grave.

Esteban felt that his mind was full of unspoken words, now arranging themselves into reasons, accusations, warnings, reproaches, and outbursts that would mount to the level of insult and remain there, ending with certain terms of a supreme opprobrium which would exhaust the resources of the language. If she stood firm under this verbal broadside—and it would be in keeping with her character to do so—then he would be left as defenceless as before.

Then vicious plans began to form in his mind. It was eight o'clock. Captain Dexter's ship would sail at five the next morning, so nine hours remained—long enough, perhaps, for something to be done. Goaded by the rancour he felt, Esteban built up a theory of where his duty lay. He was under an *obligation* to prevent Sofia from reaching Cayenne. He must not hesitate to have recourse to the most extreme methods to prevent her committing moral suicide. This adventure of hers would be like a descent into hell. Sofia was of age, but Carlos had the legal right to prevent her flight, by claiming mental alienation. There had been a case of this a few months before, when a young widow of good family had tried to elope to Spain with one of the actors who had come to sing *tonadillas* at the Coliseo. One could always count on the help of the authorities in cases which in any way affected the honour of reputable families. Impulsive love affairs were very much frowned on by colonial society, which was ever ready to avail itself of the services of the *alguacil* when its calm was troubled by an amorous intrigue or by promiscuous women. In such cases the Church became active too, and placed itself athwart the culprits' path.

Determined to resort to any means at all to prevent what he found intolerable, Esteban arrived home breathless and sweating from having run so far, and was still panting when he burst unexpectedly in on several men, with the sullen faces of policemen, who were busy prying about everywhere, opening cupboards, examining desks and escritoires, and going from the stables to the upper storey. One of them was coming downstairs carrying a packet of leaflets on his head. The searchers passed the sheets from hand to hand, and agreed that they were copies of the *Declaration of the Rights of Man and the Citizen,* and of the French Constitution, which Sofia had been keeping under her bed.

"You must get away," said Rosaura, coming up to Esteban. "Señor Carlos escaped over the roof." The young man retreated deliberately and calmly towards the hallway, on his way to the street. But two men had already been posted by the front door.

"You are under arrest," they said to him, and placed him under custody in a corner of the drawing-room. They made him wait there for several hours, without questioning him. They passed to and fro in front of him, as if unaware of his presence, looking to see if there was anything behind the pictures or under the carpet. They sank iron rods into the soft earth of the flower-beds, to see if they met with any resistance from a box buried under the grass. One man was taking books off the shelves, examining the bindings and feeling their thickness; he finally threw a selection of volumes on the ground—a number of works by Voltaire, Rousseau and Buffon, together with anything else printed in French and in prose—poetry they were less concerned about.

At last, at three o'clock in the morning, they decided that the search was finished. They had more than enough evidence that this house was a nest of conspiring freemasons, publishers of revolutionary pamphlets, and enemies of the King, who were trying to introduce anarchy and impiety into his overseas Dominions.

"Where is the lady?" they all asked now, having been told by informers that she was one of the most dangerous of the conspirators. Rosaura and Remigio replied that they knew nothing.

That she had gone out early. That she generally stayed at home but that just this once she happened not to be in at this late hour. One of the men then said that this would be a good moment to visit the ships that were anchored in the harbour, so as to forestall any attempt at flight.

"You would be wasting your time," said Esteban, raising his voice from the corner. "My cousin Sofía has never had anything to do with all this. You have been misinformed. I put those papers in her room only this evening, without her knowing."

"And does your cousin sleep away from home?"

"That is a question that concerns her private life."

The men of the search-party exchanged ironic glances. "The dead into the grave, and the living to their pleasures," said one of them with a coarse laugh. But again they spoke of going down to the ships.

At this point they asked Esteban to write a few lines on a sheet of paper. Surprised at this demand, the prisoner scrawled some lines from Saint John of the Cross, which came easily to mind as he had read them recently:

> *"Oh, quien se viese presto,*
> *De este amor amoroso amor arrebatado!"*

"The writing's the same," said one of the interrogators, brandishing a copy of *Le Contrat Social,* in whose margins, years before, Esteban had jotted down several ideas particularly insulting to the monarchy. The attention of all of them now focused on him.

"We know that you recently returned from a long journey."

"That's true."

"Where were you?"

"In Madrid."

"That's a lie," said one of them. "In your cousin's writing-desk we found two letters addressed from Paris, in which you certainly expressed great enthusiasm for the Revolution."

"That's possible," said Esteban, "but afterwards I went to Madrid."

"Leave him to me," a man said, pushing his way forward. "I'm not a Galician or a Catalan." And he began to ask about streets, markets, churches and other places of which Esteban had never heard. "You've never been to Madrid," he concluded.

"Possibly not," said Esteban, and another man stepped forward.

"What did you live on in Paris, after Spain declared war on France, and you couldn't get money sent to you by your family?"

"I was paid for doing translations."

"Translations of what?"

"Various things."

It was four o'clock. They began to talk again of Sofía's inexplicable absence, and of the need to go down to the ships.

"All this is stupid," cried Esteban suddenly. "Do you think that by breaking into a house in Havana you're going to put an end to the idea of Liberty in the world? It's already too late! Nobody can stop what is under way now!" And the veins in his neck swelled as he loudly reiterated what he had already said before, adding references to Fraternity and Equality which caused the clerk's pen to move more quickly across the paper.

"Very interesting. Very interesting. Now we're beginning to get somewhere," said his interrogators. The most important of them increased the tempo of his questions, and began to press Esteban.

"Are you a mason?"

"I am."

"Do you deny Jesus Christ and our Holy Religion?"

"My God is the God of the philosophers."

"Do you share, and have you spread, the ideas of the French Revolution?"

"Yes, in all sincerity."

"Where was the propaganda printed which we found here?"

"I am not an informer."

"Who translated them into Spanish?"

"I did."

"And these American Carmagnoles too?"

"Perhaps."

"When?"

At this point they were joined by one of the searchers who had stayed upstairs, obstinately trying to discover something more.

"Look at the fans the lady spent her money on," he said, opening one of them, which was decorated with a scene from the

Taking of the Bastille. "And that's not all. She's got a collection of boxes and pincushions in the most suspicious colours."

When he saw these red, white and blue knick-knacks Esteban felt suddenly touched by the adolescent enthusiasm which had induced such a strong character as Sofia to collect these samples of fancy-goods that had been on sale in bazaars all over the world for years now.

"We've got to lay our hands on this artful dodger somehow," said the important man. And again they spoke of going down to the quay.

So then Esteban let them have the whole story in detail: he went back to Victor Hugues' arrival in Havana, so as to slow up his story which the clerk was feverishly scribbling down. He talked about his personal contacts with Brissot and Dalbarade. About his propaganda activities in the Basque country. About his friendship with those abominable men—the traitors Marchena and Martinez de Ballesteros. Next, his journey to Guadeloupe. The Loeuillets' printing-press. The events in Cayenne, during which he had had close dealings with Billaud-Varenne, the pitiless enemy of the Queen of France.

"Make a note of it, make a note of it," said the Important Man, who was quite overcome by such revelations.

"Has Biyo got a 'y'?" asked the clerk.

"An 'I'," said Esteban, recklessly launching into a lecture on French grammar. "An 'I' because . . ."

"We won't quarrel over one 'I' more or less," shouted the important man, rolling up his sleeves. "How did you get back to Havana?"

"Everything is easy for a freemason," replied Esteban, and continued with a story that was raising him to high conspiratorial eminence. But as the hands of the clock neared five, his words took on a semblance of caricature. His questioners could not understand why a man should make such a complete confession of crimes that might well condemn him to the common garrotte, instead of defending himself. By now, having nothing left to tell, Esteban was pouring out crude witticisms, talking about Bourbon Messalinas, the horns which the Prince of Peace had affixed to His Majesty, and the fireworks which would soon be exploding up King Carlos' backside.

"He's a fanatic," they all said, "either a fanatic or a madman. America's full of Robespierres like him. If we don't take care there'll soon be a general massacre here."

And Esteban went on talking, accusing himself now of things he had never done, and boasting of having himself taken his revolutionary literature to Venezuela and New Granada.

"Make a note of it, clerk, make a note of it. You're going to run out of ink," said the important man, who by this time had no questions left to ask.

It was half past five. Esteban asked that someone should accompany him up to the roof, where he had left a personal possession inside an antique vase which adorned the parapet. Greedy for what might prove to be fresh evidence, several of the inquisitors followed him. Inside the vase there was only a wasps' nest, and several of them were nearly stung. Ignoring the curses of the men, Esteban looked towards the harbour. The *Arrow* had already sailed; the place where the ship had been moored to the bollards along the quay was empty.

He went down to the drawing-room. "Take this down, Señor Clerk," he said : "I declare before God, in whom I believe, that everything I have said is false. You will never be able to find the slightest proof that I did what I said, except that I was in Paris. There are no witnesses or documents for you to refer to. I said what I did to help someone to escape. I did what I had to do."

"You may be saving yourself from the garrotte," said the important man, "but no one will be able to get you out of Ceuta prison. We've sent people to the African quarries for less than this."

"That can be my fate too for all I care now," said Esteban. He paused in front of the picture of "The Explosion in a Cathedral", in which the huge fragments of column, sent into the air by the deflagration, remained suspended, as if in a nightmare. "Even the stones I'm going to break now were present in this picture."

And seizing a stool he threw it against the painting, tearing a hole in the canvas, which fell to the floor with a crash. "Take me away," said Esteban, so exhausted, so much in need of rest, that all he could think of now was to sleep somewhere even if it should be in prison.

CHAPTER SIX

XLII

T HE WAVES CAME silently, rhythmically, from the south, weaving and unweaving the web of their slender crests, that were like veins in a piece of dark marble. The green coastline had been left astern. They were sailing now through waters of such a deep blue that they seemed to have been made by the fusion of some wintry, glassy substance and stirred by the beating of a far-off heart. There was not a living creature to be seen on all that unbroken expanse of sea, closing in the mountains and abysses of its deeps like the First Sea of Creation, before the murex and the argonaut. The Caribbean was the only sea which at times took on this uninhabited look, teeming with life though it was. As if impelled by some mysterious necessity, the fish fled from the surface, the medusas sank, the sargasso disappeared, and all that was left to confront man was what he thought of in terms of infinity : the perpetually retreating line of the horizon; space, and, beyond space, the stars in the heavens—the mere enunciation of the words recaptured the overwhelming majesty they had once had for those who invented them; they had perhaps been the first words to be invented after those which had newly begun to denote pain, hunger, and fear.

Here, above this barren sea, the heavens took on an enormous importance, with their constellations that had been there since the beginning of time. Throughout the centuries humanity had been isolating and naming them, projecting their own myths on to the unattainable, adapting the positions of the stars to the outlines of the figures which filled minds that were forever inventing fables.

There was a sort of childish daring in thus filling the sky with Bears, Dogs, Bulls and Lions, thought Sofia, as she leaned on the gunwale of the *Arrow*, gazing into the night. But it was a way of simplifying eternity, of confining it within fine illustrated books, like the astronomical atlas on the family bookshelves, in whose engravings tremendous battles seemed to be being waged, centaurs against scorpions, eagles against dragons. In naming the constellations man had reverted to the language of his earliest myths, and had remained so faithful to it that when the men of Christ appeared, they could find no room in a sky completely inhabited by pagans. The stars had been given to Andromeda and Perseus, Hercules and Cassiopeia. There were title deeds, held in entail and not transferable to simple fishermen from the Tiberian Lake—fishermen who had no need of stars, moreover, to take their ships to where Someone, soon to shed his blood, would forge a religion that knew nothing of stars.

As the Pleiades grew pale and daylight appeared, thousands of mottled helmets advanced towards the ship, harbouring long red streamers, which formed under the water silhouettes of curiously mediaeval warriors, like Lombard princes clad in chainmail—for it was a coat of mail that the marine fibres resembled, which these creatures transfixed by splinters of light (called "men of war" by Captain Dexter) had met with on their way and now carried wrapped round them, from shoulder to hip, from neck to knee, from ear to thigh. The submarine army gave way as the ship passed, and closed its ranks again behind it, to pursue its march out of the unknown for many days, until the time would come when their heads would burst in the sun, and their trailers would be consumed by their own corrosion.

In the middle of the morning they entered a new country, that of the Sea Fans, extended like the wings of a bird on the surface of a sea turned white by their migration. And after them dark swarms of thimble-shaped molluscs appeared, some open, others closed in the contractions of hunger; followed by a floating party of snails, clinging to a raft of dried foam.

But a sudden squall transformed the sea in a moment, making it glaucous and opaque. A strong smell of salt rose from the water under the drumming rain, whose drops were absorbed by the planks of the deck. The canvas of the sails sounded like a slate roof in a hailstorm, while the ropes grew tight, and creaked in every fibre. The thunder travelled over the ship, from west to east, with prolonged reverberations, before it moved away with its clouds, leaving the sea, by mid-afternoon, bathed in a strange auroral light, which turned it as smooth and iridescent as a mountain lake.

The bow of the *Arrow* became a plough, breaking up the tranquillity of the surface with the frothy arabesques of its wake, which persisted for several hours, as evidence that a ship had passed that way. At dusk the wake stood out brightly against the already night-filled depths, and drew a map, with streets and cross-roads, on the once-more deserted sea—so deserted that those who looked on it felt themselves to be the only voyagers of their time. From now until the following morning, they would be in the Land of Phosphorescence, with its lights rising out of the depths, opening into a fan, into streams of sparks, forming shapes like an anchor, a tree-root, an anemone, a head of hair— or perhaps a handful of coins, the lights of an altar, or a stained-glass window in some far-off, submerged cathedral, flooded by the rays of abyssal suns.

On this voyage, Sofia was not troubled by the anxieties of adolescence, as she had been when she had leaned on this same gunwhale before and drunk in the breeze from above these same bows. Her decision had matured her, and now she was travelling towards something which could only be as she had imagined it. After two days during which the thought of what she had left behind had weighed upon her spirits, she had woken up, on this third morning, with an exultant feeling of freedom. Her chains were broken. She had escaped from everyday life, and was penetrating into a timeless present. Soon the great task she had waited for all these years would begin, and she would fulfil herself in the role she had chosen. Once more she experienced the joy of being at a point of departure, on the threshold of herself, just as when she had entered on a new stage of her existence on this very ship. She was rediscovering the strong smell of pitch, of brine, flour and bran, which she had known before and whose presence now was enough to abolish the passage of time. She closed her eyes as she sat at Captain Dexter's table, and the taste of smoked oysters, English cider, rhubarb tarts and Pensacola medlars brought back the sensations of her first sea-voyage.

They were not following the same course, however. Although

Toussaint Louverture was anxious to establish commercial relations with the United States, the North American traders distrusted the black chieftain's solvency, and left this chancy market to the men who sold arms and ammunition—the only goods which were always paid for in cash, even when there was not enough flour to make dough for the daily bread. Having left the coast of Jamaica on their beam, they had been sailing for several days now in the emptiest part of the Antilles Sea— making for the port of La Guaira—where the last Guadeloupan privateers only appeared once in a while, in schooners now called the *Napoléon,* the *Campo-Formio,* or *La Conquête de l'Egypte.*

One morning they thought they were in for trouble when they saw a small ship bearing down suspiciously quickly on the *Arrow.* But their momentary apprehension turned to delight when they found that it was the almost legendary *Balandra del Fraile,* commanded by a Franciscan missionary who had renounced his habit, and had been involved for many years smuggling in Caribbean waters. Otherwise they met nothing but beef ships, plying between Havana and New Barcelona, which left a powerful smell of smoked meat behind them as they passed.

To still her suppressed impatience to arrive, Sofia tried to interest herself in some of the English books to be found on Dexter's shelves—next to the Acacia, the Pillars and Tabernacle of the mason's apron, still kept in the same glass case. But the climate of *The Nights* was as alien to her state of mind as was the oppressive atmosphere of *The Castle of Otranto.* After a few pages she closed the book, not too certain what she had been reading about, and gave herself up without further reflection to anything which reached her through her pores, appealing to her senses rather than her imagination.

One morning a violet-coloured mass began to take shape against the indistinct green haze of the horizon. "The Saddle of Carácas," said Dexter; "we're about thirty miles from the Mainland."

The activity heralding an impending port-of-call began to be apparent amongst the crew; those who were not needed for any immediate duty devoted themselves to their toilet, shaving, cutting their hair, cleaning their nails, scrubbing their hands. Out on to the deck came razors, combs, soap and darning needles, and pungent essences were poured over scalps. One man was mending holes in a shirt; another was sticking a patch on a dilapidated shoe; beyond him a third was inspecting his tanned face in a woman's hand-mirror. They all displayed a restlessness which was not wholly due to the satisfaction of having reached the end of a prosperous voyage; waiting on the shore at the foot of that mountain, whose outline was growing clearer now against the high cordillera, was Woman—unknown, almost abstract Woman, still without a face, but prefigured already by the proximity of port.

Along the tall masts of the ship the sails billowed out, as if to warn the figure that rose above the roofs that men were coming. And these sails, already visible from the shore, provoked much coming and going with buckets of water from the well in the houses by the harbour, as the women prepared for action with rouge, perfume, petticoats and dresses. With no need for words a dialogue had been joined, over a sea now crowded with fishing-boats.

The *Arrow* altered course, and began to sail parallel to the mountains, which descended so steeply out of the clouds right down to the water's edge that no cultivation could be seen on their sides. From time to time their vast wall dipped down, to reveal the secret of a shady beach stretching between two rock-faces blackened by a vegetation so dark and choked that it seemed as if the night still clung there in shreds. A fabulous smell, of the humidity of a continent not yet properly awake, came from these still waters, where the seed from the sea was about to be washed up by a last thrust from the waves.

But now the mountains were receding, without having revealed what lay behind them, and leaving a narrow strip of land, on which roads and dwellings appeared between clumps of hairy coconut palms, *uveros* and almond trees. They rounded a promontory that seemed to have been carved from a lump of quartz, and the harbour of La Guaira came in sight, open towards the sea like a colossal amphitheatre, on whose tiers of seats the roofs rose in echelon.

Sofia would have liked to have gone up to Carácas, but the road was long and tiring. The *Arrow's* stay would be a short one. She waited for the sailors who were off-duty to hurry ashore, where they knew they were expected, and then got into a pinnace, accompanied by Dexter who had to complete certain routine formalities.

"You mustn't feel obliged to look after me," said the girl, noticing that the captain was showing some of the same impatience as his crew. She began to walk towards the steep streets which ran alongside a dried-up torrent, and marvelled to come upon pretty little squares adorned with statues among houses with wooden grilles and screens which reminded her of those in Santiago de Cuba. Sitting on a stone seat, she watched the pack-animals go by, on their way up to the mountain paths that climbed, shaded by sponge trees, until they were finally lost in the haze about the mountain-tops—above a fort crowned with watchtowers, one of the many which defended the Spanish harbours in the New World, all of them so alike that they seemed to be the work of a single architect.

"Until a short time ago, some masons from Madrid were kept prisoner there. They were some of Saint Blas' Mob, as it was called, who had tried to take the Revolution into Spain," a pedlar from the Canary Islands told her, as he tried hard to sell her some satin ribbon. "And you won't believe this, but they went on plotting even in the dungeons!"

So the Great Event was under way. She had not been mistaken when she foresaw that it was imminent. She was more impatient than ever now to reach the end of her journey, afraid that she might arrive too late, and that the man to whom the Great Task had been entrusted might already be in action, dividing the greenness of the forests as the Hebrews had divided the waters of the Red Sea. What Esteban had told her so many times was being confirmed : Victor, faced by the Thermidorian reaction, was taking his Spanish version of the Constitution and his American Carmagnoles into the heart of the Mainland of America, to bring them, as he had done before, the enlightenment that was now being extinguished in the Old World. To understand this one need only look at a compass-card : from Guadeloupe the squall had blown across to the Guianas, and thence to Venezuela, which was the normal route for getting to the other side of the continent and the baroque palaces of the Kingdom of Peru. It was from there in fact, from the mouths of the Jesuits—Sofia knew the writings of one Vizcardo Guzmán —that the first words had come, demanding independence for these lands which could only be conceived in terms of a revolution. Everything was becoming clear to her: Victor's presence in Cayenne was the beginning of something that would find expression in great troops of horses crossing the plains, in voyages up legendary rivers, in the crossing of high mountain ranges. An age was being born which would accomplish, here in America, what had come to naught in senile Europe. The people who were perhaps vilifying her, back in the family house, would now learn that her desires were not to be measured by the yardsticks which ordinary women used—the work-box and baby clothes. They would be talking about a scandal, little suspecting that this scandal would be much greater than they thought. There would be a new game of "Massacre them!", with generals, archbishops, magistrates and viceroys as the targets.

Two days later the *Arrow* set sail again; they left the Island of Margarita on their beam, and passed between the English possessions of Grenada and Tobago, making for Barbados. At the end of an uneventful voyage Sofia found herself in Bridgetown, in a world quite different from anything she had hitherto experienced in the Caribbean. This Dutch city breathed a different atmosphere, with its un-Spanish architecture, and its broad, wooden bilanders from Scarborough, St. George's or Port of Spain. There were curious newly-minted coins in circulation called Pineapple Pennies and Neptune Pennies. When she found that there was a Masonic Street and a Synagogue Street, she felt she was back in a city in the Old World.

She took a room in an inn recommended by Captain Dexter, kept by a sweaty mulatta. After a farewell lunch, at which Sofia felt so happy that she tried everything, not even scorning the bottles of porter, and the Madeira and French wines which were served, they took a carriage trip together through the surrounding countryside. For hours on end they jolted along the roads of a domesticated island, where the gently undulating landscape—there was nothing big, threatening or overwhelming here—was cultivated right down to the sea-shore. Here the sugar canes looked like unripe corn; the grass was as soft and well-behaved as a lawn; even the palms had ceased to look like tropical trees. There were silent houses, hidden in the woods, where columns from some Greek temple rose up to meet pediments obliterated by ivy, and where windows opened on to luxurious drawing-rooms inhabited by portraits whose varnish shone in the excessive light; there were tiled houses, so small that when a child leaned out of the window his body obscured the sight of large families gathered round the supper-table in a room where a chessboard would have seemed an enormous obstruction; there were ruins enmeshed by creepers, where ghosts met to moan on stormy nights—the whole island was haunted, according to the coachman; and above all, near the sea, there were cemeteries almost encroaching on the deserted beaches shaded by cypress trees, whose grey tombstones—very modest when a child leaned out of the window his body obscured the —told of Eudolphus and Elvira who had died in a shipwreck, and who could only be the heroes of some Romantic idyll. Sofia was reminded of *La Nouvelle Héloïse*; the Captain thought rather of *The Nights*.

Although it would take them far out of their way, and would mean their not getting home until well into the night, since the horses were tired and would have to be changed, Sofia indulged in a cajolery that seemed almost excessive to the North American, and succeeded in being taken up to the little rocky bastion of St. John, where, behind the church, she found a tombstone with an inscription that referred unexpectedly to the death on the island of a person whose name bore a crushing weight of historical association :

Here lie the remains of Ferdinand Paléologue, descendant of the last Emperors of Greece—Priest of this parish—1655-1656.

The bottle of wine he had drained during the journey had made Caleb Dexter somewhat emotional, and he uncovered himself respectfully. In the dusk, whose light was turning the waves red as they broke in a great spray against the rocky monoliths of Bathsheba, Sofia decorated the grave with some bougainvillaea which she had cut in the garden of the presbytery. The first time he visited the house in Havana, Victor Hugues had spoken at length about this tomb of the unknown grandson of the Ecumenical Patriarch who had been killed during the final resistance of Byzantium, having chosen to die rather than fall into the sacrilegious hands of the conquering Turks. And now she had found it, in the place he had indicated. Across the grey stone, marked with the Cross of Constantine, a hand now followed the course which another hand had followed years before, searching out the hollows of the letters with the tips of its fingers.

To cut short this unexpected ritual, which he felt had already lasted long enough, Caleb Dexter remarked : "And to think that the last rightful owner of the Basilica of Saint Sophia should have ended up on this island."

"It's getting late," said the coachman.

"Yes, let's go back," she said. She was amazed that her name should suddenly have occurred like that, in the Captain's stupid remark. It was too extraordinary a coincidence not to be read as an omen, a warning, a premonition. A wonderful destiny awaited her. The future had been beckoning to her secretly ever since a certain night when a Will had made itself felt by thundering on the door of the house. There were some words which did not arise by chance. A mysterious power shaped them in the mouths of oracles. *Sophia.*

XLIII

SOFIA HAD BEEN told that the rock of Grand Connétable would be visible shortly after first light, and she was up by dawn, on the deck of *The Batavian Republic*—an old Dutch merchantman, with a resplendent new name, which plied all the year round between the forests of the Mainland and the treeless Barbados, carrying mahogany for the cabinet-makers in Bridgetown, and building-boards to beautify the houses in Oistins—famous for their Norman-style, projecting upper storeys.

The girl had been waiting to leave for several weeks in her quayside lodgings; she was tormented by impatience, tired of walking about the street of the little town, and had been angry to learn of the peace treaty signed between France and the United States, which news, if it had arrived sooner, could have simplified her itinerary, by enabling her to travel from Havana on one of the North American ships that had now resumed trade with Cayenne. But all this was now forgotten, as they came in sight of the rocks and islets which heralded the Mainland, joyful in the morning air with their flocks of pelicans and sea-gulls. Already they were opposite the Mother and Daughters, which Esteban had once described to her, and the shore was showing signs of vegetation and human activity. Everything seemed extraordinary, magnificent and fascinating to Sofia, at this moment of arrival. All the greens in the world seemed to have been brought together into a single landscape to welcome her.

When the military authorities came on board, they expressed some surprise that a single woman from such a fine city as Havana should want to stay in Cayenne. But Sofia had only to mention the name of Victor Hugues for their suspicions to turn into deference.

It was already dark when the girl entered the sleeping streets of the town, making for Hauguard's inn, where she was very careful not to mention her connection with Esteban, remembering that his departure for Paramaribo had had all the features of a flight. The following morning she sent a note announcing her arrival to the ex-Agent of the Directory who was now the Agent of the Consulate. Soon after nightfall she was handed a brief message, scrawled on official notepaper : "Welcome. To-morrow I will send a carriage to fetch you. V."

Instead of the impatient summons Sofia had expected, these cold words had come, condemning her to a night of doubt. In a nearby yard a dog was barking at a drunkard who went along the street scratching his sores and shouting terrible prophecies about the scattering of the just, the punishment of the regicides, and the appearance of all before the Throne of the Lord, at a Last Judgement that was to take place—why?—in a valley in Nova Scotia. When the voice had died away in the distance and the dog had gone back to sleep, she became aware of the activities of invisible insects in every wall in the house, boring, scratching, gnawing at the wood. A tree was dropping seeds on to some overturned troughs with a noise like lead shot. Outside the hotel two Indians were arguing in voices like those of men from some explorer's tale. Everything conspired to prevent her from sleeping, and Sofia grew enervated, as she lay conjecturing late into the night. As a result, when the carriage arrived the next morning, she felt torpid and exhausted. And just when she thought they were taking her to Government House with her trunks and valises, the horses turned off down to a landing-stage, where a launch was waiting, with high gunwales, and equipped with cushions, awnings and canvas wind-breakers. She learned that she was to be taken to a hacienda a few hours away.

Although none of this corresponded with her expectations, Sofia felt almost flattered when she noticed the courtesy shown her by the crew. The boat was commanded by a young officer called De Saint-Affrique, who spent the journey enumerating the improvements effected in the colony since Victor Hugues had arrived there. Agriculture had been given a new impetus; the shops were full, and everywhere one breathed an air of peace and prosperity. Almost all the deportees had been sent back to France, leaving, as a memorial of their sufferings, a huge cemetery in Iracoubo, whose tombstones displayed the names of famous revolutionaries.

In the middle of the afternoon they entered the marshy mouth of a river on which leaves like those of water-lilies were floating, with purple flowers lying on the surface of the water. Soon they reached a landing-stage, from which one could make out a large house built in the Alsatian style, standing amidst orange and lemon trees on top of a small hill.

Attended by a solicitous swarm of negresses, Sofia installed herself in a room on the first floor, whose walls were decorated with fine old engravings depicting events that had occurred under the *ancien régime* : the Siege of Namur, the Coronation of the Bust of Voltaire, the unfortunate Calas family, interspersed with charming seascapes of Toulon, Rochefort, the Island of Aix, and Saint-Malo. As the chattering servants put her clothes away in the wardrobes, Sofia leaned out of the windows overlooking the open country; a garden full of rose-bushes gave way, after a short distance, to orchards and fields of sugar cane, surrounded by a sullen wall of wild woodland. Mahogany trees, with tall silvery trunks, gave shade to the paths, along the sides of which grew bushes of Peruvian balsam, nutmeg, and yellow pepper.

Several anxious hours of waiting went by. At last a launch tied up at the landing stage. Against the shadows of nightfall, which were already encroaching on the avenue, she saw a figure in military-looking uniform, gleaming with braid and embroidery and made to seem taller by a plumed hat. Sofia went out on to the paved terrace in front of the house, not noticing in her haste that a herd of black pigs was engaged in the delectable occupation of laying waste the flower beds opposite the front door, digging up the tulips and wallowing with jubilant grunts in the recently watered soil. When they saw the door open, the animals rushed into the house, rubbing their muddy bodies against the skirts of the girl, who tried to stop them with shouts and gesticulations.

Victor started to run, and arrived at the house in a rage. "How did they get loose? This is too much!" And, going into the drawing-room, he used the flat of his sword on the pigs, who were trying to squeeze into the other rooms and climb the stairs. The servants and several negroes emerged from the back of the house to help him, and finally the creatures were removed, one by one, hauled out by the tail or by the ears, carried, or chased out with kicks, all to the accompaniment of fearful squeals. The doors which led to the kitchen and outbuildings were closed.

"Have you looked at yourself?" Victor said to Sofia, when the porcine storm had somewhat subsided, pointing to her mud-stained clothes: "Go and change, while I tell them to clean up here."

When she saw herself in the mirror of her room, Sofia felt so miserable that she began to cry, to think how the Great Meeting she had been dreaming about all the time she was travelling had turned out. The dress she had had made for the occasion was falling off her, torn, mud-stained and smelling of the farmyard. Throwing her shoes into the darkest corner, she pulled off her stockings in a fury. Her whole body smelled of pigs, mud and filth. She had to tell them to bring up buckets of water, so that she could bath herself, thinking how grotesque this mishap was at such a moment. There was something ridiculous in being forced to wash like this, and the splashing of the water in the bath-tub must have been audible below. At last, throwing something or other over herself, she stumbled downstairs to the drawing-room, not caring what she looked like, in the sullen mood of an actor who has fluffed a big entrance.

Victor held out his hands and made her sit beside him. He had changed his gleaming uniform for the casual clothes of a well-to-do planter: white trousers, shirt open wide at the neck, and Indian jacket. "You must forgive me," he said, "but I always go around like this here. One has to get away sometimes from sashes and cockades." He asked after Esteban. He knew that the young man had left Paramaribo, and must therefore be in Havana by now. Then, as if anxious to give a picture of his life since the end of his Governorship in Guadeloupe, he described the vicissitudes of his rebellion against Desfourneaux and Pélardy, at the end of which he had been left disarmed and a prisoner and had been forcibly deported. In Paris, by means of an energetic self-defence, he had demolished Pélardy's charges. He had finally been chosen by the Consul Buonaparte to take charge of the government of Cayenne.

He talked and talked interminably, with all his old eloquence, as if to deliver himself of a surfeit of words too long suppressed. Whenever he touched on the details of his recent life, he announced their confidential nature with a too often repeated formula : "You're the only person I've told this to. Because I can't trust anybody." And then he would enumerate the obligations of Power, the many times he had been disillusioned, the impossibility of having friends if one intended to exercise real authority.

"They'll have told you I was severe, very severe, in Guadeloupe, and in Rochefort too. It had to be that way. A revolution isn't reasoned out, it's *done*."

While he talked without respite, pausing only where he found it necessary to solicit her approval, with an "isn't it?", "don't you agree?", "you see that, don't you?", "did you hear about it there?", "did you know that?" or "did they tell you?", Sofia was registering the changes to be observed in his person. He had grown a good deal fatter, although his powerful frame could carry off a certain amount of fat by disguising it as muscle. His expression had become hard, in spite of the new flabbiness which had weakened the lines of his face. Beneath his rather muddy skin one could still detect the old firmness and vigour.

The doors of the dining-room opened; two servants had just finished placing candle-sticks on the table, where a cold meal was laid, in silver dishes so thick they could have only come from the ship in which some viceroy of Mexico or Peru had been travelling. "That's all for to-night," said Victor to the servants. Then, in a more intimate tone of voice : "Now tell me about yourself."

But no significant picture, no interesting events, came into Sofia's mind in connection with her own life. Compared with the

sound and fury which had filled Victor's existence, and his
dealings with people whose names were household words, her
own life had been sadly empty. She had a brother who was a
shop-keeper; and a cousin, not made for brave deeds, whose
abjurations seemed so futile here, in face of Victor's greatness,
that the merciful thing was to hide them. Even the story of her
marriage was a lamentable one. She had acted as mistress of
the house, without even discovering a god in her cooking-pots,
as the nuns of Avila did. She had waited, that was all. The years
had passed, leaving no mark, arousing no emotion, between an
Epiphany without Kings, and a Christmas without meaning for
those who could not lay the Great Architect to bed in a manger.

"Well?" said the other, encouraging her to begin. "Well?"
But a strange, invincible reluctance kept her silent. She tried to
smile; she watched the flames of the candles; she scratched the
table-cloth with her finger-nail; she stretched out her hand
towards a glass, without finally raising it. "Well?"

Suddenly Victor went over to her. The lights changed places;
there were shadows, in which she felt herself caught, held, and
overwhelmed by a desire which restored her youthful ardour to
her. They came back to the table, perspiring, dishevelled, laughing at themselves. They talked in the language of the old days,
the language they had known in the harbour at Santiago, when,
scorning the coarse curiosity of the sailors, and ignoring the heat
and the smells from the hold, they had come together in the
narrow bunk between decks, surrounded by planks which
smelled—as these did—of fresh varnish.

The breeze from the shore was filling the house with the
scents of the sea. They could hear the noise of the water filling a
tank near by. And as the trees launched their brittle waves against
the windows, the house became a ship.

XLIV

WONDERINGLY, SOFIA WAS exploring the world of her
own sensuality. Her arms, her shoulders, her breasts, her flanks,

her knees had suddenly begun to speak. Exalted by surrender, her whole body was acquiring a new awareness of itself, obeying impulses of generosity and desire which in no way craved the consent of her mind. Her waist delighted to feel itself held; her skin shivered and contracted at the merest suggestion of an approach. Her hair, which she wore loose on their nights of love, was now something that could be *given* to this man to hold in his hands. There was a supreme munificence in this gift of one's whole body, in this "what can I give that I have not yet given?" which reduced a human being, at the moment of embrace and metamorphosis, to the ultimate poverty of feeling as *nothing* compared with the sumptuous reality of what had been received; of being so filled with tenderness, strength and joy that the mind was as if confused by the fear of having nothing with which to repay such princely gifts.

The language of the two lovers went back to the roots of language itself, to the bare word, to the stammered single word which lay behind all poetry—a word of thanksgiving for the heat of the sun, for the river overflowing on to the newly-turned soil, for the seed accepted by the furrow, for the corn that stood straight as a bobbin. The word was born from their contact, as elemental and pure as the act which generated it. The rhythm of their bodies was so closely adjusted to the rhythms of Creation that a sudden rainstorm, the flowering of plants in the night or a change in the direction of the wind was enough for their desire to well up at dawn or at twilight, enough for their bodies to feel that they had come together in a new climate, in an embrace which re-created the splendour of their first meeting. Everything was the same, the appearances of things were unchanged; yet everything was different. To-night—the night that was now slowly and formlessly beginning—would contain its own magnificence, its own bliss; it was not last night, it would not be to-morrow night. Situated outside time, able to lengthen or shorten the hours at will, the two lovers saw this *now* in terms of permanence and eternity, though outwardly it was manifested in what they managed to perceive, remotely and casually, through senses involved in the enormous task of reaching a total understanding of themselves—the rumble of a storm, the persistent cawing of a bird, the smell of the forest, suddenly brought to them on the morning breeze. It might only be a gust of wind perhaps, a fleeting sound, a breath; yet, perceived between the ascent to the orgasm and the relapse into half-sleep—the delectable calm of a state of grace—it seemed to have lasted the whole night. The lovers could remember an embrace of many hours, its rhythm quickening in time to the storm, only to find, when they awoke, that the wind could not have been audible for more than a few minutes—from the movement of the trees outside the window.

Back in the common light of day, Sofia felt supremely in command of herself. She would have liked everyone to be able to share in her great interior happiness, in her joy, in her sovereign calm. Her flesh satisfied, she turned back to people, books and things with a quiet mind, marvelling at the *intelligence* of physical love. She had heard that some Eastern sects thought that physical satisfaction was a necessary step on the upward path to Transcendence, and she could believe that now, as she became aware that an unsuspected capacity for understanding was flowering within her. After years of voluntary confinement amongst too familiar walls, objects and people, her mind was now turning towards the outside world, and finding matter for reflection in everything.

Re-reading certain classical texts, which up till now had only spoken to her with the voice of their fables, she discovered the original essence of their myths. She cast aside the over-rhetorical writings of the time, and the lachrymose novels that her contemporaries enjoyed so much, and returned to the works which had established, in language of an everlastingly valid symbolism, the ways in which a man and a woman might cohabit in the profoundest sense, in a world full of hostile eventualities. The secrets of the Spear and the Chalice, which she had hitherto looked on as obscure symbols, were now hers. It seemed as if her existence had become *useful*, as if her life had at last found a direction and a meaning. Certainly she allowed the days and weeks to go by for the sake of the present moment, completely happy, taking no thought for the morrow. But for all that she did not cease to dream of accomplishing great things one day, at the side of this man to whom she had bound herself. A man with his energy, she thought, would not be able to go long without launching himself into some splendid enterprise.

But what he did depended very largely on what was happening in Europe. And by now the reports arriving from Paris offered him little encouragement. Events were following one another so swiftly there that by the time the newspapers reached Cayenne, their information was very much out of date, and probably bore no relation to what was actually happening when they were being read. In any case, it did not seem that Buonaparte was much concerned with promoting revolutionary activities in America; his attention was focused on more pressing problems. As a result, Victor Hugues devoted most of his time to administrative tasks, giving orders for irrigation, opening up roads, putting the commercial agreements with Surinam into operation, and developing the colony's agriculture.

His régime was held to be paternalistic and sensible. The old planters were satisfied. A wind of prosperity was blowing. As the ten-day week had not been observed in Cayenne for some time, and they had returned to using the old Gregorian calendar, the Mandatory went to the town on Mondays, and came back to the hacienda on Thursdays or Fridays. Meanwhile Sofia devoted a few hours each morning to household affairs; she issued orders, set the carpenters to work, and attended to the garden, ordering tulip bulbs through the Swiss, Sieger—now an active business agent—who procured them from Paramaribo. The rest of the time she spent in the library, where there was no shortage of excellent books, along with a boring selection of Treatises on Fortification and the Art of Navigation, and works on Physics and Astronomy. In this way several months passed, without Victor ever bringing any news that could possibly disturb the peaceful, flourishing life of the colony, when he returned each week.

One day in September, Sofia interrupted her discreet country retirement in an unusual manner, and went to Cayenne to make a few purchases. Strange things were going on there. The high-pitched bells of the chapel of the Saint-Paul-de-Chartres convent had been ringing since dawn. And to them had been joined the voices of other, unknown bells, all over the town, perhaps hidden until now in lofts and warehouses, which were being struck with hammers, pieces of firewood, and horse-shoes, for they had not yet been hung. Monks and nuns were landing from a recently arrived ship. An unusual Army of the Faithful seemed to be invading the town, as they filed through the streets in their black and grey Carmelite habits, applauded by the passers-by, and carrying a forgotten paraphernalia of rosaries, holy medals, scapularies and missals. As they passed, some of the monks bestowed a blessing on the curious who were leaning from their windows. Others tried to drown the din with the verses of a canticle, but their voices failed to harmonise.

Astonished by this spectacle, Sofia went to Government House, where she was to meet Victor. But in his office she only found Sieger, buried in an arm-chair, a bottle of rum beside him. The agent greeted her with exaggerated delight, saying as he buttoned up his coat : "A fine display of capuchins, Señora ! A priest for every parish ! Nuns for all the hospitals ! The days of processions are here again ! We've got a Concordat ! Paris and Rome are in each other's arms ! The French have turned Catholic again ! There's a great Thanksgiving Mass going on in the Grey Sisters' chapel. You'll be able to see the whole government there in their best uniforms, bowing their heads to the ecclesiastical Latin : *Preces nostrae, quaesumus, Domine, propitiatus admitte.* And to think that more than a million men died to destroy what they're now giving back to us !"

Sofia went back into the street. Passengers were still landing from the friars' ship, opening large red and green parasols, while the negro stevedores piled their bundles and portmanteaux on their heads. In front of Hauguard's hotel, several priests were assembling their scattered baggage, and mopping their brows with voluminous check handkerchiefs. And suddenly a strange thing occured : two Sulpicians, who had been among the last to come ashore, were greeted by their colleagues with angry shouts of "Jurants !" Others cried : "Judas ! Judas !" And stones, filth, and pineapple peel, picked up out of the gutter, began to rain on the new arrivals. "Get out ! Go and sleep in the jungle ! Jurants ! Jurants !"

The Sulpicians, in no way intimidated, tried to kick and punch their way into the hotel, and a menacing crowd of black habits gathered round them. By now the priests who had sworn allegiance to the Revolutionary Constitution had their backs to a wall, and were making unintelligible replies to the charges levelled at them by the "recusants", the "true priests", on whom the Concordat had suddenly conferred the prestige of Soldiers of Christ and worthy descendants of the Deacons of the Catacombs, who had defied persecution and celebrated clandestine Masses.

Watchmen arrived and dispersed the ecclesiastics with the stocks of their muskets. Just when order seemed to have been restored, a young priest came out of a nearby butcher's shop and threw a bucket of fresh blood—from an animal that had just been slaughtered—over the two Sulpicians, who were now aureoled by a great red stain, as the fetid blood, having broken over their bodies, adhered to the white façade of the hotel in clots and splashes. A great ringing of bells began again. After attending the Thanksgiving Mass, Victor Hugues, followed by the members of his government, emerged in full dress uniform from the chapel of the Grey Sisters.

"Have you heard?" he asked Sofia, when he met her in Government House.

"The whole thing is rather grotesque," replied the girl, telling him what had happened to the Sulpicians.

"I'll give orders for them to be sent back on board. Their life will be made impossible here."

"I think it's your duty to protect them," said Sofia. "You ought to find them more acceptable than the others."

Victor shrugged: "Even in France no one wants anything to do with jurant priests."

"You smell of incense," she said.

They returned to the hacienda, talking little along the way. When they arrived at the house, they found the "Billauds", as they called them, who had been installed there since mid-day, along with their faithful dog Patience. It was quite normal for them to arrive unannounced on a visit of several days.

"Once again Philemon and Baucis have come to abuse your hospitality," said the former Terrorist, employing a figure of speech he had grown fond of, since he had been living as man and wife with his servant Brigitte. Sofia had noticed that Baucis' authority had been making itself felt more and more in Philemon's household in the last few months.

The negress had been artfully hedging Billaud-Varenne about with a solicitude that took the form of ostentatious exclamations of admiration and wonder at everything he said or did. Hated by his neighbours at his farmhouse at Orvilliers, near the coast, the ex-President of the National Convention had been subject for some time past to sudden attacks of mental depression. Many people in the colony sent him, anonymously, copies of the Paris newspapers, in which his name was still sometimes recalled with horror. When this happened, Billaud-Varenne would fall into despair, exclaiming that he was the victim of a terrible calumny, that no one had been able to understand the historic role he had played, and that no one sympathised with his sufferings. When she saw him thus forlorn and tearful, Brigitte had a formula ready which was better able to comfort him than anything else : "What? After all the dangers you've overcome, are you going to let yourself be affected by what these beasts write?" A smile would then return to Billaud's face, and in exchange for this smile Brigitte did as she liked in the farmhouse at Orvilliers, showing herself arrogant with the servants and overbearing with the labourers, vigilant and active in taking care of everything, and mistress of a domain whose affairs she managed with surprising skill.

Sofia found her now in the kitchen, giving orders to speed up the preparations for dinner, as if she were in her own house. She was wearing a dress as good as any to be found in Cayenne, and she glittered with gold bracelets and filagree bangles.

"Ah, darling!" the black girl exclaimed, dropping the wooden spoon with which she had just been tasting a sauce. "You're looking absolutely radiant! How can he help falling more in love with you every day?"

Sofia grimaced and turned away. She did not like some of Brigitte's familiarities, which underlined her position as the mistress of a powerful man.

"What have we got to eat?" she asked, unable to avoid, however much she might like the "little Billaud", the tone of voice of a mistress of the house talking to her cook. In the drawing-room, Billaud-Varenne had just heard about the Concordat and everything that had happened that morning in Cayenne. "That's the last straw!" he cried, drumming his fists on an English marquetry table, in time to his words. "We're sinking into the mire!"

318

LIKE A LONG and fearful roll of thunder in summer, heralding cyclones that will blacken the sky and tear down cities, the cruel news rang out around the Caribbean, amid shouts and the lighting of torches : the Law of the 30th Floreal of the Year Ten had been promulgated—slavery was reinstituted in the French colonies in America, and the Decree of the 16th Pluviose of the Year Two was no longer effective.

There was great rejoicing amongst the landowners, ranchers and planters—who were soon informed of something so interesting to them, indeed the news travelled ahead of the ships— especially when they found that they would be reverting to the system that had prevailed in the colony previous to 1789, which meant that they had finished with the humanitarian lucubrations of that filthy Revolution once and for all.

In Guadeloupe, Dominica and Marie Galante, the news was greeted with salvoes and illuminations, and thousands of "former free citizens" were led back to their old hutments once more, beneath a rain of sticks and ropes' ends. The Big Whites of the old days set out into the countryside, with packs of dogs at their heels, to look for their former servants, who were brought back to their compounds with chains round their necks. So afraid were they that mistakes might be made during this mass manhunt that many slaves who had been set free in the days of the monarchy, and possessed businesses or small-holdings, gathered their belongings together in the hope of escaping to Paris. But their plan was promptly foiled by another decree, that of the 5th Messidor, which forbade any coloured individual to enter France. Buonaparte considered that there were already too many blacks in Metropolitan France, and feared that their excessive numbers might transmit to European blood "the same tinge that spread through Spain after the Moorish invasion".

Victor Hugues received the news one morning when Sieger was with him in his office in Government House.

"We're going to have a lot of runaways," said the business agent.

"We shan't give them time," replied Victor. And there and then he sent urgent messages to the owners of the nearby haciendas and leaders of the militia, summoning them to a secret meeting that was to take place the next day. The main thing was to be the first to act, and to publish the Law of Prairial; then slavery would have been restored officially.

The plan of action having been mapped out, with a relish that threatened to translate itself into immediate excesses, they waited for sunset. The gates of the town were closed; the nearby farms were occupied by troops, and, when a gun was fired at eight o'clock in the evening, all the negroes who had been set free by the Decree of the 16th Pluviose found themselves surrounded by slave-owners and soldiers, who led them captive to a small clearing on the banks of the Mahury. By midnight several hundred bewildered and frightened negroes were massed there, unable to account for this enforced concentration. Anyone who tried to separate himself from the terrified, sweating mass of bodies was thrust back with kicks and musket stocks.

At last Victor Hugues appeared. Climbing on to a barrel so that everyone could see him, he slowly unrolled the parchment on which the text of the Law had been transcribed, and, by the light of torches, he read it out in a solemn, deliberate voice. Quickly translated into dialect by those who could hear him best, the words spread from mouth to mouth, as far as the edges of the clearing. Those present were then informed that anyone who refused to submit to his former conditions of service would be punished with the utmost severity. To-morrow their owners would come and take possession of them once more, and lead them to their respective farms, plantations and houses. Those who were not reclaimed would be put up for public auction.

A great wail of passionate despair—an outburst of collective sobbing like the ululation of hunted animals—went up from the blacks, as the Authorities withdrew, escorted by a deafening battery of drums.

But everywhere dark shapes were already melting into the night, seeking asylum in the undergrowth and the jungle. Those who had not been caught in the first haul headed for the mountains, stealing canoes and boats to make their way upstream; they were unarmed, almost naked, but determined to return to the way of life of their ancestors, somewhere where the whites would not be able to reach them. As they passed the outlying plantations, they spread the news amongst their own people, and ten, twenty, more men would abandon their work, deserting the fields of indigo and clover, to swell the numbers of the runaways. And in parties of one hundred, two hundred at a time, followed by their wives carrying the children, they moved off into the interior, through thickets and crags, in search of a place where they could build a palisade. As they fled they scattered mullein seeds in the streams and rivulets, so that the fish would be poisoned and infect the water with their miasma as they putrefied. Beyond this torrent, beyond that mountain clothed in waterfalls, Africa would begin again; they would go back to forgotten tongues, to the rites of circumcision, to the worship of the earlier gods, who had preceded the recent gods of Christianity. The undergrowth closed behind men who were retracing the course of history, to regain an age when Creation had been ruled by the Fertile Venus, with her huge breasts and her ample belly, who was worshipped in deep caves where a hand was haltingly tracing its first configurations of the activities of the chase, and of ceremonies dedicated to the stars.

In Cayenne, Sinnamary, Kourou, and along the banks of the Oyapoc and the Maroni, people were living in the midst of horrors. The negroes who had not surrendered, or who were insubordinate, were whipped to death, dismembered, beheaded, or subjected to appalling tortures. Many of them hung by the ribs from the hooks in the public slaughter-houses. Throughout the country a vast manhunt had begun, much to the delight of the skilled marksmen. Everywhere huts and thatched roofs were burning, and where so many crosses still remained to mark the graves of the Exiles, there now stood out, against a sunset made red by the flames that had spread from the houses to the fields, the sinister outline of a gallows or, worse still, of luxuriant trees from whose branches corpses hung in bunches, their shoulders covered with vultures. Once again Cayenne was fulfilling its destiny as a place of atrocities.

On the Friday Sofia learned of what had been perpetrated the previous Tuesday, and greeted the news with horror. All her hopes of what she would find here, in this outpost of the new ideas, were turning into intolerable disappointments. She had dreamed of making herself useful amongst men who were fearless, just and firm, and who ignored the gods, because they no longer needed their help, and knew that they were capable of ruling a world which belonged to them; she had thought she would be watching Titans at work, and she had not been afraid of the blood that might be spilled in such a noble cause; but all she was seeing was the gradual restoration of everything which seemed to have been abolished, of everything which the greatest books of the age had taught must be abolished. Now, after the rebuilding of the temples, they were proceeding to the imprisonment of the enchained. And all those who had it in their power to prevent such things, in this continent where they might still preserve what had been lost on the other side of the Ocean, did nothing at all, because they were too much concerned with their own careers.

The man who had defeated the English in Guadeloupe, the Mandatory who had not drawn back from the risk of starting a war between France and the United States, had now been halted by the abject Decree of the 30th Floreal. Eight years before he had shown a persistent, an almost superhuman energy in abolishing slavery, and now he was showing the same energy in restoring it. She was amazed at the lack of integrity of a man who could do both good and evil with the same cold courage. He was as capable of being Ormuzd as he was of being Ahriman, of reigning over the kingdom of darkness as over the kingdom of light. According to what turn events were taking, he could suddenly turn into his own opposite.

"Anyone would think I was responsible for the decree," said Victor, the first time he heard a tirade of bitter reproaches from her lips, and at the same time he remembered, with a certain remorse, how much he owed his present eminence to the noble Law of Pluviose of the Year Two.

"It certainly looks as though you've all given up the idea of spreading the Revolution," said Sofia. "At one time you intended to bring it here to America."

"I may have still been influenced by Brissot's ideas then; he wanted to take the Revolution everywhere. But if he, with his resources, couldn't even convince the Spaniards, then I certainly don't intend taking the Revolution to Lima or New Granada. The man who now has the right to speak for us all has already said as much (and he pointed to a portrait of Buonaparte, which had recently been hung over his desk): "The novel of the Revolution is written; our concern now is to undertake its history, and, in applying its principles, to consider only what is realistic and feasible."

"It's very sad to start that history by restoring slavery," said Sofia.

"I'm sorry about it. But I'm a politician. And if the restoration of slavery is a political necessity, then I must bow to that necessity."

The argument was still going on, with Sofia expressing the same ideas, the same anger, impatience and scorn for these degrading derelictions, when Sieger appeared on the Sunday, and interrupted an acrimonious quarrel. "It's unbelievable but true," he shouted from the doorway, in the uncouth tones of a newsvendor. He took off the old winter greatcoat, with its sweat-stained pelisse and its moth-eaten fur collar, which he wore on wet days; it was now raining in torrents, out of clouds that had come down from the high mountains, perhaps from those unknown distances whence the great rivers flowed, where, lost amongst the clouds, there were rocky monoliths to which no one had ever climbed. "Unbelievable but true," he repeated, closing an enormous green umbrella that seemed to be made out of lettuce leaves. "Billaud-Varenne is buying slaves. He's already the master of Cato, Tranche-Montagne, Hippolytus, Nicholas, Joseph, Lindore, as well as three women to do the housework. We're progressing gentlemen, we're progressing. It's obvious you can find a justification for anything when you've been President of the Convention. 'I have realised only too clearly (and he imitated the other's throaty voice) that the negroes are born with many vices, that they lack both reason and feelings and that the only principles they understand are those imposed by fear!'"

The Swiss laughed, feeling that he had given a good imitation of the former Terrorist's way of speaking.

"That's enough," said Victor ill-humouredly, and he asked to see some plans which Sieger was carrying in a pigskin portfolio.

And soon, perhaps in execution of these self-same plans, the Great Works began. Hundreds of negroes were brought to the hacienda and, urged on by whips, they began to plough, excavate, dig, hollow out and fill in the extensive area of land that was being recovered from the jungle. As the clearing extended its limits farther and farther, age-old trees fell, their foliage as full of birds, monkeys, insects and reptiles as the symbolical trees of the alchemists. Smoke rose from these fallen giants, as they were consumed by fire which penetrated to their entrails before it had finished burning through the bark; and oxen moved between the teeming fields and the newly-erected sawmill, dragging the huge wooden corpses, still full of sap and juices, and with fresh shoots growing out of their wounds; the enormous roots bumped along the ground, clutching at the earth, to be dismembered under the axe, their arms, as they flew off, still trying to catch hold of something. All was a confusion of flames, blows, work-songs and oaths, and in the middle of it the teams of horses could be seen, making a mighty effort to pull down a quebracho, and then emerging from the turmoil, sweating, gleaming with lather, their collars askew, their nostrils glued to the furrows where their hooves were scrabbling.

Once there was sufficient wood the scaffoldings were erected; against poles, trimmed by machetes, foot-bridges and terraces went up, the fore-runners of structures which were never to materialise. One morning a strange, circular gallery came to life, as yet only a skeleton, foreshadowing a future rotunda. A tower arose, destined for some unknown purpose and barely indicated by a framework of interlocking beams. Amongst the water-lilies in the river, the negroes were laying the stone foundations for a landing-stage, howling with pain when a sting-ray jabbed at them, when the shock from an electric eel made them leap into the air, or when the teeth of a moray closed like a padlock over their genitals.

Shaped stones were lying near by, from which terraces, steps, aqueducts and arcades would be clumsily built, with chisels that had to be continually returned to the forge, because they grew jagged after ten strokes and cut the workmen's hands. Everywhere there was a proliferation of braces and joists, wedges and brackets, hoists and nails. They lived surrounded by dust, plaster, sawdust, sand and gravel, but Sofia could not imagine what Victor meant to achieve with these extensive building operations. No sooner were they under way than he was modifying them, and altering the rolled-up plans, which stuck out from every pocket of his clothing.

"I'm going to conquer Nature here," he said. "I'm going to put up statues and colonnades. I'm going to make roads, I'm going to dig ponds, as far as the eye can see." Sofia deplored Victor's wasting so much energy in a vain attempt to create here, in this virgin forest, which stretched uninterrupted as far as the sources of the Amazon—perhaps as far as the shores of the Pacific—an ambitious simulacrum of a royal park, whose statues and rotundas would be absorbed by the undergrowth the moment they were left untended, and would merely supply support and nourishment for the limitless vegetation engaged in its perpetual task of dislodging stones, splitting walls, breaking open mausoleums, and annihilating the work of human hands. Man wanted to make his puny presence felt in an expanse of green reaching from Ocean to Ocean like an image of eternity. "I would be happier with ten beds of radishes," said Sofia, to annoy the Builder.

"I seem to be listening to *The Village Soothsayer*," he replied, bending over his plans.

XLVI

THE WORK WENT on amidst the mud and the dust. Tired of the din of pick-axes and saws, pulleys and mallets, which filled the confines of the hacienda, Sofia shut herself up in the house behind a barricade of newly hung curtains, shawls spread across windows, and screens acting as walls and partitions. Ever since the property had been handed over to the blacks, with their confusion of tongues, it had been overrun by guards and sentinels. Sitting on top of a step-ladder, lying on a carpet, or stretched out on the cool mahogany of a table, she had read all the books she could find in the library, only rejecting treatises that meant nothing to her—such as algebras and geometry-books, with their illustrations over-full of scientific allusions, where people with an "A" or "B" on their backs were drawn inside the figures of theorems, which linked them maybe with the trajectory of the stars, or with the amazing phenomena of electricity.

Consequently she was glad that the young officer, De Saint-Affrique, often ordered interesting new books for her from

Buisson, the famous Paris bookseller. But nothing very remarkable was coming from France these days, except for accounts of journeys to Kamchatka, the Philippines, the Fjords, or Mecca, and tales of exploration and shipwreck which perhaps owed their success to the fact that people had been glutted with so many books that were polemical, moralising and admonitory, and with all the apologias, memoirs, panegyrics, and true accounts of this or that which had been published in recent years.

In no way attracted by the truncated columns, the bridges arching over artificial streams or the temples after Ledoux which were beginning to take shape in the surrounding country-side—without, however, being able to impress themselves on a vegetation that was too hostile and wayward to ally itself with an architecture governed by lines and proportions—Sofia withdrew from reality, and, when she was not following Lord Macartney in his travels across the deserts of Tartary, she would be making imaginary voyages on board ship, with Captain Cook or La Pérouse.

The rainy season of reading indoors passed, and they returned to the days of sumptuous sunsets revealing the mystery of the distant jungle. But now these sunsets were becoming too oppressive. Their last rays marked the end of a day that had been without purpose or direction. De Saint-Affrique told her that wonderful mountains, covered in water, rose in the heart of this savage land. But there were no roads to approach them by, and the undergrowth was too full of hostile races who had reverted to an earlier way of life, and used their bows with unerring aim.

Impelled by a desire for action, for a full and useful life, her steps had led her to this life of seclusion, here amongst the trees, in the emptiest, most obscure place on the face of the earth. All that she heard talked about was business. The New Age had arrived noisily, cruelly, triumphantly in America, where only yesterday the influence of Viceroyships and Captaincies-General still prevailed. But now the men who had brought the New Age to America on their shoulders, and imposed it, without shrinking from the recourse to bloodshed which that imposition demanded, were hiding themselves behind balance sheets, so that they could forget its coming. The game went on, amidst lost cockades and tarnished reputations, conducted by men who seemed to have forgotten their proud and stormy past. This past, some people said, had been a time of excesses. But it was because of these excesses that certain men would be remembered, men who bore names too glorious to be reconciled with the wretched figures they now cut. When she heard it said that the colony might be attacked one day by Holland or England, Sofia went so far as to hope that that day would come soon, so that some event, however disagreeable, might drag the lethargic and the over-fed away from their contracts, their harvests and their profits. Elsewhere life went on; changing, wounding or exalting; modifying the fashions, the tastes, the usages and the rhythms of existence. But here they had gone back to the way of life of half a century ago. It was as if nothing had happened in the outside world. Even the clothes the well-to-do settlers wore were the same, in cloth and cut, as those that had been worn a hundred years before. Sofia was experiencing the horrible sensation that time was standing still—she had known it once before—that to-day was the same as yesterday, and to-morrow would be the same as to-day.

The summer was limping sullenly on, protracting its heat into an autumn that would be no different from any other autumn, when, one Tuesday, at the sound of the bell which was rung to summon the negroes to work, there ensued such a prolonged silence that the guards went to the huts, whip in hand. But they found the huts deserted. The watch-dogs lay poisoned, surrounded by the froth of their last vomit. When they were brought out from the barns the cows toppled to the ground, after staggering briefly about as if they were drunk. The horses, their bellies distended, put their heads under their mangers and bled from the nostrils. Men soon came in from the neighbouring haciendas; everywhere it was the same. The slaves had dug tunnels during the night, had unnailed partitions so skilfully that no one had heard a sound, and escaped into the jungle, after distracting the attention of their guards by starting small fires here and there. Sofia now remembered having heard a lot of drumming from the distant mountain-crags during the night. But no one had paid any attention to what might easily be Indians indulging in some barbarous ritual.

Since Victor Hugues was in Cayenne, a messenger was sent off to him post-haste. And just as, in their increasing dread of the darkness, so heavily charged with anxiety and menace, the

327

settlers were beginning to think it strange that a whole week should go by without the Agent returning, there appeared on the river one evening an unprecedented cavalcade of launches, lighters and other shallow-draught boats, laden with troops, provisions and arms. Going straight to the house, Victor Hugues assembled everyone who could tell him about the recent events, making notes and consulting the few maps which he had available. Then, surrounded by officers, he held a Staff Conference, and issued orders for a merciless punitive expedition against the encampments of runaway slaves which were multiplying too rapidly in the jungle.

Standing in the doorway, Sofia watched this man who had recovered all his old authority; precise in his exposition, confident of his plans, he was once again the military commander of the old days. But this military commander was placing his determination, his reborn vigour, at the service of a cruel and despicable purpose. She made a gesture of scorn and went out into the gardens, where the soldiers, having refused to occupy the huts because they smelled too strongly of negroes, were preparing to bivouac in the open. These soldiers were different from the mild and bovine Alsatians Sofia had been used to seeing up till now. Tanned and boastful, with scars running across their faces, they talked in loud voices, and fixed her with stares that left her naked. They seemed to conform to a new military pattern, and Sofia liked them, for all their insolence, because they expressed themselves in language that was virile and self-confident.

From the young officer De Saint-Affrique, who had been alarmed at seeing her surrounded by men like these and had run up to escort her, she learned that she was in the presence of men who had survived the plagues in Jaffa, and had been posted to the colony after the Egyptian campaign, although still rather shaken, because it was thought that they would adapt themselves very readily to the Guianese climate, to which the Alsatians had been succumbing in ever-increasing numbers. And now she looked with wonder on these soldiers who had stepped out of a legend, who had slept in sepulchres covered with hieroglyphics, and fornicated with Coptic and Maronite prostitutes, and who boasted of knowing the Koran, and of having laughed at the gods with the faces of jackals and birds, whose statues still stood in temples full of mighty columns. A breath of a Great Adventure had come with them across the Mediterranean from Aboukir, Mount Tabor and Acre. Sofia did not weary of asking first one man and then another what he had seen, what he had thought, during that unusual campaign that had led a French army right to the foot of the Pyramids. She felt an urge to sit down by their field-kitchens, to share the soup that was being poured into the bowls in great ladlefuls, to throw dice on to the drum where the bones rattled like hailstones, to drink the brandy they all carried in water bottles inscribed with Arabic characters.

"You mustn't stay here, Madame," said De Saint-Affrique, who, for some time now, had been behaving towards Sofia with the jealous attentiveness of a cicisbeo. "They're a rough and rowdy lot." But she remained enthralled by some story, by some heroic piece of boasting, and secretly flattered—nor was she ashamed of it—to feel herself being desired, and mentally undressed and fingered by these men, who had been saved from the Biblical affliction, and who tried to give her cause to remember their rugged faces by embroidering on their own feats.

"Have you become a camp-follower?" asked Victor sourly, when he saw her coming back.

"At least camp-followers do something," she said.

"Do something! Do something! Still talking the same rubbish! As if a man can do any more than he's able to!"

Victor came and went, giving orders, establishing objectives, dictating instructions as to using the river to supply his troops. Sofia was almost ready to admire his energy, when she remembered that what was being organised under this roof was a vast slaughter of negroes. She locked herself in her room to hide a sudden fit of anger, which soon dissolved into tears. Outside, the soldiers from the Egyptian Campaign were setting light to little pyramids of dried coconuts, to drive away the mosquitoes. And, after a night too full of noises, laughter and restlessness, the bugles sounded reveille. The fleet of launches, barges and lighters moved upstream, picking its way between the whirlpools and rapids.

Six weeks went by. And then, one night, to the sound of a heavy rain that had been falling for three days, a few boats returned. From them landed exhausted, feverish men, their arms in slings, filthy and evil-smelling, swathed in bandages the colour of mud. Many of them had been wounded by Indian arrows, or mutilated by the negroes' machetes, and were being carried on litters. Victor was the last to arrive, shivering and dragging his legs, with his arms round the shoulders of two officers. He fell into an arm-chair, and asked for blankets and then more blankets to be wrapped round him. But even after he had been wrapped, enveloped, submerged in woollen blankets and vicuña ponchos, he was still shivering. Sofia noticed that his eyes were red and purulent, and that he swallowed his saliva with difficulty, as if his throat were swollen.

"It's not war," he said finally, in a hoarse voice. "You can fight men, you can't fight trees."

De Saint-Affrique, whose unshaven chin gave a blue tinge to a skin that was already an unhealthy green, talked alone with Sofia, after draining a bottle of wine with eager gulps. "It was a disaster. The settlements were deserted. But we kept being ambushed by handfuls of men, who killed a few of our soldiers and then disappeared. When we went back to the river they shot at us from the banks. We had to wade through swamps with the water up to our chests. And then, to cap it all, the Egyptian Disease." And he explained that the soldiers who had survived the plagues in Jaffa were suffering from a mysterious sickness, with which they had already contaminated half France, where the epidemic was wreaking havoc. It was a sort of malign fever, with pains in the joints, which crept up the body and broke out through the eyes. The pupils became inflamed, and the eyelids filled with fluid. More sick and wounded would be arriving next day, more men who had been routed by the forest trees, and by weapons which, for all their prehistoric appearance —darts made from monkey bones, arrows of sugar cane, rustic pikes and knives—had defied modern artillery. "Fire a cannon in the jungle, and all that happens is that an avalanche of rotting leaves falls on your head."

At a conference of the maimed and wounded men, it was agreed that Victor should be taken to Cayenne the next day, along with the more seriously wounded. Sofia was delighted by the failure of the expedition, and, with the help of the young officer De Saint-Affrique, she collected her clothes together, and packed them in wicker baskets smelling of vetiver. She had a presentiment that she would never return to this house.

XLVII

THE EGYPTIAN DISEASE had appeared in Cayenne. The Hospital of Saint-Paul-de-Chartres no longer had room for all the sick. Prayers were sent up to St. Roch, St. Prudentius, and St. Carlo Borromeo, who were always remembered in time of pestilence. People cursed the soldiers who had brought this new plague, picked up in God-knows-what cave full of mummies, in God-knows-what world of sphinxes and embalmers. Death was in the town. He leapt from house to house and the disconcerting suddenness of his appearance gave rise to a proliferation of terrified rumours and legends. People said that the soldiers from Egypt, furious at being made to leave France, had wanted to exterminate the colony so that they could take it over; and that they were concocting unguents, liquids, and greases, mixed with all manner of filth, with which they marked the fronts of the houses they wished to contaminate. Marks of any sort were suspect. Anyone who leaned his hand on the wall during the day, and left behind the ephemeral outline of a sweaty palm, was stoned by the passers-by. Because his fingers were too black and greasy, an Indian was beaten to death, early one morning, by people watching over a corpse.

Although the doctors stated that its effects were not the same as those of the plague, everyone took to calling the disease "the scourge of Jaffa". And while they waited for it—it would be bound to come sooner or later—fear became indistinguishable from licence. Bedrooms were opened to anyone who wanted. Bodies sought each other out as people lay dying near by. In the midst of the plague, balls and banquets were given. A man spent in one night what it had taken him years of prevarication to amass. Anyone who, for all his professed Jacobinism, had hidden gold crowns away, brought them out on the card table.

Hauguard regaled the gentlemen of the colony on wine, as they waited for their mistresses in the rooms of his hotel. While the bells of the town rang out for funerals, orchestras played until dawn at balls and banquets, and the benches and tables that had been carried out into the street were moved aside to leave room for the coffins to pass when daylight came, in carts, drays and old carriages, oozing the pitch that had been daubed on their boards. Two grey nuns, possessed by the Devil, prostituted themselves on the quay, while the old Acadian, more wrapped up than ever in Isaiah and Jeremiah now that the flesh was falling away from his bones, shouted, in squares and on street-corners, that the time had indeed come when they must appear before the Tribunal of God.

Victor Hugues, with his eyes covered in thick bandages soaked in marshmallow water, went about his bedroom in Government House like a blind man, clinging to the backs of chairs, stumbling, groaning, feeling for things with his hands. Watching him, Sofia could see that he was feeble, querulous, and frightened by the noises from the street. Despite the fever which burned in him, he refused to stay in bed, afraid that he might sink for ever into a darkness even more complete than that which he already owed to the damp bandages. To prove to himself that he was alive he touched, felt and then picked up everything that came to hand. The Egyptian Disease had taken root in his powerful organism, with a tenacity only equalled by that of the man who resisted it. "No better, no worse," said the doctor each morning, after trying out the efficacy of some new treatment.

Government House was guarded by a cordon of troops, who forbade access to all strangers. Servants, guards and officials had been sent away; and Sofia was left alone with the Mandatory, in a building whose walls were covered with edicts and notices, watching the funeral processions pass by the window. He complained that his body was swelling, that he was in great pain, that the burning in his eyes was unbearable. *"Ils ne mouraient pas tous, mais tous étaient frappés,"* she replied, remembering how Victor Hugues had read La Fontaine to her in the house in Havana, when she had been practising her French pronunciation.

She knew that she was taking a pointless risk by remaining here. But she braved the danger, so that she could offer herself the spectacle of a fidelity of which she was no longer very certain. Set against Victor's fear, her own stature grew. By the end of a week she had convinced herself that the disease would not pass into her body. She felt proud, singled-out, to think that Death, the ruler of the country, was according her favoured treatment.

Another intercessor had been added to the trinity of Roch, Prudentius and Carlo : St. Sebastian was now being invoked in the town. *Dies Irae, Dies Illa.* A mediaeval sense of guilt had possessed the minds of people who remembered too well their own indifference to the horrors of Iracoubo, Counamama and Sinnamary—and because he reminded them of it only too often, the old Acadian was hounded from street to street with cudgels.

Victor sank deeper and deeper into his arm-chair, searching for things in the night of his blindness, talking already in the language of the dying. "I want to be buried in my uniform of Commissar of the Convention," he said. Then he would grope for it in the wardrobe and show it to Sofia, before draping the dress-coat over his shoulders, and setting the plumed hat on his bandaged forehead. "In less than ten years, during which time I thought I was controlling my own destiny, *they*—the people who always make and unmake us, though we don't even know them—have made me take so many parts that I no longer know which one I should be playing. I've put on so many costumes I no longer know which is the right one." With an effort he thrust out his wheezing chest : "But there is one that I prefer to all the others : this one. I was given it by the only man I've ever looked up to. When they overthrew him I ceased to understand myself. Since then I haven't tried to fathom anything. I'm like those automata who play chess, walk, play the fife or beat a drum when they're wound up. There was only one role I hadn't played, a blind man. I'm playing that now." And he added in a whisper, counting on his fingers : "Baker, trader, mason, anti-mason, jacobin, military hero, rebel, prisoner, absolved by the men who killed the man that made me, Agent of the Directory, Agent of the Consulate . . ." The enumeration, which had exceeded the number of his fingers, died away into an unintelligible murmur.

In spite of his illness and his bandages, Victor had, by dressing in some of the clothes of a Commissar of the Convention, recovered something of the youthful vigour and toughness of the man who had arrived one night to thunder on the door of a certain house in Havana. He had gone back to being his former self—the sceptical, rapacious Governor who, now that his composure was ruffled by a breath from the grave, decried his useless wealth and the vanity of men, in the language of a preacher at a funeral service.

"That uniform was handsome," said Sofia, smoothing down the plumes on his hat.

"It's out of fashion," replied Victor. "All it's good for now is a shroud."

One day the doctor tried a new treatment, which had worked wonders in Paris in curing eyes affected by the Egyptian Disease: the application of bleeding lumps of fresh veal.

"You look like a parricide in a Greek tragedy," said Sofia, seeing this figure emerging from the bedroom where he had just been treated, and being reminded of Oedipus. For her the days of compassion were over.

The next morning when Victor awoke, the fever had gone, and he asked for a glass of cordial. His bandages of bloody meat fell away, leaving his face clean and clear. He was startled, dazzled almost, by the beauty of the world. He walked, he ran, he skipped through the rooms of Government House, after his descent into the night of blindness. He looked at the trees, the creepers, the cats, as if they had just been created and he, like Adam, must give them names.

The Egyptian Disease was carrying off its last victims, who were hurried to the burial-ground, without either bells or funeral service, and cheerfully interred in the shortest time possible. Lavish Thanksgiving Masses were offered to Roch, Prudentius, Carlo and Sebastian, although a few impious people, forgetting the prayers and supplications they had made, were beginning to insinuate that more had been achieved by wearing a clove of garlic hung round the neck than by praying to the saints.

Two boats came into the harbour, and were greeted by

334

salvoes from the batteries. "You were sublime," said Victor to Sofia, telling her to get ready to return to the hacienda. But she averted her eyes, and picking up a book of travels in Arabia, which she had been reading during the last few days, she showed him a paragraph taken from the Koran : "The plague ravaged Devardan, a city of Judea. The greater part of the inhabitants took to flight. God said to them 'Die', and they died. Many years afterwards he brought them back to life, in answer to the prayers of Ezekiel. *But they still bore the imprint of death on their brow."* She paused. "I'm tired of dwelling amongst the dead. It makes very little difference that the plague has left the town. You all bore the imprint of death on your brows before it came."

And then she talked, talked for a long time, standing with her back to him—making a dark silhouette against the luminous rectangle of the window—about her intention of leaving.

"Do you want to go home?" asked Victor, amazed.

"I shall never go back to the home I left in search of a better."

"Where is this better home you're looking for?"

"I don't know. Where men follow a different way of life. Everything smells of corpses here. I want to return to the world of the living, where people believe in something. I hope for nothing from people who themselves hope for nothing."

Government House was invaded by guards, servants and officials, who returned to their duties of organising, cleaning, and waiting at table. The daylight entered once more through the windows, now free of curtains, and raised tiny worlds of dust, that climbed towards the panes in oblique shafts.

"Now you will lead another military expedition into the jungle," she said. "It's inevitable, your position demands it. You owe it to your authority. But I refuse to watch such a spectacle."

"The Revolution has altered more than one person's ideas," said Victor.

"Perhaps that's the most splendid thing the Revolution has done, to have altered more than one person's ideas," said Sofia, beginning to take her clothes out of the cupboards. "Now I know what ought to be accepted and what ought to be rejected."

Another ship—the third that morning—was welcomed by the batteries. "It's almost as if I'd sent for them," said Sofia.

Victor struck the wall with his fist: "Stop packing all your rubbish and get off to Hauguard's hotel," he shouted.

"Thank you," said Sofia, "I'd rather see you like this."

The man went up to her and, seizing her by the arms, frog-marched her across the room, hurting her, pushing her, until finally, with a thrust from his knees, he flung her on to the bed, where he had not slept since his illness.

"Don't forget my safe-conduct," said Sofia placidly, scrambling off the other side of the bed to the writing desk, where the forms were kept: "Wait, there's no ink in the inkpot." Wiping away some blood, drawn when she bit her lip in falling, she took a small bottle, dipped the pen in it, and held it out to Victor. Then she went on taking down her clothes, watching as he filled in the sheet of paper with an angry hand.

"So this is the end?" he asked. "There's nothing left for us?"

"Yes. We were strong right up to the end," replied Sofia.

The Mandatory went to the door. He stopped: *"Bon voyage."* Below, a carriage stood waiting to take him to the landing-stage. The woman was left alone, facing her scattered clothes. Beyond the satin and the lace lay the Commissar's uniform which Victor had shown her so many times during the days of his blindness. Arranged as it was, on the torn upholstery of a chair, with the breeches in place, the dress-coat displaying its oblique tricolour sash, the hat resting on non-existent thighs, it looked like a family heirloom, one of those whose contours, no longer tenanted by flesh and blood, evoke the presence of a man now vanished, who had once filled an important position. This was how they exhibited the clothes of illustrious personages of the past in the cities of Europe. And the museums were flourishing, now that the world had seen so many changes that the story-teller's "once upon a time" had been replaced by the phrases "before the Revolution" and "after the Revolution".

That night, to accustom herself afresh to being alone, Sofia gave herself to the young officer De Saint-Affrique, who had loved her with Wertherian diffidence ever since she arrived in the colony. She was once again mistress of her own body, having closed, of her own volition, the cycle of a long alienation. Now she would be clasped by other arms before she boarded the ship which would take her to Bordeaux next Wednesday.

CHAPTER SEVEN

"And behold, there came a great wind from the wilderness, and smote the four corners of the house, and it fell upon the young men and they are dead; and I only am escaped alone to tell thee".

—*Job* 1/19

THE SOUND OF heels vigorously tapping in time to guitars was coming from the floor upstairs, as the traveller stretched a frozen arm out from the folds of the tartan rugs that enveloped him, and raised the heavy knocker, in the shape of a sea-god, which adorned the great door in the Calle de Fuencarral. Although the blow resounded within, like a shot from a blunderbuss, the din upstairs intensified, augmented by a tired bass voice, vainly trying to hit on the right tune for the *Polo del Contrabandista*. But the hand went on knocking, although burned by the intense cold of the bronze knocker, and at the same time a foot, shod in a stout boot, kicked at the wood of the door, raising sparks from the frozen stone of the doorstep.

Finally a leaf of the door creaked open, and a servant with wine-laden breath thrust a candle up to the traveller's face. When he saw that this face resembled the one in a portrait hanging on the wall upstairs, the man was overcome by fright, and allowed the ghastly scarecrow to come in, breaking into a flood of apologies and explanations. He had not expected the gentleman so soon; if he had known he was coming he would have gone to meet him at the Posthouse. As it happened, to-day being the first of the year, Manuel's day—and his name was Manuel—a few acquaintances, good people though rather rowdy, had paid him a surprise visit after he had already gone to bed. They had refused to listen to reason, and, after asking God to grant the traveller a prosperous journey, had started singing and drinking "what they'd brought with them"—only "what they'd brought with them". If the gentleman would wait a few minutes, he would get all this riff-raff out down the back stairs.

Pushing the servant aside, the traveller went up the broad staircase that led to the drawing-room. There, surrounded by furniture that had been pushed back out of the way, and on a floor whose carpet had been rolled up against the wall, the revels were in full swing. Flashily-dressed *manolos* were performing an exaggerated, obscene dance, while other evil-looking youths emptied great beakers of wine down their gullets, spitting to right and left. From the quantity of empty flagons and bottles lying in the corners, it was obvious that the party was at its height. One woman was crying hot chestnuts which were nowhere to be seen; perched on a divan a *maja* was screeching out the "Marabout Song"; beyond her a man was fondling a woman rather too intimately; a drunken group was pressing round a blind man who had just been straining his voice over the long, sustained notes of a *cante jondo*.

A thunderous shout of "Get out!" from the servant broke up the party, and when they saw the head of someone who was obviously a person of quality emerging from the bundle of rugs, they hurled themselves downstairs, carrying any full bottles they had been able to snatch up as they fled. Then, breaking out into futile complaints, the servant hastened to restore the furniture to its proper place, roll down the carpet, and remove the empty bottles as fast as he could. He added some wood to the fire he had lit earlier in the day, and then, arming himself with brooms, dusters and rags, tried to erase the marks which the orgy had left on the chairs, the floor, and even on the lid of the piano— where there was a stain that smelled like brandy.

"They're good people," groaned the servant, "incapable of stealing anything. But people of very little education. It's not the same here as in other countries; there they're taught respect."

Finally, divesting himself of his last rug, the traveller drew up to the fire, and asked for a bottle of wine. When it was brought he could tell that it was the same as the revellers had been drinking. But he gave no sign of having noticed this; his eyes had just alighted on a picture he knew only too well, the one which depicted a certain "Explosion in a Cathedral". The gaping wound it had once received had been inexpertly healed over with patches, which had caused the canvas to wrinkle too much where it was split.

Followed by the servant, who held aloft a huge candelabrum with new candles, he passed into the adjoining room, which was the library. Between the bookcases there was a collection of Italian armour, crowned by helmets and morions; several pieces were missing and, to judge by the way the hooks were twisted, they had been taken down with great violence. Two large armchairs were still arranged for a tête-à-tête on either side of a narrow table, on which were an open book and a half-finished glass of Malaga, with a coloured rim round it where the wine had evaporated.

"As I had the honour of telling the gentleman in my letter, nothing has been touched since that day," said the servant, opening another door. The traveller now found himself in the bedroom of a woman recently aroused from her sleep. Nothing had been put away; the sheets were still tumbled where she had stretched her limbs, and one could deduce the speed and urgency with which she had dressed from the way her night-gown had been flung on to the floor, and the disorder amongst the dresses she had pulled from the wardrobe before choosing the one that must now be missing.

"It was a sort of tobacco-colour, with a bit of lace," said the servant. The two men went out into a wide corridor, the windows of which were white with frost.

"This was the gentleman's room," said the man, hunting for a key. What the stranger saw was a narrow room, furnished with almost austere simplicity, unadorned save for a tapestry fixed to the wall opposite the bed, which showed a charming orchestra of monkeys, playing clavichords, violas da gamba, flutes and trumpets. On a bedside table there were several small bottles of medicine, together with a jug of water and a spoon.

"I had to empty the water, because it became foul," said the servant. In here everything was as neat and clean as in a soldier's cell: "The gentleman always made his own bed and tidied his things. He didn't like any of the servants to come in here, even when he was ill."

The traveller went back to the drawing-room. "Tell me what happened that day," he said. But, for all his eagerness to tell, and his efforts to bury the memory of the orgy and the wine under an avalanche of words, punctuated by extravagant eulogies of the kindness, the generosity, the gentility, of his employers, the servant's account was of very little interest. It had all been said before, in a letter he had got written by a public amanuensis, who, though ignorant of the whole affair, had added marginal notes of his own, based on hypotheses that were far more enlightening than the meagre facts remembered by the domestic who, when all was said and done, knew practically nothing. That morning, attracted by the excitement in the streets, the servants had abandoned the kitchens, laundry, scullery and coach-house. Afterwards some of them had returned, others had not.

The traveller asked for pen and paper, and listed the names of all the people who, for one reason or another, might have had dealings with the tenants of the house : doctors, provision merchants, hairdressers, dress-makers, booksellers, upholsterers, chemists, tradesmen and workmen. He was not above recording the date on which a fan-maker had called repeatedly to sell her fans, nor the fact that a barber, whose establishment was near by, knew the life histories of everyone who had lived in the Calle de Fuencarral for the last twenty years.

From what he learned in shops and work-rooms; from what he heard in a nearby tavern, where many memories were prompted by the warm fumes of brandy; from what he was told by people of very different types and classes, he began to piece together a story full of gaps and unfinished paragraphs, like an ancient chronicle that has been partly restored by re-assembling the scattered fragments.

The Condesa de Arcos' house—according to a notary who was unwittingly writing the prologue for this patchwork narrative—had not been lived in for a long time, ever since strange, much talked-about happenings, involving ghosts and apparitions. Time had passed and the house remained deserted, isolated by its own legend, while the local tradesmen thought nostalgically of the days when the parties and entertainments its owners had given had inspired much buying of costumes, illuminations, rare foodstuffs and fine wines. Consequently, when one evening the windows of the house were seen to be lit up, it was welcomed as a great event.

The neighbours gathered inquisitively to watch servants bustling about, from the coach-house up to the attics, taking up trunks, carrying bundles, hanging new chandeliers from the ceilings. The next day painters, paper-hangers and plasterers appeared, with their ladders and scaffolding. Fresh air circulated through the rooms, driving out witchcraft and sorcery. Bright, cheerful curtains were hung in the living-rooms, while two superb sorrel horses, brought by a groom in livery, were installed in the stables, which once again smelled of hay, oats and lucerne. It was then learned that a Creole lady, who was not at all afraid of ghosts and apparitions, had rented the house.

Here the story was taken up by a lace-maker from the Calle Mayor. The mistress of the Casa de Arcos soon became known as "The Cuban Lady". She was pretty, with dark eyes, and she lived alone, receiving no visitors and seeking no contact with the people of the town or the Court. Her expression was always sad and preoccupied, yet she did not seek the consolations of religion, for it was noted that she never went to Mass. She was rich, to judge by the number of her servants and the extravagance of her house-keeping, but she tended to dress soberly—although when she bought some lace or chose a material, she always wanted the best, without regard for the price.

There was no more to be got from the lace-maker, and he had to fall back on the idle chatter of Paco, the guitar-playing barber, whose establishment was accounted one of the best places in the city to meet for a gossip : "The Cuban Lady" had come to Madrid on a delicate mission—to plead for a pardon for her cousin, who had been incarcerated in the prison at Ceuta for several years. It was said that this cousin had been a conspirator and a freemason in America; that he was a Francophile, devoted to the ideals of the Revolution, and had published subversive texts and songs, intended to undermine the authority of the King in his Dominions overseas. "The Cuban Lady" too must have had some taint of the conspirator and atheist, to judge by the seclusion she lived in, and by the way she did not even deign to lean out of the window to watch the processions pass in front of the Casa de Arcos, bearing the Holy Sacraments. It even came to be rumoured that they had erected the impious pillars of a Lodge inside the house, and that Black Masses had been celebrated. But the police, alerted by the talk, had watched the house discreetly for several weeks, and had been forced to report that it could not possibly be a meeting-place for conspirators, freemasons or infidels, because no one ever met there at all. The Casa de Arcos, already a house of mystery on account of the phantoms and hobgoblins of old, continued to be a house of mystery now that it was lived in by an attractive woman, who was much ogled by the men when she walked to a nearby shop, or went to buy Toledo marzipan on Christmas Eve in the neighbourhood of the Plaza Mayor.

The story was now taken up by an old doctor who had for

some time been a frequent visitor to the Casa de Arcos. He had been called in to attend a man who was constitutionally sound, but whose health had been shattered by his spell in Ceuta prison —from which he had just been released, as the result of a royal pardon. He had the marks of irons on his legs. He suffered from an intermittent fever, and also from a childhood asthma, which at times caused him great distress, though the attacks could be relieved by smoking cigarettes rolled in datura petals, which an apothecary in the Tribulete district had ordered from Cuba. His health had recovered somewhat, under an energising treatment, and the doctor had not been summoned to the Casa de Arcos again.

Next it was the turn of the bookseller. Esteban would have nothing to do with philosophy, the works of economists, or books that dealt with recent European history. He read travel books, the poetry of Ossian, the novel about the sorrows of Young Werther, new translations of Shakespeare; and it was remembered that he had been enthusiastic over *Le Génie du Christianisme*, a book he had described as "absolutely extraordinary", and had bound in one of those velvet bindings, with a small gold lock intended to guard the secret of the personal comments inscribed in the margins. Carlos, who had read Chateaubriand's book, could not imagine how an unbeliever like Esteban could have been so interested in a work which lacked unity, was sometimes confused, and must have been unconvincing to anyone without real faith. He searched for the book, and finally found one of its five volumes in Sofia's bedroom. Thumbing through it, he was surprised to discover that this edition included, in the second section, a fictional narrative called *René* which did not appear in the other, more recent edition, bought in Havana. And while the pages in the rest of the book were virgin of any notes or marks, a series of sentences and paragraphs had here been underlined in red ink : "This life, which had enchanted me to begin with, soon became unbearable. I grew tired of the same scenes and the same ideas. I began to sound my heart and to ask myself what I wanted." . . . "Without parents, without friends, without (as it were) having ever loved anyone in the world, I was oppressed by a superabundance of life." . . . "I went down into the valleys and I climbed up to the hills, calling on the ideal object of a future passion, with all the force of my desire." . . . "It must be realised that she was the only person in the world whom I had ever loved, and that all my feelings were merged with the sweetness of my childhood memories, and finally concentrated on her." . . . "An impulse of pity had attracted her to me."

A suspicion was forming in Carlos' mind, and next he questioned a lady's maid who had been in Sofia's service for some time. He put oblique questions which, without betraying his real interest in the affair, might lure the servant into some revealing confidence. There could be no doubt that Sofia and Esteban had been very fond of one another, and lived in a quiet and affectionate intimacy. During the hard days of winter, when the fountains in the Retiro were frozen over, they used to take their meals in her bedroom, their chairs drawn up to the stove. In summer they made long excursions by carriage, stopping to drink orgeat at the street stalls. They had been seen once at the San Isidro fair, much amused by the antics of the populace. They had held hands like brother and sister. She did not remember ever having seen them quarrel, or get cross with one another. No, never. He called her by her christian name, and she called him Esteban, that was all. The scandal-mongers—there always were some, in kitchens and sculleries—had never been able to point to any excesive intimacy between them. No. At any rate, no one had ever seen anything. When he had a bad night, because of his illness, she had more than once stayed beside him till dawn. Otherwise they seemed like brother and sister. People were only surprised that such a good-looking woman should not make up her mind to get married, for there would have been no lack of eligible suitors if she had wanted them.

"There are certain things one can never get to the bottom of," thought Carlos, as he re-read the sentences underlined in the book with the velvet binding, which could be interpreted in so many different ways : "An Arab would say that I was wasting my time; like a man looking for the imprint left by a bird in the air, or by a fish in the sea."

It remained now to reconstruct the Day Without End, the day when two individual existences seemed to have been dissolved into a tumultuous and bloody totality. Only one witness was left to the first scene of the drama, a glove-maker who, little suspecting what was about to happen, had gone early to the Casa de Arcos to deliver several pairs of gloves to Sofia. She was surprised to find only one old servant left in the house. Sofia and Esteban were in the library, leaning at the open window, listening to what was going on outside. An indistinct noise filled the city. Although nothing abnormal seemed to be happening in the Calle de Fuencarral, it could be seen that some of the shops and taverns had suddenly locked their doors. Dense crowds seemed to be congregating behind the houses, in the adjacent streets. And suddenly there was bedlam. Groups of workmen appeared at the street-corners, followed by their wives and children, shouting "Down with the Frenchmen". People emerged from their houses, armed with kitchen knives, pokers, carpenters' tools, with anything which would cut, wound or inflict an injury. Shots were already ringing out in every direction, as the human mass increased minute by minute, and overflowed towards the Puerta del Sol and the Plaza Mayor. A vociferous priest, walking at the head of a band of *manolos* holding an open razor, turned to his followers from time to time, and shouted; "Death to the French! Death to Napoleon!" The entire population of Madrid had poured into the streets, in an impromptu uprising as devastating as it was unexpected, without having been incited by printed propaganda or rhetorical speeches. Eloquence was confined to gestures, to the impetuosity of chattering women; to the momentum of this mass advance; to universal enthusiasm. Suddenly the human tide seemed to check, as if bewildered by the eddies that were forming. Everywhere the firing was increasing, and the voice of a cannon spoke for the first time, harsh and thunderous. "The French have withdrawn their cavalry," shouted some men returning from the first skirmishes, with sabre wounds in face, arms or chest. But the sight of blood, far from frightening those who were still advancing, served only to make them quicken their steps towards the place where the din of muskets and artillery showed the fighting to be fiercest.

It was at this moment that Sofia left the window : "Let's go down there!" she cried, snatching down swords and daggers from the collection on the wall. Esteban tried to restrain her :

"Don't be an idiot, they're shooting. You can't do any good with those bits of old iron."

"Stay here if you want to. I'm going."

"And who are you going to fight for?"

"For the people who've run into the streets," cried Sofía. "We've got to do something!"

"What?"

"Anything!"

And Esteban saw her leave the house, impetuous and excited, sword in hand and one shoulder bare, with an energy and an abandon he had never seen in her before.

"Wait for me," he shouted. And arming himself with a shot-gun, he flew downstairs.

That was all that was known. There followed the sound and the fury, the tumult and the chaos of a mass convulsion. The mamelukes, cuirassiers and Polish Guards had fired on a crowd which retaliated with cold steel, men and women alike throwing themselves at the horses and slashing their flanks with razors and knives. Surrounded by troops pouring out of four streets at once, people dashed into the houses, or took to their heels, leaping over walls and fences. Firebrands, stones and bricks rained down from the windows; saucepans and casseroles of boiling oil were poured over the assailants. The gunners behind a cannon fell, one after another, but the piece continued to fire, and frenzied women lit the fuses when there were no more men left to do it. All over Madrid an atmosphere as of some great cataclysm or telluric convulsion prevailed—with fire, iron and steel, anything that would cut or explode, in rebellion against their masters—amid a mighty clamour of *Dies Irae*.

And then came the night. A night of slaughter, of grim mass executions, of exterminations, in Manzanares and Moncloa. The shots which sounded now were less scattered, they were concentrated, concerted together in a fearful rhythm, as men aimed and fired in response to an order, against a sinister back-cloth of blood-reddened walls. That early May night passed slowly in a reign of terror. The streets were full of corpses, and of groaning wounded, too badly injured to stand, who were finished off by patrols of sinister myrmidons, whose slashed dolmans, lacerated braid and torn shakos revealed the ravages of war by the light of some solitary and timid lantern, moving round the whole city on the hopeless quest of lighting up the face of a particular corpse.

Neither Sofia nor Esteban ever returned to the Casa de Arcos. No further trace of them or their final resting-place was ever found.

Two days after learning what little there was to be learned, Carlos ordered the servants to close the boxes in which he had kept a few things, a few books, some clothes that still, by their shape, their smell or their folds, evoked the presence of those who had gone. Below, three carriages were waiting to take him and his baggage to the Posthouse. The Casa de Arcos had reverted to its owners, and would once more be left empty. One after another the doors were locked. And night took up residence in the house—it had been a winter of premature twilights—the half-burned logs were picked out, and the fires were extinguished by pouring water over them from a heavy red cut-glass decanter. When the last door had closed, the picture of the "Explosion in a Cathedral", which had been left behind—perhaps deliberately left behind—ceased to have any subject; the bituminous darkness merged it with the dark crimson brocade covering the main wall of the drawing-room, and the scattered and falling columns became invisible against a background which, even now that the light had gone, retained the colour of blood.

THE END

Guadeloupe-Venezuela-Barbados, 1956-1958.

349

THE VICTOR HUGUES OF HISTORY

Since Victor Hugues has been almost completely ignored by historians of the French Revolution—too busy describing what was taking place in Europe between the time of the Convention and the 18th Brumaire to divert their gaze to the distant confines of the Caribbean—the author feels it might be useful to throw some light on the historical background of the character.

We know that Victor Hugues was a Marseillais and the son of a baker, and there is even cause to believe that he was remotely descended from negroes, though this would be hard to prove. Attracted by a sea which, in Marseilles especially, has been a perpetual call to adventure ever since the days of Pytheas and the Phoenician mariners, he sailed off to America as a cabin-boy, and made several voyages to the Caribbean. Having risen to the rank of mate aboard merchant-men, he travelled through the Antilles, observing, nosing about and learning, until he finally gave up the sea in order to open a large shop, or *comptoir,* in Port-au-Prince, for an assortment of goods that were acquired, collected or purchased, either by trading, smuggling or exchange —silk goods for coffee, vanilla for pearls. Many such establishments still exist in the ports of that glittering and colourful corner of the world.

His real entry into history dates from the night when his business was burned down by the Haitian revolutionaries. From that moment onwards we can follow his progress step by step, as indeed it is charted in this book. The chapters describing the recapture of Guadeloupe follow a precise chronological plan. The passages dealing with the war against the United States—what the Yankees of those days called the "Brigands' War"—together with the activities of the privateers, both their names and the names of their ships, are based on documents consulted by the author in Guadeloupe and in the libraries of Barbados, as well as on brief but revealing references discovered in the works of those Latin-American writers who have mentioned Victor Hugues in passing.

As for Victor Hugues' activities in French Guiana, there is ample source material to be found in the memoirs of the exiles. After the point in time at which this novel ends, he was arraigned in Paris before a Council of War for having lost the colony to the Dutch, after a surrender which was in point of fact inevitable. Absolved with honour, Victor Hugues again began to move in political circles. We know that he came into contact with Fouché. We also know that he was still in Paris when the Napoleonic Empire foundered.

But it is here that we lose trace of him. Some of the very few historians who have concerned themselves with him—purely by chance, except for Pierre Vitoux, who, more than twenty years ago, devoted an as yet unpublished study to him—say that he died near Bordeaux, where he "owned lands" in 1820. Didot's Universal Bibliography gives the year of his death as 1822. But in Guadeloupe, where the memory of Victor Hugues is still very much alive, one is assured that after the collapse of the Empire he returned to Guiana and once more took possession of his property there. It seems, according to Guadeloupan historians, that he died slowly and painfully of a disease which could have been leprosy but which there is better reason to believe was a form of cancer.

What in fact was Victor Hugues' fate? We still do not know, just as we know very little about his birth. But there can be no doubt that his activities during his period of power—resolute, sincere and heroic in their first phase, wavering, mean and even cynical in their second—give us a picture of an extraordinary man, whose behaviour contains a dramatic dichotomy. That is why the author considered that it would be interesting to reveal the existence of this neglected historical figure in a novel which would, at the same time, embrace the whole area of the Caribbean.

A. C.